BENEATH THE LION'S GAZE

Maaza Mengiste was born in Addis Ababa, Ethiopia, and graduated with an MFA in Creative Writing from New York University. A recent Pushcart Prize nominee, she was named 'New Literary Idol' by *New York Magazine*. Her work has appeared in *The Baltimore Review*, *Ninth Letter* and *420pus*, has been translated and published into German and Romanian for *Lettre International*, and can be found in the Seal Press anthology *Homelands: Women's Journeys Across Race, Place and Time*. She has received fellowships from Virginia Center for the Creative Arts and Yaddo. She currently lives in New York.

MAAZA MENGISTE

Beneath the Lion's Gaze

A novel

VINTAGE BOOKS
London

Published by Vintage 2011

10

Copyright © Maaza Mengiste 2010

Maaza Mengiste has asserted her right under the Copyright, Designs
and Patents Act 1988 to be identified as the author of this work

First published in Great Britain in 2010 by
Jonathan Cape

Vintage
Random House, 20 Vauxhall Bridge Road,
London SW1V 2SA

www.vintage-books.co.uk

Addresses for companies within The Random House Group Limited
can be found at: www.randomhouse.co.uk/offices.htm

The Random House Group Limited Reg. No. 954009

A CIP catalogue record for this book
is available from the British Library

ISBN 9780099539926

Penguin Random House is committed to a sustainable future for
our business, our readers and our planet. This book is made from
Forest Stewardship Council® certified paper.

Printed and bound in Great Britain by Clays Ltd, Elcograf S.p.A.

For my grandparents,
Abebe Haile Mariam and Maaza Wolde Hanna.

And for my uncles, Mekonnen, Solomon, Seyoum,
and all who died trying to find a better way.

We are the humbled bones
Bent in the thick of your silence.
Ask of your father God who elected you
Why he has forsaken us.

—TSEGAYE GABRE-MEDHIN

PART ONE

BOOK ONE

I

A THIN BLUE VEIN PULSED IN THE collecting pool of blood where a bullet had lodged deep in the boy's back. Hailu was sweating under the heat from the bright operating room lights. There was pressure behind his eyes. He leaned his head to one side and a nurse's ready hand wiped sweat from his brow. He looked back at his scalpel, the shimmering blood and torn tissues, and tried to imagine the fervor that had led this boy to believe he was stronger than Emperor Haile Selassie's highly trained police.

This boy had come in shivering and soaked in his own blood, in the latest American-style jeans with wide legs, and now he wasn't moving. His mother's screams hadn't stopped. Hailu could still hear her just beyond those doors, standing in the hallway. More doors led outside to an ongoing struggle between students and police. Soon, more injured students would fill the emergency rooms and this work would begin all over again. How old was this boy?

"Doctor?" a nurse said, her eyes searching his above her surgical mask.

The heart monitor beeped steadily. All was normal, Hailu knew without looking, he could understand the body's silent language without the help of machinery. Years of practice had taught him how to decipher what most patients couldn't articulate. These days were teaching him more: that the frailty of our bodies stems from the heart and travels to the brain. That what the body feels and thinks determines the way it stumbles and falls.

"How old is he?" he asked. Is he the same age as my Dawit, he thought, one of those trying to lead my youngest son into this chaos?

His nurses drew back like startled birds. He never spoke during surgery, his focus on his patients so intense that it had become legendary. His head nurse, Almaz, shook her head to stop anyone from answering him.

"He has a bullet in his back that must be taken out. His mother is waiting. He is losing blood." Almaz spoke quickly, her eyes locked on his, professional and stern. She sponged blood away from the wound and checked the patient's vital signs.

The hole in the boy's back was a punctured, burned blast of muscle and flesh. The run towards the bullet had been more graceful than his frightened sprint away. Hailu imagined him keeping pace with the throngs of other high school and college students, hands raised, voice loud. The thin, proud chest inflated, his soft face determined. A boy living his moment of manhood too early. How many shots had to be fired to turn this child back towards his home and anxious mother? Who had carried him to her once he'd fallen? Stones. Bullets. Fists. Sticks. So many ways to break a body, and none of these children seemed to believe in the frailty of their muscles and bones. Hailu cut around the wound and paused for one of his nurses to wipe the blood that flowed.

The whine of police cars flashed past the hospital. The sirens hadn't stopped all day. Police and soldiers were overwhelmed and racing through streets packed with frenzied protestors running in all directions. What if Dawit were there amidst those running, what if he were wheeled into his operating room? Hailu focused on the limp body in front of him, ignored his own hammering heart, and put thoughts of his son out of his mind.

HAILU SAT IN HIS OFFICE under a pale light that threaded its way through open curtains. He stared at his hand lying palm open in his lap and felt the solitude and panic that had been eating into the edges of his days since his wife Selam had gone into the hospital. Seven days of confusion. And he'd just operated on a boy for a gunshot wound to the back. After years as a doctor, he knew the rotations and shifts of his staff, the scheduled surgeries in any given week, Prince Mekonnen Hospital's daily capacity for new patients, but he could not account for his wife's deteriorating condition and this relentless drive of students who demanded action to address the country's poverty and lack of progress. They asked again and again when Ethiopia's backward slide into the Middle Ages would stop. He had no answers, could do nothing but sit and gaze in helplessness at an empty hand that looked pale and thin in the afternoon sun. He feared for Dawit, his youngest son, who also wanted to enter the fray, who was not much older or bigger, nor more brave, than his permanently crippled patient today. His wife was leaving him to carry the burden of these days alone.

There was a knock at his door. He looked at his watch, a gift given to him by Emperor Haile Selassie when he'd returned from medical school in England. The emperor's piercing eyes, rumored to hold the power to break any man's will, had bore into Hailu during the special palace ceremony to honor young graduates recently returned from abroad.

"Do not waste your hours and minutes on foolish dreams," the emperor had said, his voice cool and crisp. "Make Ethiopia proud."

The knock came again. "Dr. Hailu," Almaz said.

"Come in," Hailu said, turning in his chair to face the door.

"You've finished your shift." She stood in the doorway. "You're still here." Almaz, in her usual custom, turned all her questions into declarations. She cleared her throat and adjusted the collar of her white nurse's uniform. She matched him in height, very tall for a woman.

"There was a teachers' union strike," he said. "The emperor's forbid the police to shoot at anyone, but look what happened already." He sighed tiredly. "I want to make sure no other emergencies come in. And I need to check on Selam soon."

Almaz raised a hand to stop him. "I already checked on her, she's sleeping. There's nothing for you to do here anymore," she said. "You've already done your shift, go home."

"My sons have to see her," Hailu said. "I'll go and come back."

Almaz shook her head. "Your wife always complained about your stubbornness." She took his coat from the hanger on the door and held it out for him. "You've been working too hard this week. You think I haven't noticed."

Almaz was his most trusted colleague. They had been working together for nearly two decades. He could feel her searching his face.

The rattle of a heavy falling object echoed in the corridor. It was coming from beyond the swinging doors, from the intensive care unit.

"What was that?" Hailu asked. He stood up and walked over to get his coat. It was then he realized how tired he was. He hadn't eaten since the night before in Selam's room, and he'd spent the entire day operating.

Almaz shook her head and led him out of his office. She closed the door gently behind them and motioned him towards the exit. "I'll tell you later. Something with one of the prisoners."

In the last few weeks, the ICU ward, headed by another doctor, had become the designated location for some of the emperor's officials, old men well past their prime who had been arrested without charges and had fallen ill while in prison because of preexisting ailments and lack of medical supervision. So far, the hospital had been able to function normally, no irregular activity to bring undue attention to their new, special patients.

From the direction of the noise came an angry male voice, a sharp slap, then a soft whimper. "What's going on?" he asked again, turning around.

"They've got soldiers watching one of them," Almaz said. She pushed him on, away from the ICU. "There's nothing you can do about it, so don't concern yourself." The expression on her angular face, with its pointed jaw and thin mouth, was determined. "Go." She walked away, into another patient's room.

Hailu looked down at the long hallway that stretched in front of him and sighed. There was a time when he could tell what went on beyond the hospital by what he heard from inside of it, when he could piece together the shouts and brake squeals and laughter and let logic carry him to a safe assumption. But these days of riots and demonstrations made everything indecipherable. And now, what was once beyond the walls had crept inside. He turned back and decided to leave through the swinging doors of the intensive care unit, a shortcut to the parking lot.

In the corridor of the ICU, a smooth-faced soldier no older than Dawit sat in a chair outside a room cleaning his nails with the edge of a faded button on his shirt. An old gun, dull and scratched, leaned against the wall next to him. The soldier glanced up as Hailu walked by, then turned his attention back to his nails. He chewed on a finger, then spit bits of calloused skin on the floor.

2

As MUSIC PULSED FROM HIS FATHER'S RADIO, Dawit danced, lost in the throaty breaths of a singer. He spun round and round, twisted and turned, shaking his broad shoulders like a bird preparing for flight. He leapt in the cramped space of his bedroom, a slender body hurling itself up, defying the pull of his own weight. He gripped an invisible spear, his heart galloped in his chest. The song had just begun but he was already spent. The first steps of his dance had started earlier, in the deadening silence that had descended on the house after his father's phone call from the hospital saying he was coming home and they would all visit his mother that night. She was no better. Those last words had sent his older brother Yonas to the prayer room, and Dawit to his room.

The day after his mother had been hospitalized, neighbors had arrived at their door to pray and visit with the family. His father had rejected their condolences. "She's on the best medication," his father said. "She'll be home soon. And we're praying for her."

"But you shouldn't bear this alone. It's not good for you or your family," the neighbors had protested. "We love Selam, let us come in and pray with you." They tried to walk through the door and Hailu had resisted, his sons watching in stunned silence from the living room.

"Thank you," his father said. "It isn't necessary. We have each other." He had shut the door softly and turned back to them, grief fresh in his face. He'd wanted to say something, Dawit sensed it in the way his eyes lingered on each of them, but he shook his head instead and sat down in his chair.

It was the lost way his father looked at his hands that made Dawit reach across the small table and cover them with his own. He couldn't remember the last time he'd made such a gesture towards his father, but on that day, in that quiet living room, Dawit ached for a parent's touch and he wanted that look out of his father's eyes.

"Abbaye," Dawit said, his voice shaking, his loneliness so sharp it made his chest ache, "I miss her."

It was the first time he'd ever seen his father collapse from the weight of emotion. He took Dawit's hand in both of his, cradled it to his face, and called Selam's name again and again, speaking into Dawit's palm. The display of sorrow had forced Yonas to turn away, then get up and leave the room.

His mother had taught him to dance *eskesta,* had spent hours and days with him in front of a mirror making him practice the controlled shiver of shoulders and torso that made up the traditional Ethiopian dance. The body has to move when the heart doesn't think it can, she'd said. She lifted his arm, clenched his fist around an imaginary weapon, and straightened his back. My father danced before going to battle; the heart follows the body. Dance with all your might, dance. She'd burst into laughter, clapping enthusiastically to Dawit's awkward attempts to move as fast as she was. You're like a butterfly, he told her, breathless from exertion. He'd reached out and laid a hand on her fluttering shoulders. He'd been eight years old and his adoration for her loving, gentle face smiling into his made him rush to her and hug her tightly.

The dancing lessons had begun after Dawit flung himself at his older brother one day. He'd kicked the much bigger boy with such pointed vengeance that Yonas had stumbled back, dazed, then fallen over completely, his hands still at his side. Selam's response had been swift and decisive. In two simple movements, she warded Hailu's blow away from Dawit and dragged the screaming boy up the stairs and into the master bedroom. She'd held his shaking body, letting Dawit's tears soak into her dress as she patted his back and hummed his favorite lullaby. Then, without a word, she started clapping, her hands and feet moving to a silent rhythm that seeped into Dawit and soon enveloped them both. Like this, she commanded, bringing her hands to her hips and moving her shoulders up and down. Like this. Now faster. Don't think, move the way your heart wants you to move, ignore the body. Let the muscles go. There is no room for anger in our dances, pretend you are water and flow over your own bones. His tears stopped, his attention focused on his movement.

These days, Dawit was forced to stay in the confines of his father's house each night. It was Hailu's attempt to stop him from attending meetings where students planned their demonstrations against the palace. The tensions between them were drawn tighter lately. Only dancing seemed to ease his agitation. He felt trapped in his small bedroom, in his large house that spoke, if nothing else, of his father's dominion over the family. There would be another rally tomorrow afternoon. He was determined to go, no matter his father's orders, despite his promise to his mother to stay away from all political activity.

Dawit could hear his father in the living room, walking towards the stairwell. He wondered if he only imagined footsteps hesitating in front of his bedroom door. He kept on dancing. He whirled, his arms flung wide, extended wings in search of a rhythm to send him up, away from the reality of a house without his mother.

One day, Emaye, my mother, I will put water into my bones and dance until my heart obeys. Dawit spun, eyes wide open to take in the slowly darkening sun.

A FAINT MELODY slid from Dawit's room into the living room where Hailu was resting, and threw him back to the days of his youth, when his and Selam's families had gathered inside his grandfather's *tukul* and drunk honey wine in celebration of the new couple's impending first child. His cousin's *washint* had filled the small hut with tunes of love and patriotism, the hollow reed instrument needling a plaintive voice into the revelry. She had been seventeen; he, an arrogant twenty-eight-year-old with an awkwardness around this girl who sometimes looked at him with childish mockery. I am your husband, he'd told her, sitting on the steps of her father's house, and I will remain faithful to you even while in medical school in England. She'd grown quiet, unimpressed by his chivalry.

You'll be changed when you come back, she'd said. Will you let me leave if I want? Will you let me come back to my father's house if I ask? Will you ever keep me against my will, as my father once kept my mother? And he'd sworn to her then that he would let her go, that he would never force her to stay with him. It was this promise, however, that Selam reminded him of last week, and it was this promise that he knew he could never keep.

Seven days ago, Selam had clung to his hand as she pushed words out with shallow breaths. There is this. This. It is silent and I am alone. This. She was shaken and weak, panicked to find herself back in the hospital room she'd been discharged from only weeks before. Hailu promised her then that there would be no more attempts to nurse her back to health, that he would finally obey her wish to be allowed to rest, that he would become, in the moment when she was her sickest, her husband and not the doctor he also was. The promise made more sense back then, when there was hope and the possibility of life, when he knew he was under no obligation to follow the path his words had made for him.

There is this to know of dying: it comes in moonlight thick as cotton and carves silence into all thoughts. She'd finally been able to form the words fully and lay them before him with a desperation that bordered on anger. This dying, my beloved, is dark and I am tired and you must let me go. Seven days ago, he'd stood in Prince Mekonnen Hospital gripping his ailing wife's hand and heard from his mouth a promise that was already on its way to being broken. His wife was giving up and was asking him to do the same.

Hailu stared at the long shadows in the living room he once shared with Selam. How many nights, how many of these moons did I watch shrink back into sunlight, then dusk with that woman by my side? It is 1974 and I am afraid without you, he admitted for the first time. Nothing I have ever learned has prepared me for the days ahead if you leave me now.

He stood and walked through the living room into the dining area, resisting the urge to pause at Dawit's door and reassure himself that his son hadn't snuck out of the house. He'd told Dawit and Yonas to get ready to visit their mother. He'd seen the sullenness that had settled in Dawit's face at his strict insistence that the three of them go together.

"We're a family," he'd reminded Dawit, the words an echo of the many times he'd had to force Dawit to visit Selam with the rest of the family. His youngest son wanted no one around when he spoke with his mother, protective of their bond.

3

HIS FATHER WAS TALKING but Yonas was trying not to listen. They were waiting for Dawit so they could leave, the wait made longer by Hailu's voice cutting through the early evening heat.

"It happens to many people." Hailu was matter-of-fact, his words clipped. "Their heart weakens, it fails to pump enough blood to the brain. Perfusion. The changes are dramatic. But it's normal. If I can control the blood pressure for long enough, she'll recover." He smoothed his tie and adjusted his suit jacket. He'd dressed his best to visit Selam in the hospital. "I don't understand what's going wrong."

A numbing weight pressed on Yonas and settled into an ache. "You've gone over this so many times."

His father continued as if he hadn't heard, a man trapped in his own language of grief. "Congestive heart failure," he said. "Nothing more than the weakening of the heart."

"It's time to go." Yonas stood up.

Hailu raised his prayer beads close to his chest. "She can be strong again. The doses of furosemide should have helped."

Yonas sat back down and let his eyes roam across the living room and settle on his father's polished prayer beads. His father had started carrying his beads with him everywhere only a week ago. It had once been a point of contention between his parents, with Hailu insisting that religion was a private matter for doctors, not to be put on public display. But you need prayer, too, Selam argued, looking to Yonas as her ally. Hailu had been resolute: no one in his hospital or anywhere else should ever see that he had any doubts whatsoever about his capabilities. There are some, Hailu said, who mistake prayer for weakness.

"We should go before it gets dark." Yonas stood awkwardly in place. "Those soldiers stop every car at night"—he looked at his watch—"and we don't want to be late."

Hailu moved towards Dawit's room but Yonas held him back.

"Not today," he said. "We'll be back again. You're too tired for another fight."

Hailu shook his arm free. "If he doesn't go with us, you know where he'll go. I treated a boy his age today."

Yonas wrapped an arm around his shoulders and led him towards the door. "We have to get home before it gets late. Did you see the car that was burning on the street last night? With the university closed, these students have nothing to do but plan more trouble. And besides," he added, "Sara said she'll watch him for you." After his mother, Yonas's wife Sara was the only one Dawit listened to, if he chose to listen to anyone at all. "You look exhausted," he said.

A BLUE HAZE drifted from eucalyptus trees dotting the hillsides of Addis Ababa and clung to the horizon like a faint, tender bruise. It was dusk and a hollow wind whistled through a crack in the driver's side window of Hailu's Volkswagen where he sat. Yonas was in front next to him, both of them quiet. Dawit hadn't responded when he'd knocked on his door, and only Yonas's pleadings had prevented him from getting his key and forcing his way into his youngest son's room. He slid his car out of the garage onto the wide dirt road used by motorists and pack animals alike.

Hailu's neighborhood was a series of newer houses with sprawling gardens and lush lawns, and the more modest old Italian-style homes made of wood and mud with wide verandas and corrugated-tin roofs much like the one he'd inherited from his father. Some owners with large gated compounds rented single-room mud-and-wattle homes to poorer families. The neighborhood had neither the opulent villas nor the decaying shanties of other areas, and it was where Hailu had spent much of his years as a young, newly married doctor. It was a community, and one that, more and more often, he didn't like to venture far from.

The car dug into potholes on the rocky terrain, straining from the weight of two grown men. Ahead of them and all around, the green hilly landscape, crested with bright yellow *meskel* flowers, rolled against an orange sky. From this point on the road, Addis Ababa's hills blocked Hailu's view of the drab concrete-and-glass office buildings that had sprung up in the sprawling city in the last few decades, their ugly façades dominating every street, crowding out the kiosks and fruit stands that struggled to maintain the spaces they'd occupied for decades.

He'd grown to dread driving, the stalls, the false starts, the thick noise that pushed through the confines of his car and competed with his thoughts for attention. Everything seemed too loud these days: the exhaust fumes and engines, the brays of stubborn donkeys, the cries of beggars and vendors. The endless throngs of pedestrians. In his car, in the shelter of the regulated heat, he was comforted by the familiar parameters.

Yonas pointed out the window towards the stately high walls of the French Legation that were slowly shrinking in the distance. "I used to cut through the estate to go to school before they put that wall up." He chuckled. "The *zebenya* almost caught Dawit one day when he tried to follow me. He chased him with his stick. Dawit wanted to come back and find the old guard." Yonas shook his head, smiling and staring at the wall.

"I'm not used to seeing that stone wall, even after all these years," Yonas said. There were dark circles under his eyes and he tapped the fingers of one hand into the palm of the other, a nervous habit Hailu saw only rarely.

They were on a smoother road now, rocky bumps giving way to a paved flatness that was far less damaging to his tires. If he had been alone, he would have sped up, but he wanted to linger in this moment in the car with his son and hear him talk of better days.

Along the side of the road, street vendors were taking down their stalls for the day, pulling out their long poles from the ground, folding large plastic sheets that served as awning against rain. Hawkers called out reduced prices on their wares, competing for attention in the noise and congestion. One young woman delicately balanced a baby on her hip as she arranged her neatly stacked rows of cinnamon sticks and *berbere* on a thin cloth in front of her, the bags of crushed red pepper bright as rubies. Shoeshine boys planted on every street corner squatted and whistled at businessmen rushing towards crowded parking lots. A lone voice climbed above the din and clamor, a prayer, and for a moment, a deep hush fell upon the scene and all that was heard were the churnings of engines.

They were approaching Yekatit 12 Martyrs' Square at Sidist Kilo, near Haile Selassie University where Yonas taught history and Dawit was studying in the law program. In the square was an obelisk monument that honored the victims of an Italian-era massacre. At the top of the obelisk, a stone lion gazed proudly across the city, defiant. Four imposing tanks rested at each corner of the intersection. Two soldiers paced, their gazes lifting from their shoes as Hailu drove by. They watched the Volkswagen pass, then turned their attention back to their boots.

"They're younger than some of the university students they're supposed to be watching," Yonas said. "Boys." There was an overturned bus in the distance and a small crowd of street boys milling around with stones in their hands, kept at bay by soldiers' kicks.

Hailu knew if Dawit had been there, he would have said something, would have made a passionate declaration about the need for a new constitution and freedom of expression, for land reform that gave the farmer ownership of what he tilled, for the removal of an old, tired monarch. But he wasn't, and there was nothing in the brief pause that followed Yonas's words but the rumble and rattle of trucks and cars whizzing past them and out of sight. Hailu slowed to let a young boy and his sheep pass. He stared at his hands, age spots now dotting the skin above his wrist, and he thought back to the day he first saw Selam's tattoos, inked into her hands a week before their wedding.

"It's God's mark on me," she'd said, blushing as he ran a thumb over a tattoo that was as green as a fresh leaf. "It keeps evil away."

His own mother had similar crosses gracing the lines of her jaw, but he'd wanted to goad the young girl into showing the temper her older brothers complained about. "What if I don't want a wife with a cross carved into her skin?"

"I'll tell my father to find someone else for me. He'll choose another man."

"And what if no one wants a rejected girl?" He had been a brash student, feeling very bold in front of this beautiful girl from his village.

She stayed calm. "God doesn't take without giving." Even back then, her confidence had shaken his.

"God doesn't take without giving," Hailu repeated now to himself, wishing he could summon up her certainty.

"Did you say something, Abbaye?" Yonas asked.

"Your mother's tattoos, the crosses," Hailu said. "I love them, I always have." He shook his head, and drove the rest of the way in silence.

YONAS HAD EXPECTED his father to disappear into his office and change into his white coat as soon as he entered the hospital, to perhaps tuck his prayer beads into the large pocket in front, then hide his anxiety behind a professional demeanor. Instead, Hailu took the beads out of his pocket the moment he stepped out of the car. He held them in plain sight. Then he headed for Selam's room and became just another nervous husband on his way to see his wife, his steps so wide and fast that Yonas was left several paces behind him.

In the hospital room, in a small bed tucked beneath a small window, Selam slept with an IV snaking out of her thin arm. She was dressed in a blue hospital gown. Her gold cross necklace rested on a chest that rose and sank with the help of an oxygen tank. Hailu stood by her feet, poring over her medical chart. Yonas reached for her hands. He kissed the tattoos on the back of her wrists, and he closed his eyes.

I told your father these crosses needed their own space, his mother said to him long ago, holding up her wrists and angling the inked crosses into the sun. Yonas had been forced to squint against the light that seeped into the prayer room adjoining his parents' master bedroom. I told him he must build me a room big enough for the angels that watched over me, a place we could talk. Selam said this with a teasing smile, but as a young boy, Yonas had believed her and he'd held his own hands into the sun and wondered if his wrists, absent of crosses, were also worthy of holy ground. The story his mother told was that his father built the prayer room for her. Carved the space out of their large bedroom and erected a wall and door to mark where holy ground began and the physical world ended.

His father had traveled the 748 kilometers from Addis Ababa back to Selam's former home in Gondar, in northern Ethiopia, to find the wood to make the door. He used the bark from the largest tree on her father's land. It had roots that dug into the earth like hungry fingers, and I wanted to make a door from a tree that refused to let go of life, Hailu once said. He brought the trunk back himself, tied to the top of his first car, a two-door with a grumbling engine, then dragged it on horseback from Debre Markos when the car had stalled on the treacherous winding roads back to Addis Ababa. The door was thick and knotted, it held scars that polishing could not remove, and Hailu allowed no one else to construct and cut it into shape. The last bit of wood from the tree was used to make the long rectangular table that was the prayer room's only piece of furniture.

Yonas was a thirty-two-year-old man now, with a daughter and a wife, but he knelt in the prayer room every day, held his naked wrists to the sun, and wondered again about his worthiness. His mother had been in the hospital for a week, but the slowing down of her heart had started years before. He alone witnessed the countless afternoons she came into the prayer room to weep by herself, unaware that her eldest son was pressed against the thick wooden door, listening. He was also the only one who knew that she'd stopped taking the medicine his father prescribed for her heart. He'd caught her throwing her daily dose down the sink one day, and had been so shocked and confused he'd merely stood there and stared. She'd looked up to find him, and given him a slow smile of resignation.

"My son," she'd said, her hand gently twisting the pill cap on. "You understand, don't you?" The light from the morning sun had been cold and gray on her face. "I'm tired of fighting what God wants."

She'd hugged him, then gone downstairs to make his father coffee. Selam had needed no words from him, had asked for nothing except silence from this son who abhorred lying. And it was this silence that fed a guilt that had become nearly unbearable as he watched his mother grow sicker and his father become more desperate to keep her alive. He let the soft ache in his chest die away before opening his eyes.

His mother was stirring, her expression changing from placid to tense. Her eyes were closed but she turned her head towards the window, then hid her face in her pillow with a sharp jerk of her neck.

"Emaye," Yonas said, laying a hand on her shoulder, "are you dreaming?"

Hailu moved to her side and held her face in both hands, cupping it tenderly. "*Emebet*, my lady," he said, "it's the medication. It's not real. Wake up." He glanced at the heart monitor, watched its rhythm increase. "Wake up, Selam. I'm here."

"Is she in pain, Abbaye?" Yonas asked. "Should I go get the nurse?"

"She's just waking up, that's all." Hailu kissed her cheek. "Selam."

She opened her eyes, recognition softening her frown. She looked around her. "Am I still in the hospital?" she asked. Her large eyes, her most striking feature, were focused on Hailu, who lowered his gaze to check her pulse. She looked around the room. "Why?" She let a finger trace the oxygen tube to her nose.

Hailu put her hand down. "You're getting better," he said. He cleared his throat and looked again at the medical chart, stern and professional. "The medicine will work. It's just a matter of time. I'm watching the dosage."

Selam looked at Yonas and took his hand. "Your father made me a promise, did you know this?" She had set her full mouth in the stubborn line Yonas recognized as one of his own angry gestures. "When we first married—"

"Selam," Hailu cut in, "this isn't the time. You need rest and you need to eat." He walked to the door and pointed at the bed. "I'm getting Almaz, she'll get your food ready." He walked out, running a hand over his face then letting it move to the back of his neck and knead tired muscles.

She looked at Yonas. "Yonnie, I want to rest, you know this. Talk to him." Her eyes were pleading, desperate.

Yonas patted her hand. "God knows what to do, Emaye," he said. "More than we do." He dipped his head and hoped she didn't notice the way he grimaced as he leaned in to kiss her.

"Dawit, tell him for me—" she said, then stopped. "Where's my other son?" She tried to rise and groaned in frustration at the tubes that stopped her. "Dawit's not here?"

Yonas brushed her hair from her forehead and kissed her cheek, he rested his face against hers. "Emaye," he said affectionately. "Emama." He heard above his head, through the small window, the faint sound of a car door slamming, a goatherd's whistle, the padded thump of a noise that could have been a distant rock thrown, a distant shout, another rifle discharging above the heads of restless students marching forward. "He'll come," Yonas said, because there was nothing else to say.

4

Sara heard the gate creak open and keys rattle. She wondered who was foolish enough to wander outside after sundown since patrol cars had begun to roam through the neighborhood. The police were everywhere these days, looking for possible suspects in the rash of bus burnings and shop lootings that had been taking place around the city. These bold acts of violence and rebellion, growing increasingly more persistent, kept most citizens locked behind closed doors once the sun dropped into the horizon. An unnatural quiet now descended on Addis Ababa's nights. She heard the side door groan open and soft footfalls in the corridor. Dawit. She checked the clock above the TV; it was close to seven. Soon the family would be sitting around the television trying to ignore Dawit's silence and Hailu's stares.

Sara waited for Dawit to go into his bedroom, then got up and knocked on his door. She sensed the hesitation on the other side. "It's me," she said.

The door swung open and Dawit stood in front of her dressed in dark trousers and a black long-sleeved shirt. "What?" he asked, feigning a yawn.

"Why are you dressed like that?" she asked. His nonchalance, more pronounced since Selam had gone back into the hospital last week, was irritating.

He looked down at his clothes with a raised eyebrow. "Like what?"

She pushed past him and into his room. "Are you going to try to treat me this way too?" She and Dawit, though eight years apart, had always been close. When he didn't answer, she sighed. "Abbaye keeps asking me to make sure you're home at night. He's trying to do so much all by himself. Help him."

"I know," Dawit said. "I'm being careful." He set the notebooks on the floor and sat on the bed facing her.

She eyed his clothes. "I didn't go to college but even I can tell you look like one of those troublemakers burning buses and cars." It was when Sara looked closer that she saw his eyes were red, that streaks lined his cheeks. "Where were you?" she asked. She'd long suspected that Dawit grieved intensely and alone for his mother.

"At Lily's," he said, referring to his longtime girlfriend. "After a meeting," he added.

She noticed a small red book next to his lamp. "You've been to three meetings already this week. At least that I know of. And now you're reading Mao? You're never home."

She was struck by how age and muscle had chiseled his features into a more angular version of her husband's, eight years his senior. There had been a time when the family could hardly distinguish a childhood photo of Yonas from a recent one of Dawit. The wide forehead was now more pronounced above thick eyebrows, and he'd developed a sharp, strong jaw. The brothers shared the same mouth, the same gentle curve of the bottom lip, the same mouth her daughter had inherited.

"There's an important rally tomorrow. We want to force the emperor to give us a meeting and discuss reforms," he said.

She laughed. "The emperor meeting with students?" She caught the hurt look on his face before he hid it with an arrogant shrug. She softened her tone. "We're all going to the hospital tomorrow, even Tizita. Please come, just for one day."

"I have things to do." He was having a difficult time meeting her gaze.

"You'd rather go to a rally? You already missed going to the hospital tonight." She watched his features harden, his mouth set as firmly as Tizita's before a temper tantrum.

"You don't know how lucky you are to have a family, and all you want to do is push them away," she said. If her parents were still alive, there would never be a day of disagreements between them.

He stared at the floor the same way he used to do when she would lose her temper with him when he was a child.

"If you're worried about another fight with Abbaye," she said, keeping her voice gentle, "I'll be there to help."

He shook his head. "I have to go." He sat back down on the bed and wrapped his arms around his pillow, becoming the small boy she'd grown to love like a brother.

———

THERE HAD BEEN a new kind of confidence that fueled Dawit at the meeting. He'd relayed the latest statistics about the famine without faltering. He'd waved articles from foreign presses, explained their criticisms about ineffectual aid distribution plans in detail. He'd shouted in a voice he'd barely recognized as his own, its sharp fullness reminiscent of his father. He'd watched his peers nod and whisper furiously. And he'd felt a sense of purpose, an assurance that a path was being laid out for him, something all his own. Dawit let himself dwell on the memory of his outrage and exhilaration. He needed that charge in this room that was ultimately his father's.

His father still didn't understand his need to fight for those too poor and overworked to demand their basic rights. It's a phase, his father said. You don't know what you're doing, you're only following others.

But he had a reason. There had been a fight. The boy was the son of a neighbor. The rich family lived in a house bigger than Dawit's, and there were two cars in the garage, one a Mercedes that a chauffeur cleaned and waxed every day. The boy, Fisseha, was older—fifteen to Dawit's twelve—and at school he carried a thick wooden club and a smirk he worked to perfect into an adult sneer.

Dawit and his best friend Mickey were walking home when he saw a girl sitting at the gate, near the wheel of the polished Mercedes, sobbing. Dawit recognized her as Ililta, the daughter of one of the house girls who worked in the home. She and her mother came to his house sometimes to visit their aging servant Bizu and trade neighborhood gossip. He heard a frantic cry coming from the other side of the opened gate. The sound carried something Dawit would later tell his mother reminded him of a baby, trying to explain what happened next.

"It was small," he would tell her.

He told the frightened Mickey to wait at the gate. "I'll just go check," he said.

"It's not your house," Mickey said. "Let's go."

Dawit had gone into the compound anyway. There was a shuffle and rustling coming from the open door of the servants' quarters, and again the desperate, pinched cry. He ran in and it took a few seconds for him to comprehend what he was looking at.

There was a woman, older than his mother, sitting naked on the bed, tears running down her face and trailing between her heavy, sagging breasts. In front of her, holding his penis, was Fisseha, equally naked, the familiar smirk on his face.

"Mulu?" Dawit said. He didn't recognize her without her clothes on, without the bright smile she usually had whenever she came to visit Bizu.

"Get out of here!" Fisseha said. "Go!" He still had his hand on his penis, his scrawny hips still arched towards Mulu.

And in that second, Dawit would have turned and run, would have grabbed Mickey and gone home and hidden in his room until his heart quieted, but Mulu said: "Please."

And he saw the panic and shame and terror in her eyes and he knew he couldn't leave, that he would stay where he was and fight his way out. He attacked Fisseha with a vengeance he reserved for his older, stronger brother. He kicked him, stomped on his toes, kneed his groin, pulled his head up off the ground and bashed it back down, then punched his bloody lips, his bleeding nose, his swelling eyes, and he didn't stop even after he caught sight of the polished club passing from Mulu's hand to Fisseha's weakened grip, then slipping on the floor and rolling under the bed.

"Go home!" Mulu begged. "Go, you'll get me fired. Go!"

Dawit kept hitting, the naked body beneath him squirming, then slowing, then finally still, bare to his blinding rage. He hit until Mulu's daughter Ililta ran in and threw a *shamma* over her mother's nakedness. Mulu's suddenly blanketed body made Dawit pause, then shrink away from the battered, immobile Fisseha. He was shocked by the damage he'd inflicted. Before he could say or do anything else, Ililta pushed Dawit out of the room, her "thank you" muffled by her crying.

When he got home, his father opened the door, saw the blood on his clothes, and immediately started shouting, asking loud accusatory questions Dawit refused to answer, shaken still by what he'd seen and done. When he tried to explain to his mother later, leaving out the part about Mulu's nakedness, she'd hugged him, sad.

"This is how many boys learn how to become men," she said. "House girls are sometimes expected to do more than cook and clean. You could have cost Mulu her job."

"But she was crying," Dawit argued.

"She'd be crying without work too. Where would she go with a young daughter? Fisseha's father pays for Ililta's education." His mother kissed his cheeks. "But your temper," she continued, holding his chin tenderly in her hand. "You hurt him, it was too much. His father took him to the hospital and Abbaye treated him for free." She shook her head. "No more. Please. For your sake and mine. And thank your father for what he did, stitching up that boy's face to save you trouble in school. Thank him."

He never thanked his father, afraid that he would describe in his flat medical voice all the injuries this latest patient had sustained at the hands of his own son. After that day, Mulu never came back to their house, and he and Mickey took an alternate route home. Fisseha slunk away anytime he saw him, though his eyes glowed with hatred. The scene of that fight played over and over again in Dawit's head, even after all those years.

His father would soon walk into the house and Dawit knew he'd face another fight. Dawit would try to tell him that he hadn't wanted to go with him and his older brother, but that simple reason wouldn't be enough for his father. It wouldn't be enough that he wanted to be alone with his mother, that he wanted to talk to her privately the way they'd always done. His father would never accept that his mother was also his friend.

Dawit wanted to tell his mother things he had a hard time telling anyone else, even Lily. He'd remind her of Fisseha and people like him who took advantage of others and needed to be stopped, and explain why he'd had to break his promise to her and continue to be politically active. He wanted to show her one of the letters from Mickey, sent to him from his trip to one of the famine sites, and prove to her, if not to his father, that his fight was just, that he was doing the right thing. She would understand in a way no one else in his family could. She would remind him that in his veins ran the blood of her father, one of Gondar's fiercest fighters, and she would tell him that hope can never come from doing nothing.

5

THIS WASN'T HOW MICKEY REMEMBERED WELLO. The rolling hills of his childhood had been a lush patchwork of greens and browns, rich soil had blanketed the gentle slopes as far as he could see from his aunt's small hut clustered in a ring of other thatched huts as round and perfect as coins. The farmland, tilled by obedient cattle pushed and prodded by men and boys with strong, thin frames, had once sprouted tall waves of teff, the wheatlike grain growing a pale gold in the sun. The ground had been a deep brown. The sun had been a shimmering yellow. The sky's blue had been broken by rain clouds and the soft songs of sparrows. He had run through tall grass and hidden in the overgrowth of wide bushes. He'd scattered seeds with his uncle, and raised his face to the first drops of rain that fell as thick as beads. Under the wiry shade of a thin tree, he'd buried a dying bird and sealed the grave with small stones. There had been color in this land that stretched out before him now in deathly paleness. There had been the brays of cattle, the birds and the shrill whistles of herders urging their animals forward. There had been life with all its noises and shades. What was this he was looking at now?

His instructions were to assess the famine the emperor's officials claimed was under control and easing. The military committee in Addis Ababa had been in a meeting at the Fourth Division headquarters, discussing the latest developments in a city exploding with demonstrations and union strikes. He'd gone into the building, a bag of mail slung over his shoulders to deliver to his superior officer, when he'd walked past the open door of the meeting room.

"You," the officer at the head of the table had said, his sharp eyes looking him up and down. "Have you ever been to Wello?" His voice seemed louder than it should have been in that small room, in the tense quiet of that table of soldiers and mid-level officers who peered over photographs and documents. "Have you?" he asked, impatient.

"My aunt lives there, in Dessie," Mickey said, feeling heat crawl up the back of his legs and over his head. "She used to," he said, correcting himself, the officer's stern face suggesting a man who would show no mercy if given misinformation. "She died last year."

The rest of the men all mumbled their condolences. A few dropped their heads in respect, then sighed in sympathy before looking at him again. The officer talking to him did not move his direct gaze from his face.

"Cholera," the officer declared. "It was cholera that these elitists should have prevented, they had the means to stop all of this." He pounded on the table, his back to Mickey, the full force of his anger rolling out in front of the men who leaned into him and nodded vigorously. "It was cholera, wasn't it?" He turned again to Mickey.

It was old age, it was a peasant's bitter existence, it was too many children housed in a body daily wearing out, it was many things, but not cholera. But Mickey said nothing, the man's confidence and simmering anger forcing him into a reverent silence. Dawit had this confidence, and there was nothing to do in the face of it but stand still and let it sweep over him.

The man pounded the table again. "What's your name, soldier?" he asked, though he was already gathering his papers and stacking them in a neat pile.

"Mickey," Mickey said, the bag of mail heavy on his back. His superior officer would surely be angry at his late delivery. "Mikias Habte."

The officer nodded to the rest of the men around the table. "He'll go to Wello and bring back a report," he told them. "Do you know what it means to serve your country?" the officer asked Mickey.

Mickey nodded quickly. "Yes, I do."

"You can go," he said, gesturing for Mickey to leave the room. "Report to me when you get back from Wello. Close the door."

Now, in front of him was a small child with a head bigger than the rest of his body, crouched in a posture of fatigue that only dying old men should know. His bony skull rested on frail wrists, and he stared into the distance blankly, his sagging mouth host to flies and holes where teeth once grew.

Mickey pulled out his notebook and scribbled furiously. Dawit, he wrote, we eat too much in Addis Ababa. We don't know hunger like this. My thick body feels like a scar in this village. I'm embarrassed that I haven't eaten during the long drive from Addis Ababa, and all I want is to go back to my tent and eat the food my mother packed.

Patches of brown cracked earth had been dug out of the flat dryness of the landscape. They dotted the dead land like pockmarks, craters dug by desperate hands in search of shriveled roots and insects or any stone that could sit in their mouths and remind their tongues of the weight of bread. Mickey's boots felt tight around his sweaty socks and swollen feet. His rounded belly suddenly an obscenity in this land of rotten animal carcasses and inhuman hunger. The smell of dead cattle forced him to put a handkerchief over his nose and mouth.

"You'll get used to the smell," the clerk from the local administrator's office said to him, pointing him in the direction of a small tent. "It's the carcasses . . ." He stopped and pulled out a piece of paper from his pocket and handed it to Mickey. "These are some basic facts about the village," he said, his eyes earnest. "They don't want to know anything about what's happening here, those officials. I've tried to tell them, but they're afraid of bad publicity if the news spreads." He grunted and shook his head. "I've been forbidden to tell you the truth, but you can read it." He pointed to the paper and shoved his hands in the pocket of his white overcoat. "I was told to dress like a doctor in case any reporters come here."

"What about this boy?" Mickey said, pointing to the child. "Shouldn't we take him somewhere?"

"His mother left him there to look for food. There's nothing here." He spread his hands as if the landscape were an empty table, then gestured again towards a small tent where a tired nurse leaned against the wooden post and watched them with flat eyes. "And with all this, there's the cholera outbreak." He walked on without a glance at the child.

"The emperor came here to visit last year. He must have seen this. Isn't he helping?" Mickey had to quicken his pace to keep up.

"It's not enough." The clerk shook his head. "And it's come too late. When you are convinced that everything that happens is the will of God, what is there to do but wait until God has mercy?" He stopped at the mouth of the tent and turned to Mickey. "People are walking to Addis to beg for food, if they can get there alive. Maybe that's where that child's mother went." He stared into the horizon. "Nothing will change if others don't help. Tell your people for us," he said. "Tell them what's happening."

BACK IN HIS TENT that cold night, shivering under the pale yellow glow of a weak kerosene lamp, Mickey wrote with urgency and anger, scribbling his words onto the blank paper.

This is how a man tills his land: behind cattle that are tied to one end of a plow that he uses to dig and lift and turn the ground. He holds a stick in one hand and the end of the plow in the other. At the end of that stick is a rope that he uses to whip the animals when they tire from the hot sun and the lack of water and simple hunger. A man works like this every day, every month, year after year, behind his cattle, his hand attached to a plow that has dug its own imprints into his calloused palms. He speaks to no one but himself, he hears nothing but his own slavish grunts as he pushes his plow into dirt, willing a crop to grow from unforgiving ground, praying daily for more rain. But it didn't rain in 1972 in the north, my friend, and the farmer had no crops. The rains did not come as they should, and when the rains failed, the crops failed, and when the crops failed, the farmer grew hungry, and when he grew hungry, his cattle also grew hungry, because a farmer will feed his cattle before himself. When the cattle began to die, the farmer gathered his family and tried to walk to the nearest village, the nearest aid shelter, the nearest anywhere where he could hold out his proud hand and beg for food. But everyplace he went was the same as what he had left. They are starving here in Wello, Dawit. They are starving in Tigre and Shoa. We have lived in the city and we have forgotten about these people. And imagine, now, a farmer far from Wello, in the south, where the rains are more forgiving and the land has not been cursed by famine. This farmer plows land that isn't his, that was never his father's, which was never his grandfather's, and will never be his son's. He works as hard as his animals day after day to pay a landowner's taxes and to glean enough crops so his family has enough grains for food after they've given the landowner his share. The landowner's share is always large. It is always more than the landowner needs. It is a selfish share created by a selfish system that preys on the weak and makes them servants to the rich. Dawit, we live in a feudal system. Our country exploits those who work the hardest to stay alive. Our emperor has built the myth of this land on the blood of those who have been too tired to voice their own truths. Is this my country? We have grown up together, Dawit, but I was someone else before you knew me. My father was this farmer from the south, he died on a rich man's plot of land tied to the wrong end of his plow because he'd been forced to sell his cattle to feed his family that harvest. My father died like an animal, still tied to those ropes when I found him, swallowing with his last breaths the dust of another man's land, broken by the burden of his labor. The rich think this land is theirs though they have never earned the right to call it theirs. Not like these farmers. Not like my father. Most of those who are here, on the ground dying, are the ones who were strong enough to walk out of their villages and get here. The roads are littered with our people who died on the way, their bodies rotting in the sun if the vultures haven't gotten to them first. We dishonor our dead and our workers, Dawit. The rich have kept this secret, the emperor has stolen this truth from us and we have to fight to get our country back and save these people. A man told me today as many as two hundred thousand will die. They will die. It is too late for them. Do we even have as many alive in Addis Ababa?

6

EMPEROR HAILE SELASSIE LEANED into his cupped hand and listened to the empty pocket of air that blew like dry wind against his ear. He adjusted the pillow behind his back on his hand-carved chair and sank into the soothing gentleness of silence. He was in his wide, marble-floored bedroom, the thick wooden doors of his closets revealing rows of identical tan uniforms and intricately embroidered velvet capes. There was no sound but this air, there was no one here but him, there was nothing to do but sit, and he sighed in relief.

Mercy. This, we have prayed for, the emperor thought. This has been all we have wanted. When those treacherous sons of Neway fought our bravest of men and tried to steal our rightful place on this throne, we begged not for justice but for mercy. Mercy on this throne and this humble one, your appointed. Didn't your own most blessed King Dawit beg to you in his darkest days, did he not sing your praises when you answered? Surely goodness and mercy shall follow us, he said. We ask only for mercy, not even for the blessing of rain.

Rain. It had always been his country's curse. Centuries of floods, then drought, thunderous rain, then sun-bleached farms. There had always been too much or too little, seeds floated out of soil or split in half from a burning heat in this land. It shouldn't have been surprising, the emperor thought, that this new trouble had started, only a few months ago, with water.

Prime Minister Aklilu Habtewold, elegant and prim, his hair slicked back, had been the one to tell him.

"We have problems in Neghelle," he said. Years of French diplomacy had helped him cultivate his naturally regal, controlled bearing, but the prime minister's words that day had been crisp and sharp, even rushed. "The soldiers are rebelling. Their well has broken."

The emperor had been irritated by this triviality. He had gone back to his papers, an inquiry from the minister of finance about ways to handle taxi drivers' demands for lower petrol prices. It cannot be, the emperor wrote, oil prices are higher worldwide because of the OPEC oil embargo of 1973; they must share this burden.

"Your Majesty," Prime Minister Aklilu said, "they have taken the officers hostage. They say their water well is unsafe and they're not allowed to use the same well as the officers. They say they're forced to eat rotten food while the officers dine well every night. I'm afraid this will escalate. We shouldn't rely on any assistance from the United States, they have their own problems with President Nixon's scandal."

The emperor did not look up from his papers. "Send the planes, tell them to fly low. Don't hurt them."

The prime minister had been hesitant. "The bombers? But that will cause more anger. There's—"

A simple twitch in his eyebrow was enough to silence the prime minister. "Then you will tell them change will come. Don't punish them. Tell the other ministers that nothing must be known of this." He had gone back to his papers, to his documents, to his piles of inquiries and respectful requests and forgotten about these soldiers and their dirty water.

Less than a month later, it had been the Debre Zeit Air Force that demanded more money, and Prime Minister Aklilu had granted that, then another increase. Two salary increases for these lowly soldiers in less than a month, from money that did not exist for those purposes. Then Asmara's entire division had risen up and taken control of the radio stations. The voices speaking through the radio, their unschooled accents rough, had had the arrogance to make more demands of the throne, to air their complaints. The voice on the radio had asked for a higher minimum salary, free medical treatment, timely pay, a change in regime, and—a pause—the bodies of privates to be returned to their home village, just as was done for officers. The emperor had seen in this the awareness of his might. They understand we will crush them, he said. They had not forgotten the Neways, they had not forgotten, and still they dared to rise up.

"They've shut down the airport? Closed the roads? Taken over the city? You have allowed this to happen?" The emperor's rage had been focused on the prime minister. "You have allowed this to happen in our country?"

"It is a mutiny," Prime Minister Aklilu said. He'd kept his head low, his eyes lower, his small mouth was pursed in a thin line. His blue suit, tailored by an Armenian he'd had trained in Paris, sat perfectly on his broad shoulders; the fit was impeccable. In his hands was an envelope. "Your Majesty"—his voice was clear, only his soft eyes betrayed his emotions—"they want a change, they want a new cabinet, and things will only get worse until they see something. I respectfully and regretfully give you my resignation. I see no other way." The lines had been rehearsed, the emperor could tell. "It is with a profound sadness that I submit this letter. You have been a father to me, my education could not have been if not for you. I have had the honor of serving this country at home and abroad, I have been blessed to stand before the United Nations and to assist in the reunification of our country."

The emperor silenced him with a raised hand. "You are leaving? After so many years?" But in the distance, beyond his window, he heard the restless growls of his caged lions, and he understood what was happening was right.

THE EVENTUAL ARRESTS of former Prime Minister Aklilu and his cabinet should have quelled the soldiers. His drive to Mercato to press money into the open hands of his poorest people should have stilled the rumblings. His appointment of Endalkachew Mekonnen, with his Oxford diplomacy and aristocratic assurance, to prime minister should have steadied his shaken country. But from a sky that lay bare and hot under the sun, leaflets fell from helicopters like torn feathers. They dropped from the emperor's air force and army aviation helicopters, addressed to all of his people, crisp sheets of carefully typed demands. These soldiers wanted more and they wanted a committee to make sure those demands were met. To make sure those responsible for corruption and the famine were brought to justice. To make sure a new Ethiopia could rise up from under the heavy weight of an aging, decaying monarchy. The demands were never-ending, a thick white fog across his city.

The emperor had felt a small, sharp pain in the center of his chest as he watched the spiraling pages settle in his garden from his library window. He saw, in the grace of their descent, his last days laid flat before him. It will come, he told himself. It will come as softly and quietly as these papers, and we must prepare.

7

THE RALLY BEGAN IN MESKEL SQUARE, in a flatland of concrete and asphalt that sat in the center of the city. Five hundred students moved restlessly in anticipation of military trucks and howitzers. Down the wide roads that shrank into smaller streets, the distant pitch of trucks and sirens blazed in the morning sun, and everywhere whispers of courage and defiance drifted over stone. The marchers carried placards and flags, waved empty hands and fists into the air. Behind the fence of nearby St. Joseph's prep school, thunderous voices lifted, light as feathers. Schoolboys ran to join the five hundred. And from Meskel Square rose full-bodied shouts that shook the city and seeped into the walls of Jubilee Palace where Emperor Haile Selassie pondered this latest noise from his subjects.

Traffic was at a standstill, a line of metal insects baking in the sun. Onlookers leaned out of windows, car doors opened, hearts sped in the growing cacophony. Passersby made way for the procession of armed soldiers jogging in perfect unison toward the square, their footfalls surprisingly nimble. The five hundred students, milling no more, stood frozen in place and let a collective gasp speak for their fear. Placards drifted down, soft clouds in a brisk wind. Rifles raised, caught the glint of the sun and sent light hurling back into the sky.

Dawit moved through the crowd of students, tall and fast. Empty-handed. His broad shoulders parted the way for each step as he searched for a familiar face. Lily had promised to meet him near the fence of the prep school. He stood on his toes looking for her ringlet curls and the red shirt she said she would be wearing. A solid hand, cool against his arm, stopped him.

"Over here." It was Solomon, an economics student, older than most, more sullen than any.

Dawit was surprised. The man had never spoken to him before.

Solomon rarely addressed anyone, seldom looked beyond the invisible wall he'd built around himself and walked within every day.

"I'm looking for someone," Dawit said.

"Get in front," Solomon told him, pointing to the head of the crowd. "They're not going to shoot. Not today." He shoved a pamphlet in his hand. On one side of the pamphlet was a photo of a starving child with painfully swollen limbs. On the other, Emperor Haile Selassie fed his Chihuahua meat from a silver platter. "Keep it in your pocket. You don't have time to look for anyone, it's starting."

"Are you sure they're not going to shoot?" Dawit asked. Rumors said Solomon was one of those coordinating protests with students across Ethiopia and throughout Europe and America.

"Soldiers rebelled in the north because they don't have clean water to drink while the emperor's officers get beer and wine." He nudged Dawit forward and pointed at the row of soldiers standing ahead of them, "A hundred thousand marched for the rights of Muslims and no one was hurt. Everyone wants the emperor out. We're all on the same side. Move to the front."

Dawit did as he was instructed, felt the low murmurs and excited talk rise at his back like a breeze. He swept his gaze once more across the square for Lily, but it was impossible to see her, there were so many and the crowd was getting larger. He focused on those who seemed to have been waiting for him, who nodded briefly and made room in the front, ready to march or fall with him. Dawit felt the first shivers ride through his body in waves and he let his shoulders loosen.

The first footfalls started from the right, a gentle thud on cracked concrete. Followed by another. Then the brush of arms raising fists. Solomon handed him a placard and Dawit grabbed it and held on tight. LAND FOR THE TILLER it read, its bold black letters crisp on stark white. Solomon raised his own, A PEOPLE'S GOVERNMENT FOR ALL. The five hundred, multiplied, faced the soldiers in ready silence. A thousand eyes staring into the barrels of two thousand loaded rifles.

Dawit looked across the front lines, into the faces of classmates familiar and unknown, glanced at the schoolchildren who flanked them, and he felt his heart swell and a feeling close to gratitude forced tears into his throat and he had to raise his voice with the chorus of others to stop from weeping at this sight of so many who for one moment were joined in a bond as strong as family, perhaps in a union even stronger than blood.

His first jump was involuntary, so instinctual that he scarcely knew what he had done. Dawit leapt again, chest pushed forward, and felt the surge of bodies moving with him and voices ringing like a thousand clanging bells. He didn't know when the first shakes of his shoulders started, but he felt the tremors from those next to him, heard the deep-throated warriors' cries that rose and fell, and his shoulders moved with a weightless rhythm, soft waves against a trembling wall. The students surged ahead, their ecstatic leaps growing wilder and free as the soldiers backed away in awkward, faltering steps.

8

DAWIT LOOKED DOWN THE BRIGHT hospital corridor. It was strangely quiet, even though it was past visiting hours. There were a few nurses clipping their way from one task to another. He turned into the hallway that led to his mother's room. It, too, lacked its usual activity. He stepped inside the room and shut the door softly.

She was asleep under a window that framed the angry voices and shrill whistles from the street. The curtains could not soak up all the noises coming from citizens who would soon flee into the shelter of their homes. Police sirens streaked past, and he squinted to sharpen the outline of his mother's body in the rise and fall of light from outside. Herders' campfires, newly lit, flickered in the distant hills, flaring and waning like bursting stars, and the warm glow of headlights broke the flat expanse of dark in the unlit room.

Dawit moved closer to the bed and touched his mother's hand, held it and let his warmth soak into her cool skin. He laid his head next to hers and kissed her cheek, then traced the crescent-shaped scar he'd made next to her eye as a young, careless boy. The scar, once plumped by flesh, now folded into itself, evidence of the weight his mother had lost in the last week. An old shame came back to him, clung to him as strong as any smell in the building. His tantrums as a child had never been easy for her to control, and the scar was proof of the emotional damage he must have wreaked on this small woman. Dawit straightened the sheets and blankets that clung to her, then pulled a chair to sit at her feet.

"Emaye," he said. She didn't stir. "Forgive me."

There were days when he'd spent entire afternoons like this, leaning against her legs as she sewed or stared out the window, listening to the hypnotic lilt of her voice as she told him of her Gondar, a land of noblemen and castles. The melody of her favorite lullaby stepped forward from his memory and into the room. Dawit hummed the tune, a series of simple notes. He draped his arms over her legs, then laid his head on the bed, making sure that a part of him touched a part of her. He relaxed, the crown of his head solidly against her leg, he let his breaths deepen and then slow into soft sighs. His song ebbed into silence, and Dawit fell asleep, comforted.

HAILU'S PRAYER BEADS dragged on the ground, hooked to the arm of the chair; his radio was off. It was late afternoon, the sun was tipping into the shadows of night. A tepid breeze floated through an open window, and tension pressed on all sides of the house, bearing down on Yonas.

"Why isn't he home yet?" Even though Hailu's voice was pinched, it was smooth, frighteningly soft. It shook Yonas's nerves and settled his senses back in a jumbled order.

Hailu switched the radio on. Voices sputtered and then flattened into crisp sentences. An announcement from a reporter: Churchill Road was blocked; all roads to Meskel Square were closed due to the rally. No injuries to report. Patrols would be extra rigorous tonight.

"Students set three buses on fire this morning. Do you know why?" Hailu asked. "Because they're government-owned. But their parents need buses to go to work. What sense is in that? And they broke the windows on two Mercedes parked near Banco di Roma; shops in Piazza and everywhere else are staying closed, we can't buy things we need. Ethiopian Airlines flights have been grounded. The emperor already dissolved his cabinet and created a new one, but they're not satisfied. And now they have this rally." He turned down the radio. "That's where he went, isn't it?" Hailu paused and looked out the window. "How do I handle him?"

Yonas wanted to shrink away from this agitated voice that spoke to no one in particular. He turned the radio off instead.

His father turned to him. "The rally called for the resignation of the emperor." Hailu was incredulous. "Do these children think they can take down a monarchy of three thousand years? Do they think all they have to do is raise a few signs and the world will change?" He was counting his prayer beads one by one. "That their ideas can stop bullets?"

His father's statement reminded him of one of the few fights they'd had, fourteen years ago. It had been in 1960. He was eighteen then and the country was at the height of a coup attempt. Two brothers had waited until the emperor had flown out of the country to stage their rebellion with the help of the Imperial Bodyguard. The Neway brothers. One was a brigadier general, the other a graduate of Columbia University in America. Yonas had believed in the brash and vivid dreams of these courageous brothers, had taken up their galvanizing calls for change and marched with full-throated shouts through the streets of Addis Ababa. His father, back then, had sat at the door and waited for him, too, had stayed awake at night and gone to work the next day without sleep. He had asked Yonas the same question: What can you do to take down an entire government? You have eighteen years, the emperor has three thousand. But Yonas believed until the very end, even as the country watched a poorly planned coup turn into a bloody showdown. In a matter of days, the Neway brothers and their men were dead, three of the corpses, including that of one of the brothers, Germame Neway, hanged, then put on display in St. Giorgis Square as a warning. All hopes of change had been extinguished with them, but the rumblings left by their calls for revolt had managed to snake their way from 1960 to 1974. And now here was his father once again questioning a son's ideals.

Sara came into the living room, smoothing her long skirt and tucking hair back into her orange scarf. "Tizzie won't sleep," she said. Just the way she walked, with sturdy, graceful steps, eased his anxiety.

Yonas made room for her on the sofa. "Didn't you try to get her to lie down earlier?" He wrapped an arm around her and drew her close to him. "She'll fall asleep when she's tired."

"Selam started getting sick as soon as Tizita was born," Hailu said. He hadn't taken his eyes off the door.

"Was it at the same time?" Sara said. "I was so weak." She laid her head on Yonas's shoulder. "Those early days," she said, shuddering. "Tizita was so tiny."

"It was Emaye's first trip to the hospital," Yonas said.

"Tizita will be four soon. Shouldn't we give a party?" Sara asked. She looked up at Yonas. "She's old enough to remember it later."

Yonas was surprised by the idea. He looked at his father but Hailu was staring into the distance. "It doesn't seem right. Not now."

"Emaye likes parties," Sara said. She smiled gently at him. "She was talking about giving Tizzie a party. Abbaye needs to relax, seeing his friends will be good for him."

"Abbaye, what do you think?" he asked his father.

"Four years," Hailu said. He shook his head, the lines of his mouth lengthening. He stood with effort. "I'm going to lie down."

A HARD RAIN FELL. Thick drops that pooled and shimmered on the asphalt road. A bright moon hung in the starless pitch. Dawit drummed on the steering wheel of Yonas's Fiat, speeding when he shouldn't have been. He'd left the hospital and gone to meet with the organizers of the student union in a small house near the Sidist Kilo university campus. Solomon had tapped him to head recruitment for the next rally.

"People like you," Solomon had said, grim-faced though he gave a compliment. "Talk to your friends, tell them to talk to their friends. We're gaining momentum, we need more people. Choose them wisely."

Dawit made a mental list of his friends: Lily, Meron, Markos, Teodros, Zinash, Anketse, Tiruneh, Gebrai, Habtamu, Getachew—there were so many who would be willing. He ran through the names of those he knew in passing, and as the asphalt road crumbled into dirt in front of the stately French Legation, he thought of Mickey, the friend who was a brother in all but blood.

They were seven years old when they met. He was a thin, wiry child with a reputation for fights and inattentiveness; Mickey was the son of a widow, a heavy-breathing boy with a soft heart and nervous eyes that never seemed to stop blinking away the light. They'd met at the bottom steps of Dawit's veranda, Dawit staring, along with the rest of the compound, at this newest addition to their community. Mickey and his mother carried only one bag between them, a small leather case no bigger than Hailu's medicine bag. Mickey waved shyly to Dawit and squinted, his neck jutting forward like a chicken, and Dawit realized he had poor vision. Hello, Mickey said, my father died, so I'm going to live here. Dawit had returned his wave and said he had a father, and given the new boy a tentative smile.

Mickey had followed his mother to their one-room home, a tiny structure squeezed between others just like it on a thin pathway barely wide enough for two people. He set their bag at the door, then came back to the veranda. Can your father be mine, too? Mickey asked.

His father had accepted Mickey's offer to be his third son with a seriousness that left Dawit jealous.

"What happened to your father?" Hailu asked, bending low to meet Mickey at eye level. He was holding the boy's chubby hand.

"He's dead," Dawit had said, leaning closer to his father. "He told me."

"What happened?" Hailu asked, his smile fading, his hand moving to a firm, gentle clasp around Mickey's shoulders, drawing the boy near.

"He fell down," Mickey said, squinting at nothing, looking away. "He was working and then he fell." Mickey looked past Dawit and his father and took in the house. Its two-story structure suddenly seemed too large and imposing to Dawit, who followed Mickey's eyes. "Your house is big," he said.

Hailu guided the boys up the veranda, Dawit holding on tightly to one of his hands, looking for a way to get his father's attention back. "You'll go to school. You won't have to work like your father."

Mickey's mother, Tsehai, had been watching. "Mickey, come here!"

Hailu had let his hand go. "Tell your mother we're all a family. If she needs anything, just let me know." He'd patted Mickey's head, pulling his hand out of Dawit's grip to give Mickey a hug.

The two boys grew inseparable. At school, Dawit's protectiveness of him prevented many of the other children from saying anything about Mickey's shabby clothes and worn shoes. In the classroom, while Dawit's mischief and laziness earned him lashes or kicks, Mickey's earnestness warmed even the strictest teacher's demeanor. The two boys were closer than brothers and Dawit shared everything with him: his marbles, his lunch, even his pet turtle. It was only after they'd finished secondary school that things changed. Mickey had to work and could not attend university, though his grades and scores had been better than Dawit's. He'd joined the military, waving aside Dawit's guilty looks and mumbled condolences.

"I have new clothes, now," Mickey had joked. "Finally, I look as good as you."

And now Mickey was in Wello. His letters becoming increasingly enraged, showing Dawit a side of Ethiopia, and his friend, he'd never seen.

9

THE EMPEROR WASN'T SURE HOW these soldiers had crept into his meetings. Somehow they'd managed to crawl out of their barracks and into Menelik Palace, their distaste for educated and cultured men clear in their haughty glares. They had been meeting at the Fourth Division headquarters when one day a few of their select had driven in their jeeps onto his grounds, pushed past his startled guards, and settled themselves around his table. This defiance brought Endalkachew's already-dwindling cabinet to stunned paralysis. Endalkachew, stripped of all semblance of power, most of his ministers jailed, was forced to resign, and then was arrested himself. These low-level officers selected another one of his men, Mikael Imru, as prime minister, all the while bowing in deference and murmuring their unending loyalty.

He'd become confused by how many they were, these men in dark green fatigues who now cradled his elbow in palace meetings and whispered that he must remember their demands, he must remember his people. He no longer knew their numbers. Did not know which of these earnest soldiers had taken control of his radio station and breathed these words into every home and restaurant in his city: "We do not believe in an eye for an eye. We will bring to trial all those who misused their power. There can be justice without bloodshed." And was it only the wind or had his people sent joyous shouts into the night sky? In the whirl and speed of so much happening so fast, the bodies of these men had disintegrated into mere voices in his ear. They seemed molded out of the shadows that clung to dark corners of his palace, drifting in and out of his line of vision, leaving traces of smoke and the scent of burning wood in their wake. They talked to him in his sleep, their words nestling against his head and burrowing into his brain. The emperor slid through his days shaking the noises loose from his ears, trying to bat the prodding requests away. Let us help you lead the country, you are old and we are young, you are one, we are many. We will do everything you ask.

The pressure built in Emperor Haile Selassie's head, drilling behind his eyes. Thoughts collapsed into a hundred scattered words floating in front of his face, pinned onto pages that were shoved under his pen. He found himself numbed by the honeyed smiles that sliced his resistance more than their hard, sharp eyes. Your name here. And here, these officers he'd never known before said. Sign this and dissolve your ministry and the Crown Council, we have a new and better way for you to rule. They were mere men instructing God's chosen, the monarch with blood that could be traced to wise King Solomon of the Bible. Soon, the voices floated from the radio and called his best men to submit to the wishes of all and go to jail. There will be no bloodshed, the radio said, only justice. His senators and judges, cabinet members and ministers, his noblemen, began to leave their posts and walk with grim confidence to turn themselves in. Sign here, and here, no time to read, we must hurry, trust us. Don't sit, there is no rest. We must show that change is coming. Don't you hear your people? The emperor stood. The emperor walked. The emperor followed the backs of the uniformed men from one meeting into another. What has become of us? he asked himself. When will angels lead us out of this fray? Emperor Haile Selassie tried his best to become immobile. To stand rigid without following. To sit without signing. To watch without nodding, without expression, without revealing the panic that fluttered through him. But things kept moving forward. We must not be anything other than what we are, he reminded himself. We are and so we will be. We are here, in these days of locusts and noise, but it has been written that this shall pass, and so it will.

THERE WAS NO ONE IN Jubilee Palace today. No footsteps approached his room in the hallway, no shuffle of servants' slippers moved through cavernous rooms. There was only the scent of overdried wood dying into ash, pungent and strong. A faithful servant shifted restlessly in front of him, waiting for his next orders. Emperor Haile Selassie held a crisp white piece of paper and extended it to the man. Write this, he said to his servant, and heard his own voice drift back to him. Write this, it said, floating to him, fading. They must remember, my subjects must be reminded that I was once in exile in a country beyond these borders and even from afar, I ruled victorious. Remind them of those terrible days of Mussolini's mustard gas and tanks, when I stood before nations and battled bigotry with truth. Write. Write, the echo returned, softer and less insistent. Emperor Haile Selassie handed a pen to the old servant and watched the man tremble. Write, he ordered. Write so they are reminded, so that they know the Conquering Lion of Judah still sits on his throne. Tell them I have not left my people, that I rule still, over eighty years old and wise, kin to God's most blessed of kings. The emperor looked outside his window at his lions pacing in their cages, their growls like far-off thunder. We have not finished our time. The servant, eyes cast low, bowed. Call the minister of the pen, the emperor said, looking to the red sun falling in the distance. He will write for us. Call him here. The servant whispered: He is gone. Where is he? the emperor asked. Where are they all? Where are my people?

10

THE LIVING ROOM WAS MORE crowded than it had been in a long time. This celebration was to honor New Year's Eve and Tizita's birthday, but all Hailu could think about was that his watch was slow—once again, he hadn't wound it. He was forgetting his most routine habits.

"We needed this party," said Kifle, a pleasant-faced man with a long scar near his ear. "I'm glad you invited us, in spite of everything you're going through." He smiled. "We're all praying for Selam. These days, that's all we can do." His smile wavered.

Kifle's gentleness, so characteristic of the man who was one of the emperor's most trusted financial advisors, threatened to bring tears to Hailu's eyes. "We're supposed to listen for a report at five o'clock," Hailu said as he stirred the ice in his fresh glass of whiskey, careful not to spill any on the traditional white tunic and white jodhpurs given to him by Selam. "My watch isn't exact." He'd been walking through his days disorganized, unprepared for what lay ahead.

"It's about the famine, and the emperor. The whole city's been so quiet today," Kifle said. "My sister in Gondar said they're all waiting to get the news. None of the officials up there have come out of their houses all week."

The doorbell rang and Kifle stiffened. No one moved until Sara came in from the dining room.

"It's just the children," she said. "Even though there's no bonfire tonight, at least all traditions won't get thrown out this year." She opened the door and smiled down at a group of little girls holding *meskel* flowers, the yellow petals vibrant against their new *habesha* chemise. She fished in her pocket for coins as they started singing. *"Abebaye Hoy!"* she exclaimed. "I used to go to every house in my neighborhood and sing the same song on New Year's Eve," she said to them, taking the flowers and dropping coins into their palms. The little girls squealed excitedly and ran to knock on another door, their new white dresses stark against the setting sun.

The record scratched to a stop.

"I'll put the music on when the announcement is over," Dawit said to the guests.

Hailu swallowed his anger and forced himself to smile. "Wait and I'll fix it." The record was one of Selam's favorites, the collection of 45 singles among her most prized possessions. "You've ruined it."

Radio Addis Ababa blasted on and a breathless announcer reminded all citizens to watch special programming on Ethiopian Television that night.

"Hailu," Kifle said, "let's enjoy. It's a little girl's birthday and tomorrow is the beginning of a new year." He raised his glass. "To Ethiopia." He extended his glass in a solitary toast and froze as yet another announcement came on asking more government officials to report to the palace and turn themselves in.

"If they don't call your name, then they come to your office or find you at home," Kifle said. He rubbed his neck. "No one's safe."

"Nothing's going to happen. Their lawyers will clear everything," Hailu said, patting the man's arm. Some of those whose names were read aloud were close friends of Kifle. "Tefera will be released soon, you'll see."

Yonas walked to the group of men, his camera in hand. "It's purely symbolic. These military advisors want us to know who's in charge." He adjusted the lens. "Did you hear the new name they have for themselves?"

"I forget. It's not an Amharic word, is it? It's much older," Kifle said.

"Derg," Hailu said. "They're calling themselves the Derg. It means committee in Ge'ez."

"Why use the ancient language of priests for this debacle?" Kifle muttered.

Yonas held up the camera. "A picture, please." The men gathered close together and stared sternly into the camera.

"Kifle!" One of the women on the sofa gathered her purse and hat as she called to him.

Kifle turned to Hailu. "We have to get home."

Kifle's wife Aida approached Hailu. "Prime Minister Endalkachew was arrested. Did you hear?" she asked. She glanced in the dining room where Mickey sat in his uniform. "The military makes me nervous."

"Mickey?" Hailu said. "You've known him since he was a boy."

In the dining room, Dawit, Mickey, and Lily watched the elders with curious intensity.

"We turned in a timetable for a transition to civilian government after the emperor's gone, but the Derg hasn't responded." Dawit turned to Mickey. "Is the military going to talk, have you heard anything?"

Mickey shook his head and smiled proudly. "The major was happy with my report. He wants to give me a chance to rise." He waved cordially to Kifle, who took one last glance at the party before leaving. "The committee said people would be punished." The smile slid from his face.

"Only those who should be." Dawit patted his leg. "I'm glad we're fighting these people together. You and me," he said.

SARA LIT THE FOUR CANDLES on the round, freshly baked *dabo* she'd decorated with small plastic yellow flowers the way her own mother had done for her birthdays, and ran a hand down her daughter's back. "Who am I if not your mother?" she whispered. She kissed Tizita's forehead and took the knife before the excited girl tried once again to grab it. She cut the loaf of bread.

Lily clapped her hands and hugged Tizita. "You're grown up now!" she exclaimed. She turned quickly to kiss Sara's cheek. "Congratulations," she whispered. She kissed her cheek again. "You have a beautiful girl."

Sara felt herself reach up to pat her hair in place. Lily's energetic personality, her wild curls and exotic beauty made her feel plain and simple. The younger woman was dressed in the popular denim jeans and wide-collared shirt favored by college students, an American style that contrasted with the more formal Ethiopian way of dressing. Sara's skirt suddenly seemed matronly.

Hailu called Tizita into the living room.

"Let's go," Yonas said, taking Tizita's hand. Sara let her daughter go.

Lily hugged Sara. "I have to go soon, I'm sorry."

"Can't you stay?" Sara grinned. "We haven't started asking you when you'll accept Dawit's marriage proposal."

Lily sighed. "Mickey started that fight already this afternoon." She shook her head. "How can I think of anything else when I have these exams?" She checked her watch. "Tell Dawit I'll call him later. Mickey's leaving, I'll follow him through the side door." She went down the corridor.

In the living room, Yonas and Dawit were glaring at each other. Sunlight spilled and widened in the gap between them. Sara approached with square slices of *dabo,* hoping she could defuse what seemed like an escalating argument.

"What do you know about peasant rights?" she heard Yonas ask Dawit. He had both hands shoved into his pockets. Yonas's temper was as volatile as Dawit's, but his control over his emotions was far better than his brother's, though today he seemed close to an outburst.

"Here," Sara said, handing him a plate.

Yonas pushed it away. "Have you ever been outside the city? Have you ever tried to learn about the people you say you're speaking for? All your demonstrations are about higher pay and lower petrol, middle-class elitist concerns, how does that help the poor in the countryside?"

Sara shoved a plate towards Dawit. "Take it," she said. "And remember we have guests."

Dawit lowered his voice. "Who's going to speak up for them?" he asked. "People like you, who just want to hide until things get better?" He tore the square chunk of bread angrily and shoved a piece in his mouth. "At least we're trying to get things changed."

ALL THE GUESTS WERE gone and the rest of the family was changing clothes. Sara sat alone in the living room and smoothed the place next to her where Selam used to sit. She missed Selam's friendship, her vibrant womanly presence in a house otherwise dominated by men.

"It's just me again," she said to herself.

She switched on the television and watched the static skip before settling on a bland-faced newscaster. She didn't want to think about Selam. It would only revive memories of her own mother and rekindle a loss that was as sharp as fresh sorrow. She frowned. What puzzled her was that more and more, she had to struggle to hold on to her father's memory, even with the help of a faded photograph. She'd nearly forgotten his face. She could only hear, on the best of days, the faintest traces of his voice, remember the smallest fragments of his stories.

Sara curled her legs on the long floral-patterned sofa and traced the edges of a low-hanging beam of moonlight that laced through the empty living room and fell into shadows across her arm. The window was open, a cool breeze seeping through thin curtains to curve over her chest and soak into her blouse. She closed her eyes and waited for memory to come back to her.

Her father plants his finger in the middle of her palm and traces the longest lines of her hand to her wrist. Your mother and I ran away from here to there. We rode to here—he lets his finger draw a path up the length of one arm, across her back, down the other arm to rest in the center of the opposite hand. Then we did this—he takes her hands and presses them together in prayer—and then you came to us. My daughter. You are my daughter, he repeats.

Sara flexed her hands and found that years had darkened the paths on her palms; calluses now formed rounded hills on the journey her parents took to safety during the Italian Occupation. She was eleven when she began to wonder how her father could run away from an Italian contingent searching for a tall boy in resplendent white and a frightened girl who'd strangled an Italian general in his bed. He laughed when she asked, his eyes filling with a soft sadness she didn't understand. I would have died to help her escape, he said. The nature of love is to kill for it, or to die. He stared at her then, his eyes turning liquid with emotion, one day you'll know what a life is worth.

When Sara was seventeen her mother died, joining her father in their family plot and leaving her all alone. Sara cut her hair for the first time. She loosened each row of braid and watched it unfold behind her, dark and thick. Then she took her mother's old scissors and hacked fists of hair. She stared in the mirror when she was finished and felt the prickly roughness of her naked scalp. Then, slowly, she dug the end of the scissors' blade into soft skin. She dragged the blade across the middle of her scalp and watched as her pale brown skin became wet with blood. Then she said a prayer for her parents' souls and asked

Angel Gabriel to guide them to the girl with the scarred head, to tell them that even from the clouds, they would always know which girl was their daughter. She wanted them with her until it came time for her to have her own family, her own children. Until she was no longer alone.

Sara touched her scar and traced a path to her stomach. There was a pocket of warmth that still held the shape of two babies that had died inside of her. Every month during her cycle, she imagined her stomach contracting, trying to push them out once again. Some nights, the spasms were stronger than others. Her father would have pointed to his lame leg, an injury from war, and told her that what is left holds its own promises, that what remains will give birth to hope. Her mother would have understood the grief, would know, as only a woman knows, that it burns hot and rests close to the heart. Maybe, she thought, maybe the body can only contain so much of a given memory before it begins to make room for more. Maybe it is better that I forget some things, maybe there is not enough room in me for two parents, just as it was with those children.

II

THE FAMILY SAT TOGETHER IN FRONT of the television, their cups of tea untouched in front of them. They were leaning forward towards the screen, repulsed and transfixed by what they were seeing. Vultures cawed and screeched, greedy and vengeful. They beat their wings furiously and fast, sent feathers tumbling into the eye of a camera. The steady glare of the sun shot balloons of light into the lens, forced shadows to skulk back into the sky. Under the vicious heat were flesh-covered skeletons that breathed. Covered in rags the color of dust, children crawled on all fours. Grown women with bones for breasts clung to emaciated babies. Defeated men let ravenous flies feast on their eyes. Naked bodies lay crumbled on cracked earth, scattered like ash.

"My God," Yonas said, pressing a hand over his face, wiping dry eyes, "my God. These poor people."

The camera was merciless. It swept past gaping faces, over destitute land, swung into the belly of the relentless heat and then down again to another body, another helpless mother, another bloated boy.

"Mickey was there, he saw for himself what this government has done. These thieves! These money-hungry bastards!" Dawit had stood up. Now he was pacing next to the sofa, watching the screen in intense fury. "All along, the emperor has been watching these people die like this. He was there last year, he didn't do anything. This is why we need a change. How many more have to die before Ethiopia wakes up?" He pointed to the television, then sat back down. One knee jiggled uncontrollably. He chewed on his bottom lip.

"It's because of the drought and some officials, you're right," Hailu said. "But not the whole government. Our leaders aren't evil, not like this." He straightened the table setting in front of him. "And this Derg committee, why didn't they tell us sooner? They're the so-called advisors of the emperor aren't they?" He shook his head. "They couldn't do something before tonight?"

The documentary suddenly jumped to grainy scenes of lavish palace halls, glided over tables heaped with steaming delicacies, spun past the emperor feeding his lions extravagant foods, his numerous Mercedes. Then back to the hungry, the skeletal, the dead littering the paths that led out of one dried-up village into another. One small girl, her stomach so distended it looked like it would split, gnawed on a stone.

"Did you see that?" Hailu said, pointing at the screen.

Yonas frowned. "Those parts in the palace are from years ago, aren't they?"

"More propaganda," Hailu said.

"He's a rich man who's lost touch with his people," Dawit said. He'd gone to his room to bring letters back. "Look"—he flipped one page open—"Mickey wrote me, he heard rumors of grain being sold in other towns." He poked a finger at one line. "That grain was supposed to go to these people!"

Hailu shook his head again. "Haile Selassie loves his country. We're not being told everything."

"There's more," Yonas said.

The family listened to the choked voice of the British journalist recount the numbers dead, devastated by the unimaginable famine. Biblical proportions, he whispered. A desolate valley, the sun too bright for shadows of death. Who will help them? he asked. Why haven't they been helped by their government? he continued. Why has the emperor forgotten his own?

In the unblinking eye of the camera: a sea of bodies bleaching under a fisted sun.

Bizu, their elderly maid, was pressed against the archway of the dining room, her hands at her cheeks, her gray filmy eyes floating in unshed tears. "They're in Wello," she whispered. "That's Wello." Her hands beat her chest. Wello was a province far from Addis Ababa, in the north. "That's where they're dying like this." She leaned against the wall. "That's my home." It was the first time she'd ever spoken of her life before coming to live with them. "They're my people."

Sara rushed to her side. "Bizuye, Bizu, let's go into the kitchen." She took the tiny woman in her arms and tried to lead her out of the room. Bizu resisted, her sobs growing louder.

"I can't leave," Bizu said. "Did you see them? I can't leave." She stayed by the doorway, Sara helplessly rubbing her back.

"He couldn't have known how bad it was," Yonas said. "There's no way."

"How could he ignore this?" Dawit asked. He was standing again, pointing towards the television, his eyes on his brother. "All those ministers he made rich should be charged with a crime! That's what a new government will fix. These rich elites are nothing but traitors to their people, and until we get rid of all of them, nothing will change!" He spoke with such force that a vein throbbed in his forehead.

Hailu's eyes were fixed on the screen and the rolling credits. "It's true," he whispered.

"What's true?" Dawit sat down again with some effort.

Hailu turned, snapping out of his reverie. "Does it matter?" he said. "All your protesting and marching will do nothing for these people. You want to call the ministers traitors, you want another new prime minister, a new constitution? What happens in the meantime? The problem is too big. We need help immediately, not a new government and more disruption." He wound his prayer beads around his wrist.

Outside their window came a rising tide of voices. A young man shouted in the distance, followed by an answering yell, then a responding howl. Women called to each other in high-pitched tones. Families had already stepped into the courtyard of Hailu's compound, their murmurs growing louder to rise above the noises beyond the gate. Heavy footsteps pounded down the road. A sharp rock crashed against the gate. Cars sped by, loud music blaring. No one would be locked in their homes that night. It seemed the entire city was slowly opening their doors and windows, their surprise and stunned anger too volatile to be contained within four walls.

12

THERE WERE FIVE OF THEM AND they smelled of fresh sweat and gunpowder. They came to him in the dead hours of the morning, speaking in whispered tones. He was waiting, his back to the door, a Bible under his pillow, prayers for the hungry spilling from his lips. He didn't move when the doorknob twisted, pliant and well oiled. He pretended not to hear the first shuffle of hesitant feet into his bedroom.

"Emperor Haile Selassie," one of them said, his tone as solemn as a prayer, "please get up."

The emperor forced his legs straight and smoothed his military uniform, the rows of shining medals swaying against his chest. He held out his hand for his coat and waited calmly. The day had finally come.

The man who spoke coughed softly. "Get your coat and come with us, please. Your Majesty."

The emperor squared his shoulders and raised his eyes to look into the shadowed faces of the five. His advisors. Fully molded bodies in army fatigues, with sharp eyes and teeth, strong hands and firm feet. They could not meet his gaze, and he realized he could not remember their names. Only the man furthest to the left, shorter and darker than the rest, dared to glance in his direction once. An unfamiliar face, the emperor thought, but the look of him, that haughty defiance of a caged animal, he'd seen in some of his fiercest generals, and it was then that the emperor understood.

"Our era is over," he said. "Yes." He stared into the dark, his back rigid. He let his eyes linger on each of the officers until they shifted uncomfortably and one of them sneezed. He noticed that all of them kept their heads bowed, maintained a respectful distance from him, his subjects once more. "There's no use fighting the Almighty. Let us go," he said, and led them out of his room and into the wide marble hallway, their footsteps echoing like a volley of gunfire.

A perfect triangle of light crawled from under his library door and the emperor stepped into its path and out of the shadows as he entered his last day as the King of Kings. In his library, two groups of noblemen and soldiers, pressed into their chairs like windblown birds, rose and bowed deeply as he sat down at his desk.

A trembling police officer dressed in shabby trousers stumbled in his haste to stand at attention. Sweat dripped freely from his temple into the neck of his ill-fitting shirt. The tallest of the five men shoved a document in his chest and instructed him to read. The officer took the paper, gripping it so hard it doubled into sloppy folds in his shaking hands. Another soldier held the policeman's wrists to keep them still so the frightened man could read.

"Recognizing that the present system is undemocratic; that Parliament has been serving not the people but its members and the ruling and aristocratic classes; and that its existence is contrary to the motto 'Ethiopia *Tikdem,*' Ethiopia First; Haile Selassie I is hereby deposed as of today, September 12, 1974."

The emperor felt the heat of a thousand eyes fall on him, and he looked from one minister to another, from one nobleman and relative to the next, and he folded his hands in front of him, index fingers and thumbs touching, an unbroken trinity. He remained seated, refusing to believe the end would be so undignified and without ceremony, announced by a man who carried traces of dirt under his fingernails. He said, "We have raised you up. Have you forgotten?"

From the back of the room seeped the sound of tears breaking into uneven sobs.

One of the noblemen walked to him and tenderly kissed his cheek. "Go," he whispered. "Don't make this more difficult." He led him to the door, that simple gesture releasing chair scrapes and whispers, sending the noises crashing against the emperor, who found himself spiraling in the deafening cacophony.

Dazed, the emperor trailed the five men outside and waited for his Mercedes. One of them motioned him to the back of a blue Volkswagen, and Emperor Haile Selassie needed no words to convey his contempt for the order, for the officers, for the treasonous plot. The shortest of the men, his movements spare and tightly coiled, pointed towards the car and swung the back door wider, his skittish eyes the only evidence of his impatience. Under a rising sun furiously beating its way through clouds, the five stood, neatly ordered and stiff, sweating, waiting, then waiting some more until the old man finally slumped, defeated, and squeezed into the back of the small car.

Despite the onlookers who cheered as the Volkswagen drove past, despite the ringing in his head and the chorus of shouts that greeted him through the thick glass, despite the deep thud of drumbeats from hands as fast as wings, nothing could have convinced the emperor that heaven had not fallen into a sudden hush at this betrayal of his kingdom, and he knew that it would be in this absence of sound that God would hear the prayers of his Chosen One and heed his call.

Overhead, the first crack of thunder rolled through the Ethiopian sky and then the rain. The emperor watched his beloved city blur and grow dim, and then everywhere, the quiet.

13

"**W**E'LL HAVE A HARD TIME GETTING HOME," Hailu said to Sara as he opened the windows in Selam's hospital room for fresh air. The thick smell of smoke and petrol drifted in. "Tanks are blocking most of the roads." He stared outside for a moment, at the unusually congested roads and the gray haze that stretched across the hills like a stubborn stain. "Did they really arrest the emperor?"

"It's hard to believe, isn't it?" Sara felt Selam's temperature. "She's sleeping more," she said, frowning. "Yesterday, she told me she's been having strange dreams."

"It's the medicines," Hailu said. "She's stable." Below them, he watched two young boys ambling down Churchill Road towards the Commercial Bank of Ethiopia with a large bundle of branches strapped to their backs. They paused to stare at one of the tanks resting at a corner, then continued on, their high-pitched chatter rolling into the room during a brief lapse in street noise.

"That documentary was horrible, but why arrest Princess Tenagnework and the other princesses? What do they have to do with it?" Sara angled Selam's face away from the glare of sunlight. "We should leave. Sofia started today," she said. "Bizu's not happy, but she's too old to do all the housework herself."

Hailu sifted through pill bottles. Selam had lost weight, her skin was pale, her face was slack and dull. She looked much older than him. "Almaz keeps telling me to take her home," he said, shaking pills into his hand and counting them.

"She's right," Sara said, watching Hailu separate pills by color and size in his palm. She held out her hand. "Let me have them. You should call home and check on everyone."

"I called. Dawit's out." He shook his head in disgust and let his gaze follow Churchill Road's long path from Piazza to the railway station.

Just a few months ago, protestors had marched on this road with their cries for reform. They'd worked their way from City Hall past the post office, turned towards the hills of Entoto at Meskel Square, passed Jubilee Palace, Parliament, and Arat Kilo, and made their way from De Gaulle Square to St. Giorgis Cathedral, completing a nearly perfect circle. The city had felt under siege by that steady onslaught of marching feet. Their shouts had been like rolling thunder breaking again and again, so deep and loud that residents had locked their doors and stepped away from windows. It had all been full of fury and noise back then, but he'd been sure that diplomacy and respect for the monarchy would triumph. Today, however, the emperor, his only surviving daughter, his grandson Commodore Iskinder Desta, his granddaughters, and hundreds of his ministers and officials were under arrest.

Hailu shook his head and turned away from the window. "Did Bizu have you write down rules for Sofia to follow?" he asked. Bizu had never learned to read or write.

Sara smiled. "She drew a line on the floor in the kitchen that Sofia can't cross. She can't get to all the spices."

"She used to make my life miserable when I was a boy with her rules." He tried to return Sara's smile and failed. He watched her gentleness with Selam as she held a cup to his wife's mouth and tilted her head to help her swallow the pills. She wiped the corner of Selam's mouth with her finger when she finished. The simple gesture made Hailu look away. His wife was completely helpless.

"Emaye's lost more weight," Sara said.

"She's stable," Hailu repeated, then held the door open for Sara. "Let's get home," he said as they left the room. He looked back at the closing door. "I've almost forgotten what she was like before."

SELAM DIPS INTO THE crevice of a rolling cloud, sourness coating her tongue. A dry whirlpool threads dust through its hollow middle and a thousand startled crows flood the sky. A sad owl coos and moans, its wings beating against powerful gusts. A feather falls in wide circles to the earth. Selam tucks herself behind a veil of clouds and sinks into the gray. She flies over Legehar train station and sees a dingy square building with peeling paint and a long line of men shuffling in front of soldiers seated at metal tables, their soft leather shoes kicking dust, sending puffs of dirt into the air. Selam descends towards a small window and a hungry dog gnawing on stone. She hears a string of prayers resting on the wings of a white-tailed swallow hurtling into the heavens. She listens, breaks the words apart, a mother once again, and hears a man, once God's chosen, caught in the choke hold of despair.

FLAMES CHEWED INTO a large portrait of Emperor Haile Selassie. A throng of people, those older draped in *shammas* and more hesitant, shoved closer into the wild circle, hypnotized by the embers that curdled and spewed. Some raised their fists and shouted, some stomped their feet, clouds of dust floated across wide-eyed faces. Others broke into ululations, and the shrill excited shrieks of children pierced the deepening celebratory rumble. Mercato's open-air market was in chaos, vendors' tables and goods cleared away to make room for the masses of people who ran and leapt and hugged each other. Solemn, cautious soldiers watched the crowds with blank faces, tanks behind them on the streets. A military truck screeched to a halt at a nearby office building and soldiers jumped out and ran in, their guns leading the way.

It was September 12, 1974, the first day of the new year, and Addis Ababa's dreams and frustrations lay bare, finally exposed, to a hot sun that seemed brighter and more powerful than it had ever been before.

Hailu and Sara pushed through the people, bags of food in their arms.

"I don't understand this," Hailu said to Sara. "What do they think is going to happen now?"

They made their way to a street corner, under the shade of a tree, and stared at the flames leaping over the heads of onlookers. Planks of wood and more portraits burned in the middle of the circle. Heat shimmered in the air, giving the jubilant crowd the flatness of a mirage.

Hailu looked across the spectacle in shock. "I never imagined . . ." he began.

"Let's keep moving," Sara said. "These soldiers should do something." She linked arms with Hailu and stepped closer to him. "What will they do next?" she said softly.

He glanced once more at the crowd. "Did they forget all the emperor has done for this country?"

—

TIZITA WAVED TO THEM from the veranda, grinning and jumping up and down as Hailu pulled the car into the garage.

"I thought she was with Yonas," Sara said, frowning. "She's alone?"

"Emaye, watch!" Tizita called.

Sara walked towards her daughter and smiled. Tizita's arms flapped like wings. "I can jump far," she said. The veranda was four short steps.

Sara ruffled her hair. "Come inside, you can play with Sofia's little boy, Berhane."

Tizita twirled in circles. "I'm dizzy."

THE SCREAM SCALED the walls and exploded into every room. It held the panic of a trapped animal: high-pitched and agonized, sharpened by fear.

"What was that?" Hailu asked. They were in the kitchen waiting for Sofia to put her sons to sleep for a nap.

"Tizzie!" Sara yelled, jumping up from her stool near the oven.

It came again, rising, then splintering like broken glass.

Bizu paused at the kitchen door. "Where is she?" She held a hand to her ear.

"Emaye!" Tizita shrieked.

"Tizzie!" Sara raced out of the kitchen, nearly colliding with Bizu. "Tizita!"

There was no response. Sara flung the front door open. Her daughter was writhing on the ground, just below the veranda, her head tucked into her chest. "Get up, it's okay," she said. "Get up."

Tizita started shivering.

"What's happening?" Sara asked. "Answer me! Tizzie! Tizita, get up. You just fell." Sara stumbled down the few steps of the veranda. Tizita's eyes were closed. "Wake up," Sara said. The little girl wasn't moving. "Wake up!"

Tizita felt cold, her breaths came in shallow puffs.

"Abbaye! Yonas!" Sara tried to carry her daughter but the little girl was too heavy, her own legs too weak.

"Sara, I'm right here, calm down," Hailu said. "Let me see her."

Sara wouldn't let go. "What's wrong with her? Tell me!"

Hailu put a hand on her face. "Pay attention. Sit down or you'll drop her."

"She's not moving," Sara said. "She's having trouble breathing."

Hailu pried into the grip Sara had on Tizita. "Let me see her. You're frightening her." She resisted. "Let me look at her. Now!" He used the voice that made his nurses jump.

Sara dropped back to the step, ashen and trembling. "She screamed."

Hailu laid his granddaughter on the veranda and listened to her heart. Her eyes had rolled into the back of her head. She was breathing quicker, sweat collected on her upper lip. There was no scratch on her.

"Where did you find her? Are you sure she only fell down?" He started to pick her up but Sara pushed in front of him.

She cradled Tizita. "Let's go to the hospital . . . Where's Yonas?"

14

THE SAGGING MATTRESS PROTESTED UNDER Mickey's shifting weight, his shoes gaped empty next to his bare feet. The news that the emperor had been deposed was not a surprise. The documentary had broken open the flood of outrage against the monarchy. He'd known it was inevitable, that the Derg, these officers from the Fourth Division, were merely biding their time until they removed him from the throne and maneuvered themselves into seats of power. The radio announcement only verified what had been known by the city much earlier. But no one had considered what would happen to the emperor after he was overthrown.

The call came from the same officer who had ordered him to Wello, Major Guddu. The words rolled into sharp bursts that flared from static: Meet me at headquarters. The emperor is under arrest. More prisoners on their way. Come immediately. Hurry.

"What?" he'd asked. Not because he hadn't heard, but because he couldn't believe what he was hearing.

"Come to the base!" Major Guddu shouted.

Mickey stammered a response, then dropped the phone. He hadn't considered the fact that someone would have to watch Emperor Haile Selassie, walk in front of those eyes that could strike down a man with a simple blink. Never had he thought of the possibility that he would be the one ordered to guard him. His work as a soldier was merely a job, consisting of nothing more than a series of menial tasks authorized by manhandled paper and smeared stamps.

Now the phone's crackling beeps came through, muffled against his thigh.

"Mickey," he said to himself, "Mickey, get ready." His uniform hung on an old wire hanger from a bent nail in the wall, its dark outline a stiff-angled silhouette of his own body.

"This is your chance. You deserve it."

But the declaration rang false. His whole life had prepared him to accept the fact that in nearly everything, there would always be someone better. There were too many others in positions much higher than his, with connections stronger than he had, with a fervor for competition he could never teach himself to stomach. He assumed the military would be another series of missed chances. His life was a long list of privileges never meant for him. It was the way things were in Ethiopia for countless others. He was no different, nothing special.

But now, there was this call, and Mickey found himself ordered to assume duties no mortal would have wanted. The emperor was God's chosen, that the blood of King Solomon and King Dawit flowed in his veins, and Mickey imagined that anyone who dared to corner and trap one of God's own, who dared to defile that divine blood, was committing a blasphemous act for which there would be no forgiveness.

DUST FLOATED AND DRIFTED in the air, veiled everything in an ashen brown. Mickey stood in front of a thick door with peeling paint. Beyond those doors, through a slender hallway, in a musty room with a dirty cot and an unclean blanket, was Emperor Haile Selassie. He let the dust accumulate on his glasses, drop a glum, dark haze on his entire day. Muscles spasmed and jerked in his eyes.

"Go on," said Daniel, another officer who'd been called to duty. "He's lying on the bed, he hasn't moved since they brought him. I think he's praying." Daniel's voice relaxed him; Mickey felt his fatherly assurance. He put both hands on Mickey's shoulders and pushed him forward. "I'll take over as soon as I'm done with the new prisoners." He sighed. "So many."

Mickey was frozen in place, his bladder ached. He squeezed his legs together and his rifle fell to the ground. "Can I sign them in instead?"

Daniel picked up the rifle. "I pulled a chair into the corridor for you. It's next to the room, but it's far enough away so you won't have to see inside it."

"If he looks into my eyes, I'll be cursed." Sweat collected under his arms, he could smell himself. "He's the emperor. Janhoy. Who am I?"

Daniel smiled, his eyes gentle. "My oldest son has eyebrows that join in the middle." He put two fingers in the space between Mickey's eyebrows. "You're fine, no bad luck for you." He tried to widen his smile but it was strained. "He's sleeping. He's old and tired. He can't hurt you."

Mickey resisted the move to open the door.

"He'll know you're not one of them," Daniel said. "You don't have that look." He patted his back. "Be kind to him. He'll remember you when this is over."

IT WAS COLD in the corridor. The slanting wooden chair was splintered and the sharp edge of the faded seat dug into his thigh and numbed his leg. Mickey plugged his ears to drown out the erratic breathing zigzagging from the emperor's cell into his chest. The tiny room was directly behind him, its interior exposed like a hungry mouth, its door no restraint for the man who could have easily called angels to his aid. A soft wind brushed against his neck and Mickey jumped and scraped his chair forward.

A low moan slid across the floor. It seemed to dangle in front of him, then weave around his throat. He fought the urge to wail. His chest jerked. He couldn't tell if the emperor was crying or praying. He'd heard other soldiers contend that despite the permanent chill in the building, the emperor's cell pulsed with subtle heat, and he wondered if that was why he couldn't stop sweating, why his shirt now clung to his back, why he felt as if he were suffocating under a pressure as thick as a hot towel.

"Mickey," he called to himself, "Mickey."

He remembered the day his father collapsed in the fields he tended for the landowner. They had been living outside the town of Awasa in an uneven thatched hut his father had tried to shape into a perfect circle to please his mother. Plastic sheets over the windows served as their only protection from rain and wind. He'd seen his father stumble, then go down. His slingshot still in his hand, the target bird forgotten, Mickey had rushed to him as fast as his seven-year-old legs could go, and lowered his head to his father's mouth. His father was flat on his back, and Mickey had listened for what he was sure was his name coming through the strangled breaths. But his father was mouthing his own name. "Habte. Habte. Habte," he said again and again. He must have seen Mickey's questioning eyes, noted his confusion over a dying father who could only speak of himself, to himself, with his last breaths. "Say your name, force yourself to exist," he'd said. "Make life come back."

"Mickey," he repeated now, trying to remind himself that he was alive, that soon he would leave this chair and exist somewhere else, far away from the heat, safe.

15

Sara clasped her palms between her knees, shivering as if she were sitting in a cold breeze. She was a frightened girl again. "Yonas should have been watching her," she said. She dug her knuckles into her stomach.

Hailu frowned. "Are you feeling okay? Can I bring you something to drink?" He put an arm around her.

The pale green waiting area of Prince Mekonnen Hospital was nearly empty except for an old woman tucked into a corner, sleeping with her head on a bag of clothes. Almaz, calm and reassuring, had met them at the emergency entrance and whisked Tizita away on a gurney, her rubber-soled shoes squeaking loudly on the marble floor. She'd refused Hailu's request to do an examination himself.

"Stay with your daughter," Almaz said. She'd always called Sara his daughter. "She needs you."

Hailu felt restless and agitated, useless.

"They're taking a long time. Please go find out what they're doing," Sara said, rocking in her seat.

"They'll let us know." He stood up, then sat back down. There was nowhere to go. "You can't rush them."

"I never told her not to run on those steps." Instructions, reminders, a mother's duties. She'd forgotten that one, the most important.

"It's not your fault," he said.

She stared at the fist in her stomach. This child had been tangible proof that God listened. Tizita was evidence that she, Sara Mikael, was worthy of mercy and pity. Her daughter's life meant that this vengeful God, who had already taken her parents, was capable of compassion.

"It was a simple fall," Hailu said, but she heard in his voice his own disbelief and confusion.

A young physician made his way to them in strides at once wide and sauntering. He had a thin frame, slender face, and shoulders that seemed to slope down and tip him forward as he walked. Both Sara and Hailu jumped from their seats. "Sit down," he said, standing with more authority once he'd stopped moving. "I'm surprised you could get here so fast. Demonstrators have blocked most of the roads. Did you hear the shooting?"

"How is she?" Sara asked. She sat only to maintain eye contact with the young physician, who had found a seat next to Hailu.

"What happened?" Hailu asked.

The physician leaned forward, his long fingers clasped together. His eyes were bloodshot. He had the bland expression of a man accustomed to delivering bad news. "Her intestines twisted, Dr. Hailu," he said.

"What? I don't understand." Sara noted the doctor's youthful face and fatigue. "Abbaye, what does he mean?"

"Intussusception?" Hailu had heard of this happening only once, from a doctor who'd treated a child in Dire Dawa.

The physician nodded. "The fall happened in such a way that her stomach shifted. A segment of her intestine slipped inside another segment. It happens sometimes to children."

"That means she's in pain." Sara stood and took hold of Hailu's arm. "That means she's hurting."

The physician walked them to the swinging doors. "We've given her medicine for the pain. She's asleep. She needs to be under observation, no food can get past the obstruction. There'll be swelling." He opened the door. "She's a small girl, maybe that has something to do with it."

"I can't make her eat," Sara said, biting her lip.

"I only meant she's young," the doctor said. He stepped into the hall and looked both ways, frowning. "Soldiers came to take Lieutenant General Essayas and Dr. Tesfaye out of the ICU. They can't survive back in jail."

"What can we do about Tizita?" Hailu looked down the long corridor for Almaz. He wanted to talk to her, not this young doctor with so little information.

The doctor shook his head, turning his attention back to them. "We can control the pain. The rest is up to God."

"No," Sara said.

"She's strong," the doctor said. "We have to wait, but she's got every advantage on her side." His voice was mechanical, his concentration focused on the door leading to the quiet corridors of the ICU.

"She's so small, she's not strong at all," Sara replied.

SARA HELD HER DAUGHTER'S HAND and looked around the over-crowded room. Sick adults lay quietly on thin cots with metal rails that rose like jail bars around them. Her small child slept in this cold, ugly room that smelled of disinfectant and sweat. Sara wanted her out of here and home before she woke and saw these listless patients with tubes pushed down their throats. She noticed one young patient, a man with a bloodstained bandage over his eye, raise his head and let his other eye wander over her. She turned her back to him.

"The bed's too big for her." Sara kissed Tizita's cheek and looked to Hailu. "Can we get a private room, will you ask Almaz?" She looked at the young doctor. "What did you give her? What do we do now?"

The doctor folded his hands in front of him. "Something for the pain. She'll sleep it off, then we'll check her again."

"We can't wait until something happens, we have to help her now. Abbaye, tell him. Check her yourself. Go find the nurse!" Sara's voice was shrill and loud.

The patient with the bandaged eye grumbled. "This isn't Mercato." He turned towards the wall. "Quiet."

"He's come," Almaz said, leading a pale and shaken Yonas with her into the room. "He didn't even park the car, it's sitting in front of the door. Dr. Hailu," she said, dangling keys on one finger, "go park it properly. Hurry." Her voice was clipped, competent. "You, sit," she commanded Sara as she pushed Yonas gently towards his wife. "Doctor, let me talk to you outside." Within seconds the nurse had managed to bring a sense of order.

Once they were alone, Sara pulled out of Yonas's arms.

"Almaz told me she fell, but I don't understand," Yonas said, trying to reach for Sara.

"You left her alone." Her mouth trembled as she stepped further away from him. "You left us."

"She didn't want to go." Yonas's face was stricken. He leaned on the bed rail. "She said she wanted to stay home." He sat down on a chair near the bed, his head in his hands.

"How could you leave her?"

"They're moving us to a private room," Yonas said, glaring at the curious patient watching them intently. He turned back to Sara, his face stunned and sad. "I was only gone for a short while. Melaku didn't have milk so I had to go somewhere else, and this traffic, with the tanks . . . How is she?"

"From now on, I'm going to be the one to watch her. Not you."

He stood to kiss Tizita's forehead. The effort seemed to drain all his energy. He slumped, his hands gripping the rail, and thought for a moment. He looked like he was about to speak, then stopped. "I'm going to call Lily and see if she knows where Dawit is." He walked out.

In the corridor, a soldier came out of the intensive care unit with a coat and suitcase in his arms. He stared at Yonas as he went by.

CARS WERE MOVING SLOWLY and Dawit had to roll the window all the way down to let a breeze into the hot taxi. They had passed Meskel Square and turned onto Churchill Road, where people milled around the edges of traffic, constantly looking over their shoulders while whispering in tightly clustered packs. Gunfire popped in the distance, followed by a faint roar of shouts, then police sirens. Tension was high in a city still reeling from the arrest of the emperor and the sudden restriction on demonstrations and free speech imposed by the military regime.

A military march, sung by enthusiastic children, came on the radio.

"I hate this music," the taxi driver muttered even as he turned up the volume. As the song played, the traffic stilled. Other cars turned on their radios. Radio Addis Ababa's announcer came on and all cars shifted to neutral as he read from a list of names of captains and generals, commanders and nobles.

"Please report immediately to Menelik Palace. Repeat, report immediately to Menelik Palace."

"The wine cellars at Menelik Palace are being used as a prison. Jubilee Palace is now being called the National Palace. What's next?" the driver asked. He turned to look at Dawit in the backseat and pushed his sunglasses above his head. "Who's left to rule if everyone's in jail?" He was a young man with a lazy eye. He caught Dawit looking at his face and slipped his sunglasses back down. "When did all of this go bad?" he asked, turning back to the traffic, agitated. "And now there's a midnight curfew."

"Can you hurry?" Dawit asked. "I have to get to the hospital."

"Nobody's moving," the driver said.

The announcer continued to read a list of names, now expanding to include more government officials, civil workers, and other members of the royal family. The names echoed in stereo, multiplying by the cars on the road. No one moved. Pedestrians stared in discomfort at each other. In the traffic lanes, hands hung out of cars, their angry gestures forgotten.

The driver looked out the window, agitated. "Why do they do this on the radio?"

The song began again, a signal that the announcement was over, but it wasn't until a shepherd walked through the row of idle cars with his lazy flock, one drowsy sheep slung across his shoulders, that drivers began to honk and shout. The taxi tried to maneuver around an ambling mule.

"They need to run away," the driver said, poking a finger into the steering wheel for emphasis. "Why are they turning themselves in so willingly?"

"There'll be a fair trial," Dawit said. "Students and union leaders have already made the demands." He couldn't help feeling proud of his role in making those demands.

"You think a country with a curfew and a ban on demonstrations cares about fair trials?" The driver laughed.

The Derg had arranged for special military courts to try the prisoners after a civilian inquiry. They were being held on suspicion of corruption, abuse of office, or participation in the famine cover-up. The legal process would be orderly and timely, the Derg promised. But Dawit hadn't expected so many important military men and dignitaries to be arrested.

"Can you hurry?" Dawit said.

He checked his watch. He'd gone to a meeting that had run over and come home to find Bizu pacing, nervous from his father's angry calls looking for him. He needed to get to the hospital quickly.

HAILU WALKED INTO the small room Almaz had prepared for Tizita, his steps slow and heavy. The walls were the same pale green as the waiting room and light blue curtains hung against large square windows. She'd made sure to get a room close to Selam's and Hailu said a silent thanks for her constant attentiveness.

"I couldn't find Dawit," Yonas said. "He's not at Lily's." He looked like he'd been awake for days.

Hailu checked Tizita's temperature. "He's on his way." He saw that there was an empty chair next to Sara, but Yonas had made no move to sit.

"What have I done?" Sara whispered. "Leave me alone." She looked from one man to the other. She touched her shoulder and realized she'd left her *netela* at home. She bent over her knees in the chair, wanting to do anything to feel warm again, safely covered.

"This is no one's fault," Hailu replied, exasperation creeping in.

Yonas steadied her, refused to let her go. "She won't stop blaming herself."

"You don't know," Sara answered. "Even you don't know. I know. I feel it." Sara began to beat a steady rhythm on her chest. Her words fell into the room with a deep thud. "Nothing twists by itself."

Hailu pulled her arm down. "Stop it." The sound reminded him of the days after Sara had lost her second baby, when she'd mourned with a fervor that had stunned the neighborhood and brought him and Yonas to their knees with grief.

"It's the only way God will hear," Sara said. She wanted to turn her whole body into a drum so every word could vibrate and pound into heaven like a thunderous wind. "Even this isn't enough."

"That's not true," Yonas said. "Praying is enough." He stood in front of her but didn't sit down.

"It isn't," Sara said. "Your God," she added, "has shown me no mercy."

Yonas shook his head. "Do you think he wants your pain?" He tried to reach for her hand.

Her look was contemptuous. "What do you know about pain?" She pulled away.

"Sara," Hailu said. "Enough." He turned to Yonas. "I'll be in Selam's room."

"I haven't done enough," she said. "I didn't do enough to keep my second baby after the first one died, and I didn't do enough to show my gratitude when Tizita lived." She grasped Hailu's hand. "I want to go to St. Gabriel's." Her new secret, tucked safely near her breast: at St. Gabriel's she would crawl around the church and let her blood fall on holy ground. She would make this sacrifice to a God who demanded from his children before he gave.

16

THE HOSPITAL SMELLED LIKE DISINFECTANT. The floor felt sticky under his feet. Dawit looked at Tizita, still asleep with an IV snaking into her arm, and he hid his queasiness by turning towards Sara. They were alone; Hailu and Yonas had gone out to get food. He'd just told her the good news, that he'd been made head of the communications committee in the student union. He would be responsible for all the newsletters and information circulated on behalf of university students.

"It's enough. Even I think it's enough," Sara said, smoothing Tizita's hair back from her face. "Abbaye worries about you too much as it is."

"He tries to control me."

"Did anyone in your family ever fall like this?" She rubbed Tizita's arm.

Dawit looked at Sara's beautiful face, a more mature and earthy beauty than Lily's. Even when they first met, when he was ten and she eighteen, he'd felt they were the same in many ways. The years separating them, he liked to think to himself when he was younger, did not separate them at all. When he and Lily had first met in secondary school, he'd talked so much of Sara that Lily had been jealous.

"She'll be okay," Dawit said. "You have the best doctor in Addis in the family."

Sara was pale. "Did you learn about this sickness in school?" she asked. "What do you think we should do?"

Dawit shook his head. Sara hadn't gone beyond a high school education, and her ideas of what he learned in university were sometimes exaggerated. "The doctors will help her get well."

She stared out the window above the bed. "He's going to take her away from me."

"Who?"

"I was born in Qulubi," she said. "My mother made a *sílet* to God that if she escaped from that Italian into safety, she'd baptize me at St.

Gabriel's Church. She told me I'd always be protected because she kept her promise. A mother's blessings go down to her daughter, she said. But now, look"—she motioned towards Tizita. "Something happened. He wants to take her away."

"Why do you think God has anything to do with it?" Dawit asked.

Yonas and Hailu walked in carrying a large plate of steaming stew covered with warm *injera*. Yonas looked tired, his eyes were red-rimmed. "Almaz said we can stay here overnight," he said. "She'll have cots and blankets brought in. Stay out of the hall, soldiers are still here."

"I'm not going to sleep," Sara said.

"They arrested more officials," Dawit said. "They still haven't named any charges, and there are no plans yet for a civilian government. Did you hear the announcements on the radio?" he asked his father.

Hailu didn't respond. He handed a plate to Yonas instead.

"The Derg just asked the courts to consider the death penalty for those found guilty of the famine cover-up," Yonas said. "Aren't they quoting from the reports Mickey filed when he was in Wello?"

"I think so," Dawit said. "I haven't seen Mickey since he's been at the jail." He watched his father serve food in disapproving silence.

"Let's pray, Abbaye," Sara said. "I'm tired of all this talk."

Hailu frowned at Dawit. "Where were you?"

"At Lily's," Dawit stammered, watching disgust settle in hs father's eyes before he shook his head and turned away.

17

No light seeped through the window above his cot. The dank smell of mildew clung to the emperor's lungs. Only the howls of the dog that scraped its bony ribs against the mud walls outside during feeding time let the emperor know that another day had passed. No one spoke to him and fewer dared to look towards him; none approached his cell. In the first days of his imprisonment, he'd had a regular visitor. A military official in a wrinkled uniform who would stride into his cell and demand to know the whereabouts of money that had never existed.

"You have it in a Swiss bank account," the official insisted. "Where is the money? Where is it? You know. Give us the account number."

He stared at him, confused. There was no money. Finally, he'd thought to ask, "How much money?"

The official scoffed, then replied, "Over a billion American dollars." His tone was triumphant. "It could have fed all those people you let starve."

It was the emperor's turn to scoff, to rake his eyes over the soldier's poorly ironed uniform. "Do you even know how much a billion dollars is?" The official left in a disgruntled huff, pulling his belt over his paunch. Eventually, he stopped coming and the silence grew.

The emperor spent hours sitting still, wheezing through a dry rattle in his chest that was growing deeper. He kept himself wrapped in a thin blanket that did nothing to shield him from the chill, and let his mind wander across decades to his victorious return from exile after the end of the Italian Occupation in 1941. He let himself dwell in those days, reliving half-forgotten conversations and once-insignificant details. He recalled the processional walk to his throne, the women who wept at the sight of him, and the unbearably proud and fierce gazes of his warriors as they welcomed him back to his country and his crown.

The emperor shuffled back and forth in his cramped cell and reenacted his own stately walk. He waved to onlookers on his way from his home in Jubilee Palace to meetings in Menelik Palace, and searched, out of habit, for small boys with joined eyebrows for his bodyguards to push out of his view. He marched every day, hourly, to his library and sat on rich padding and brushed velvet. Emperor Haile Selassie walked through his marble halls and to his royal throne, removed himself from the mustiness of mud walls and the undignified stench of his own body, and let memory seep into the present, then dissolve into a glorious dream.

HE COULDN'T REMEMBER when he'd been moved from the Fourth Division military base back to Menelik Palace. But he would never forget the drive through the streets of Addis Ababa and the way there had been no evidence of his absence. None of the hollow, directionless stares he'd come to imagine in the faces of his people; none of the longing for his return. There had been the sunlight, brighter than normal, almost blinding and painful to him. There had been the fast-paced symphony of trucks and taxis, of rubber and metal scraping over asphalt; wooden carts pitching over rocks, the shrill wails of street vendors. There had been the smells: eucalyptus and incense, oranges and exhaust fumes, sweat and pack animals. All of this would always be there. Ethiopia would remain, despite even his absence.

He'd been overcome for a moment by the sheer force of life and energy in this country he loved so much. He wanted to embrace it, open his arms and let children run to him, let men and women kiss his hands. If he could have, he would have paused long enough to let his people bow and lay prostrate before him, and he would bless each and every one and shed tears with them. But in front of him and pushing at his heels were soldiers who were leading him away from the small mud room he'd lived in for months, towards a small Volkswagen guarded by heavily armed soldiers who would not look at him.

In the car, he had tried to ask the guard beside him where he was being taken, but a sharply dressed officer had turned around from the front seat and shone a flashlight into his face to silence him, making his eyes water so much the collar of his dirty jacket was soaked. No one spoke for the rest of the ride. He looked out the window instead, his view shadowed by the guard's rigid profile, and became the only one in this forsaken city who wanted the King of Kings to reign supreme once again.

He'd been taken to the great hall that had once belonged to the late Empress Zewditu. All of the furniture had been emptied out of the big room and only a small cot with thin sheets and a blanket sat in its center. Soldiers were posted outside his door, which was locked in triplicate and then chained. Their fear of him was heartbreaking, compounding his loneliness and the largeness of this empty space he was trapped inside. They walked backwards into the room whenever they escorted his old servant inside with his food, doubly armed and wearing sunglasses. They scurried out as quickly as they could, too afraid to glance his way. The mournful whimpers of his old lion, Tojo, lulled him to sleep, and he tried to make himself forget about the garden just outside his window which he was no longer allowed to walk in. Under the weight of this solitude, all of the emperor's hours, minutes, and seconds blurred and ran together like a slow, dying river.

18

How would emperor haile selassie later describe the moon that night? Voluminous, as thick as milk, a thousand melted stars that sliced the sky with razor-sharp edges. Even in the dark, from his window, he could make out the outlines of trees shivering in the breeze. A truck with squealing brakes pulled up and a barking order, followed by the confused mutterings of soldiers, made the emperor move back to his cot. There was nothing here he would want to see. Lying on the bed, he raked his fingers over the spider-bite scabs that dotted his arms, picked at one, and took comfort in the tiny pinch of a peeling wound. This was evidence, he reminded himself, that he was still alive. They hadn't killed him yet. He closed his eyes, let himself float in the darkness, and picked at another scab. He couldn't help smiling.

Quick footsteps echoed beneath his window, then came an order: "Why aren't they ready? Get them into the truck. Tie them up. With this." The thud of a heavy object falling to the ground.

Silence. Then a voice. "But they're officials and royals. Major Guddu, they're—" the man said, his voice trembling.

"They're traitors. Their greed created the famine. Put them in the truck, Mickey," Major Guddu said.

Guddu. The emperor recognized the name of the short, dark man who'd been one of the five to take him out of his palace and place him under arrest.

"Major, what about the trials . . ."

"The Council agrees with me. Are you a traitor like them?"

"But—"

Footsteps, then a gentle click.

"I can start with you, if you'd like." Guddu was calm.

The emperor drew his knees to his chest. He pushed himself as far from the approaching footsteps as possible and hunched into the corner. He mumbled a prayer, louder each time he heard the jingle of keys, then the creak of a door, then the grunts of prisoners herded past his window. He tried not to listen, but for a moment he stopped praying long enough to note the soothing rhythm of their footsteps. Their shuffling feet sounded like the rustle of fallen leaves in the wind.

THE CITY WAS QUIET that night. There was no sound but the crunch of gravel splitting under the weight of military trucks full of frightened prisoners. Nothing to break the thick black of night except a large wide moon. Mickey sat towards the front in one of the trucks, next to Daniel, holding his rifle and pressed against a glass window that revealed their path from Menelik Palace to Akaki Prison. The prisoners huddled in the center of the truck bed, shoved together by the prodding rifles and sharp kicks of other soldiers who dangled off the sides. A thin wind cut through Mickey's shirt and flattened against his chest like a cold hand.

"Give them room," Daniel instructed. "Come over here." He pushed himself deeper into a corner, tucked his legs tighter.

The prisoners were all shaved, still dressed in the same clothes they'd been arrested in, now torn, stained, and hanging limp on thin bodies. A thick rope snaked around and between their hands and legs, connecting one man painfully to the next. The rope cut each time the truck jerked over a rock.

"I can't move," Mickey said. He tried to get closer to Daniel and looked up to find himself staring across heads and straight at Hailu's friend Kifle. The long scar on the side of the man's face glistened in the moonlight like a string of oil as it curved over his jaw. Mickey felt his throat tighten and he dropped his head, ducking out of view.

"My shoulder might be dislocated," Kifle said, his whisper carried by the wind to Mickey. "I can't breathe." Kifle tried to raise his hand to his chest, but the man sitting next to him whimpered.

"You cut me when you move," the man said.

Some of the prisoners tried to hunch into themselves and further away from Kifle.

"Someone help me," Kifle said, starting to cry. "There's a mistake. They arrested me last night. What did I do wrong?" He tried to rest his head on his own shoulder.

"Sit up," an angry voice commanded. "Die like an Ethiopian."

Mickey recognized the sharp tones of famed war veteran Colonel Mehari. Next to him, he saw the stoic, grim profile of ex-prime minister Aklilu Habtewold, dressed in a tattered suit and shoeless, sitting upright and gripping the hand of his brother, the former minister of justice, Akalework. Mickey flattened himself against the glass plate and hoped Kifle would stop crying. In front of their truck was another truck, and in front of that truck, another, then another. All were packed with prisoners, and Mickey was sure each prisoner was surrounded by vengeful angels who sat amongst the soldiers and memorized their faces. He hunched as low as he could, dipped his head into the heat trapped by the sweating bodies, and gagged from the stench of fresh urine.

Some of the men were biting the rope that was mercilessly tight around their wrists, splicing bloody stripes across their mouths. He caught the frustrated sobs of one man who couldn't curl himself into a ball, every move he made knocked his companions over. Mickey saw the silhouette of the heaving man, a body squirming on its side. Then he closed his eyes to blot it all out.

The truck lurched into a pothole. Prisoners screamed. Mickey opened his eyes. All he could make out were tumbling arms and legs connected by the steady straight rope.

"Slow," Daniel whispered, his hands cupped over his face. "Go slow." He tapped on the driver's side window. Tears were rolling down onto his neck. "Do you see the men who are here?" he said to Mickey. "We're not worthy of their company."

"Why is God punishing us?" a man said.

Mickey saw a man old enough to be his grandfather start to move in the huddle of bodies. Prime Minister Aklilu and his brother shifted to their knees so he could kneel. The old man faltered, then slowly raised his hands. His movement lifted the others' arms.

"Let him hear all his children," the man said. One by one, hands closed around each other in the dark. Mickey imagined a thick-rooted tree pushing through dirt. Kifle moved with the men next to him, and it was then that he finally saw Mickey.

"Help us!" Kifle said, his arms spreading, moving with the men next to him. "Mickey!" he pleaded. He knelt with his hands in the air, arms wide like naked wings. "Mickey," he repeated again and again, sobs shaking his thin frame, digging rope into skin.

"Our Father, who art in heaven . . ." The men prayed loudly, their voices drowning out Kifle.

Mickey felt shivers run through his body and put his hands over his ears and turned to Daniel to say something, to cower with him, but saw that he, too, was kneeling with his lips moving rapidly, his head shaking from side to side in his own private protest.

19

THE OLD WOMAN WAS DRESSED in black and carried a small horsetail fly swatter on a handwoven leather handle. She stood at the door of Hailu's house silhouetted by a bright moon, knocking.

"Emama Seble, please come in," Hailu said. "I'm sorry I didn't hear you. I was listening to the radio. Mogus called and said he heard shots near his house, but there's no news about anything like that." He bowed to the woman.

Emama Seble offered no greeting. She moved past Hailu into the living room and sat down in his chair, next to the radio. "Everything's censored anyway," she said. "What do you expect to hear?" She flicked the swatter and turned off the radio. "Two sick people in one family must be very hard."

"We're grateful Tizita's home." Hailu frowned and sat on the sofa next to her.

Emama Seble was the great-aunt of one of Yonas's friends, and she lived alone in the compound. Childless, she'd moved in when her husband died. All of the children in the neighborhood tried to avoid the heavyset woman who, since her husband's death ten years ago, dressed only in black, even though the mourning period was only one year. Stern mothers frightened their children by claiming she had the *budah* and that she would lay a curse on anyone who misbehaved or dared look into her evil eye.

"Has she improved?" Emama Seble asked, wiping her forehead with the edge of her long-sleeved sweater. She stared at the frayed ends while waiting for an answer.

"No." Hailu sank into the soft cushions. "They don't think there's anything left to do. She eats very little that stays down." He adjusted the pillows.

"How is Sara?"

"Not good. She goes to the church every day before even Yonas wakes up. She hardly eats. She doesn't sleep."

Emama Seble twirled a black thread on her sleeve. "She wants to die with the little girl."

"How do you know that?" Hailu asked.

Emama Seble smiled. "I was once a mother."

"I'm sorry," Hailu said. "I didn't know."

"These things happen." Emama Seble met his gaze. "It must be very hard for you. There's no logical explanation for what's happening."

"Some tea or coffee?" Hailu stood up. "How rude of me not to ask."

"No need. I want to see Sara." She hoisted herself up with Hailu's help.

EMAMA SEBLE BOWED three times in front of the prayer room. An edge of moonlight peeked through the door to her right.

"She went to church early this morning. I moved Tizzie in my room to let her rest." He knocked on the door as he opened it. "Sara, Emama Seble has come to visit you."

Sara had lost weight, her eyes stared ahead vacantly, and her skin had the ashen coat of dried tears. Emama Seble enveloped her in a hug.

"*Lijjay,*" she said. "My child. You feel as if you've fallen into this hole alone, don't you?" She held on despite the young woman's stiffness.

"Move. I want my daughter," Sara said.

"I'm watching her," Hailu said.

"No one can watch her but me." Sara reached for the door. "Let me go."

The old woman's broad hands traveled over the knots in Sara's back. The look on her face was tender. "Let me talk to her alone, Hailu."

Sara struggled against her embrace, a frantic light in her eyes when she saw Hailu walk out.

"Sit," the old woman said once Hailu left. "You don't think I know? Let me see your legs." She was brusque again.

"No." Sara gathered her skirt around her.

"Lift your skirt so I can see," Emama Seble commanded. She shook Sara's shoulders gently. "Lift it or I'll do it myself."

Sara pulled the hem of her skirt up slowly.

There were tiny punctures all over her legs, bright and deep. As Sara lifted her skirt, the holes deepened and lengthened. Pockets of pus poked through broken skin and the tiny shards of glass still embedded in her legs sparkled.

"How many times have you crawled around the church?" Emama Seble asked, wiping her brow, then her upper lip. She was sweating.

"Six," Sara said, staring at the wall in front of her.

"What God would want this?" Emama Seble muttered. She took Sara's skirt and pulled it higher. Sara's knees were open wounds. "Oh no, no. You can't do this anymore."

"I promised Angel Gabriel I would go seven times," Sara said, her voice small and thin. She tried to cover her legs but Emama Seble held the skirt tight.

"Nobody else in the family knows about this? These foolish men think you're just walking?" Emama Seble glanced at the door. "They haven't asked you anything?"

"They don't need to know anything."

"Let me clean these wounds for you," Emama Seble said. "I'm not letting you go to the church again."

"No." But Sara's voice was flat; it held no force. "My daughter's dying. Another one is dying, Emama. Leave me alone." She tried to stand but Emama Seble pushed her back down on the bed.

Emama Seble rang the bell near the bed. "Bizu, my dear, bring me warm water and a clean towel," she called out.

"Lie down." Emama Seble motioned. "Close your eyes. Let me take this weight for now."

"She's mine." Sara looked at her knees. "He's not taking her away."

It had been six days since they brought Tizita from the hospital. Six days: so much time in the life of a small girl. Six days of barely any food or water, continual shivers, and never-ending pain. In those six days, Sara had felt her own stomach sink further against her hips, her breasts ached. In those six days, Sara had begun to beg at the foot of the statue of Saint Mary. Tell me how you did it, she pleaded. Tell me how you watched this son of yours die his death, and you did not curse his father. Tell me how you listened to his cries and did not offer yourself in his stead. Tell me what you knew that I do not know. Tell me how you could call yourself a mother, then become a spectator on that spiteful day. Tell me. And it was on the sixth day that Sara remembered, finally, that even Mary had not mourned alone. She'd been sheltered in the arms of her other children, full-bodied evidence of mercy and grace.

"My only child is dying," Sara said.

"Here's the water and a towel." Bizu climbed the stairs with slow steps. She lifted filmy, graying eyes to Emama Seble. "If you need anything else, don't bother with Sofia, she doesn't know where anything is. I'll do it."

Emama Seble squeezed a steady stream of warm water over Sara's knees. Sara cringed as it made its way into her cuts.

"Bring the girl to me," Emama Seble said. "If you insist on going to the church, do it tomorrow." She spread the cloth over Sara's legs and poured out the remaining water. "What you've taken must be replaced."

"This one is mine," Sara said. "This one, I'm keeping."

"She's a thread woven into a larger cloth, like all of us. If you take one, you break the others along the way. It must be fixed." She shook her head. "I can try to help her get well. And the rest, we'll see . . ."

IN THE LIVING ROOM, Hailu was back in his chair, hunched over his radio. Yonas was next to Emama Seble on the sofa. They listened in concerned silence.

"The Education Ministry announces that the last two years of secondary school and the university will remain closed in preparation for student deployments across Ethiopia to assist in reforms. Counterrevolutionary agitators were arrested for the intent to incite riots. Haile Selassie University has been renamed Addis Ababa University. Victory to our struggling masses! *Hebrettesebawinet!* The only true means of equality, Ethiopian socialism!"

Emama Seble shook her head. "Now they're sending all the troublemakers away? Those villagers aren't ready for them."

Yonas nodded. "The Derg just wants them out of its sight. Close to fifty thousand *zemechas.*"

"I've already made a request that Dawit stay here because of Selam," Hailu said. "Lily's going."

"You have to watch him," Emama Seble said. "Zeleka told me her daughter, the smart one, Sosena, not the useless one, is writing letters from America to give advice to these students. Others are sending money from everywhere. Put that pride away and start treating him like a man, respect him, he'll listen to you then," she said. "This sofa needs new pillows." She shifted in her seat.

Hailu turned off the radio. "Did Sara talk to you?"

"She needs to sleep, that's all," the old woman replied. "I need rest myself. This shooting, how can anyone sleep at night?" She stood.

Yonas followed her. "Let me get the door."

At the front door, she leaned towards Yonas. "You were right to help your mother," she said. She searched his face. "Sometimes life isn't what we should be hoping for."

"What do you mean?" He took a step back.

"Open the door, let me go home." Her ankle-length dress swayed as she turned. Yonas watched as a fly landed on her thick waistband and was quickly enveloped by the billowing material, disappearing against the sea of black cotton like a pebble in a dust storm.

20

D AWIT WOKE TO THE SPLATTER of stones against his window. He knew the signal. He crept down the corridor to the small door next to the garage. His father was still asleep, but he imagined he could hear Yonas's voice coming from the prayer room. Two telltale creaks above his head told him Sara was awake, pacing in front of Tizita's bed. The little girl had developed a fever the day before.

Dawit opened the door and shivered. There was a bitter chill despite the rising sun. Mickey was slumped against the wall, dressed in fatigues. He looked shorter and heavier in uniform. His cheeks were smudged with dirt and sweat and he wasn't wearing his glasses.

"What's wrong?" Dawit asked.

"Let me in," Mickey said. He pushed into the house. "Did you hear the trucks go by?" He was out of breath. "Close the door!"

"What trucks?"

Mickey rushed into Dawit's room and sank to the ground. "Did you hear them? Close the curtain."

Dawit closed the curtain, suddenly nervous. It was rare for Mickey to be so distraught. "What's wrong?"

Mickey blinked rapidly. "I lost my rifle and my glasses." He moved his hand to push up invisible frames. "They're gone."

"Do you know where?" Dawit knew Mickey well enough to understand that he was trying to explain something else.

"He made us tie them up and drive them away and shoot them." Mickey held his head, his voice was low, a trembling boy's cry. "They kept asking me not to do it."

Mickey's face was drawn, the skin across the fleshy curves of his cheekbones seemed tighter. Dark circles gave his eyes a sunken stare, his lips were cut from biting them. His fingertips were black. Blood dotted the back of his hands. His breath smelled sour.

"Mickey?" Dawit said. "What are you talking about?"

Mickey's hands were clasped tight around his head, squeezing so hard that Dawit was afraid he'd hurt himself. "They told me their wives' names and how many children they had at home. We know them. They went to our school. Some were so old." He was shaking. "Major Guddu ordered everything. He was standing next to me the whole time. They all died."

Dawit felt his whole body engulfed in a blast of heat. He couldn't understand what Mickey was saying. "What are you talking about?" He wiped his neck, the sweat sticky and thick. "Who's this Major Guddu?"

"Daniel. Daniel refused. He tried to untie some of them. The major put a plastic bag over Daniel's head and shot from inside the bag. He said the revolution didn't waste uniforms. My uniform was so bloody the major made me put on Daniel's uniform." Mickey's words were strangled between coughs. "Look how dirty it is."

"Who died?" Dawit couldn't say "killed." "Mickey?"

"He was so brave, he didn't say anything. He knelt and prayed for forgiveness. He was my friend."

Dawit stumbled to his bed. The sweat was drying quickly, replaced by a chill. "Who were the prisoners?" he asked. "Do you know any names? We've been petitioning to have some of them released, there weren't any formal charges—"

"I killed them myself. Can't you hear me?" Mickey wiped his eyes impatiently, roughly. "He made me. He put the plastic bag over me and told me to shoot." He touched his hair, and that's when Dawit noticed the flecks of dried blood on his forehead. "They didn't want to die. They moved so much. The rope kept cutting them. It was too tight."

"Who?"

"The emperor's grandson, *Lij* Iskinder Desta. Prime Minister Aklilu, Prime Minister Endalkachew. The other officials. Even . . ." Mickey grimaced and choked on his words. He dropped his head and rocked back and forth. "Even other people."

These were the men who'd once ruled Ethiopia with the emperor, graduates of Harar Military Academy, Oxford, the London School of Economics, the Sorbonne, and Harvard, dignitaries to European nations, speakers at United Nations forums, proud warriors in the fight with Italy.

"Are you sure?" Dawit hugged his friend, but a fracture as thin as a strand of hair had snuck between them, separating him from the full sorrow he should have been feeling. Mickey's sweat was odorous, sharp, mixed with another strong scent. Dawit turned his head. "How did you get here?"

"I jumped out of the back of the truck. I dropped my rifle. It was too hot to hold. He made me shoot so much." Mickey reached into his shirt. "I still have this." He pulled out a pistol, holding it flat in his palm as if it was soiled. "There are no more bullets."

Dawit took the pistol and, unsure what to do with it, shoved it quickly under his bed. He noticed, for the first time, how yellow the whites of his eyes were, how small and darting his pupils.

"How could this happen?" Dawit asked.

"I'm telling you what happened. You think I'm lying? Look under my nails, look!" Mickey shoved his hands into Dawit's face. Underneath his fingernails were dark threads of dried blood. "Don't you smell their shit on me? The bag was over my face, it was hard to breathe."

Sweat stains trailed down Mickey's back and under his arms. Dawit smelled the bite of urine and saw a wet patch on the floor.

"Get up, wash here before going home." He patted his back, a limp gesture. Mickey had become enemy and victim all in one night.

"I know what you're thinking. They were so scared. They begged so much, they were going to give us everything, all their money. I couldn't hold my rifle long, it was burning my hands, the metal was so hot it kept jamming. He kept saying the Russians would have to give us new guns now. He kept saying you can't have a revolution without uniforms and new guns and all the traitors and cowards must be killed. I'm a coward, I'm the one he's talking about."

"I'll get the bath ready. Take off that uniform." Dawit handed Mickey a robe to put on.

"I'm a coward," Mickey said.

"You didn't have a choice." Dawit rubbed his shoulders. "Take off the uniform." He held him tight and felt Mickey's heart beating fast against his chest. "You couldn't say no."

"Promise me you won't tell anyone." Mickey stepped away from his embrace. "Promise me, as a brother." His nearsighted eyes narrowed.

He'd stopped blinking and his hands were still. "And we'll never talk about this again.

"Say it!" Mickey shouted.

"Be quiet. Tizzie's sick," Dawit said. It was his turn to take a step away from Mickey, the two of them suddenly felt too close. "I promise we'll never talk about this again."

Mickey dropped his head. "What do I do with the messages for their children? What do I do with them? We know some of them. What do I tell them?"

Shaken, Dawit walked out of the room, into the bathroom to run the water for his friend.

21

SARA LAY NEXT TO YONAS, SUFFOCATING in the wordless space that had grown between them in the days since Tizita's fall and her escalating fever. Their bed felt too small. Yonas's breathing sounded too loud. The room was too hot. And in this oppressive dark, her anger stirred. They hadn't spoken to each other since Emama Seble's visit, hadn't touched in over a week. She bit her lip to keep from calling his name. He wasn't sleeping, she could feel his mind racing, could sense the tension in his body.

"You can move as far away as you want, but I'm still her father," he said suddenly. "You can't change that."

"I'm not trying to," she said.

"You are." He was flat on his back, speaking to the air above him, refusing to look at her. "What you don't like, you try to change. You don't want to share this child but she's mine, too, just like the others."

Sara wanted to remind him it was her body that held two dying babies. Her stomach that felt like it was splitting into pieces. Her blood that flowed. Not his.

"I know that," she said.

Yonas shut his eyes. He couldn't argue with her when she stared at him. Her eyes reminded him of all the reasons he loved her. "What about my mother?"

"Emaye?" Sara asked.

"Didn't she take care of you after your pregnancies? Didn't she cook special foods and take you to visit your parents' graves?" he asked.

His hand was tracing her back with a pressure that made her want to scream. She sat up. "I don't understand why you're asking."

"You've been so focused on yourself, you don't ask about her anymore. You haven't gone to visit her. You're selfish with our daughter." He stressed the word "our." "You think you're the only one suffering, when there's me and Abbaye and Dawit. You never ask how I am. Never."

She counted the small cracks that branched from the peeling white paint on the ceiling, illuminated by a soft gray moon.

"You don't know what you're talking about," she said, listening for cries from Tizita.

"You don't think I love my daughter? I don't want to lose her." Yonas was getting louder. He sat up to meet her gaze. "Half her blood is mine."

"Don't talk to me about losing someone," Sara said, letting her anger breathe and grow. She moved farther away from him.

"Why?" Yonas pressed. "Tell me why I can't talk to you about it."

"What do you know about losing anyone? You've had such an easy life that when something happens, you collapse like a child and start praying." She spat out the words.

"Tell me this, since you don't lie," she continued.

She leaned closer to his face. Her features were tight, sharpened like stone, her eyes flat and cold. Her light skin was flushed.

"Are you praying for your mother to live?" She gave him no room to escape her gaze. "I hear you. Only an ignorant person wishes for their mother's death. If you knew about losing someone, you'd do everything to avoid it. You'd never pray for it. You'd rather die than feel it again. How could you do that?"

"I've never prayed for my mother to die." He spoke in a calm voice. "I've prayed for what she needs."

Though they were in this room, in their marriage bed, together under the same moon, Yonas suddenly felt as if he'd walked away, as if he'd already stood up and gone out the door, and left behind everything these four walls contained. He no longer knew this woman, and maybe that meant he no longer loved her.

"You pray for Emaye, your own mother, to die without pain," Sara said. "I've heard you." Then, so softly that Yonas almost didn't hear, she said, "Is that what you've been praying for my daughter?"

Yonas swung his right hand. Sara's mouth was still open when his palm connected with the side of her face. The blow was hard. Its momentum threw her against the wall with a thud.

Sara charged at him. Yonas stumbled backwards, dazed, startled as much by her ferocity as by what he'd just done. Never had he raised a hand to Sara.

"What is wrong with you?" She hit, hands swinging accurately, without mercy, kept on hitting, couldn't seem to still her rage. She attacked with her fists. She aimed for his face, his head, his neck, wherever she could find tender flesh.

"What have you done?" Tears spilled down her face. Her lips trembled. "You don't think I'll fight back? You forget I'm my mother's daughter?"

Yonas ducked, shielded his eyes from her blows, but did nothing else.

Finally out of breath, Sara stepped back, her body tightly coiled. "You don't know me."

Yonas stepped towards her. She raised her chin, a red welt already evident near her jaw. She didn't flinch. He stood so close she could hear the wheeze at the end of each breath. She resisted the urge to rub his chest and kiss it. He took her in his arms and held her close; her own arms were pressed stiffly to her side. He rocked gently and Sara felt the soft brush of lips on her head. He was praying. Then he turned and left the room.

22

THE TAXI DRIVER WHO PICKED UP SARA in front of the French Legation was crying.

"To St. Gabriel's Church," Sara said as she got in the backseat. She avoided his open display of grief.

"I can't believe it," he said, shaking his head and wiping his eyes as he put the car into gear. "All of them." He looked into the rearview mirror to talk to her. "Even General Amman," he said. "That great man helped us win the war with Somalia. He wanted to avoid a war with Eritrea."

"What happened?" Sara asked, shifting her legs to ease the pain in her knees, and looked out the window. They were on one of the many roads carved out of the side of a hill in Addis Ababa. Below, a sprawling community of shanties with corrugated-tin roofs rose from what had once been a lush valley. The gray sky hung heavy and thick above them.

Sara glanced out the window as they drove by Arat Kilo and the university's Faculty of Science. There was a row of tanks with soldiers hanging off the sides, their rifles pointed into traffic. Another group of tanks waited at an intersection ahead, more soldiers walked back and forth at another street corner. The few people passing by were moving with haste, their faces hidden by the *shammas* they'd draped over their heads and across their shoulders.

"Why so many soldiers?" she asked.

The driver tapped his radio. "You didn't hear?" he asked, turning around, then back to the road again. "The Derg killed sixty officials last night. Just shot them like criminals." He wiped his cheeks. "Even the prince and the prime ministers. Ex-prime ministers. No trials." He ran a hand over his face but the stunned expression in his eyes remained. He couldn't stop shaking his head. "They killed General Amman in his home. They killed them . . ." His voice trailed into silence.

"That's why it's so quiet," she said.

It was morning and the sky felt empty without the melodic prayers that would normally be rising from the copper-domed Holy Trinity Cathedral at the break of dawn. Only the faint lingering wails of street beggars, especially plaintive that day, hovered over the startled city.

Sara touched the side of her face as she leaned her head on the window and stared at the ground. She flinched when her fingers pressed into the bruise left from Yonas's blow. She fought her tears and watched the tires swallow, then spew small stones, leaving them behind for the next traveler.

"I cried when I heard, too," the taxi driver said. "I can't stop. How is this possible? They promised no bloodshed."

They drove the rest of the way in silence. The taxi driver frowned at a group of soldiers in front of the Parliament building as he approached St. Gabriel's Church. "They should be ashamed to come out today." He glared at one, who dropped his head and walked to another corner of the street. "My neighbor's son is a soldier," he said, pulling over to let Sara out. "He wore civilian clothes to work and carried his uniform with him. They should all be that afraid of us."

"Thank you," she said, dropping extra coins in his palm. She avoided the stares of the soldiers and waved the taxi on.

A SLENDER EUCALYPTUS LEAF spiraled to the ground and twirled gracefully in perfect circles. Sara saw the leaf land on an old beggar crouched on one row of steps surrounding the eight-sided church, his blind gray eyes roving in their sockets like hungry rats.

"Are you back again, my daughter?" he asked, pushing his nose into the air.

"It's my last time." Sara fought the urge to turn away from the stench of rotting skin surrounding him.

At his side, a little girl shuffled on scarred knees that extended to a pair of shriveled legs trailing limply behind her.

"Raise your voice so the angels can hear you." The man looked directly into the rising sun. "Keep whatever promise you make, there's no other way. Otherwise . . ."

He nudged his chin in the direction of the small girl who was dragging herself to a smartly dressed group of women. One of the women kicked her away with an irritated huff.

"God blesses all who give. Give and you shall be blessed," the girl cried out as she hobbled towards the elegant group of women again, careful this time to keep a safe distance.

"Abbaba, I'm very sorry for your troubles." Sara dropped coins in the center of his wrinkled palms. The silver shimmered in the light, dulled by the man's closing hands.

"May God bless you, my daughter. May you never see days like mine," the old man wailed.

Sara blinked back the tears that threatened to fall and made her way to the small road that encircled the octagonal church.

DAYS AGO, Sara had paid one of the beggars to bring broken glass and scatter it along the path, and shards still sparkled against the sun. Her knees on that first crawl around the church had been merely bruised, spotted with tiny red cuts. She'd prayed quietly, in murmurs respectful of the other worshippers who prayed with their foreheads touching the walls of the church, their lips brushing stone.

The second day, her hands were cut and her back ached, she'd had to raise her voice to help relieve her pain. By the third, she was hunched low on her arms. She'd had to stop several times, lie flat in the dirt until she could pray in words worthy of her anger. On the fourth visit, she was so focused on the effort to move she ignored the crowds of people who stopped to stare at her, at once shocked and compelled by her determination. Her bleeding legs no longer shook, the pain had dulled into a thick ache across her body, only her voice was sharp, getting louder with each move.

By the fifth day, she was immobile, a shivering body in the dirt.

A group of elderly monks, wearing faded robes and long white beards, approached her. "We'll pray with you," the eldest of them said, his sad deep-set eyes almost hidden in folds of wrinkled skin. "One of ours has been jailed." They sank to their knees on all sides of her and nudged her ahead.

It was on the sixth day that a woman knelt beside her and held out two woven pads of eucalyptus. The leaves were layered and carefully sewn together with a thick thread as red as blood.

"For you, sister," the woman said. "When the leaves split, the juice will help your knees heal." She was one of the beggars, a doe-eyed hunchback with no front teeth. Sara had noticed her intense stares each morning.

"Go away," Sara said.

"There is enough of your blood on this road." The woman nudged the leaves towards her, then finally set the pads down in front of her. "Didn't Christ also bleed so we wouldn't have to?"

Sara slid on top of them and instantly felt their coolness. "Thank you." Her mouth was dry and tears had caked inside her throat and left her hoarse.

"I see you here every day," the woman said. "So many people come to church before they visit their family in prison. Even our monk is in jail. Is it the same with you?" Sara didn't respond, and the young woman sank to her knees and began to crawl next to her. She refused to leave her side even when her back hurt and rendered her mute.

A BREEZE FLICKED along the path, sent dust blooming over the group of well-dressed women. Their muttering drifted past Sara as they stepped gingerly over rocks, careful not to scar their leather shoes. Their voices mingled with the buzz of hovering flies, dipped again into delicate whispers.

The gravel cut into Sara's feet. She let her eyes circle the span of the church, and her legs shook from dread. Her pads were nearly shredded, streaks of sap and blood had dried along their thin branching veins. She knelt, the pressure on her wounds making her break into a sweat at the same instant that she shivered. A bird's thin screech sailed high above her head, and she thought of Tizita, lying in her bed. She began to crawl and pray.

You. You have cursed this womb and torn yours out. Mixed my blood with premature ash. You have heard my bitter cries and sat silent to my prayers. You have made me into nothing but the mother of one, the daughter of none, a woman carrying twin monuments of grief. Leave me alone. Let me be as I am. I ask for no more. Sara prayed. If this

God demanded blood, if her father and mother and two babies weren't enough, then she would give of herself until he was forced to concede, if not out of compassion and justice, then out of a damning guilt born of having watched his own son die on a cross while pleading to a father who had forsaken him.

A gentle hand touched her shoulder and pressed softly.

"My sister, I've come again." It was the hunchbacked woman. "I have more leaves for you today."

Sara hadn't realized that she'd stopped crawling. Her skirt was ripped and the padded leaves were now shreds of green laced in frayed red thread.

The woman knelt beside her. "My mother did this when I was born, too. Sometimes your pain isn't enough. All the blood you spill, it might not be enough. This is a hungry God we beg for mercy." She turned her soft eyes towards Sara.

"Leave me." Sara continued her slow shuffle. The high-pitched shriek of a bird floated in circles above her head. She tensed her back to still the shivers.

"I'll go with you the rest of the way," the young woman said. Her eyes traced Sara's face and she smiled a gentle smile. "Today, we'll make our voices loud. Today, we'll shout into the clouds. Today, for your daughter, and for my monk, we'll do this, and may God have mercy on our pain. May God forgive and help us forget these days."

Sara and the young woman crawled around the church. Deafened by each other's prayers, they didn't notice the monks had come again to make the journey with them. Their voices rose in waves—a rippling chorus beating against the sky. Drops of thickening blood marked their path around the road, a brilliant red border glistening in the sun.

23

A RED RING OF FIRE FLARED AROUND the burning end of a dying cigarette. Solomon paced, his stride assured. He smoked in three quick inhalations, then a long exhale, the release drawing his energy taut. Dawit felt himself suffocating in this man's power. Frightened and awed by his command of every step.

"What do you understand of what I've said?" Solomon asked.

Dawit stepped forward, then backed away from his cutting glance. They were in a small house near the university. City lights blazed and dimmed in the haze of a cool fog. Dogs wheezed and coughed outside the door.

"I'm going to collect pamphlets from the printing press and deliver them to the house," Dawit said. He tried to make himself sound confident. "After you tell me where the house is."

"What else?" Solomon asked, disappointed. "What is it that I haven't told you? What do you understand without being told?"

Dawit's heart raced. No answer came. Sweat collected in pools under his shirt and he knew Solomon noticed, so Dawit did what he did when he didn't want his father to see him nervous: he trained his eyes forward, jutted his chin, pressed his arms to his side. He became a young tree that refused to be bent by the push of the wind.

"What else?" Solomon was impatient, dismissive. He turned the dying cigarette in his mouth, finished it off, and started another one.

Dawit struggled. "I don't know."

Solomon let the cigarette sag. "Pick a code name, or I'll give you one."

"I don't understand," he said. The pamphlets he'd be passing out were simple ones, there was nothing illegal about them.

"There's no law against pamphlets," Solomon echoed Dawit's thoughts. His dark hair was sprinkled with white strands, and tiny wrinkles creased the edges of his black eyes. "Not yet, but the day will come. It's inevitable when a military junta won't allow a civilian government. If you get caught, we've got to make sure you can't give anyone else away."

"I wouldn't do that," Dawit said.

Solomon sighed. "Pick a name, no one in the organization can ever know you by anything else."

Dawit considered for a moment, thought of names he'd wanted, warriors he admired: Adane, Amare, Menelik, Kassa, Teodros, Alemayehou, Getachew.

Solomon clapped his hands. "Enough. You're Mekonnen," he said. "Like your father's hospital, though I heard they're changing the name."

Dawit repeated the name softly, the hard, crisp letters snapping in his mouth. It sounded strong, full, the name of a man. He smiled, nodded. "I'm Mekonnen." He paused. "Your real name's not Solomon?"

"We're finished here." It was when Solomon dug in his pocket for another cigarette that Dawit noticed his hands for the first time: shaking, uncontrollably loose-limbed. There was a pause and then a look from the other man before both shifted their eyes away from the momentary shame.

"Go home," Solomon said, both hands in his pockets. "I'll let you know when we're ready."

DAWIT MET SARA AT THE GATE, agitated. "The Derg sent five thousand men from the Imperial Bodyguard to Eritrea." He held a newspaper in his hand. "It's not right." He looked down at a headline and held the gate open for her. "Teferi Bante is the new chairman, but Guddu seems to be the one in charge." He stared in disgust at a front-page photo of two men in military uniforms marching across a field, fists raised. "Have you heard of him?"

Sara felt weak, her back ached, deep scratches on her knees had broken open, they were bleeding. "I'm tired," she said. She leaned against the gate. "I need to sit."

Dawit was still looking at the newspaper. "Doesn't this make you angry?"

A military truck spit rocks and dust as it barreled down the road in their direction. She met the glance of a soldier. He dropped his head and rolled up the window.

"Let's talk later," she said. She ignored his surprised look and went into the compound and sat down on the veranda. She and Dawit had spent many hours recently discussing the day's headlines. She felt his curious stare and let her hair fall over her face. She knew this man who was a brother to her would be able to read her expression; he'd always been able to see a part of her that Yonas overlooked. If he'd been older when she'd first married and moved to this house—in those days when her homesickness rubbed against the old pain of two dead parents—she would have confided in him about everything, would have found in him that person strong enough to understand the scar that ran across the top of her head.

"Where did you go?" he asked, moving to sit by her.

Sara took in the place she now called home. It was large, a two-story house amongst the many one- and two-room mud homes that circled it. The rocky paths that led from one home to the next were well worn from years of countless neighborly visits. A large water jug, rubbed clean, leaned against one door. The residents of Hailu's compound shared what they had, and trusted to get it back.

"I was at St. Gabriel's," she said. She settled her legs further under her skirt and tried to ignore the pain.

Dawit took her hand. "You look sad," he told her. He followed her gaze around the compound. "I'm going to be very busy for a while."

Sara sensed the electricity in his words, heard in what he said the power of those things he wasn't saying. They sat together, warmed by companionship that asked no questions. Around them ran children's footprints, scattered over once-muddied paths. Dawit's dog lay sprawled over a bone, his head resting on top of Tizita's make-believe castle. To their right, colorful threadbare clothes swung in the breeze like old flags.

EMAMA SEBLE LIVED IN a single room behind a door painted the deep brown-red of sunburnt flesh. It swung open before Sara had a chance to knock. She was holding Tizita.

"Hurry up." Emama Seble pulled her inside. She adjusted the black scarf around her head. "Give her to me." Tongues of fire flickered above a melting candle in the center of the room.

"What are you going to do?" Sara asked.

Loose shadows swept over Emama Seble. "I'm going to help her."

"I'm not leaving," Sara said.

"I didn't ask you to, now give her to me. I have hot water and it can't get cold," Emama Seble said.

The old woman took the shrunken girl to the courtyard, towards a large pot used by the women for boiling water. The thick scent of euca- lyptus rose from the pot.

"What are you doing?" Sara asked.

"You should have brought her yesterday as soon as you came back from the church." The old woman stepped closer to the pot. The fire at the base hissed and sighed under a mound of coal and wood, it was dying. Soft ash crumbled to the ground.

"Give her back to me," Sara said.

"I won't hurt her, I promise you." Emama Seble's voice was sooth- ing. "Haven't you tried everything else?"

Sara reminded herself that this was her last hope. Her daughter was still losing weight. She spit out as much food as she managed to swallow, her skin was tinged a dull gray, and her breathing was shallow. She'd lost the energy to do anything but sleep.

Emama Seble leaned towards the steam while Tizita slept in her arms, peaceful and calm above the heat.

"You'll burn her," Sara said.

Emama Seble closed the girl's nostrils and forced Tizita to open her mouth and fill her lungs with the warm, healing aroma of eucalyptus. She let the little girl breathe like this, then massaged her stomach. She repeated the process, her eyes roving behind her eyelids, her face intent.

"There it is," Emama Seble suddenly said. She stopped just below Tiz- ita's heart. "A knot. Right here." Emama Seble pushed against the lump.

Sara's stomach ached. Emama Seble pressed again, harder, and Sara doubled over, the sharpness of the pain taking her breath away. "What's happening, Emama?" she asked.

Emama Seble put her whole hand over Tizita's stomach. She held the girl in a strong grip and pushed. "It's you," she said to Sara.

Sara moaned, rigid from the pain in her stomach. Her body remem- bered this agony. It had visited twice before. She felt pressure building in her womb and shooting into her head. "I don't understand," she said.

"It's your fault she's sick." Emama Seble's stare was unflinching.

Sara curled a fist into her stomach. She felt something unwind like a spool of thread; she was unraveling.

"You took this child," Emama Seble said, moving her hand away from Tizita's stomach.

"She's a gift, my gift." It was hard to speak. Sara's throat burned, her eyes were watering from the steam.

"Gifts are given. You've forced yourself into a space that doesn't belong to you, and pushed everyone out. It isn't right. You know what you've been doing, you've known from the beginning."

"Give her back," Sara said, holding out her arms but afraid to take a step towards the woman.

Emama Seble flicked beads of water onto Tizita. She grabbed leaves from the pot and followed the steam that rolled off the leaves and into the sky.

"You're doing this to her," Emama Seble said. "You're suffocating the life that's trying to grow. You're too angry." She turned to her house. "Come."

Emama Seble disappeared into her home. By the time Sara walked into the room, the old woman was already seated on a stool. Tizita was lying on her back on the table. The flickering candle sat on the floor, its blackened wick trapped in wax. A slow sun sent amber ropes of light into the room.

"Hold her by her feet so she's completely upside down."

Sara hesitated, overcome by the urge to take the child and run back home. Emama Seble waited. Sara lifted her daughter by her feet.

Emama Seble smoothed the leaves on Tizita's stomach, then massaged. She started near her groin and moved towards her chest, firmly pressing the girl's belly. She unrolled a *netela* and wrapped the white gauzy shawl over the girl's midsection like a bandage. Satisfied, she leaned back, exhausted. She helped Sara set her down on the table. Tizita was still sleeping.

"Why didn't she wake up?" Sara asked. She felt new panic rising.

"She's okay. Leave the *netela* on for the next three days."

"And then?"

"Let her father unwrap her. Not you. I'm tired." Emama Seble got up and moved to her bed.

24

THE ASCENT IS A THRILL THAT pushes itself from the secret spot between her legs and settles into a song. Selam sings with a fullness she can only compare to lust—shivering ululations that splay against the stars. It's a freedom she's never known, an unruly, sweet beckoning she can't resist. Each sweep of her wings propels her onward upward skyward.

Then her name presses on her like a heavy hand; presses down again.

"Selam." It is one voice, two, there are many. "Selam."

The voice draws her to a path so dark she knows she's reached *yealem beqayn*, the end of the world. She comes to a flat white building, to a space behind the building, to an area gilded by drying trees where the ground has been stripped of grass. Mounds of dirt piled high as anthills are caked in blood, patted down with shovels she knows once shook with guilt.

She sees scraps of finely woven cloth, broken glasses, a flung cross pendant.

There is the stench of betrayal and pain. She tries to fling herself up, away from it all. But the voices wrap their sorrow around her, and they repeat her name.

"Selam! Selam! Selam!"

I am struggling. Cannot move. Why this taste in my throat? What has become of sweetness and honey?

It is only after she's nearly given up and given in to the downward pull of their grief that she realizes they aren't calling her name but the meaning of her name, hurling it into the heavens for the angels to hear, and to act.

"Peace! Peace! Peace!"

Then, just as suddenly as they'd pressed against her, they let her go. Selam lets the momentum of her fear fling her farther into the sky than she's gone before. She flies again, spirals towards stars that crackle with heat, weaves through the breeze, her heart so strong it sends flashes of red past her eyes, propels her deep into the comforting freedom of the dark.

SHE WASN'T BREATHING.

"Selam," Hailu repeated. His mouth covered hers as he tried to breathe into her again. "Selam!" He pushed against her heart with flat palms, then listened for a heartbeat. Nothing. There was nothing. He felt Yonas grab his hand and Sara put her arm around him. Dawit was in a corner across from them, his eyes wide and frightened.

"Let her go," Yonas said, tugging at his arm, pulling him away from the bed.

Hailu gripped his son's hand, drew Sara closer, and searched the dark corner for Dawit's eyes. With the devoted patience of a believer he waited for his wife to die.

But then there was a gasp. He was sure of it. Selam struggled for air and that was all Hailu needed to propel him out of his family's reach and towards her bed. He took a syringe from his pocket and felt a stab of guilt so strong that his hands shook as he gave his wife an injection intended to stun her heart into regular beats.

Dawit began to sob and dropped his head in his hands. Yonas backed away and sank into a chair. The family watched the flat line of the heart monitor.

"You promised her," Dawit said. "You promised!" He ran out of the room.

"I'll get him," Yonas said, his voice tight and small.

"Abbaye, sit down," Sara said, her arms around him. "Please sit." Tears ran down her face.

"Selam," Hailu begged, refusing to be moved. "Selam."

A gust of air from the open window swayed the curtains. The dull gray of moonlight broke into the room, slid over the bed.

"Abbaye?" It was Yonas, come back to wrap his arms around him. "Sit down, Sara's right."

"Close the curtains. Close them!" Hailu struggled out of his son's embrace and leaned over to take Selam in his arms. "Help me," he said, looking down at his wife.

Yonas raised his mother so Hailu could put his arms around her. She felt light and fragile, her arms swung loosely in his grip.

"Help me carry her to the hallway," Hailu said.

Dawit's sobs echoed in the corridor. It came from deep within him.

"I'll get blankets and a pillow," Sara said.

Hailu and Yonas lifted Selam off the bed, her head cushioned against Hailu's chest. Her skin cool to his touch. "Is a window open?"

Yonas shook his head. He couldn't meet his father's eyes. "Why do you want to take her out?"

"Open the door," Hailu said. "Open it."

DAWIT SAT ON the floor in the hallway doubled into himself, his hands locked into a tight fist. The bright lights pressed on his head like an unforgiving sun.

"Dawit." Hailu stood at the door, his wife in his arms. "Stand up." He looked next to him, to his elder son. "Come here, both of you."

Hailu had prepared himself for this moment, had thought carefully of his last words to Selam, of the way he would hold her and ease her breathing until she slipped away. He'd put on paper the verses he'd share with his family after it was all over, which priest from Entoto Kidane Mehret he'd call, who he'd get to inform the rest of their friends and distant relatives of her death. He knew which blue embroidered dress he'd insist she wear for burial, which wedding photograph he would send with her, which of his rings he would put on her finger. Hailu had thought of it all because he knew that leaving one detail unplanned would render him paralyzed. It was in not knowing what came next that Hailu felt at his weakest.

So he didn't know why he'd never imagined Dawit next to him when Selam died, only Yonas. Sara behind them felt natural. Dawit's presence was a detail he had to take into account and he wasn't prepared to do so.

"You have to look at her," he said to Dawit.

He wanted to hide the fact that his son's presence sent a wild panic through him. Dawit reminded him too much of Selam, he had her nose and forehead, the tilt of his head was hers. Hailu could accept a dying wife, he could continue to hold this slowly cooling body for as long as he needed to, but he couldn't cope with the living traces of his wife in his son. It reminded him of what he would always miss.

"Help me put her down," he said.

Sara unfolded a blanket and laid a pillow on the floor. Down the hall, a young soldier watched in uncomfortable sympathy.

"If you don't look, you'll never be able to forgive yourself," he said to Dawit, praying that his son didn't realize he was talking to himself.

"Don't turn away." Hailu forced himself to look at him and try to let go of the familiar. "Look."

The family knelt around Selam's body. Hailu reached across his wife to grab Dawit's arm and squeeze it. Their hands settled on her chest.

"She's gone," Hailu said. He kept his focus on Yonas. "She's left us."

25

ONCE, I WAS BELOVED OF GOD, the King of Kings. I was the Conquering Lion of Judah, a descendant of King Dawit. My blood, rich and red, is kin to that other King of Kings, the most Beloved. I ruled my kingdom in honor of His. We were as we were because He was. In this kingdom of men, angels walked amongst us, flesh and spirit side by side, fiery swords next to spears. Wings beat back bullets, bent Italian rifles, flattened tanks. Under a poisonous rain dripping from warplanes flying as low as insects, we have run and triumphed, shielded by feathers, our skin still whole and splendid under the sun. Abyssinia. Saba's blessed children multiplied, scattered into hillsides and castles, buried in obelisks and caves, mummified as perfectly as pharaohs. Ethiopia, the most loved of the Beloved, do you hear the drums above the clouds? Do you know that angels approach, and they come for you? Mercy will be no more for this blasphemy against us. There will be the day, Beloved, when we will rise again, and a divine rage will pour itself on you and we will not stop the tide, though you will beg. And after the storm, after the cleansing, we will open our arms again, and you will come, eager once more, and angels will guide our next steps, and we will move together.

IN HIS PALACE, time moved in swoops, curled seamlessly from one hour to the next. He woke at six, met with officials at nine. He had afternoon tea at four, dinner with his family at eight. Every minute was accounted for, every need anticipated by invisible bodies who tiptoed in and out of his presence noiselessly, their swallowed thoughts escaping only through their eyes, discernible if he'd been concerned enough to notice. But he hadn't been. We did not see the beast, he whispered into the endless quiet punctured only by the guard's whistle. It stood before our eyes, but we did not see.

—

THE WHISTLING SOUNDED like the distant siren of an oncoming train that night. It was hollow, thin, and the rapid tap of the soldier's rifle as he walked the hall mimicked the rattle of worn rails. Something wasn't right; Emperor Haile Selassie could feel it. There was too much noise coming from outside. Inside, it was too still and every sound magnified relentlessly. Even his faithful lion Tojo, who usually whined outside his window, did nothing but jump and claw at his cage. It had been quiet since Major Guddu had ordered the emperor's family and friends into trucks that roared away into the night, but this was different. This was the silence of a muffled scream, a strained soundlessness.

This is why it didn't surprise the emperor when he heard the whistling suddenly die down, the rifle suddenly stop tapping, the guard's steps slow, then come to a halt. This is why it didn't surprise the emperor when he heard the guard snap to attention, then spit out, "Major Guddu, good evening." It didn't unnerve him to hear footsteps make their way towards the large room that was his cell, nor did it make him shiver, the way it normally would, to hear the jangling of keys, then the creak of his door opening.

What did surprise him was the young boy Major Guddu had brought with him. A fat boy stuffed into a military uniform much too tight for him, wearing glasses that rested on a flat nose. A poor woman's son, the emperor could tell by the look of him. Another one of those who'd joined the military in hopes of steady, increasing pay, and instead found themselves at the mercy of an uncontrollable beast. The boy shuffled in behind the major and stood with his back against the wall. He blinked so fast the emperor was sure he'd soon squeeze out tears. The boy didn't look at him, and the emperor suspected it wasn't respect that pushed the boy's head into the creases of his fleshy neck. It was fear.

Major Guddu thrust a hand behind the boy and shoved him forward. He flashed a pearl-handled pistol, and it was then that the emperor began to shiver. It was General Amman's pistol, a gift he'd given to the war hero during the 1964 conflict with Somalia. So even this friend, the bravest, was dead.

"Mickey. Do it," the major ordered the boy.

The boy named Mickey flung himself back against the wall, away from the pistol, and stood there again, blinking.

If he hadn't seen the pistol, the emperor would have thought that time had run backwards and he was reliving the last few moments before the brandishing of the weapon. The boy was standing, quivering chin in neck. The major's hand was positioned in the thick of the boy's back, ready once again to shove. But from down the hall, the soft slide of leather-soled shoes floated into the room and the emperor knew this was a brand-new moment and everything that happened from now on would happen only once.

The emperor didn't understand the significance of the bloodied plastic bag the major waved in front of Mickey, but he could understand the terror that wrapped around the boy's face. It was a fear stripped naked of pretense, pure. He'd seen it in grown men only on the field, and usually it was replaced by a veil of courage that guided most to their inevitable fate. But this, this was the look of a boy not yet a man, of a boy who might never fully become a man and who now found himself exposed in the worst, most terrifying way.

The major held the plastic bag and the gun in front of Mickey. "You or him," he said. "Remember your friend Daniel."

Mickey seemed to glance at the window above the emperor's bed, contemplating escape. And the emperor felt as if he himself was witness to a macabre pantomime, a silent play in which he was both curious audience and reluctant star.

Mickey looked at the pistol. "No."

The major slipped the plastic bag over Mickey's head and tucked the mouth of the gun inside the plastic, against the thick vein pulsing on the boy's neck. Then the major stepped so close to the soldier's fat, heaving chest that the emperor considered the possibility that this was all a dream and the two had merged into a double-headed demon.

It wasn't until the major jerked his hand back that the emperor realized Mickey had knocked the gun onto the floor. And it wasn't until Mickey ripped the bag off his head and sank to his knees in prayer that the emperor realized the major had moved to his bed and was looking down at *him*, his own pillow in hand.

It couldn't have been his voice that said, "What has taken three thousand years to build can't be destroyed in one night." But he didn't know who else could have said it.

And it couldn't have been he who looked at the cowardly fat boy and said, "Be a man, watch this." But it was his mouth moving, though the rest of his body was as still as a statue.

It could have been that the whistling was also in his imagination. That it actually didn't get louder, that the major's footsteps didn't shuffle to his bed, that Mickey didn't actually say, "How can you? He is the emperor." The emperor wasn't sure of anything anymore, and he told himself that it wasn't a pillow pushing against his face, flattening him to the mattress, pressing down so hard on him that he could feel the bedsprings. He told himself it was Angel Gabriel, come down to bear witness. He convinced himself that the soft feather that floated out from a tear in the pillow was proof that angels existed and legion were helping him right now, easing the pain of airless lungs. And it all happened so quickly, so quietly, so effortlessly, that Emperor Haile Selassie believed that it was all a dream, just another act in the silent play, and the heavy sleep that engulfed him was due to nothing more than an old man's fatigue.

PART TWO

Mother of the strong boy, tighten the belt around your waist.
Your son is for the vultures only,
Not for burial by your relatives.

—ETHIOPIAN WAR SONG

BOOK TWO

26

H E WAS NEARLY THREE YEARS a widower now. He'd lived through thirty months of loneliness in a churning city. He'd grown weary in those months of jeeps and uniforms, marches and forced assemblies; his patience worn thin from the constant pressure to mold his everyday activities around a midnight curfew. He'd had to contend with identity cards and new currency, a new anthem and even a new flag. He'd come to detest Radio Addis Ababa and Ethiopian Television and the announcements of the arrests and even executions of intellectuals and city leaders, and increasingly, students. His daily commute was punctuated by a constant stream of propaganda posters with star-and-sickle emblems and large-fisted, determined workers. Pictures of Guddu were everywhere. Communism had couched itself comfortably in a country that once boasted of a Solomonic monarchy.

This morning, in the dry heat of another arid day, Hailu tried his best to shrug off his restless agitation and ignore the caw of newspaper boys that broke above the blaze of moving traffic:

"Defense Ministry Prepares for Cuban Officials!"

"Soviet Friendship Stronger Than Ever!"

Soviet friendship and Communist sentiment had helped nationalize his hospital, had helped strip it of its name, Prince Mekonnen Hospital, and impose a new one, Black Lion Hospital. The Derg had imposed itself on his work and passion, turned it into a wasteland of haughty Soviet interns and underserved Ethiopian patients. The few doctors who hadn't fled or had been excused from the war against Eritrea and Somalia were overworked; medicine was in such demand it had become a luxury. He had tried to defy one of those Russians by insisting in writing that his performance would be jeopardized by the introduction of new medical theories. "We are Ethiopians and have always done things the Ethiopian way," he wrote. "I have healed and taken care of some of you and your family," he told the nameless, faceless officials who'd ordered these changes in his hospital. "I have trained with the best in Africa and Europe," he reminded them. He'd received notice two weeks later that his floor and his staff would remain unchanged.

Hailu sat in his car on Churchill Road and watched the newspaper sellers. He wondered which of these too-thin, ragged boys carried anti-government pamphlets tucked between the pages of their newspapers. These sheets of paper were printed in dark printshops in the dead of night, then furiously distributed into the streets, dropped on doorsteps, and thrown into office buildings and into car windows overnight. They blanketed Addis Ababa's roadsides, benches, and tables.

"Castro Praises Ethiopia's Progress! North Korea Donates Uniforms!" the boys cried, a shrill chorus in the blue dawn haze.

One lanky boy motioned in Hailu's direction, raising a newspaper like a flag. Hailu shook his head and tried to push thoughts of Dawit away. His youngest son had made an absolute break from his influence, had become so entrenched in his secret meetings and whispered phone calls that nothing Hailu did could bring him back into the family fold.

Intermittent car horns melted into a long, sustained blare. Buses and trucks dodged the boys. Irritated pedestrians brushed against blue-and-white taxicabs. It was crowded as usual. Everything was noisy. Sound traveled from car to pedestrian to pack animal, rising and falling over the hilly street. Aged trees dotted the roadside and drank in the cacophony. Ethiopia would remain, despite all outside influences, a mix of ancient and modern, progress and ritual sitting as uncomfortably next to each other as Communist ideals and Coptic beliefs.

"Anarchists Jailed for Threats to State!" the boys called out. Several drivers waved from car windows, eager to read this latest development. Hailu saw one boy slide a sheet of paper into a newspaper as he approached a truck.

Dawit, too, passed these raging pamphlets from doorstep to outstretched hand, though he denied this when asked, unconcerned that his ink-stained palms exposed him as a liar. Hailu shifted into gear and drove towards the hospital, rolling the window up to dampen the boys' voices. His son was no different from the thousands dissatisfied in Addis Ababa. Like so many, he hadn't returned to his classes once schools reopened, choosing to spend his time protesting the Derg. Resistance was the growing murmur amongst the young and the agitated.

In the beginning, the Derg had promised the people a "bloodless coup," yet had done nothing but prove its own viciousness and murderous spirit. Though benevolent declarations and benedictions filtered out of its headquarters in Menelik Palace, the people no longer trusted the military regime. No one believed the announcement that the emperor had died from natural causes. It was a known secret that the mounds of dirt on the outskirts of the city were mass graves. And those gun battles—rapid-fire volleys between soldiers and fighters— were unrelenting proof of a growing rebellion. There was noise everywhere, and not even a curfew could stuff the silence back into Ethiopia's nights.

Hailu could see the silhouette of Black Lion Hospital ahead of him. He tried to focus on the building's façade, steer himself away from the Tiglachin Memorial that was now planted in front of the building. The monument was an elongated semblance of a lion shaped like an obelisk, topped by a red star, a stone nova that snaked its way to the sky. It was a five-pointed testament to Major Guddu's new military prowess, strengthened by Russian and Cuban military support. Ethiopia had fallen victim to the Cold War scramble for the Horn of Africa.

The red star greeted Hailu every morning from his office window, its sharp points cutting into dense fog. It was thrust atop a metal pole, and that pole jutted from the concrete slab that climbed its way higher with a precision that was frightening. In front of it was a statue of young soldiers standing with a flag, also topped by the star, draped behind them. One soldier had a rifle raised, still strong and ready after battle. The red star, as bright as a spilled drop of blood, cast its shadow over a hospital that was no longer a familiar place. This monument was, thought Hailu, a distorted obelisk, an emasculated memorial to one man's growing rage against his own people.

EVER SINCE THE Russians had come into his hospital, he'd stopped using the front entrance. Most of them looked at Ethiopians with the same disdain his people felt for them. They had come into his country and begun to help destroy it. He didn't want to see them, or be seen, didn't want to go through the motions of professional camaraderie and respect when he felt none. He chose instead to go directly from the parking lot to the stairwell that led to the intensive care unit on his floor.

Once inside, Hailu moved through the silent corridor with clipped steps, conscious of the sharp echoes trailing him as he walked to his office. Everything in this building sounded more hollow, more cavernous and empty lately. Some of his colleagues used to think it strange that he found comfort in these four walls, and he'd try to explain it wasn't the presence of illness he focused on, but the possibility of life. Now, there was nothing. He'd barely sat down at his desk when Almaz knocked on his door, a stain across her normally immaculate uniform.

"There's a new patient," Almaz said. She remained in the hall, an old habit she refused to break.

"Come in," he said. He swiveled to push a thick book upright on the shelf. Like everything else in his office, his shelves were organized, his medical books neatly ordered by size. Nothing was out of place and all unnecessary files and notes were put away daily. The bareness of this small space comforted him.

"There's a new patient," she repeated. "A girl."

Light streamed through the windows in a long bright strip, a pale red glow seeped onto the floor from the star outside. Hailu closed the curtains.

"And?" he asked. He straightened a pile of papers and readjusted a paperweight.

"It's not normal." Almaz was as efficient with her words as with her actions. She was his best nurse, the most reliable under pressure, to see her worried was cause enough for him to worry.

Hailu sighed. He wanted to ask her what was normal these days. "You should be used to things by now," he reminded her.

"Soldiers are asking for you," she said, looking down at the stain on her uniform. "They usually stay on the other floors, with the Russians," she pointed out. "They've come here now."

"What do they want?" he asked.

"They don't want to talk to anyone else," Almaz said. "You should go." She wiped the front of her uniform with quick, nervous strokes then stopped when she saw nothing would remove the stain. "There's a girl," she said again, looking at him, then away.

—

A SILVERY SPIDERWEB clung to a corner of the hallway. Large drops of water and muddy footprints traced a sticky path from the hall into a room. Once again, Hailu was momentarily stilled by the changes that had taken place. He pointed to the mud on the ground.

"Someone should be cleaning this up," he grumbled.

"Everyone's been assigned to the Cubans and Russians from the front," Almaz said. She knelt down to wipe the spot with a handkerchief. "What about our own people?"

Hailu winced at her earnest attempt to scrub the stubborn stain out. "We don't have time for that," he said.

She wiped her hands on a clean handkerchief. "She's being guarded," she said as they stepped into the elevator. "She's very bad." Almaz seemed to be getting more agitated as the elevator doors opened.

HE HAD BEEN a doctor for nearly thirty-five years, treated infections and war wounds with calm efficiency, battled unknown illnesses with cunning and forethought. He knew the sight of a body better left to die on its own, could decipher the clues that spoke to a life still struggling to hold on. But what could have prepared him for a girl wrapped in a clear plastic sheet? What medical book could have taught him that a sheet of plastic as big as a body could dig into wounds like this? That wounds this deep and vicious could be on a young girl? He looked at her again. Clumps of hair had been pulled out of her head. Blood had soaked through her trousers and bright, flowered blouse. Her swollen feet hung off one end of the gurney. All of this was covered and displayed in plastic like a butcher's oversized trophy. Seeping out of the opening of the plastic bag was the smell of excrement and burnt flesh, shit and cruelty, a new obscenity.

"What is this?" Hailu heard himself say. A sour taste coated his mouth. "What's happened to her?" Automatically, he reached for his stethoscope and put the plugs in his ear, then found he couldn't move. "Why is she here?" he asked. "Almaz?"

Two soldiers he hadn't noticed before stepped out of a corner of the room. They glared menacingly at Almaz. She dropped her gaze and stared at her folded hands.

"Who are you?" Hailu asked. He cleared his throat and lowered his voice, trying to portray a semblance of calm. "We are not equipped to treat her. There's been a mistake." He could hear the panic in his voice. "What happened to her?" He turned to his nurse but she was stiff and silent, stripped of her usual authority.

"She needs to get better as quickly as possible," one of the soldiers said. "So we brought her to you." He was thin and deep wrinkles draped around his eyes like extra skin. The rest of his features were smooth.

Hailu took him and his partner to be a little older than Yonas, maybe close to forty years of age. He stayed quiet for so long he caught the faint strains of a radio in the room next door. The rigid beats of a military march told him it was tuned to another Marxist-Leninist lecture.

"She has to stay alive," the second soldier said. His gaze wouldn't settle on the girl lying exposed on the hospital gurney. "We all know the story."

But that story that had built Hailu's legend in the early days of his career was false. The man had been very much alive, only temporarily so deep in unconsciousness that his breathing had slowed, then nearly stalled altogether. Hailu had been the only doctor amongst the roomful who had taken the time to wait and listen for the faintest pulse on the man's wrist. He hadn't refuted any of them when they signed medical documents accounting for the exact time of the patient's death; a humble farmer who had collapsed in front of his frightened wife and children. Instead, he'd let the room clear quickly, as it tended to do on Friday night shifts, then he'd slid the white sheet off the man's face and called for Almaz to bring in an IV. Every Christmas, the man still brought a goat to his house as a present. But that story had circulated around Addis Ababa and beyond, and though he'd tried for years to explain what really happened, Hailu found himself slave to a myth he had helped to make as powerful as truth.

"I don't understand this," he said in a whisper. "What has happened to her?" he asked again. He noted the nervous twitch in the second soldier's large hands. He looked at the girl more closely. She was most likely one of those whom the Derg labeled an anarchist. She'd been arrested for suspicious activity, dragged out of her home or pulled from

a café as she drank tea with friends, given no time to change out of her
flowered shirt and stylish trousers. She had been taken to prison and
questioned endlessly, all night. Now, she was here. "What did you do to
her?" Hailu asked. He saw both soldiers flinch.

The first soldier stepped forward. "You delivered my baby boy, we
named him Hailu," he said. "He's four now, a strong boy. A good boy."
He was slender with a potbelly and knees that bowed awkwardly.

Hailu refused to look his way. He stayed focused on the girl. Her
interrogator had been careful not to touch her face.

The second soldier, thick-limbed and deep-voiced, stepped closer
to Hailu. "She has to stay alive. No one can know she's here, make sure
this hallway is blocked off. This is between you and your nurse," he said,
clearing his throat. "We're under strict orders." He looked at Almaz
sternly. "Do you understand?"

She nodded, her face expressionless, her hands still folded in front
of her.

Hailu walked around the bed to look out the window. Addis Ababa
returned his gaze, sunlight twinkling like a watchful eye. He drew the
curtains.

"Did Russians train you how to do this to people?" he asked, his
chest so full of anger he was sure his voice was tight. "I heard these East-
ern Europeans have been teaching you how to interrogate your own
people," he spat out. "Is this what happened?"

The bowlegged soldier stayed silent, his head low. Neither spoke
until the soldier with the deep voice stepped forward again. "There will
be no questions," he stated flatly. "Do what you do best. Heal her."

He opened his mouth to reply, then shut it when he saw Almaz
shake her head. "She needs a bath. Leave us with her for a few minutes," he said.

The soldiers walked out. The girl moved her head. Hailu lifted a
corner of the thin plastic away from her hand. It drew a small patch of
burned skin with it. He saw one of her fingers shake.

Almaz wrung her hands, eyes finally gazing around the room. "This
isn't good."

"She's trying to say something," Hailu said. He wanted to step close
to her, but couldn't. "See if you can hear her," he said.

Almaz pressed her ear against the girl's mouth. Hailu saw the girl's chest expand, her eyes fluttered to slits, her pupils rolled under her eyelids.

"Come here," Almaz said, grabbing his arm and pulling him near the girl. "Listen."

The girl's breath was sour and smelled like dried blood. She spoke faintly: "Abbaye."

Hailu drew back sharply and shoved his hands in his pockets. He searched instinctively for the prayer beads he still carried with him every day. "God help her," he said. He started pacing, rubbing his eyes, a headache growing in a thick band around his temples. "Help her. Who is she? Ask her name, quick, before they come back." He didn't want to think of the father who was frantically looking for his little girl right now. He stopped, frustrated by Almaz's slowness. "Find out who her father is!"

"What did you say, my daughter?" Almaz whispered soothingly, hovering close to the girl. "Who is your father?" She waited, then shook her head. "Nothing. She's out." She looked at Hailu with terrified eyes. "What do you think they'll do to her once they get her back?"

Hailu turned away from the bed, stared at a cobweb draped in one corner of the room. "We have to take the bag off," he said. He wiped his brow; he was sweating. "It's going to take some time."

Through the curtains, trees shook shadows onto the hospital lawn. There was the sound of leaves rustling in the wind, the blaring horns of traffic, and the shouts of farmers and vendors. Life outside these walls went on as always. Inside, it seemed the world had shifted off its axis and was breaking into two.

27

TIZITA, NEARLY SEVEN YEARS OLD and long-limbed, skinny, and temperamental, kicked a ball and jumped, twisting and twirling in that leap, causing Sara to gasp. Sara tried to focus on *Democracia* and an article about rebel control of major cities in Eritrea. The capital city, Asmara, and the port of Massawa were under siege. Cubans were training new recruits of the Ethiopian army. The Derg, the article said, was using fascist tactics against civilians.

"Emaye, I'm kicking higher than Berhane!" Tizita yelled. "Look at me!"

Sara let the somersaults of her heart still before allowing herself to watch her daughter play with their servant Sofia's son. She tried to remind herself that her daughter was healthy, that her prayers had been answered. She wished she could accept Tizita's recovery as a gift, and not a concession she had forced from a grudging God.

"I'm the winner!" Tizita ran towards Berhane. A grin as wide and open as Sara's stretched across her face. She had her bright eyes, Yonas's thick eyebrows, and lips whose gentle fullness echoed Selam.

Sara set the newletter aside and pretended to cheer the children's earnest game of soccer. Her body was tense and she didn't understand why. She'd kept a careful eye on Tizita as she played outside all day, afraid this anxiety was a sign that her daughter might get sick again. The close scrutiny was exhausting. She was sweating and her back ached. She glanced at her watch, a gift from Yonas to her on Tizita's sixth birthday, and clapped her hands loudly.

"Dinner," she called out. "I need to go inside and get ready. Come help me, both of you." She didn't want to let her daughter out of her sight.

"I'm not finished," Tizita said. She tossed the ball to the boy.

Sara clapped her hands again, more emphatically. She recognized the ready pout on Tizita's face. "Get in," she said.

"No," Tizita said, her lips jutting out, frowning. "I don't want to."

Sara took the ball away from Berhane.

"I told her," Berhane said. He raised a handsome, alert face to Sara. "I'm hungry." His sincerity made her smile and she hugged the boy to her. She regularly begged Sofia to move in with them and out of their shack, but the younger woman had refused, citing her husband Daniel's disappearance, though Sara had suspected it was also a question of pride.

"If we've moved, how will he find us when he comes back?" Sofia responded, her dark eyes sad.

"Emaye, look," Tizita said, pointing at the gate.

The gate was shaking. Its bottom scraped the hard ground. There was a struggle on the other side to open the gate through sheer force. Every resident in the compound knew the latch would stick if not jostled just right.

"Someone's trying to come in," Berhane said.

Sara stepped away from the gate, opened her arms, and let the children run to her.

"Go inside, get Abbaye," Sara said, pushing Tizita towards the front door. She picked up the copy of *Democracia* and handed it to her daughter. Sara pushed her harder. "Hurry!"

Tizita didn't move. "Bad soldiers are coming," she said, whimpering and standing closer to Sara.

"Go inside!" Sara shouted. "Take this"—she tucked the newsletter under her daughter's arm. "Go. Go get Abbaye." The children scrambled up the stairs. "Yes?" she said, stepping back and unlatching the gate. "Who is it?"

She saw the barrel of a gun probe through the open gate, then a hand, calloused and ashy, a thick leg, heavy boots, an entire body, and she tried to piece together the man's grim eyes, his high forehead, the military uniform, his words: "There's an order . . ." Papers unfolded in his hand, grew from a perfect square to a neatly creased declaration. "Residence nationalization . . . new *kebele* rules . . . mandatory."

The soldier stepped in. Following him was a thin man with a long, slender scar that ran from cheek to cheek, extending the edges of his mouth.

"I got your letter," Hailu said; he'd walked up without Sara noticing. "But I thought I had a week." He gave the soldier a disdainful look. "Can't you follow your own instructions?"

"What's going on?" Sara asked, surprised by Hailu's terseness and noting his red-rimmed eyes. He looked tired.

"They're nationalizing the house in the back, where Bizu sleeps," Hailu said, settling his eyes on the thin man next to the soldier. "As if they haven't taken enough. All of my grandfather's land is gone. So is the land Selam's father gave us. Now this."

The soldier cleared his throat and raised the papers higher. "Orders," he said.

"Nationalizing the house?" Sara asked.

"Anyone with an extra house is now required to offer it to the Derg as part of our efforts to help all of Ethiopia's poor," the soldier said.

"But it's not extra," Sara said. "It's Bizu's. That's where she sleeps. She's been sick lately and needs it."

The soldier smirked and pointed to the man who'd moved to stand beside him. "This is your new *kebele* officer, Shiferaw. He's proven his true revolutionary spirit to us and he'll be here to collect taxes, just like the old *kebele* officer. But you must also report any deaths, weddings, or births in your household to him. He'll be giving weekly classes on socialism. He'll live in your compound."

Shiferaw nodded his head in eager obedience as the soldier pushed him forward for all to see. His mouth pulled into a smile when the soldier looked his way, the thin scar moving higher across his cheeks, distorting his grin.

"What's this?" It was Emama Seble, her black figure making its way to them, her eyes resting on Shiferaw. "Hailu, you should check his mouth."

The soldier took Shiferaw's arm and shook it lightly. "A strong state begins with its people."

"The Derg has new rules for their neighborhood associations," Hailu said. "They want to control everything we do." His eyes hadn't wavered from the soldier, but Sara sensed an air of resignation in the way he spoke; his shoulders slumped slightly.

"It's a necessary step in our progress," the soldier said, matching

Hailu's tone. "Unity is a guarantee of sure triumph." He smiled stiffly, mechanically. "Do whatever he says," the soldier added, pointing to Shiferaw.

A bewildered crowd had gathered around the two men, Hailu's community of families now a quiet circle watching the spectacle cautiously.

"But that house"—Hailu turned towards the courtyard—"it's not empty."

The small house hidden in a corner of the courtyard was where his mother had died. She had found a peace in that dark home that no one could understand. It held for Hailu all his childhood fears and hopes, those moments when he saw life doggedly maintaining its grip on a body that was resisting all such effort. His mother lay in that single room whose windows swallowed up the sun, and she waited for the battle to rage, then end over her existence. "It isn't up to me," she said, daily forcing him to cross each arm over her chest in preparation for her last breath. "It is only up to me to wait." But every day she lived, the disappointment and sorrow in her face became harder for him to bear. He began to feel responsible, to see an accusation in her eyes that none of his hugs and kisses could erase.

It was in the days and months after his mother's death that he decided to become a doctor, determined that one day, he would help tip the scales towards the patient's wishes. No one would be helpless anymore. It had not been simple with Selam, he had broken his own vows to himself, but the possibility of her full recovery had pushed him. Hope, he'd decided while caring for his wife, was the only exception.

The house had been locked tight, its curtains forever drawn, until Bizu, sunken into a sadness since she'd seen the documentary about the famine in Wello, had begun to sleep there. "It's warm here," was her rebuff to them. "It's nice and dark."

In the courtyard, two pretty young women hanging clothes to dry stole shy glances at the soldier, whose chest inflated with each flirtatious look.

"His name is Shiferaw," the soldier said again. "He's an important man, but you can come to me if you have any questions." His eyes lingered on the tallest girl, who smiled and then went back to her clothesline. "I'm stationed in this neighborhood."

"Let's go inside," Sara said to the children. "Your mother's made us dinner," she added to Berhane, pointing to Sofia, who stood at the doorway with her hand over her mouth.

"Berhane, come here," Sofia said, frantic. "Hurry!"

Berhane, fascinated by the rifle and the soldier's uniform, stood gaping at the older man as if staring up at a looming mountain. "You're a soldier?" he asked.

"Berhane!" Sofia shouted, running down the steps of the veranda to get him. "Stop talking to that man!"

"Yes, do you want to be one?" the soldier said, ignoring Sofia. "My son does." He smiled, revealing a toothpick-sized gap between his lower front teeth.

Berhane nodded. "My daddy's a soldier. But we can't find him." He held up three fingers. "It's been three years."

The smile disappeared from the soldier's face.

"Berhane, get over here!" Sofia grabbed her son and dragged him into the house.

28

A WHISPER FLOATED INTO THE LATE afternoon sky and settled back on Dawit and Lily lying in a thick shaft of dying sunlight. Soft shadows played across the rounded curves of Lily's face as she looked at a small stack of letters next to Dawit.

She shook her head. "There was no way to get letters to you except through another *zemecha* who was running away and coming back to Addis," she said. "I wanted to see if I remembered everything. Thank you for bringing them."

Lily had been one of the tens of thousands of students sent across the countryside of Ethiopia to teach peasants about land reform and other changes made by the Derg. She'd come back gaunt and frightened, her hair cut short, it seemed, to highlight her startled stare.

"Sometimes, I was just writing to myself." She held the letters gingerly, weighing them in her palm. They were folded sheets of paper without an envelope, dotted with fingerprints around the edges. "You felt so far away. We were so far from the city." She pressed her naked body against Dawit's.

She unfolded one letter. "Our first day Tariku called a mandatory meeting of the village elders." She started to grin. "He spoke for one hour before one of the men stood up and walked away." Her smile widened. "They didn't speak Amharic, they didn't understand anything Tariku was saying. It was a beautiful speech." She let out a sharp laugh, her eyes alert and cold. "You're so lucky your father found a way to keep you in Addis," she said.

Dawit watched her open the next letter.

"It rained so much I used to think the farmers prayed for storms to drive us back to the city," she continued. She took his hand and held it tightly, talked to him as if he'd never read the letters, as if he hadn't memorized every fact and imagined the terror of a young girl stuck in a village full of angry people. "The night Tariku and Meseret destroyed their altars, they came after us with guns. The police just watched. I found out later they had orders from the Derg to arrest any of us who survived."

Her eyes were closed. She shook her head slowly with a finality Dawit couldn't understand and picked up the third letter, then put it down. This was the first time she'd talked about that night.

"You're back," he said, hugging her close. "You're home now."

"The Derg executed some of the *zemechas*," she continued, holding her head. "Meseret was jailed. They almost suspended me from exams, but they said they'd give me one more chance. Tariku . . ." Her mouth quivered. "Enough of this." She sighed and smiled softly at him.

He kissed her and watched her wipe her eyes. She'd gained back the weight she lost in the countryside and styled her growing hair to show its curls to full effect. She was once again the immaculate, groomed girl he knew, but across her cheeks were spots where her skin had darkened, *madiat*. It was, his mother had once told him, the physical evidence of a woman's deep distress.

"We should go," she said, looking at her watch. "It's almost sundown." Her troubled eyes, slanted slightly at the edges, followed Dawit's hand trailing a path down her body under the blanket.

"Curfew's at midnight." He wrapped his arm around her.

She leaned into his chest, composed again. "I have an exam tomorrow," she said. "And there's a *kebele* meeting in my neighborhood." She stared at him and let her eyes linger on his. "I have to speak at the meeting. That's why I needed these letters."

Dawit sat up, surprised. "Since when did you start doing what the Derg wants?"

"It's not for the Derg," she said, pulling the blanket closer around her bare shoulders. "Don't you know me by now? It's about the women's associations we tried to start in the village. I'm explaining what we can do to make sure it works in the city. I have to."

"You're helping the Derg," Dawit said. He moved away from her.

She shook her head and put an arm around him to draw him close. "Teaching women about their rights is a good thing. And since *kebele* meetings are mandatory, we might as well use it to our advantage. We can take them over one day, or at least get close enough for a clear shot," she said coyly, kissing his shoulder. She was quiet. "Maybe the way to fight is from inside. As long as we keep fighting."

Dawit drew his knees to his chest and stared at his feet. "Everything's become another way to fight. Every rule is there to break," he said. "But how are people being helped?" He reached for his shirt.

Lily handed Dawit his jeans and watched him dress. "Sara said Mickey came looking for you." Her voice was carefully controlled. She slipped on her blouse and skirt.

"I'm not talking to him." Dawit stomped his foot as he tied his shoes and a cloud of dirt leapt and hung in the light streaming from the window.

"He made sure you didn't get caught distributing pamphlets when you first started." She put her jacket on and wrapped her arms around his waist. She was much shorter than him and had to raise her head to look him in the eyes. "You owe him something."

Dawit pulled out of her hold and put on his belt.

"You can't blame him for a promotion," she said.

"You don't get a promotion for doing nothing. It's a reward. What do you want me to do? Congratulate him?" Dawit said. "I'm not doing it."

Lily grew quiet. "It's getting more dangerous with these *kebeles* watching everything. People are scared. They're turning in anyone just to avoid jail themselves. You need him."

"I don't need a lecture. You don't know what I know." Dawit thought back to that early morning when Mickey had come to his door in a blood-splattered uniform, a rifle lost and a gun in his belt, confessing to acts that neither of them spoke of again. It was after that that their friendship had begun to unravel; quiet moments were no longer comfortable, and conversations stumbled into stilted, awkward silences. Then, when news of Mickey's promotion traveled through the compound, Dawit had refused to talk to him at all.

"So he's your enemy?" she asked, walking to the door.

"Do you understand how bad things are?"

"I'm going to the same meetings you are. I'm passing out the same newsletters." She paused. "I'm the one risking a medical school scholarship."

"And of course that means everything," Dawit said.

She stood at the door with a tight grip on the handle. "Don't you think about a better future for yourself?" She was curious, then defiant.

He sighed and moved to wrap his arms around her. "I'm sorry," he said.

Lily pushed him away and grabbed her shoes.

Dawit opened the door and waited for her. "One day you'll cut your foot walking outside without shoes."

A smile played across her face. It was a rhyme they'd made up together, a way to end any fights. "My feet are tough." Her response was lyrical, a practiced song.

"And what would happen if you stepped on a nail and started bleeding?" He put his arm around her as they walked to the car.

"I would jump up in the air and scream like a monkey . . ." She rested her head on his shoulder and wrapped an arm around his waist.

"And then what?" he asked.

"You would catch me," she said, giggling.

"How do you know?" He held her closer to him.

"Because you promised me you'd always be there," she said, serious and quiet in his arms.

Dawit kissed the top of her head, then let his mouth find hers. They kissed, the tension forgotten for a moment, then drove down the hill into the city. The sky burned a deep orange, empty of the sun and not yet ready for the moon.

HAILU COULD HEAR the faintest moans of a *washint* in his head, the hollow reed instrument spinning what had been Selam's favorite song, "Tizita," a melancholy tune of memory and home. He was in the bathroom adjoining his bedroom, unwrapping a new bar of soap. There is a girl in the hospital, far from home, calling for her father, he thought, looking at his palms, and I have done nothing but cause her more pain. Hailu let cool water run over his wrists and trail between his fingers. He turned on the hot water and coolness slid into a pleasant warmth that ebbed into a searing heat. He kept his hands under the tap, watched suds bubble and cascade into the drain, then disappear. No matter how many times he washed his hands, he'd have to go back and inspect wounds no human being should have. Animals in this condition would be put out of their misery. He lathered the soap again. What gave the Derg the right to tell him when he should be home, what he could listen to on the radio, what he should read, and now, who he could treat in his own hospital, and how?

"Abbaye, time to eat," Tizita called.

Hailu began to scrub his hands. "Get started without me," he said. The water gurgled as it drained. What kind of man could do what was done to this girl? How was it that he had become another instrument in that process?

"Abbaye says we always have to eat together," Tizita said, her words muffled as if her mouth were pressed firmly against the wood door.

"Go see if Dawit's home, then I'll be ready." He dried his hands on an old, rough towel and inspected his nails. There was nothing on them, he told himself. You can go eat *injera* with clean hands, he reassured himself. A new thought nudged itself awake from a corner of his mind, bent him over the sink: his mother's home was no more.

29

THE NEWS CAMERA SCANNED PAST A GROUP of soldiers from the hundred-thousand-man peasant army, the People's Militia. Wearing North Korean uniforms and carrying Soviet machine guns, they marched into arid, dusty hills, their sweat visible even at a distance. Lining the roadside where they walked, women and girls clapped and raised their voices in encouragement as other soldiers, less tired, monitored the cheering with pointed rifles. The soldiers dragged themselves over the road, mechanical and obedient.

"Turn the volume down, Tizzie," Yonas said.

The camera cut to Guddu, crisply dressed, his green fatigues perfectly tailored. He paced in front of another large group of hunched soldiers, his smoker's lips enunciating words with sharp precision. His eyes, small and furious, darted back and forth with barely restrained agitation; the rest of his body was kept under strict control. He shouted at his men, pumped his fist into the air, then pointed to the flag hanging limply behind him. The screen flashed to a map of Ethiopia and a yellow line snaked a path north, into the Eritrean region, and ended in a big red X.

Dawit got up from the sofa and sat on the floor next to Tizita, who was playing with her doll. "What's Guddu thinking?"

Yonas looked towards the door. "Has Abbaye come home yet?"

Dawit shook his head. Hailu usually sat in his chair watching news with them.

Yonas watched trucks loaded with soldiers rattle down a dirt road. "Guddu's got Soviet support."

"But to fight Eritrea and Somalia at the same time? Then battle with other rebel groups within our the borders?" Dawit pointed to the soldiers walking listlessly in a single row.

"I don't know why you're so shocked," Yonas said. "This is the man who let Qaddafi attack the Sudanese from Ethiopia. He closed Kagnew station and ordered all U.S. military personnel out of the country in seventy-two hours. Guddu's becoming famous for his arrogance."

The television cut to Guddu shaking hands with Soviet dignitaries, their smiles bright under camera lights.

"I don't trust him," Dawit said.

"It's the Soviets I don't trust," Yonas said. "Not long ago, they were giving arms to Somalia to fight us." He sighed. "Guddu thinks all he needs is their support to drive the Eritrean rebels back and fight the Somalis in Dire Dawa and Harar. But with the U.S. behind Siad Barre, it's not going to be so simple."

"The Soviets aren't the problem." Dawit pointed to the screen and another map of the northern Eritrea region. Guddu needs to let Eritrea go."

"So you want to break up Ethiopia?" The laugh out of Yonas was mocking. "Now you're sounding like one of your pamphlets."

Dawit jumped up and took Tizita by the arm. "Go upstairs." He led her into the dining area and pointed her towards the stairwell. "Go to bed," he said, insistent.

"No," she said, pulling against his grip. "It's not my bedtime."

"I'll be upstairs to pray with you soon," Yonas said to his daughter. "Go on."

Tizita reluctantly went to her room.

"Never mention pamphlets again, especially in front of her," Dawit said. He pointed at the stairwell and glared at Yonas. "She could say something in school."

Yonas returned his glare, his mouth a firm line. "You keep leaving them in my trunk," he said. "They're searching cars randomly at the university. They took Professor Shimeles, and didn't you hear about the high school students they beat in front of the class and then arrested? How careless can you be?"

"I didn't think," Dawit said, looking away.

"You never do," Yonas said. "When have you ever thought about anyone but yourself? When?"

"It's not about me."

Yonas smiled and shook his head. "Not about you? Then who? Every single cause you've taken up has been to benefit the middle or upper class, people just like you. What do you know about what the poor really need? Didn't Lily's experience teach you anything?" He drew closer to his brother. "You talk about a socialist future, but tell me how it's different from this socialism the Derg is pushing down our throats. How can you fight them when you don't even know which ideology you're following?"

Dawit cut him off with a flick of his hand. "The Derg is a dictatorship clothed in socialist propaganda. Whatever it takes to get the Russian money. You should know that, Professor," he spit out.

Yonas held Dawit's wrist, his grip tight. "You make pamphlets that do nothing but criticize, and don't consider what to do if this government stays in power for a long time." He loosened his hold and seemed to consider his next words carefully. "And Mickey . . . he can protect you from yourself, and you refuse to talk to him. Do you know how many times he's been here? You want to pretend you're some hero from one of those American soldier movies you love so much. Next, you'll be running through the streets with a gun like these other revolutionaries."

"I don't kill people. I'm trying to save them," Dawit said, his voice suddenly quiet. "And how can you talk to me? You still give history lectures to an empty classroom. What do you think is happening to all your students? Stop trying to convince yourself things are normal." He stood up. "Always trying to hide behind something."

"You are putting my wife and daughter, all of us, in danger," Yonas said, watching Dawit retreat to his bedroom. "Are our lives less important than those of people you've never met?"

Dawit paused at his door. His head dropped. "I'll check the car next time," he said, then walked into his room.

HAILU SAT IN THE hospital room, the soldiers posted outside the door, and watched the sleeping girl jerk herself out of a nightmare, then drift back into unconsciousness. He was sitting on his hands, his palms plastered flat to the chair, his body made heavy by the weight pressing into his chest. The sight of this girl frightened him more than anything he'd ever seen. The sound of her moans and quiet whimpers was as terrifying as any scream he'd ever heard. He was staring at evidence of the body's wondrous and cursed gift for withstanding abuse. She was testimony to the stubborn endurance of nerves and tissue, proof of one man's sustained cruelty. We have both caused her pain, what makes me better?

Two weeks ago, he'd peeled the plastic wrap off her. Those hours had been agonizing and tedious, the work delicate and painstaking. He'd scraped and pulled the plastic off centimeter by centimeter, praying as he worked, realizing for the first time how indelicate his hands were, how clumsy and imprecise their hold on a scalpel. Each time he'd paused, he found his own body was burning, aching, and there was the sense that all the water in the world would never be able to coat his dry throat. Once, he'd leaned down to kiss her cheek, and couldn't bring himself to utter an apology for work he'd been commanded to do, he couldn't acknowledge, in that apology, his own complicity in her suffering. That day, two weeks ago, he'd done the job alone, had demanded that the soldiers leave the room, and he'd answered her sporadic calls for her father with simple whispers: "I am here, I am here."

RUMORS FILTERED THROUGH the compound about Shiferaw: that he'd spent two nights in jail and come back with that slender grin. This was how they forced him to talk, the women said. He gave names of those he'd never met, the coward, the men added. He'll eat you, the children squealed. The old men and women nodded and pointed to his military fatigues. He betrayed his friends and received this position, they said. Our *kebele* is run by a traitor.

Shiferaw dressed every day in faded military pants and an overstretched sweater. He conducted his mandatory meetings with relish, his sliced mouth upturned as he led unenthused men and women in revolutionary songs and doctrine. He had annexed another house down the road from the compound for these meetings, and daily he moved back and forth between the two places, carrying papers and posters of Guddu, Lenin, and Marx with the air of someone who knew he was being stared at, but tried to pretend he didn't care.

Neighbors were careful what they said when he was nearby; women let their gossiping drop to niceties, men lowered their political complaints into talk about the weather, children tiptoed around him and never looked at his face. Only Emama Seble refused to curb her abrasive tongue, pulling at his frayed sweater and poking into a moth-eaten hole with a frown anytime they crossed paths.

"Your precious Russians can't dress you better than this?" she chided.

Shiferaw had learned to cower around her just like everybody else, and during meetings, he never forced her to join in song, allowing her instead to sulk with folded arms, sullen in her black attire.

30

SARA AND EMAMA SEBLE WATCHED Tizita and Berhane playing marbles from the veranda.

"How can these people say they're for the rights of all when they don't let us vote?" Sara said, waving a slip of paper in front of Emama Seble. "Because Abbaye owned and rented homes, none of us in the household can have a say in what's decided in our *kebele* for a whole year?" Her cheeks were flushed. "And Shiferaw said he'll fine us double our taxes if we don't show up for the rally for the Derg next week."

Tizita took her turn and pushed her nose close to the ground as she aimed. Her finger nudged a nearby marble. A bright smile lit up the earnest boy's eyes.

"What will a vote change?" Emama Seble asked. She took the slip of paper and squinted. "This Shiferaw is trying to make me go to literacy classes."

"Tizita, sit up straight!" Sara called out. She patted Emama Seble's leg. "Bizu has to go, too. Melaku had Tizzie read a book aloud to him, then he carried it to the *kebele* meeting and showed Shiferaw he could read." Sara sighed and focused on Tizita. "I keep trying to convince myself something good can come out of this. I was talking to Dawit yesterday and—"

"What good thing?" Emama Seble handed her the slip of paper. "There's nothing good that can come from the devil." She shook her head. "When the Italians were here, at least you could tell who the enemy was."

The women fell silent and watched the children fight over their marbles game.

"It scares me every time she bends like that," she explained to Emama Seble.

"Don't punish her for your fear," the old woman said. "She's growing up. Sofia's son, too." She narrowed her eyes. "Any news about her husband?"

The two children ran into the courtyard.

Sara shook her head. "Nothing."

Sofia came from the courtyard carrying a bag of food and holding Berhane's arm. "I told you not to do that anymore, it's not good for your eyes," she said, bending down to wipe his face. "Stop doing that." She smiled wearily at the two women. "He keeps turning his eyelids inside out."

"I can see better that way," Berhane said.

"If a fly lands on it, you'll get stuck like that," Sofia said. She resisted a smile as the little boy touched his eyelids with a worried frown.

"Come here," Emama Seble said to Berhane, her eyes squinting in mock seriousness. She pretended to wipe her eyes with the edge of her black sweater. "Let me see something."

Berhane, curious, stepped forward. Emama Seble raised his chin and peered into his face. She grinned when she saw him move his lips over his teeth.

"They'll shrink to their right size soon, don't worry," she told him gently. "Now, let me see something, hold very, very still." She turned his face from the left to the right. "Ah yes, I see it," she said to herself.

The little boy started squirming in excitement. "What is it?" he asked.

"Hold still or she can't finish." Sofia laughed.

"Do you see my magic?" he asked.

"I see . . ." Emama Seble held the boy away from her and sat back. "I can't tell you, it's too much."

"Please, please tell me! I know it's my magic." Berhane grasped her arm.

"Go away," Emama Seble said suddenly, wiping her brow and turning serious. "Leave me alone."

Sara was startled by her tone. "Emama?" she said.

Emama Seble wrapped the boy in a long hug. She pushed him away just as quickly, then pulled him to her again, more gently this time. "I'll tell you about your magic," she told him, then whispered into his ear. The boy smiled.

"He keeps talking about magic, I don't know where he gets it from." Sofia shook her head. "Maybe Tizita brings it from school."

"What will this magic do?" Sara asked, drawn to the earnestness in the boy's face.

"Bring my daddy back." He moved out of Emama Seble's arms and put his head down. "But I'm not supposed to let Emaye know, my brother told me."

Sofia's face fell. She knelt and held Berhane tightly.

"Sofia, go home," Emama Seble said. "There's no use in making the boy sad like this." Emama Seble turned to Berhane. "Remember what I told you."

Sara and Emama Seble watched the young mother and her son walk out of the gate and down the road.

"This country has grown too many teeth," Emama Seble said.

"HAILU!" IT WAS Melaku shouting from his kiosk, a wide grin on his face. He spit out a fig seed lodged in one of the many toothless spaces in his mouth and waved to Hailu in his car. "I have to ask you something," he said, flagging the Volkswagen.

His hands were broad, calloused and cracked, but his long fingers and tapered fingernails hinted at a man once comfortable in the world of royals and palace intrigue. He held out two bright oranges as he ran to the car. "Take some to work, they're ripe."

Hailu slowed down but didn't stop. "Not today, thank you." He crawled forward.

"They're your favorite," Melaku insisted, leaning into the car. "I even have one peeled." He stared at the road in front of them. "And I got a notice today, can you read it for me?"

Hailu shook his head. "Aren't you taking those literacy classes?"

Melaku winked. "I passed the entrance exam." He fished a letter out of his pocket. "Here it is, and take these oranges." He dropped the oranges onto Hailu's lap.

Melaku was the neighborhood kiosk owner. His stand was located at the end of Hailu's street. Many years before, he'd been a rising musician, famous for his skills with the stringed *masinqo* and the mournful tremor in his voice. He played in a band that performed regularly for the emperor. But his career was cut short when he fell in love with Elsa, the young daughter of an official, and dared to ask for her hand in marriage. The angry father demanded Melaku never set foot on palace grounds again.

Still single, Melaku had become as much a part of the neighborhood landscape as the trees that grew alongside the road. No one seemed to recall a time when they couldn't run to the kiosk for a bottle of Coca-Cola or a small bag of sweet dates. He was the eyes and ears of the close community, relaying information when necessary, defusing harmful gossip when needed. He was everyone's grandfather, elder uncle, and for some of the women, their favorite former lover.

Hailu unfolded the letter and glanced quickly over it. There was an official Derg stamp at the bottom, then a sloppy scrawl that substituted for someone's signature. The letter was short and direct.

"It says they're opening a *kebele* store, all private shop owners have to close down," Hailu said, frowning and looking up at the startled older man. He reread the notice. "You only own a kiosk."

Melaku turned around to look at his kiosk as if making sure it was still there. "What do you mean 'close down'?" he asked. He was shaken. "Close down my kiosk?" He took the letter from Hailu. "Let me see this." He frowned and let his eyes wander aimlessly over the paper. He pointed to the signature. "Who is this? I have to talk to him."

Hailu turned off the ignition. He read the signature carefully. "I don't know," he said. He hoped Melaku didn't see the surprise that made his ears burn and his face flush. The name at the bottom of the letter was Mickey's. "We'll see what we can do. Don't worry." Hailu turned on the ignition and shifted into gear, his nerves jangling, already careening towards the moment he'd walk into the hospital and see the girl again.

"They're building a new jail down the street," Melaku said, pointing behind Hailu. "Good news every minute with this Derg."

DAWIT CROSSED THE wide street in front of Addis Ababa University and wondered at the crowd that was gathered on one side of the school's imposing stone archway. In his brother's car was a new batch of pamphlets that called for an end to fighting in Eritrea. Solomon was to meet him inside the entrance of the school, near the steps of what had once been the John F. Kennedy Library, to give him new drop-off locations. Soldiers now manned his usual distribution areas, their watchful eyes alert and unrelenting, and Solomon insisted on strategic locations. Nearly at the archway, Dawit approached the growing crowd and pushed his way towards the front, curious.

A woman sobbed, cradling the body of a young man.

Dawit felt his eyes close and his knees weaken. Ahead of him, the expansive stone gates of Addis Ababa University blurred in the heat.

"What happened?" he asked, seeing Solomon and feeling himself pulled out of the crowd.

Students gathered around the body, knelt beside the mother, and picked her up. They led her away, some shielding her eyes, others holding her tight, their cries muted behind tight mouths.

Solomon patted his back. "The blood?"

Dawit nodded, dizzy. "It hasn't happened since I was a boy."

"You better get used to it." They walked to the parking lot. "Did you see who it was?" Solomon asked. He opened his car door and unlocked Dawit's side.

Dawit shook his head. "Not clearly," he said, getting into the car.

As they drove, Dawit regained his composure, his vertigo slid away. Buildings stiffened to square forms, the road unwound and laid straight before them. He breathed evenly again. Solomon turned up the radio and drummed on the steering wheel as the announcer boasted of an assault and air raids against an Eritrean town.

THE CAFÉ WAS SIMPLE, a small one-room establishment with faded posters. Short wooden stools lined the walls. Behind old coats of cracked, peeling paint, a patchwork of newspaper scraps and torn magazine pages had been layered onto the walls for reinforcement. Except for a bored waitress who served them tea without asking, the place was empty.

Solomon fished in his pocket for a crumpled slip of paper. He flattened it carefully. "Here," he said. It was a clipping from *Addis Zemen*, the state-owned newspaper, and it showed the typical headshot of a student, a serious, dignified stare from a young face. "Recognize him?"

"No," Dawit said, letting the sweet cinnamon tea settle in his stomach.

Solomon took the clipping and stuffed it in his pocket as wrinkled as ever. "He's another student." He looked at Dawit for a moment. "He was helping us with pamphlets, too." He sipped his tea deliberately. "I'd just heard he was taken into custody last night." He held a shaking spoon, then put it down and hid his hands under the table. "They work fast."

Dawit fidgeted, nervous and lost.

"You wanted more work from us," Solomon said, stepping into Dawit's silence. "But this is why I insisted you wait. I didn't think they'd leave him out in public like this."

"He's the body." Dawit felt the tea turn into ice in his stomach.

Solomon nodded, both hands around his teacup now, steam reddening his fingers. "It's just the beginning." Another look. "We'll have you finish the last batch of deliveries. Get them to the house by the end of the week, then take a break."

"What about him? Shouldn't we do something about the body?"

"No one's allowed to move it, not even his mother." Solomon's newly lit cigarette pulsed a bright red as he inhaled. He exhaled long and hard. "Leave it alone."

31

SARA STARED AT THE SMALL SQUARE CARDS in her hands. Hailu's name, house number, and *kebele* number were typed in smudged ink at the top. Below that, the names of each member of their household and their ages, even Tizita's. Typed at the bottom were the staples each household was allotted, and the amount of each.

"We're supposed to take these ration cards to the *kebele* store opening down the street starting next week," she said to Lily. "I don't even get enough teff to make *injera*. Yonas asked Shiferaw for more"—she paused—"but he couldn't convince him."

She threw the cards on the table and looked helplessly at Lily, who sat across from her in quiet sympathy, their pot of coffee growing cold in the hot room. The house smelled of sweet incense and cinnamon. A cool breeze flowed from the open window and sifted together the rich, thick scents.

"My mother and I get almost as much as you," Lily said, "I think our *kebele* leader likes me." She made a face. "We don't need so much teff, I'll give you some whenever I pick up my ration." She was dressed in a miniskirt, platform shoes, and a wide-collared shirt, looking very much like the student she was. She patted her short hair. "Does it suit me? I had to cut it in the countryside. It's growing, but so slowly." Lily's hair used to brush her shoulders, now it bloomed fluffy and soft around her small head.

Sara felt worn beside the stylish woman. "Afros are the latest style. It makes your hair look thicker." She took safety pins out of her pocket and began to pin the curtains together. "I can feel Shiferaw staring into the house sometimes, even when he's not around," she said.

"It's better to be safe. Too many people getting nosy these days." Lily ruffled her curls. "It's not curly enough for a real Afro. Bizu said her grandmother used to tell her that a person with wavy hair was dangerous. I hope the Derg doesn't know this." She smiled weakly.

"What did Dawit say?" Sara asked, putting the ration cards in her pocket. The square corners protruded, made her feel sloppy. She took the cards out and laid them back on the table. "Maybe I'll talk to him about these," she said.

"He likes it long," Lily said.

Sara adjusted the sealed curtains. Shiferaw had begun to spend more and more time in the courtyard just outside the window, watching them all with serious eyes and that thin grin. He'd already reported two men for not singing in *kebele* meetings with the right "revolutionary" spirit. The men had been beaten and taken to jail. She flattened the yellow cloth over the glass pane. It blocked out the sun and draped the living room in shadows.

HAILU UNWRAPPED A flag and unfurled it in the living room. The green, yellow, and red stripes were faded from years of sun. The Lion of Judah, wearing his tilted crown, was emblazoned in the middle, proud against the yellow background. It was the old Ethiopian flag, the one used under Haile Selassie. He hooked the flag on the wall furthest from the window where it used to hang before the new regime banned it from public and private display. There was still an outline of its shape on the wall.

Yonas put an arm around his father. "Don't you know this is the flag of reactionaries?"

Hailu smoothed a crease that ran through the center. "Your mother gave this to me on my first day at the hospital. You were young. I'd just come back from England," he said. He stepped back from the flag. "It feels like ten years since we had to take it down."

Yonas followed his father's gaze, frowning. "It's illegal to hang this up," he said.

Hailu's eyes were gentle. "My office was so small back then." He bent to wipe dust off his shoes. "My hospital was the best in Africa." He stood up and glanced at his hands. "No one would know that now."

"Shiferaw or one of the neighbors could see it." Yonas eyed the curtain. "Sara said he's been trying to look inside the house lately."

Hailu shook his head. "I've seen the ones we should be afraid of." He adjusted the curtain. "I invited Mickey to our house for a talk."

"Without telling Dawit?" Yonas asked, looking uncomfortable. "You know they haven't spoken in a long time. And since Mickey's new promotion—"

"If he says something about the flag, I'll know Dawit was right." Hailu wiped his hand across the coffee table and inspected it for dust.

"Haven't you heard the rumors? They say Guddu favors him because of his complete obedience."

Hailu sat in his blue chair. "By the end of all this, who's to say any of us will be blameless." His eyes were on the flag.

ON MICKEY'S FACE was a thin layer of sweat; underneath his arms, two wet spots that soaked through his uniform. He waited for Hailu at the front door.

"You can wait for Abbaye inside, he'll be downstairs right away," Sara said, looking around to make sure none of the neighbors saw the uniformed officer standing politely on their veranda. This would look exactly like what it was—a requested visit—and could brand them as traitors.

"Come in," she said, opening the door wider and extending a hand. "Please. Before the neighbors see you."

"Oh, of course," he said, embarrassed. He stepped into the living room and caught his breath at the sight of the flag.

"Sit down," Yonas said, watching him carefully. "Would you like something to drink?"

Mickey sat in the middle of the largest sofa, perched on the edge with his hands clasped between his knees. He undid the top button of his shirt, then fumbled to button it again.

"Something to drink?" Yonas asked again.

"Oh no. No thank you. I'm okay," Mickey answered, waving his hands in front of him for emphasis. "Not thirsty." He coughed. "Is he coming?" he asked, sneaking looks at Dawit's bedroom door.

Hailu walked through the dining room and strode towards Mickey to envelop the young man in a tight embrace. "Thank you for coming," he said, kissing both cheeks. He smiled warmly. "It's been some time."

"Gash Hailu," Mickey said, using the term for "Uncle," "it's good to see you." He returned Hailu's embrace and held on.

Hailu guided him to the empty seat next to his chair. "How are you?"

"Fine, fine," Mickey responded quickly, nodding his head as he spoke. "Everything's fine." He sat down next to Hailu and put his hands on his knees, then put them down by his side. "You're well?" he asked, staring at the flag.

"Things are as good as can be expected," Hailu said. "Considering all the changes," he added. He paused and waited for Mickey to respond.

Mickey stayed silent and looked again at the flag, then back at Hailu. "Yes."

"How is your mother?" Hailu asked, walking to the window. "No sun gets in when we do this," he grumbled. He began to unpin the curtains.

"No, no," Mickey said, nearly standing out of his seat. "Don't do that. It's better to keep it closed." He cleared his throat. "In case some-one sees me," he explained, nodding towards the flag. "I don't mind it like this." He sat straighter. "People talk too much without knowing anything."

"I see," Hailu said. He sat back down next to Mickey. "Sara's bring-ing tea." He pointed to the dining room table where Sara was arranging teacups on a tray. "We don't have much sugar, I'm sorry." He held out empty hands. "It's hard to buy anything these days."

"It is," he said.

"Even Melaku is finding it hard to keep stocked." Hailu inhaled deeply and took the tea Sara offered. He waved aside the biscuits. "He's had that kiosk for so long, we depend on him for everything."

"He's been there since I was a boy," Mickey said. "He's in good health?" He played with the buttons on his military jacket.

"He's been having some trouble," Hailu said.

Sara handed Mickey a cup of tea on a saucer. "It's hot, careful."

"He received a letter the other day," Hailu continued.

"How much sugar?" Sara asked, holding a spoon.

The teacup rattled in Mickey's hand as he set it down on the table. "No sugar," he said. He turned back to Hailu and thought for a moment. "Melaku received a letter?"

"Do you remember all the food he used to give your mother without charge?" Hailu asked.

Mickey looked down. "There are orders to follow."

"If he's out of business, there's no way for him to live," Hailu said. "And what harm is a simple kiosk?"

"This government is trying to do its best," Mickey said. "We take care of our people. He'll get ration cards."

"Ration cards?" Hailu leaned in, their faces so close Mickey had to look down. "You know him. He's a friend, and you still signed the letter."

"I had to." Mickey drew away and squinted at the flag. "But I didn't want to."

Hailu grimaced. "What would you do, if you could?"

"Some people have been given more rations than they can use. It's the way the system works sometimes, even when we try. Maybe Melaku can find a way to help redistribute them properly. To those who need it most, of course." Mickey sipped his tea, his eyes never wavering from his hands holding the cup.

EMAMA SEBLE COULDN'T keep her eyes off Mickey. The old woman, leaning back in her chair at the dining room table, had angled her body in the heavy boy's direction to stare at him. Mickey ate his dinner like a man under surveillance. Emama Seble's small, dark eyes moved over his hunched figure.

"New uniforms?" she asked, her fork stopped mid-twirl with spaghetti.

Mickey swallowed a mouthful of salad and took a gulp of beer. "I have to wear it." He shifted uncomfortably under her scrutiny.

Hailu had insisted Mickey stay for dinner, and Emama Seble had invited herself to the occasion, having heard from neighbors that Mickey was at the house. "How are things since your promotion?" she asked.

"Seble, that's enough," Hailu interrupted. He moved his spaghetti around on his plate.

"I'm asking about his mother," she retorted, and turned back to Mickey. "She must be proud of you. There's more pay." She waited for a response.

"Mickey, do you want more food?" Hailu said. "Yonas and Dawit can eat when they get back."

Sara handed the bowl of salad to Hailu. "Abbaye, you asked for spaghetti again but you're still not eating. You're losing weight." She frowned, concerned. "Isn't it good? Sofia made the sauce special for you."

Just then, Dawit came out of his bedroom. The two old friends stared at each other until Mickey dropped his gaze back to his plate.

"You're here?" Hailu asked. He moved a chair for Dawit.

"I was taking a nap," Dawit said, his attention concentrated on Mickey. "Why is he here? Get out of my mother's chair."

"Gash Hailu—your father invited me," Mickey said, getting up quickly, the chair scraping behind him.

"You shouldn't have come. And why do you call him Gash, as if you're close to this family? You're no one to us." Dawit spoke softly and ignored the seat Hailu offered him. He stepped closer to Mickey and pulled him so his arm dangled in his tight grip. "How can you eat with those hands?" he asked, shaking Mickey's limp arm.

Mickey slumped against the force of Dawit's hold and looked at Hailu. "Gash Hailu," he pleaded.

"Dawit!" Hailu said. "He's my guest."

Mickey tried to jerk out of Dawit's grasp, but the slender man was stronger. Dawit's grip was fierce. He seemed to take pleasure in Mickey's obvious pain. "He's a traitor," he said to Hailu. His mouth was smiling, his eyes cold. "Get out of my house," he said to Mickey, dragging him away from the table.

Dawit shoved him so hard that Mickey nearly fell backwards into the cabinet on the opposite wall. Hailu stood up and reached for Dawit, but Emama Seble put a hand on his arm.

"Let them deal with this on their own," she said. "You've done enough already."

Hailu sank back into his chair, resigned. "This had to be done," he said. "There was no other way."

Dawit kept prodding his old friend until Mickey stumbled out the door and onto the ground. His glasses landed next to him.

Mickey slipped on his glasses, then sprang up. He wiped the dirt off his trousers. "It's only because of your father that I'm not reporting you," he said quietly, voice shaking. He spoke softer. "They've been watching you. We can help each other, like we used to." He raised anguished eyes to Dawit and searched his face. "I'm not a bad person."

"You're a coward," Dawit said. He poked Mickey's chest and punctuated each word with a push. "You always have been, and you know it. Nothing will ever change that."

Mickey pulled himself upright and adjusted his belt and jacket. He inspected his sleeves and smoothed away imaginary wrinkles. He slipped a handkerchief from his jacket and wiped his upper lip with meticulous care. He stood straight and soldierly and saluted Dawit. Then he strode towards him so fast Dawit didn't have time to react.

They were suddenly face-to-face. Mickey blinked and focused through his glasses. "My mother knows how much I care for her," he said. "I work so she can buy food. You sent your mother to her grave thinking her favorite son couldn't even look at her while she was dying. Who's the coward?"

Mickey pushed Dawit so hard that Dawit fell backwards and hit the ground. Then he turned and walked away without another glance at his former friend.

32

HIS OFFICE WAS COMFORTING WITH the curtains drawn, when there was no red star to spill its colors across his walls and onto his floor. No hot sunlight to remind him of a helpless girl who came in wearing a bright floral shirt, recovering slowly. It had been days since he'd gone into her room, repulsed by his own efficiency. He hadn't been able to bring himself to slow her recovery. He'd counted instead on the girl's weakened resistance to infection. But her body had fought off illness with a spirit that normally would have made him proud. She was healing and it was thanks to him.

Beyond the thin glass pane that separated him from the world outside, he caught the lilt of a sparrow. He reached into a small drawer in his desk and dug towards the back until he found what he was looking for: a photograph of Selam and himself when Dawit was born. It'd been taken on the front steps of this hospital, back in the days when there had been a short lawn thick with blooming bougainvilleas and roses.

Selam was tired, it was easy to tell the birth had been difficult and she'd exhausted herself trying to push Dawit out. She leaned on his arm, her tiny hand gripping his, and her face, staring into the camera, was beautiful, serene. Her eyes were gentle. Her eyebrows were perfectly plucked, a routine she'd developed after moving to the city, her full lips parted but too sore from biting to fully widen into a smile.

Far in the background, half hidden behind a pole and staring stiffly ahead, was Almaz, and he remembered now how reluctant she'd been to be photographed.

"It's bad for you," she'd protested.

Yonas was taking the picture and had pleaded with her to join them, but she'd agreed only after Selam's insistence.

Hailu smoothed down a creased edge of the picture and stared at the younger version of himself. His hair back then, just starting to gray at the temples, was shorter, neatly trimmed to his head in a style Selam disliked. It was only as she grew sicker that he'd relented and started to let his hair grow longer. He was proud that day, happy, confident he could do whatever he needed to provide for his growing family and keep them safe. It was evident in the arm he draped possessively over his wife's shoulder. The other hand rested softly on Dawit's leg, his fingers cupping his son's small foot. He wasn't looking into the camera, his head was bent towards his newborn son and his wife, his smile only for them.

THERE WAS A SOFT knock at his door.

"She's awake," Almaz said as she pushed the door open. "You need to see her this time, Dr. Hailu."

He'd begun to resent her reminders.

"I'm not allowed to treat her," she continued. "And she needs stronger medicine. She's still in pain." Almaz stood just outside his office. She wouldn't step in unless asked, and this morning he took some small pleasure in keeping her out.

"Why can't you take care of her today?" he asked, putting the photograph in the back of the drawer. "There's nothing different, is there?" He strained to keep his voice even. "We don't have any new medicine anyway."

"She hasn't eaten, she refuses," Almaz said.

"Make her eat." The soldiers had begun to grumble about his absence. He'd assured them repeatedly that she was in capable hands.

"I think you need to see her, Dr. Hailu. She needs more than my supervision. Her injuries—"

"I want you to make sure she eats."

He remembered when it had become difficult to get Selam to eat, how the simple act of feeding her meant prying her jaw open and shoving food into her mouth as if she were an animal. He'd been unable to do it without Sara's help. Those were moments his family never talked about, moments when he'd been reduced to a paralyzing helplessness.

"How hard can that be," he muttered to Almaz. He hoped his tone hid the tightness in his throat. It wasn't until just now that he realized the girl was nearly the same age as Selam had been when they were married.

"You know how hard that can be," Almaz said, angered. "I've tried," she added, her voice shaking.

He felt a sudden rush of sympathy for his nurse. "I'm sorry," he said. "You're right."

"WHY IS THE WINDOW OPEN?" he said as he walked into the room. There was too much light falling on her bed, beads of sweat had collected on her forehead. Her damaged collarbone was dusted with a faint sheen of perspiration as well. Sunlight was pressing on her mercilessly. He closed the curtains with sharp tugs, yanking at the resistance of the curtain clips to slide easily over the rods. What he saw made him want to throw himself over the girl and shield her.

"It's such a nice day," the soldier with the bowed legs said. "We wanted to get fresh air."

"The sun's too hot," Hailu said. "She's been burned enough, don't you think?" He watched the way his words twisted the soldier's face and he relished his discomfort. "Go outside if you need to."

"You haven't been here lately," the soldier with the deep voice said. "We were waiting for you."

Almaz went around him to the girl. "She might have a fever," she said, settling the back of her hand on the girl's forehead tenderly. "She shouldn't be sweating like this." She checked the girl's vital signs, her concern motherly, professionalism discarded long ago. "It might be an infection."

"Weren't you leaving to get fresh air?" Hailu stared from one soldier to the other. "We need to dress these wounds," he said. He didn't say any more until he heard the soldiers' chairs creak as they rose, then their footsteps in the hall.

Almaz turned away from the girl. "She won't last one night when they take her back."

Scabbed cigarette burns dotted her arms and legs; the bottoms of her feet were crusted with darkened skin and pink scar tissue. Hailu could tell by the intensity of the rope burns that circled her ankles and wrists that she'd tried to resist. There had been no mercy shown.

"This isn't healing so easily," Almaz said, pointing to deep puncture wounds on her thighs. "I think it's where they used something to attach the electric wires to her. A neighbor told me they've picked up new tricks and equipment from these *ferengi*. They're coming in planeloads. Animals."

Almaz smoothed hair from the girl's forehead and wiped fresh sweat away. The girl's eyes were closed. Her breaths rattled in her chest as if the effort shook her ribs.

"She's the same age as my Alem. God take care of my girl," she said as she crossed herself.

"Has she said anything else?" Hailu asked. He stood near the window and wondered how he didn't recognize Selam in this girl earlier.

Almaz leaned into the girl's ear. "They're not here now. Can you talk?"

The girl stayed immobile.

"I gave her something for the pain." Almaz sighed. She felt gently around the girl's stomach, drew the sheet back to reveal a large bandage. "I heard the soldiers talking. The person who does this puts all of them in a plastic bag first so he doesn't soil his clothes." She unwrapped the bandages and dusted off peeling skin with a damp towel.

"Be gentle." He could see her skeletal figure poking through the thin gown. The pale blue flowers were dingy from wear and sweat.

He heard Almaz take a deep breath. "I try to forget how small she is," she said.

This girl was too weak to survive another round of interrogation. Even if she lived, she'd bear the scars for life. There would always be deep gashes on her thighs, her feet would never wear delicate heels. She would always walk with a limp. She had been raped, violently. She'd be so ashamed she'd never marry. Her days would be spent trying to prepare for the nightmares that would awaken when the sun died.

"What are we keeping her alive for?" he suddenly asked, surprising even himself. But as soon as it came out of his mouth, he felt the words work themselves into meaning, then logic. What was there for her but more of this?

Almaz was startled. Her hands stilled above the girl's stomach. "What do you mean?"

"This one is a special case," Hailu said. He turned to the hallway and pointed at the door. "They've told us that much. Do you think they'll let her live after all of this? And what kind of life—"

"She's important to them," Almaz stammered. "She's very important."

"It means they'll show even less mercy this next time. They've killed her already." He counted the number of lacerations on her chest, the severity of the burns on her legs, the depth of the wounds on the bottoms of her feet. "Give me her chart."

He took the progress report Almaz handed him and wrote each detail in medical terms that could never possibly describe the human capacity for viciousness and this girl's own heartbreaking endurance.

"We're treating a corpse," he said. He shoved the clipboard back in its place at the foot of the bed.

"It's better than dying," Almaz said. But Hailu noticed that her hand had moved to lace fingers with the girl's.

"I don't think so." He covered the girl with the sheet again. "I don't think you believe it either."

"I'm going to the bathroom to clean this towel." She folded the sheet under the girl's neck, then headed for the bathroom. "God help us."

SELAM SAID DEATH CAME IN MOONLIGHT. There is this to know, she said. There is silence and no thought. All is carved away and swallowed in the dark. This is death, she told him each time she thought she'd breathed her last. It is like this, and I am leaving in this way. But this girl in front of me, Hailu thought, still soaking in sunrays, knows that life is in the moonlight, even in the silence. That death holds thoughts. It gouges and violates. Death is not in the absence and oblivion of letting go, but in the crash and tear of depravity and brutality, as electrifyingly putrid as excrement and rotting flesh. And what have I given her? What have I given her but another moment in the stink and mire of horror and noise?

THE LION RACES BERHANE OVER THE HILL, rushes so fast he feels the wind lifting both of them high above the leafy tree, and soon they are running on clouds. His father barrels across the hill on a white horse, dressed in his white jodhpurs and tunic, a spear in his hand, his hair long and billowing from his head in proud curls. He looks up and waves, then turns and gallops through a field of yellow flowers. From the clouds, Berhane hears the sun call his father's name. "Daniel," she says. "Daniel."

BERHANE WOKE to find his mother holding him against her chest, rocking.

"Daniel."

She was far from him even though her heart beat against his ear. He closed his eyes and left his mother alone in her thoughts. He pushed himself deeper into her embrace, drifted back to his bright fields and yellow flowers.

Sofia held her son all night and hummed songs she'd forgotten since marrying Daniel. The sounds flowed like water, simple childhood melodies that calmed her and held back fears. Near her, her eldest son, Robel, turned fitfully, then pulled the thin blanket closer to his chin and continued sleeping. Outside, the long coo of an owl fell against their window.

THERE WAS A NEW jail rising on the horizon near his home, a slab of concrete and steel carved into the forest where Dawit once played amongst tall trees and thick grass. Constant activity swarmed around the area. Men and women carrying concrete blocks trudged up and down the road, burdened by the added weight of sun and sweat. Dawit stood at his gate, on the way to Melaku's kiosk, and watched the latest procession of tired workers. Their wide-brimmed hats cast shadows on the road.

There was a long line at the kiosk when Dawit got there.

"Dawit! Good morning, what do you want?" Melaku's wide smile revealed the empty spaces in his mouth.

Melaku's small shop had become an alternative means for people to buy what ration cards wouldn't allow. Shiferaw's grumbling did nothing to deter the old man, who chose to irk the *kebele* officer further by taping Mickey's notice ordering the kiosk closed onto one wall.

"If the palace couldn't destroy me, do you think you can?" he quipped to the man with the deformed smile. "And watch your wife around me," he'd added for extra injury. "Women don't want a man who smiles in bed."

The scowl Shiferaw's mouth couldn't form was nonetheless evident in his eyes.

"Dawit, tell me what you want, I'll hold it for you. These people are greedy today!" Melaku said, angling himself to look past the row of customers to the back where Dawit stood, embarrassed.

"Am I invisible?" It was Emama Seble. She threw Dawit an irritated glare.

Dawit offered her a smile. Seeing the black-clad widow still frightened him as much as when he was a boy. He couldn't understand how Sara managed to be friendly to the sour, frowning woman.

"Seble, shut up," Melaku said, "or you'll have to beg Shiferaw for more sugar this week."

"Melaku," a man in front of them said, "I need to get home."

"Which woman are you taking eggs to today? You need a ration card for wives, Taye." Melaku grinned as he watched the man's mouth drop open. "Next," he called out, counting money with vigor and continuing to hurl barbs at customers.

"You have to be careful," Dawit said to him once he was at the counter. It was just the two of them—and Emama Seble, who'd decided to linger. "One report is all it takes, and they'll put you in jail." Dawit felt uncomfortable under the woman's stare.

"They can go to hell." Melaku wiped dirt out of his eyes, his long fingernails clean and carefully filed. He looked at Emama Seble. "Go home, old woman."

"I'm walking back with him," she said, pointing at Dawit.

Melaku turned back to Dawit. "I'm just an old shopkeeper," he said.

"That doesn't matter, you know that," Dawit said.

"When I see the jailer, I'll ask for his mother." Melaku ignored Emama Seble's snort.

Dawit patted the old man's arm. "One Coca-Cola." He put coins on the counter.

"None today, I ran out."

Dawit looked at him, surprised. "It's only noon."

Melaku nodded. "A group of soldiers took everything, didn't even pay for the ones I tried to hide." He motioned to his shelves. "They bought some of my rations, too, complaining that soldiers weren't getting any more than the rest of us, it's all going to the officers. Imagine, just like old times."

"They're from the new jail?" Emama Seble asked. Her arm rested between the two men.

Melaku waved her question away, irritated by her presence. Dawit could feel her lean in. There were rumors that Melaku and Emama Seble had once been lovers, and it embarrassed him to stand next to them now and listen to the bickering he suspected covered a history of intimacy.

"They use this road every day," Dawit said.

"Military jeeps. I saw Mickey in one. They've been patrolling this area more," Melaku said.

Dawit cringed at the mention of Mickey's name.

They all looked to the road as if expecting a jeep to rumble past them at any moment. There was only a row of women hunched with firewood on their backs and a boy herding his sheep.

"Have you seen your friend lately?" Emama Seble asked.

"No." Dawit kept his eyes on the road in case her *budah* could detect his resentment.

Melaku put a bottle of Fanta on the counter. "I'll try to save Cokes."

Dawit and Emama Seble walked home without speaking. He caught the backwards glance she gave the kiosk before getting inside the compound and shutting the gate. He waited until she entered her house, then he stepped outside the gate and scanned the landscape for signs of a military truck or a group of soldiers. There was nothing but the silhouettes of his neighbors pressed against the outline of the jail.

35

FROM AFAR, THEY COULD HAVE BEEN mere sheets of paper, flimsy pages with crudely printed letters. But on these pages were words deemed treasonous and illegal. And there was a box of papers with those words tucked under a heavy blanket in the back of his trunk; anti-government pamphlets that his brother, irresponsible, arrogant Dawit, had left in his car. A thousand ways to go to jail and disappear, bundled under neat cardboard flaps. If I close this trunk and sink back into the darkness of this garage, I can walk away and forget they ever existed.

For a moment, still staring into his open trunk, Yonas didn't hear the knocks. They came again.

"Yes?" He slowly shut the trunk. "Yes?" He checked his watch, there were still hours until curfew.

The knocks again. One, two, three in rapid succession. Yonas stood for a moment trying to decide what to do, then opened the door and braced himself for a row of military fatigues.

On the ground curled into himself was a man older than he but younger than his father. His mouth was swollen; gashes crisscrossed his shaved scalp. He reached for Yonas with a hand from which one broken finger hung.

"They're coming," he said at the same time that Yonas heard a truck screech and felt the shudder of thick military boots stomping towards them. It was when a soldier broke away from the line of others that everything froze.

Then Mickey put his hand out to Yonas. "He's escaped," he said. His extended hand dangled in the space between them as he blinked behind thick glasses. "We're just taking him back. That's all." He dropped his hand and looked down at the man. "It's my job."

The man tried to raise himself on all fours. "Please," he said. "Peace."

Yonas saw a boot crash into his ribs and heard the crack of a rifle butt connect with skull. The man tried to shield his head with his arms, but the blows came from all directions.

Mickey flinched. "Go back inside," he said. "Please."

It was the sharp crease in Mickey's new uniform that brought Yonas's memories rushing to him, images of a young Mickey dressed in worn trousers with the same sharp crease, watching Dawit fight another boy for him, begging them to stop punching.

"Leave him alone," Yonas said. But he spoke too late. They were already dragging the man to the truck. And Yonas would have shouted, would have taken Mickey by the shirt and slammed him against the wall and beat him the way he deserved. For once, he would have relished the giving up and giving in to his blinding rage without guilt. But in his father's garage, hidden under a heavy blanket, were cartons of pamphlets, and that cut off any other protest from him.

DAWIT WAS SITTING at the dining room table talking with Tizita and Sara when Yonas walked into the room. He pulled Tizita away from Dawit.

"Go play upstairs," Yonas told her.

"I was telling Dawit about school," Tizita said.

"What's wrong?" Sara asked.

"Are you okay?" Dawit asked.

Yonas's brown eyes, usually soft with kindness, were stony; his full lips were folded tight against his teeth.

Yonas leaned into Sara's ear. "Get her out of here."

Sara stood right away. "Tizzie, help me roast coffee." She nudged the girl towards the kitchen. "Go."

Tizita ran into the kitchen.

Yonas moved towards Dawit so quickly that he pushed Sara against the table. Dawit jerked up, remembering boyhood fights with his brother, and shielded his face with one hand and made a fist with the other.

"What the hell is wrong with you?" Dawit's voice cracked. His head was tucked into his chest. One hand now rested on his skull to protect it. "What's wrong with him?"

Sara had seen Yonas mad. His temper was intense but always brief. This was different. It frightened her. She shouldered herself between them and turned to Dawit.

"Get out of here," she said.

"What the hell is wrong with him?" Dawit asked again. He was ready now for Yonas's next move.

Yonas grabbed Dawit's arm and pulled him close, knocking Sara away. With one sharp swing, he slapped him hard across the face. The force sent Dawit crashing into the china cabinet.

"Stop!" Sara screamed. She covered Dawit's body with her own.

Yonas looked past her to Dawit, his expression rigid and blank, his mouth curled in distaste. "Do you think I'm a coward?" he said.

Yonas swung again, this time with a knotted fist. It landed squarely on Dawit's chin and Sara heard the crack of teeth knocked against each other. Yonas reared back, yanked Dawit by the shirt, threw him to the ground, and knelt on his chest. He had a choke hold on Dawit's collar, jerking him up till they met face-to-face.

"Am I a coward to you?" he hissed. He slammed his forehead into Dawit's.

"Stop!" Sara tried to pull him away. "You're hurting him!"

Dawit roused and tried to push. He bucked and kicked, but Yonas deflected each move. Sara finally threw herself on top of Dawit and screamed at the first blow that fell into her back.

"Emaye!" Tizita came running from the kitchen holding a bag of coffee beans. "Don't hit my mommy! No!" She ran to her mother and clutched her waist, her face buried in Sara's back.

Yonas recoiled. He looked from his sobbing daughter to his wife, and then to his brother, still on the floor, his forehead bruised, his mouth bloody. "Tizita," he said. He stood up to hold his daughter.

She inched herself away from him and closer to Sara.

"Move." Dawit got to his feet, using the table for support.

"No more, please." Sara wrapped her arms around her daughter and lifted her up.

The two brothers stared at each other in silence, fists curled, until Yonas spoke.

"I warned you," he said. "Your stupid, childish games." He sank into a chair and put his head in his hands. His knuckles were cut and swollen. "Your stupid, senseless ideas." He made a noise and then his shoulders shook. Dawit saw him wipe tears away.

"What the hell is wrong with you?" He was afraid to move closer.

Hailu walked in cupping a small brown paper bag. He looked at Dawit's bleeding mouth and the angry purple welt on his forehead.

"Explain yourself," Yonas said. He balled Dawit's hands around a crumpled pamphlet. "Show him."

Dawit went slack. "I was going to get those out."

Yonas shoved him.

"This was the last time, anyway!" Dawit shouted.

"It's too late," Yonas said. He walked upstairs to his bedroom and slammed the door. The house rattled from the impact.

SARA RUBBED YONAS'S BACK. His body jerked in spasms so forceful and sharp that a few times he'd almost fallen off their bed. He hadn't spoken a word. His eyes were fixed on a point beyond anywhere she could see.

"Talk to me." Sara pressed herself against him. He was cold. "Tell me." She draped an arm over him and felt his heart beating so hard she grew alarmed. "What happened?"

Yonas began backwards, and told her about his encounter with Mickey.

"His mother said he got another promotion last week. I thought it was just in an office," Sara said.

"I didn't do anything," he said. He sat up. "Nothing. Nothing."

"What could you do? Nardos's husband was shot for trying to pull their daughter away from them. Then they took both the children." She wrapped her arms around his neck and kissed him.

Yonas shook his head. "I could have stopped them. I could have made Mickey leave the man alone, but I didn't."

She stroked his face. "He would have taken you in, he's changed."

Yonas stood. "Next time you drive my car, check inside the trunk. Be careful."

"Why? What's there?"

He walked out. "I'm going to pray," he said.

36

THE HUMAN HEART, HAILU KNEW, can stop for many reasons. It is a fragile, hollow muscle the size of a fist, shaped like a cone, divided into four chambers separated by a wall. Each chamber has a valve, each valve has a set of flaps as delicate and frail as wings. They open and close, open and close, steady and organized, fluttering against currents of blood. The heart is merely a hand that has closed around empty space, contracting and expanding. What keeps a heart going is the constant, unending act of being pushed, and the relentless, anticipated response of pushing back. Pressure is the life force.

Hailu understood that a change in the heart can stall a beat, it can flood arteries with too much blood and violently throw its owner into pain. A sudden jerk can shift and topple one beat onto another. The heart can attack, it can pound relentlessly on the walls of the sternum, swell, and squeeze roughly against lungs until it cripples its owner. He was aware of the power and frailty of this thing he felt thumping now against his chest, loud and fast in his empty living room. A beat, the first push and nudge of pressure in a heart, he knew, was generated by an electrical impulse in a small bundle of cells tucked into one side of the organ. But the pace of the syncopated beats is affected by feeling, and no one, least of all he, could comprehend the sudden, impulsive, lingering control emotions played on the heart. He had once seen a young patient die from what his mother insisted was a crumbling heart that had finally collapsed on itself. A missing beat can fell a man. A healthy heart can be stilled by nearly anything: hope, anguish, fear, love. A woman's heart is smaller, even more fragile, than a man's.

It wouldn't be so surprising, then, that the girl had died. Hailu would simply point to her heart. It would be enough to explain everything.

—

HE'D BEEN ALONE in the room, the soldiers smoking outside. He could see their shadows lengthening over the bare and brittle lawn as the sun swung low, then lower, then finally sank under the weight of night. It was easy to imagine that the dark blanket outside had also swept into the hospital room, even though the lights were on. It was the stillness, the absolute absence of movement, which convinced him that they, too, this girl and he, were just an extension of the heaviness that lay beyond the window.

She'd been getting progressively better, had begun to wake for hours at a time and gaze, terrified, at the two soldiers sitting across from her. The soldiers had watched her recovery with relief, then confusion, and eventually, guilt. Hailu could see their shame keeping them hunched over monotonous card games.

It hadn't been so difficult to get the cyanide. He'd simply walked into the supply office behind the pharmacy counter, waved at the bored pharmacist, and pulled the cyanide from a drawer that housed a dwindling supply of penicillin. Back in the room, Hailu prayed and made the sign of the cross over the girl. Then he opened her mouth and slipped the tiny capsule between her teeth. What happened next happened without the intrusion of words, without the clash of meaning and language. The girl flexed her jaw and tugged at his hand so he was forced to meet her stare. Terror had made a home in this girl and this moment was no exception. She shivered though the night was warm and the room, hotter. Then she pushed her jaw shut and Hailu heard the crisp snap of the capsule and the girl's muffled groan. The smell of almonds, sticky and sweet, rose from her mouth. She gasped for air, but Hailu knew she was already suffocating from the poison; she was choking. She took his hand and moved it to her heart and pressed it down. He wanted to think that last look before she closed her eyes was gratitude.

IT WAS ONLY ALMAZ who'd recognized the vivid flush of the girl's face, the faint hint of bitter almonds, and known what had happened. She'd walked in just as Hailu was explaining to the soldiers how the electric shocks she'd received had damaged her internally.

"Oh," she said, "yes." She collected herself. "It was too much for her. Too much infection."

The soldiers were agitated. They paced back and forth. They asked Hailu again and again to explain exactly what had happened.

"The infection was climbing from her feet to her heart," he repeated. "There was no way to stop it. She was too weak to fight it."

"But she was waking up, getting better."

Hailu's palms were sweaty. He heard a ringing in his ears that seemed to get louder as he talked. He cleared his throat. "It was a surprise for all of us."

The girl's body was still in the bed, covered completely in a sheet. They hadn't filled out the necessary forms, the soldiers had yet to acknowledge these next steps.

"You have to do something," the deep-voiced soldier demanded. He grabbed Hailu's arm and shook it. "We reported she'd be able to leave in a few days. People are expecting her." He tightened his grip. "Do something."

The skinny soldier sat back down in his chair and began to rock. "What are we going to say? They'll send us to jail." He shrank back against an imaginary blow.

"I'll write up the death certificate," Hailu said. "Everything will be explained there."

"I'm a witness," Almaz said. "There was nothing we could do."

The soldier stopped rocking and looked at his partner. "We can't say anything for a few days." He nodded to the girl. "Just yesterday we told them she was fine."

The other soldier nodded. "We should wait." He looked at Hailu, his eyes growing cold. "They'll want to ask you more questions, I'm sure of it. She was an important prisoner."

So it was that the girl was still in the hospital room tonight, dead, being watched by two frightened soldiers who could do nothing but stare in front of them and shudder at the reaction their report would bring. Hailu had wanted to stay, to sit with the girl, but Almaz had ordered him home.

"Nothing changes," she advised. "I'll be here anyway." She'd handed him a small brown paper bag just before he walked out of the hospital. "It's the girl's. She had it on when she came here and I was keeping it for her." She squeezed his arm. "Keep it."

Inside the bag, in the brown hollow of space entirely too large for it, was a slender, delicate gold necklace with an oval pendant of Saint Mary holding her child. He held up the necklace and watched as it swung daintily under the glow of his lamp. Cold, bright light caught the pendant and shot glints against the windshield.

37

Sofia pinched Robel's cheeks to get him to smile as she poured water into the large can she used as a teakettle. She pushed a wooden stick through two holes she'd cut into it. The can swung on the stick like a bottom-heavy bridge. She lit the small mound of charcoal and twigs and let Robel blow on the coals, smiling as his eyes brightened when the coal flared a brilliant red. She hugged him tightly.

"It's your brother's first day of work," she said. "Go wake him up."

They were outside their small shanty, in front of the dugout Sofia used for cooking meals.

Robel hesitated. "He should go to school," he said, pulling out of her embrace and frowning. He added twigs to the fire and stared into the sputtering flames. He was twelve years old but had already begun to carry himself like a man since Daniel's disappearance.

"We need the money," she said, rubbing the bridge of his nose where his eyebrows met as he frowned. "It's bad luck," she reminded him.

He relaxed his face, his brows wide apart again. "But I promised I'd make sure he went to school."

"If Berhane sells newspapers, it'll help." She kissed his cheek. She knew of the silent promises Robel made to his father. He'd begun keeping a growing list of them on a sheet of paper he carried everywhere. "He'll go to school one day," she assured him. "You, too." She dropped a few leaves of tea into the water. "Go on, wake him."

Robel went inside.

"Emaye, I'm ready for work," Berhane said, stepping out with his arms open wide for a hug.

She held him, squeezing until he giggled. "Come have tea." She poured even amounts of the pale, sweet water into two smaller cans.

"I'm big now," he said.

Sofia's stomach turned at the thought of her youngest son selling newspapers on the street. Things were never supposed to be this way.

Both her sons should have been in school. Daniel had taken the job as a guard to pay for the best education for Robel and save for Berhane's. Now everything was different. Every plan she'd ever had had collapsed into a pile of dust.

She could cope with the hollowness of Daniel's absence. She'd already begun to learn ways to mask the empty side of her pillow. She'd started to sleep with one of Daniel's shirts next to her head. She vowed to do this for the rest of her life. She planned to wake each morning before her sons, tuck the shirt back in a plastic bag, and preserve a bit of her husband every night. She could do this until the day she died. It would not be enough, but it was something. But the children. Our sons were born poor, Daniel, but they were never meant to stay poor, she thought.

Berhane slurped his tea and smiled. "It's sweet." He touched his stomach.

Today, her youngest son, her special boy, was going to start selling newspapers on the same street Robel shined shoes. They would work until she came home. Long days like these were never meant for children.

She leaned in to kiss his cheek. "Wear your shoes, you'll be walking a lot."

Berhane held up a calloused foot. "Tizita says my feet are the strongest."

"I still want you to wear the shoes," Sofia said, referring to the worn pair of slippers that had once belonged to Robel. They were too big for Berhane, but they'd protect him from the glass and rocks on the road. Robel, at her insistence, had finally agreed to wear a pair of Daniel's shoes on cold days, stuffing the toes with cloth to keep them from slipping off.

Berhane stood up to reveal dark red shorts that were much too large for his thin frame and sagged around his waist.

"Why aren't you wearing your blue ones?" she asked.

"Red is Tizita's favorite color," Robel said.

"Give him your belt." Sofia motioned to the worn leather belt around Robel's waist. "I'll try to find you another one so you don't have to share."

Sofia watched her two boys run back into their home to prepare for their day. She angled her face towards the sun rising in the horizon. Out of habit, her eyes raked the road that stretched around their cluster of shanties, searching for Daniel.

DAWIT AND HAILU stared at each other in the shrinking space of Dawit's bedroom. The air was charged.

"I found this," Hailu said. He raised his hands to his chest. In the center of his open palms lay a pistol. "Where the hell did you get this?" His hands shook as if the weapon was too heavy. He stood so stiff he was sure his son could see the pounding of his heart through his hospital jacket.

"I asked you a question," Hailu said. In his nose was the smell of cyanide, in his pocket, the girl's necklace, and now, in his hands, his son's pistol. Selam, what am I doing wrong?

Dawit was taken aback and out of breath. He'd just witnessed two armed men leap from a car and gun down two others. He hadn't stopped to watch the bodies fall, hadn't asked whether the gunmen were part of the opposition or the government, hadn't wanted to do anything but get to the safety of his home as fast as he could. And now, here was his father, in his room, holding the gun Mickey hadn't wanted back since that terrible day of the executions. The gun that fell into Dawit's hands depleted of bullets and that he'd hidden deep under his bed, repulsed.

Dawit let moments pass as he looked at his father. "Do you really think this is mine?" He was starting to sweat. "Do you think I'd use it?" Anger was rising in him again at the accusation, the violation, the arrogant demand for answers that should have been obvious.

His father held the gun closer to him and Dawit stepped back against his desk.

"Don't lie to me," Hailu said, his face flushed and determined. "I already know what you're doing. Tell me the truth!"

"You'd rather believe a lie than the truth," Dawit said, taking a step towards him, raising his voice. "I could tell you it isn't mine, but that's not what you want to hear. You want to hear what you think you already know. And you don't know anything!"

"You think you're strong enough to fight them with this?" Hailu dangled the gun in front of Dawit's face by the grip, holding it with two fingers as if he didn't want to stain his hands. "Where do you keep the bullets?" He bent down and stretched an arm under the bed. He stood up and dusted a mark off the front of his jacket. "Get the bullets and give them to me." He put the gun in his pocket, adjusted the drag on his collar, and waited with folded hands.

"I don't have bullets. There was a boy from my school," he said softly. "They left him near the road like trash. They're the killers, not me."

"So you want to carry a gun now? I'll take you to work," Hailu said, shaking his head, then looking at the gun in his pocket. "I'll show you what I have to fix." There is no room in this country for youthful errors. Nothing but me protects you from them, he thought. "You're all making yourselves easy targets."

He wanted to shake the defiance out of his son's proud shoulders and push logic into a mind that had closed long before. A year ago, he would have hit him. Today, he felt too tired. "I forbid you to have anything to do with those groups. I'm keeping the gun, and from now on, you'll be home by dinner and you won't go anywhere without permission," he said.

Was that a scream coming from another house raid or the cry of a father looking for his daughter?

Dawit spoke over the noise in Hailu's head. "You can't do anything and you know it. You don't understand. You don't even know the right questions to ask. You want to control me and try to pretend there's nothing happening in this country." Dawit wiped his eyes, swallowed the pain in his throat. "We have to keep fighting. We're different from your generation. Just because someone has authority doesn't mean they should be respected." His mouth opened, then closed, and slid into a straight line. He kept his eyes level with his father.

Hailu saw in that move his own youthful arrogance come back to visit him.

"Dawit," Hailu said. He sank down onto the bed. He put his head in his hands. "Stop this. I beg you."

My father doesn't know what he can't see; he can't see what he can't understand. I'm a son to him only in name. Dawit strode out of his bedroom and slammed the door, leaving Hailu alone with that distant cry.

———

A DARK RIBBON of bodies slunk down the road towards his kiosk and Melaku's heart caught in a beat and shook. Soldiers. He hid Coca-Cola in an empty box, then tried to prepare himself for his newest and most regular customers. It was early morning but they were already making their way to his window to be served. He opened his shutters, drank in the cool dewy breeze, then prepared himself for the routine exchange of money for goods. He conducted his business with a set of movements as choreographed and precise as in a stage play: a sharp grunt, the hiss of coin on counter, the slap of bottle against palm, another grunt, then shuffling footsteps, another uniform, then it began all over again.

He tried to hide his inventory of rations from the soldiers when he could, and save his stock for the neighborhood. He pretended to these soldiers that he was a struggling kiosk owner selling only cigarettes, gum, and such, surviving on the good graces of an old friend who was now a high-ranking official—not one of the many black-market vendors who'd begun to flourish in the city. Every morning, Melaku turned himself into a performer, a shell of moving body parts and a pasted smile. He stared only at the coins, at the soldiers' hands, at the Coca-Cola they loved so much. He avoided their uniforms and their eyes.

But this morning, the beat was broken at the very end of the line by soldiers he'd never seen before. They were a trio of too-skinny boys. There were no sliding coins, no soft slap of palm on bottle, no grunt of thanks, then retreating footsteps. There was only the spare, tight shrug of shoulders and the gentle, womanly clearing of throats.

"Coca-Cola." They spoke as one. "Three."

He held a bottle towards them. No hand met his halfway. One of them planted a palm on the counter and slid coins towards him. He had eyes the color of new leaves and those eyes watched Melaku's every move.

"Anything else?" Melaku asked as he produced one bottle, and another, then another, and stepped back.

They shook their heads. The bottles and coins sat untouched. They stood rigid as stone, a neat row of shoulders and necks. Melaku felt the heat of six eyeballs darting over his face in what seemed like six different directions.

"You know a man named Hailu," they said.

"Who?" Melaku felt his knees begin to shake.

"Dr. Hailu, the father of Yonas and Dawit." They pointed in the direction of Hailu's house, three bony fingers with curved, sleek nails.

Melaku couldn't tell the difference between them. "That's a common name," he said. "I get many customers every day. This area's growing quickly." Fear bent his resolve, shook his voice.

They draped their hands across the countertop and leaned forward. "Tell him we must see him today. We'll be waiting at the jail."

Melaku smelled the hint of myrrh, saw mouths singed brown from too much smoke. Their words wrapped around his chest.

"I don't know if I'll know which one he is," he said. "Not everyone comes here, especially since the *kebele* store opened." He gave them the look of a confused old man.

They swiveled towards the road. "He drives past here every morning."

The soldier with the pale eyes pushed another coin towards Melaku. "For your work," he said.

Melaku shook his head. "Keep it." But they were gone by the time he could get the words out.

THEY'D TAKEN THE girl's body yesterday. The soldiers had gone to make their report and had come back hours later, dumped the body onto a gurney, and wheeled it into a waiting jeep, their frightened whispers falling behind them.

The girl's departure had been abrupt and lacking ceremony. Hailu had said a quick prayer over her, tucked the sheet around her shoulders, and told them to be careful.

"She's been weak," he said. "Tell her father she asked for him often," he added. "She was brave considering the pain," he reminded them.

But he'd been ignored, and within minutes her hospital room was empty, leaving a shallow dent in her pillow.

In the car driving to work, Hailu took a deep breath. It would be a while before he'd be able to forget the sound of the girl asking for her father. He honked a greeting to Melaku. He was running late.

Melaku dashed out of his kiosk and pounded on the car's hood. "Stop!"

"What is it?" Hailu said. He braked abruptly. "I could have hit you!"

"Soldiers came asking for you." Melaku's voice was thin. "I told them I didn't know you, but I don't think it worked. They wanted you to come to the jail." He ran a hand over his head. "That means they've built it already . . ."

Hailu felt his chest tighten. "When did you see them?"

"This morning." Melaku pointed to Hailu's house, just as the trio had done. "They know you have two sons, they called them by name."

"They know my sons?" Hailu stared ahead of him. "What else?"

Melaku wiped his forehead. "I didn't think to ask questions." He lowered his eyes. "I wanted them to leave."

Hailu wanted to be alone. He wanted to let his anxiety unfold so he could examine it in private. "I'm running late."

Through the rearview mirror, Hailu caught Melaku's reflection. The man was standing next to the road, his hands hanging at his side, stark fear plain to see even from the growing distance. Hailu rolled down his window to dry the sweat that soaked the back of his shirt.

38

A LION IS FAST AND STRONG. A lion can jump into the sky. A lion is brave like a soldier.

"It's brave like me," Berhane chanted while he struggled with a bundle of newspapers stacked as high as his chin. He stumbled and bumped into Robel.

"Let me carry them," Robel said. He took a few out of Berhane's arms. "Don't trip on the rocks."

They were near the Sidist Kilo campus of Addis Ababa University, and the road in front of them was a wide asphalt circle that bent around Yekatit 12 Martyrs' Square. Short concrete steps led to a tall obelisk. At the base of the obelisk were scenes from the 1937 Italian massacre that followed an assassination attempt on the ruthless General Graziani. Further up, a granite lion stood proud on a ledge above the fray, his paw curled around his scepter.

Berhane's heart raced. "It's a flying lion!"

"That's where the emperor used to live." Robel pointed to a large, imposing building across the street, tucked behind a thick stone wall, hidden by thickets of lush purple and red bougainvillea. "He had many houses so he gave it to the students."

Berhane shifted the newspapers in his arms.

Robel grabbed several more. "You can't see anything and you'll miss the lion zoo."

Berhane stopped. "Where?"

"Smell," Robel instructed, wrinkling his nose. "Can you smell them?"

"Lions stink?" Berhane asked.

"They eat rotten meat. They're over there behind that wall." Robel pointed to a pair of metal lion statues that sat dulled and gray on either side of a dirty gate. A red sign arched above the entrance. Yellow letters in shaky handwriting were scattered unevenly across the curve.

"Are they in jail?" Berhane asked. He noted the short, brush-covered wall. He could climb that wall and take a lion from there. "Soldiers can't kill lions."

"It's a zoo." Robel guided him across the street. A taxi stopped and let out three students in front of the school. "Come on, I'll show you where you have to be."

Robel set his wooden shoeshine box down, then opened the lid to take out polish and his brush and a stained cloth. He flipped the box lid down and patted it for Berhane to sit. "You'll be over there." He pointed to a corner near to him. "I'll be able to see you. Don't run into the street. Just sell to the students. If you see a truck with soldiers, come back to me."

"What if we see Abbaye on this road? What if a jeep comes to buy my newspaper and he's inside?"

"Pay attention." Robel took two coins out of his pocket. "This is how much a newspaper costs. Two of these."

"I'm hungry," Berhane said, sitting obediently until his brother gave the command that he could go to his station and start work.

Robel patted his arm. "I'll buy you food once I get a customer." He hugged his brother. "Don't be scared, okay?"

"I'm not scared," Berhane said, staring at the granite lion.

HAILU SAT AT HIS desk in the dark. He'd been summoned to the jail officially. His presence was requested in writing, delivered to him by three skinny soldiers who spoke in unison. They'd walked into the hospital and gone to his office. They stood in a straight line, their shoulders even. Their identical uniforms, the way they each planted their feet the exact same width apart and had their hands folded in front of them, fingers plaited together, made Hailu think he was looking at triplets, though they were nothing alike in appearance. One was darker than the others, another was heavier, and the third had strange see-through eyes that looked like chips of stained glass. Watching them address him had been as confusing to Hailu as the order itself, handed down by a man most only knew as "the Colonel."

"You were told to come in, we spoke to your friend. Here is a written order. Come to the jail tomorrow, arrive by dawn," they said. "The Colonel wakes up early."

They kept their eyes lowered, but even then, Hailu felt their indifference to his status and age.

"What's this about?" He looked at the inked signature at the bottom of the letter and tried to imagine the man whose hand moved across the page with such jagged sweeps of the pen. "I have to work tomorrow morning, I'm scheduled for surgery."

Two of them turned to look at the third soldier. He stepped forward. "Please don't disobey orders," he said. His eyes were the color of a premature leaf, his pupils black coins floating in a pool of green water.

"Should I bring a suitcase?" Hailu asked.

Most prisoners were ordered to bring a suitcase of clothes under the pretext that they'd return home eventually. Soldiers took the suitcases and added to their wardrobe, many of them wearing to bars and parties the clothes of those they'd executed.

"You won't need to," the third soldier said.

Hailu tried not to think about the fact that no one he knew ever returned from a summons to jail.

"Tomorrow," they said before walking out of the office. "Don't disobey this time."

Now, Hailu was in his chair with the lights off. He sat with his back straight as a tree and waited, though for what, he wasn't sure.

YONAS WAITED IN the middle of the noisy traffic. The roads were packed in every direction; it was impossible to move. In the distance, tanks and trucks crawled in perfect symmetry. Pedestrians milled and pushed around cars, strained to see what they could of the roads; a cautious, curious mass.

"What's going on?" he asked a driver near him.

"I don't know," the man said as he wiped his forehead with his tie. "Someone said there are dignitaries, Cubans. Maybe even Castro."

"More Cubans?" Yonas said. "For what?"

"To help us kill each other faster. They'll be in the north, Eritrea." He turned off the engine and got out of his car. "We'll be here a while," he said as he leaned against his door.

"I want to see what's ahead." Yonas stepped out of his car. "Do you think my car will be safe?"

"Communism has been the best thing for crime, my friend. What thief wants to be in jail these days?" He pulled a cigarette out of his pocket and lit it.

Yonas couldn't see through the throng of people. He was squeezed in every direction. The crowd was impatient, no one was moving, people pressed from behind. There was a surge forward, a stumbling backwards, an impatient kick. Tension was high.

A loud bray brought a groan from the crowd.

"I'm stuck just like you," a man standing near his donkey retorted. He held a stick in one hand and the animal's rope in the other. "It's not my fault."

"Peasants," someone said.

Yonas smiled at the farmer. "I need to see how far this goes. Can I stand on your donkey?" Yonas pulled out coins from his pocket.

The farmer grimaced and shook his head.

Yonas took out more. "That's it."

The farmer grumbled but took the money.

Yonas looked over the ocean of heads. At the edge of the crowd were rows of tanks and groups of soldiers sitting on top of them at attention. A cavalcade was rolling through, a sleek, shiny entourage of Mercedes and jeeps. The new Ethiopian flag flapped from each antenna, its green, yellow, and red stripes free of the proud lion. In one of the jeeps was Major Guddu, wearing a tan government uniform and pumping his fist into the air emphatically, his smile determined, his teeth flashing. The crowd remained still, silent. A fat man wearing black glasses sat next to the major, and when the man shoved his glasses higher on his nose it was then that Yonas recognized Mickey, smiling blandly, waving meekly. He could have been mistaken, but he thought that for a brief moment Mickey looked at the man standing above the crowd, and recognized him as well.

39

A GIRL KNOTTED IN TIGHT ROPES was dumped in Yekatit 12 Martyrs' Square. Her skirt was lashed to her legs with rope that dug into her wrists and ankles and brought her limbs to an unnatural point.

Students gathered around her, their fear carefully draped. Dawit pushed through them and forced himself to take a better look. He could count her ribs through her bloodied shirt. One earring was ripped off. In her face, as swollen as it was, was a full beauty and something else. Dawit stared at her. He remembered her. Ililta. Once, Ililta's face had been tear-stained and her wide eyes had been shut to block the image of her naked mother, Mulu, with a cruel, cruel boy. Once, this girl had kissed his cheek and smiled. She had joked with Bizu and served his father coffee on visits, her legs skinny and ashen as she tiptoed through his dining room. Dawit dropped to his knees in front of her and began to untie the ropes.

"Leave her alone." The voice was gruff, authoritative behind a rifle. "Get out of here."

Dawit felt the circle close around him as spectators bent down for a closer look. The mouth of a rifle pressed into his shirt. He pulled away.

"I know her," he said. "She's my neighbor."

In front of him in the crowd, Solomon dangled a cigarette in a shaking hand. His head moved back and forth. His eyes begged Dawit's obedience.

"But I know her," Dawit said again, this time for Solomon.

"Get away from her before we arrest you," the soldier said, smelling of raw steel and petrol.

"I want to move her out of the square, out of the sun."

The soldier shook his head. "She's a lesson to all of you. And there will be others unless all of these anarchists stop their bourgeois assaults."

Solomon's eyes narrowed, his mouth set in a straight line. He shook his head again, more emphatic.

"Get up!" There was the sound of running, more soldiers. "Now!"

Dawit refused to let go of the rope. The soldier lifted it with the end of his rifle and dropped it back on the girl. He pushed Dawit, sending him backwards into the crowd.

"Get out of here," the soldier growled. "All of you!"

SOLOMON AND DAWIT sat in the old, dark teahouse, a cup of sweet tea in front of them. "Are you crazy?" Solomon asked, pounding the table. "Are you that stupid?"

"I knew her," Dawit said.

"It doesn't matter who she was." He paused. "Especially if you knew her, you keep away. You keep the hell away, do you understand me?!" He shook Dawit's arm. "You pretend you don't notice. Idiot!" He glanced around the room and lowered his voice though there was no one there. "They're watching us and now they know to look at you every time you're on campus. If you do anything like this again, you're out."

"It's not right to leave a body."

"You want to save people, then save the living." Solomon stood up, pushed his chair into the table. "Those who are dead aren't worth dying for." He strode out, his tea untouched.

HAILU LAY IN BED fully clothed, a suitcase at his feet. He was dressed in layers: two pairs of socks, three shirts, two pairs of briefs, and one jacket on top of a thick sweater. He could feel the sweat collecting under his arms. He hadn't slept all night. He'd spent his time looking through photographs, walking barefoot, felt the smoothness of wood under his feet. He'd traced his path with fingertips pressed on sky blue walls. Selam's favorite color.

They used to paint the room together once a year, and as their sons grew older, it had become a family project. There were no more new coats after she died. He had come to hate the color. He'd hoped that sunlight would have dulled the brightness to a shade closer to a solemn dusk, but it hadn't happened yet.

He sat up and imagined floating in an expanse of sky. He held his breath as long as he could, wanted to feel light, even light-headed, when he woke Yonas.

HAILU AND YONAS knelt in front of the statue of Saint Mary. "You have to drive me there," Hailu said.

Yonas turned to his father, then back to the statue. "How could this happen? I don't understand."

"Let's go," Hailu said. "I have to hurry." He stood up.

"Why? Why do they want you? We've stayed out of things."

"Get up." Hailu was rigid.

"Let's hide you," Yonas said, still kneeling. "I'll wake Dawit and we'll hide you." He wrapped his arms around his father's legs.

"I don't want to be here when Tizita wakes up. You'll explain for me." Hailu pulled Yonas up.

"I'll go instead," Yonas said. "I can go talk to them. I'll take Dawit and we'll go together."

"I'll be back by this afternoon." Hailu cleared his throat. "They've told me that, there's no reason to believe anything else."

"You can hide with Melaku until I get you. Hurry." He pushed Hailu out of the prayer room, nearly stumbling in his haste. "We'll go to Melaku's, then we'll take you somewhere else."

"Stop it," Hailu said, his voice shaking. "They'll come here for you and Dawit, maybe even Sara, if I don't go."

Yonas reached out to embrace his father, but Hailu made no move towards him. He let his arms drop. He was not the son his father needed. He understood, finally, what his mother had always known about Dawit, that this son of hers was the strongest of her children. Dawit would have fought with Hailu, instead of wanting to hug him like a child. Dawit would have burst into the jail and demanded they leave his father alone.

Yonas gripped his father's hand. "I won't let you go."

"They'll arrest you if I don't go. There's no other choice." Hailu hugged Yonas and held on with fierceness. "I know you. Remember there was no other way." He let go just as quickly and turned around, composed and collected.

They walked into Hailu's dark bedroom. Yonas turned on the light, illuminating the anguish in Hailu's face. It sent him back to the days of his mother's illness.

"Abbaye, when Emaye was sick—"

"There's nothing to say," Hailu said, his mouth trembling. "Turn off the light. Hand me my suitcase. I want to take my car."

Yonas switched the light off and felt for the suitcase. "But why did you pack if—" He found Hailu's firm hold already on the handle. "Give it to me," Yonas said.

Hailu didn't let go. They left, both clutching the suitcase, Hailu leading Yonas with steps that had long ago memorized the way out.

DAWIT CRAWLED AGAINST THE WIND, feeling for a hand, a foot, the edge of a torso. The handkerchief around his mouth drowned the stink of corpse in the scent of his father's cologne. He brushed against stone and dirt, fallen branches and dung. He worked his way to the center of the square, where the body still lay. He cut ropes loose with a knife.

Dawit wrapped a large blanket around and under the body, then hurriedly dragged it out of the square to Yonas's car. It was his luck that there was no one to witness this. Soldiers in the area broke orders to see one of the only bands still allowed by the Derg to perform. He braced himself to face Mulu's wrath and confusion and asked his own mother for help in convincing Mulu to bury her daughter without ceremony.

THE JAIL WAS a concrete building rising out of a dusty meadow shorn of trees. The parking lot was a patch of dirt carved out of the dry landscape. Hailu's small Volkswagen was dwarfed by the military jeeps and trucks lined along one side like slumbering crocodiles. Though the building had windows, no light shone through. What a familiar sight they must have been for the soldiers who worked inside: two men in a small car in the parking lot, sitting in silence with stricken faces.

Yonas felt his father's distance and didn't know what to say.

"Hailu," Yonas said; his father's name meant "his power." He felt his father shaking beside him. "Hailu," he said, softer.

Hailu clung to the hand of a son who could not stop repeating his name. He pulled himself back from the space beyond clouds and let sorrow and fear wash over him.

THE DINING ROOM TABLE FLOATED WIDE and long between them and made Dawit feel like a small boy again. Finally he shook his head. "I don't understand," he said. "What are you saying?"

"I already told you," Yonas said. "I have to tell Sara," he added, looking into the empty living room as if expecting Hailu to emerge, "but I wanted to talk to you first." He wiped his face and reached for Dawit's hand.

"It doesn't make sense," Dawit said, drawing back his hand. "How could he be summoned like that? For what?"

"Don't you know someone who can help?" Yonas put his head in his hands, pushed his palms into his eyes. "Don't you know someone?"

"How could you just let him go?" Dawit stood up and spoke to the top of his brother's head. The news began to settle in. His father was in jail. "Why did you just drive him there?" He could make out the shape of his father's radio, square and small, in the living room.

Yonas hunched over his hands. "I tried to stop him."

"And you could have woken me." Dawit went into the living room and felt the vastness of the room devour him. He could still smell the thick odors of musk and body, dirt and sweat, still hear Mulu's guttural wails at the sight of her daughter. He wiped his nose, took in his father's chair, the silent radio, the emptiness of it all. "I should have been with you. I could have done something."

"There was nothing you could do. I tried everything," Yonas whispered. "I had to take him. They would have come for us."

"I'm going to the jail," Dawit said.

"I tried everything," Yonas repeated, his eyes unfocused. "He wouldn't let me do anything." He thought for a moment. "There's Mickey."

Dawit remembered Mickey that day they had passed a sobbing Ililta and heard Mulu's small cry, thought of how this fat, cowardly boy had wanted to do nothing but walk away, how he'd stood by and watched, then run away when Dawit fought Fisseha.

"No," he said.

Yonas stood and pushed his chair in. "I'm not asking you."

The living room was still filled with the smell of their father, his sharp, clean scents, the lingering odors of a man fastidious in his habits, dignified in all his manners.

"Did he ask for me?" Dawit suddenly asked.

DAWIT UNFOLDED HIMSELF slowly out of his father's car and gazed at the massive hulk of the jail, a gray slab of imposing thickness built with Soviet money. It was planted on flat land that seemed to crack from the unaccustomed weight. There were people crowded around the entrance, men and women and girls and boys, swarming and colliding with each other, only a few bothering to form any semblance of a line at the door. He felt his stomach twist.

A short man wearing a tailored business suit beat on the thick door. "Open the door! Open up, we're not leaving."

Dawit walked over to him. "My father's in there. Did you see a tall man with white hair come in last night?"

The man gave him an impatient look and returned to pounding on the door. He looked back at Dawit. "The window," he said to him, pointing above his head. "Can you reach it? See if there's anyone in there."

What Dawit saw through the small, high window made him break into a fresh sweat. The office was a display of military precision. There were no stacks of papers lining dirty, cluttered desks. No groups of soldiers sat in clusters smoking cigarettes and playing cards. No cigarette butts lined the floors. It had the bland orderliness of a vacant hotel with its glossy floors and shiny countertops. Dawit turned back to the businessman.

"It's empty," he told him.

"They see us," a man dressed in a security guard uniform said, coming to stand near them. He inhaled on a bent cigarette. "It's the same every morning. They make us stand here for hours, then they let a few of us in."

"My father's in there," Dawit said. "He was summoned."

"You're lucky. They took my daughter from class," the security guard said. "I work in the same building, they used the back way, no chance to see her."

Dawit turned away. "Where do they keep them?" he asked, taking in the milling crowd. "All these people are looking for someone?"

The security guard took a long drag of his cigarette and let the smoke billow out of his nose and mouth. He shook his head. "It's small."

The talking faded and then a hush fell over the crowd. In the parking lot, a young woman in a floral dress lifted a suitcase out of her car. She had a suit jacket draped over her arm. She tottered on high heels.

"They told me to turn myself in. How do I get in?" she said.

A sympathetic murmur lifted from the crowd. They cleared her path to the door.

The young woman went to the door and began to knock.

"Why are you here?" the security guard asked. "Don't you know what they do?"

"My husband's inside," the young woman said. "They told me if I didn't come, they'd kill him." She bit her lip. "I don't know what he did."

Dawit stood next to her. She was the same height as Lily, but more slender. She had fragile wrists with sharp bones that looked like they might snap with too much pressure. "Stand here," he said, pointing to the other side of him. "If the door opens, it'll hit you."

"How do I tell them I'm here?" She rapped against the heavy door.

"They hear you," the security guard said.

The young woman sat on her suitcase, her jacket still folded neatly over her arm. "He gave this to me," she said, caressing the material.

"Did they tell you why your husband's in jail?" Dawit asked. "Did they give any reason?"

"Get out of here," the security guard said to her, lighting another cigarette. "Make them find you."

She ignored them both. Dawit fought the urge to hold her arms and force her to pay attention to him. He wished he'd brought a picture of his father.

"Is your husband a doctor?" Dawit asked. He didn't know what answer he wanted, and he flinched as the question came out of his mouth.

"A cook," she said. "We have three children." She ran her eyes over Dawit's fashionable jeans and shirt. "We're not rich."

Together, they watched the sun burn pale, then yellow, then gold in a darkening horizon. Then the front door swung open just long enough for three soldiers to grab the young woman and drag her inside.

THIS IS FEAR. I know this taste of bile and sweat in my mouth. I have run against Italian bullets with this taste thickened on my tongue, I have raised a rifle and a scalpel and my hands with its familiar sting and stink, I am no stranger to this. This is fear, Hailu said again, but it didn't ease the tightness in his throat. It didn't loosen the veins that swelled and throbbed from the pressure of a heart beating much too fast. There is nothing here that is not the sum of its most minute parts, there is nothing here that logic and rational discourse cannot put back into place. But each breath seemed to shove him deeper into the jail despite the fact that he hadn't moved from this solid chair in what felt like hours, maybe days.

So Hailu started counting. *And, hulet, sost, arat.* He couldn't understand why the Colonel would be so interested in a small, quiet girl who was fragile, so fragile, much too fragile to live in these times. He would tell the Colonel that she was brought to him already near dead. How do you expect me to keep a dying body alive, he'd ask. I'm nothing but a simple doctor, a mere man. Like you, he'd remind the Colonel. We two are only men. It is God we need to question, to interrogate, to beg for answers.

Hailu lifted his face to taste a fresh breeze. The cane is tall in my fields, so tall it blocks my vision, closes off the sun, and curtains me in darkness. He didn't listen to the heavy door that shut behind him. He dug himself even deeper into the steadily increasing numbers instead. He searched his pockets for prayer beads he realized he'd forgotten at home. He took Tizita's hand. Count with me, Tizzie.

"Quit praying," a soldier ordered. He shoved him out of the small room into a long hallway, then into a wide reception area with fluorescent lights so bright not even sunlight could compete. The air was weightless and chilly, it burned his nose to inhale.

The jail was cleaner than his hospital lobby. It held no smells; there were no noises. Soldiers were attached to chairs, hunched over documents that sat atop perfectly arranged desks, rigid as statues. Not one looked up to take in this latest prisoner, flanked by two of their stern-faced comrades. Hailu faltered for a moment, but a hand pushed him forward, and he heard inside the noiselessness that was making his head ache, tiny telltale signs of life: the scratch of pen on paper, the deliberate thump of a stamp, the opening of a freshly oiled drawer, the slow hush of a chair pushing across a concrete floor.

"Sit," a voice ordered behind him.

Hailu slumped into the metal chair pushed under him. The slant of light that pushed into the room from a strip of space in the curtains was crisp, nearly bleached of all golden color. It settled on a soldier carefully thumbing through a stack of papers with a back as straight as a ruler. Hailu looked around him. Gone was his sugar cane field. Tizita's hand had evaporated. The air bore down in all its coldness. He hugged his suitcase to his chest, begged his body to produce heat to replace the chill he already felt settling into his bones. The urge to run overtook him again, but the very order of things, the symmetry of motion and stillness in the dark gray office, made even the thought of resistance illogical.

"You won't need this." One soldier took his suitcase away. "Or all the layers you're wearing. We'll keep it safe for you." A small smile spread across his lips.

Hailu held on to the handle. "Why can't I keep it?" He spoke slowly, careful not to lose count of the numbers in his head. Out of the corner of his eye, he could see the bright stream of light glinting off the other soldier's black shoes, ricocheting back against the wall. "It has all my things."

The soldier took the suitcase from him. "Orders. The Colonel's very strict about these things." He reached into Hailu's jacket pocket and fished out his keys. "I'll take this, too." He wrote a note on a sheet of paper. "The list"—he held up the sheet—"will keep track of everything."

Hailu watched him print in an awkward, childlike script. "When do I see the Colonel?"

The soldier smiled again. "You're eager?"

"I have work tomorrow morning." He paused for effect. "I'm a doctor."

"We know who you are."

Hailu closed his eyes and visualized each numeral, drew their characters on an imaginary blackboard.

"Follow me," the soldier said. He motioned to the long corridor.

THE CELL WAS the length of his dining room and nearly airless. It had a heavy door that was indistinguishable from the flat concrete wall. There was no window, only a low ceiling that cupped a lightbulb entwined in what looked like an iron web. The floor was just a continuation of the walls: smooth, polished, the color of dirty water. There was a plastic bucket in a corner. It was too cold to be barefoot, though he was, and the hardness made the arches of his feet ache. The cell felt like a coffin, a box created to hold the forgotten dead.

"Enjoy," the soldier said. "It's not as bad as it could be, you're lucky." He walked out carrying the extra clothes Hailu had been wearing, and left Hailu immobile in the center of the tiny room.

He stared at the lightbulb caught in the iron web, tried to find the edge of it, that point where dark gave way to bright. He strained to hear something, anything besides his beating heart. He listened so closely, and for so long, that the buzz of the bulb grew until it made his ears ring and shot slivers of pain through his head. Then the light suddenly vanished, shut off by an invisible hand somewhere outside his cell, and Hailu sat on his cot, blanketed in darkness.

BOOK THREE

42

THE NEWS OF HAILU'S SUMMONS had traveled like a current from open door to swinging window to shuttered blinds until routine morning greetings had dissolved into dead silence. No one had come yet to offer condolences to the family. They'd shut themselves away, suspicious and afraid that the next person betrayed might be them. Emama Seble sat next to Sara with her trusted horsetail fly swatter flicking from one leg to the other. At their feet, Tizita played marbles by herself.

"Sit up," Sara told her. Tizita sighed and straightened her shoulders.

Emama Seble glared in the direction of Shiferaw's house. "Tell him to petition for us. Hailu hasn't done anything." She pointed to the other homes. "They haven't come to see how you are?"

"People are scared," Sara said.

"Of what? It's them we should be scared of," the older woman said.

"Melaku's been here." Sara noted the brief pause before Emama Seble spoke.

"Any news?" Emama Seble nudged a rolling marble towards Tizita.

"He's asked some of the soldiers. They shut up when he mentions the Colonel." Sara reached down and pulled Tizita's shoulders straight.

"I can't play like that." Tizita shrugged off Sara's hands. "Where's Berhane?" she asked, settling herself against Emama Seble's chair.

"Do you miss him?" Emama Seble asked.

Tizita nodded. "Sofia said he's working. Can I work, too?"

Sara smiled. "You're in school."

"Is Abbaye working?" Tizita's bright eyes held on to Sara, she clenched large marbles in her hand and waited for the answer.

"Don't lie to her," Emama Seble said.

"Look," Sara said, holding Tizita's arm and pointing at her bracelet, "how can you miss him when you have this beautiful bracelet he gave you?"

"You know, don't you?" Emama Seble asked.

Tizita nodded. "He was packing his suitcase, that means he had to go to jail."

"You're right," Emama Seble said, "but he'll be back."

"Will Daddy have to go?"

"Let's go inside," Sara said. She wasn't sure how to explain what she still couldn't fully comprehend.

MICKEY'S TINY BOX of a house seemed even smaller than Dawit remembered. He and Yonas hunched on short wooden stools in the living room that also served as Mickey's bedroom. Mickey's mother, Tsehai, hovered over them, a thin woman with wrinkled arms and loose skin. She walked slightly bent, a hand resting on her waist when it wasn't flying into the air, punctuating her agitation.

"Mickey should be home soon, but these days, it's hard to say." She adjusted a neatly pressed khaki uniform that hung near the door. She wiped a speck of dust from her faded pink walls. "He's been given so much responsibility." Tsehai sat down, fidgeting in the silence. She scooped spoonfuls of vegetables, *misser*, and *shiro* on the large plate of *injera* in front of them. The flavorful lentils and crushed chickpeas filled the room with spiced scents.

"We haven't seen you in a long time." Yonas pushed the plate her way. "Please eat," he said.

There was a time when Tsehai visited regularly. As Mickey progressed in the military, she'd avoided all unnecessary contact with neighbors.

"Dawit, how's school?" she asked. "Mickey always wished he could have gone to university like you."

"Abbaye's in jail," Dawit said. "He was summoned."

Tsehai's face gave nothing away. She picked at her food with skeletal fingers.

"He's done nothing," Yonas said. "We don't know what the charges are, they won't tell us. At least if we can find that out—"

"I don't get involved in those things," Tsehai said.

"When will Mickey be home?" Dawit asked.

"I don't know." She watched them eat. "It's so hard to get good cabbage these days, isn't it?" she said, pointing to the vegetables.

"We need reasons, no one seems to have any." Dawit pushed the plate away. "I've had enough." He looked at the half-eaten plate. "I'm sure Mickey's position gets you plenty of vegetables. Don't you care about what he's paid to do?"

Tsehai muttered as she took the plate and walked towards the kitchen. She turned back suddenly. "My Habte died working in the fields. You think I wouldn't trade all these ration cards for his life back?" She stared at a faded photo on the wall. "You want reasons? You come here asking Habte's son for reasons?" She spat. "We're getting justice, finally." She stopped, biting her bottom lip

"We've had enough." Yonas stood and pulled Dawit up.

"I'm sorry. I didn't mean anything about your family," she said.

"We're leaving," Yonas said. They walked out.

MELAKU'S OLD, cracked radio sat on the ground next to his feet. The room was dark. "They take Radio Voice of the Gospel off the air and give us Radio Voice of Revolutionary Ethiopia. Communist lectures instead of American music. Didn't Marx enjoy himself once in a while?" he grumbled. He set a steaming cup of tea next to Dawit and lit a candle. "What does it matter anyway? No electricty again."

"She'll never tell Mickey we came," Dawit said, deep in thought.

"Probably not. That woman is very angry," Melaku said. "Has Mickey come home yet?"

Dawit shook his head. "I've been watching the house." He stirred his tea. "I would have made Abbaye stay."

"You know Hailu when he says something, that's the way it is," Melaku said. He dropped another sugar cube into Dawit's tea. "My last cube until I can get more. Enjoy it."

"What does he know about the way it is?"

Melaku smiled, the wrinkles creasing his eyes. He patted Dawit's arm. "I remember when your mother used to fight with him. She'd complain about the same thing. Your father's a strong man, stronger than you think," he said. "They would have come after you or your brother if he didn't report to jail."

"Let them come."

Melaku raised his palms to the sky. He rolled his eyes dramatically. "To be young and foolish again."

"I would have done something."

"With what, a slingshot?" Melaku asked.

"I'm not scared."

"Fools die unafraid." Melaku came in close, a hand on Dawit's shoulder. "And what makes you think you can do something better men haven't been able to do?"

Dawit shrugged off his hand. "I can."

Melaku let out a bitter laugh. "Are you better than the men born before you? Do you think the rest of us just sit by, sipping tea, while the people we love die? Melaku began to pace. "Is that what you think? That you're better than me, than the patriots who made sure this country didn't become Italian? You think you're stronger?"

"Sit down." Dawit patted the stool. "I didn't say that."

Melaku sat. "You don't know anything. Don't promise your life away so easily. You're like my son. I'm telling you this for your own good."

"What if something happens to him?" Dawit's chin quivered.

"They need doctors in the hospital. They need him, can't you see that?" Melaku asked, though his face, too, was drawn and worried.

43

"IT'S TOO BRIGHT, TURN OFF THE LIGHT," Sara said. "Why can't you just use the candle? You should be used to it."

Yonas held up his Bible. "The candle isn't enough. And who knows how long the electricity will be on. I want to read while we have it."

She moved across their small bedroom to the window and closed the curtains. "It's too much." She switched off the light. "I'll bring a bigger candle, I bought more today." She sighed in relief at the sudden darkness that descended into the room. It felt warm, and even the blasts of gunfire outside seemed to dim. "They've started early tonight," she said. The back-and-forth rattles shook the windows.

"Reading with a candle gives me a headache, you know that." Yonas switched the light back on. His eyes were bloodshot and he looked drawn. He had aged ten years in one week.

The crunch of tires, then a sharp horn broke into the room. Sara quickly shut off the light again. She grabbed a sweater and pulled it over her nightgown. "I'll get the candle," she said.

They hadn't talked about Hailu since his arrest. They'd fallen into a ritual of silent protests and unspoken tensions. Each time Sara tried to talk about his father, Yonas retreated into himself and answered her with a blank stare. Their interactions consisted of noting the absence of things: rain, visitors, their daughter's laughter, and now, light.

Yonas set the Bible on the table next to their bed. "Forget it. I'll go to the prayer room."

"You'll wake Tizzie, she insisted on sleeping in Abbaye's bed," Sara said.

"I'll bring her here," Yonas said. "I'll sleep in the other room."

"You don't want to come back?" she asked. "I have a hard time sleeping." She swallowed.

"I'll be back then." He made for the door, then paused. "You're scaring her." He turned to her. "She's scared at night now because of you."

"There's reason to be scared. They can make us do anything they want." She regretted her words when she saw him flinch.

"She's too young to understand," he said. "You should tell her that sleeping in Abbaye's room isn't going to make him come back faster. You should talk to her."

"Why can't you tell her yourself?" she said. "You don't talk to anyone anymore."

Yonas shut the door behind him without a word.

HOW MANY SECONDS? How many days? How many weeks? There was no marker in time, no night and day, nothing to help him shift from one minute to the next except those moments he shuffled his eight steps to urinate in the plastic bucket that had long since begun to overflow, then dry around the edges with his waste. It stunk of him in this cell, the worst parts of him: the fear and paranoia, the regret and loneliness, the uncontrollable tears that came unbidden and stopped just as suddenly. Did she feel like this? Hailu wondered. Did she feel her sleep guided only by the weight of her eyelids? Did her chest cave into her spine when she lay on her back? Did she ache, before the torture and the beatings, for pain as proof that she was human and living? Had her stomach, too, known this gluttonous gnawing that only the starving understood? Soon, soon, there will be nothing left of me, nothing except my sons, my Dawit—

How many days he'd been in the cramped cell, Hailu didn't know, but in that time he'd only eaten handfuls of dried bread. Urine-sprayed water served in a rusting can was in plentiful supply, however. The can was set just inside his door by a pair of hands he'd come to imagine as disconnected from a body, set on the floor with a silence so complete, so cushioned from any threat of noise, Hailu hummed to convince himself he hadn't grown deaf. But my eyes have flattened in this terrifying small room, they have been robbed of color and distance, shapes and textures. How it hurts to look at these corners and edges and find crisp lines bent and blurred.

He'd begun to forget the sound of his own voice, though he spoke to himself continuously.

"How long, Doctor?" he asked himself. "How long have I been here?"

And in his best professional voice, he'd reply, "Days. Weeks. Perhaps months. The body doesn't understand time the way we do."

"What does it understand, Doctor?"

"The body knows itself," he said.

"But it doesn't," he challenged. "How can it, when I can't hear myself?"

"Listen, listen, listen," he said. And he did, and he waited, and he heard nothing, not one sound that could hurl him out of this lightless well and into life.

THE HOUSE WAS located on the outskirts of the city. It sat behind an imposing stone wall peppered with shards of broken glass. Its manicured lawn was crowded with thick rosebushes and wild bunches of African lilies. Its windows gleamed in the sun. It was small, Dawit thought as he peeked from his crouched position in the backseat of Solomon's car, too small to be the headquarters of the Revolutionary Lion Resistance.

"Stay down until we get inside," Solomon said as he rolled up to the gate and flicked his headlights. "Listen to me for once," he added. Dawit ducked back to the floor when he heard the metal gate creak open, but he couldn't help peeking through a hole in the blanket that covered him.

"There's no one here," the *zebenya* said. He was slight with a delicately chiseled face, a mouth that dropped down on one end, and eyes that never stopped moving over the car. "Go away."

Solomon leaned out his window. "Engineer Ahmed is my uncle and it's his birthday. I have a small gift for him, from his sister, my mother."

"Which sister?" the *zebenya* asked.

"I'm the eldest son of his eldest sister."

The guard swung the gate open.

Once inside, Solomon turned to Dawit. "Be polite to Kidus, he guards us with his life."

Dawit could feel the old man's ink black eyes on his face. Kidus kept an Italian-era rifle tucked under one armpit. A former soldier, Dawit realized, a patriot from the Occupation. Kidus locked the gate, then sat with his hands on his knees, his old rifle next to him, his bare feet perfectly even. He stared at Dawit with intense suspicion.

"Here?" Dawit asked Solomon, pointing to the front door. He saw the guard give a subtle nod. The door opened.

INSIDE WERE PILES of clothes, blankets, dirty plastic bags, tired men of different ages hunched in groups of two or three, heads tipped in list-less conversation, bloodshot eyes that followed Dawit's every move as Solomon led him down the hallway.

Solomon paused to adjust a crooked charcoal sketch of two warriors with headdresses made of a lion's mane. "In there, third door," he said.

It was a bedroom with a plush bed and thick silk curtains. The wood floors were polished to a pristine shine and a cream wool rug lay in the middle of the room. A young man with a boyish face and open smile stepped out of the adjoining room.

"So Solomon says you're ready," he grinned.

"For what?" Solomon asked. "What I said is he's spoiled."

The man clapped Dawit on the shoulder and sent him tumbling into Solomon. His mouth still curved though his eyes were suddenly serious. "Spoiled?"

Solomon nodded. "He doesn't listen." Dawit felt a chill settle behind the man's pleasant demeanor.

"Sit down"—the man pointed to the floor. "Engineer Ahmed doesn't like us on the bed." He slid to the ground and folded his legs casually. "Who are you?" he asked. "What are you doing here?"

"I want to help," Dawit said.

The man shrugged. "So? Why should we trust you?"

"You can trust me." Dawit couldn't catch Solomon's eyes, he had his back turned observing a closed window.

The man smiled ruefully. "Would you tell us if we couldn't?"

Dawit had heard rumors about the leader of the Revolutionary Lion Resistance, that the man was large and forbidding, stern and ruthless. That he'd shot through a roadblock just a month ago help-ing a former judge and his family escape out of Addis Ababa. The city waited every week for more news about the leader they'd begun to call Anbessa, "lion."

The man frowned and Dawit saw lines around his mouth. He was older than he looked. "Why should I trust you?" he asked again.

Dawit stared down at his hands. "I believe this is a dictatorship, not a people's government. I believe in your fight."

The man burst out in laughter. "Our fight? Haven't you been reading *Addis Zemen*?"

"That's the government's newspaper," Dawit said.

"That's exactly why you should be reading it. How else would you know that we're all fighting the same fight? They've gone left, my friend." He chuckled. "They've jailed us, they're killing us, they've started dumping us like trash on the road, and now they've really done it, they're stealing our ideology. Can you imagine? Those bastards! Creating socialist advisory boards with some of my own former friends, trying to create a joint forum." He pulled out a cigarette. "We don't have a fight anymore, we're all saying the same things." He lit a match. "What the hell do you believe that's different from them?" The cigarette tip flared and darkened.

"My father's in jail." His declaration didn't stir the man.

"That's not a belief. Did you turn him in?"

Dawit flinched. "I'm not like that."

"How are you with blood?"

Dawit swallowed hard. "My father's a doctor."

Solomon and the man exchanged a brief nod. "Anbessa. Or at least that's what the people call me." He grinned wide and winked. "Guns?"

"I can learn." Dawit sat taller.

"He's not the type," Solomon said. "He can't do this."

Anbessa turned back to Dawit. "Who helped you get that girl's body out of the square?"

"No one," Dawit said, nervous in the face of Solomon's stare. "I made sure nobody knew."

"Start training him," Anbessa said to Solomon.

"He's good with organizing. I thought that's why we came," Solomon said. Solomon's eyes seemed to move over Dawit anew, reassess all the flaws and shortcomings that had frustrated him since they'd met.

Anbessa frowned, and it was in the flare of his nostrils and snapping eyes that Dawit saw a hint of the rage that might have razed a dozen soldiers at a roadblock. "We'll have new assignments soon."

"They're watching everyone. Especially students." Solomon threw an angry look at Dawit. "And he argued with a soldier after seeing that body."

"Have you looked in the living room?" Anbessa pointed towards the door. "There were forty more we couldn't save," he said. "Tomorrow, there will be more."

"He needs time," Solomon said.

"We've run out of time." Anbessa put an arm around Solomon. Solomon fell silent and Dawit could feel his resistance and resentment. "My friend, we're being cornered," Anbessa continued. "Plans have to change. You're too inflexible sometimes."

Anbessa took out another cigarette and turned to Dawit. He slipped it between his lips but didn't light it. "I have a good feeling about you."

"I won't let you down," Dawit said, feeling a deep loyalty already for the friendly-faced man. "I'm a fighter." And as he said it, he realized his father's arrest and Ililta's death made it easier for him to imagine himself shooting a gun and feeling no regret.

"Good," Anbessa said. "Until next time. God guide you, and us all."

Solomon led Dawit out of the bedroom and back into the living room. "Don't try to recognize anyone." Solomon ignored the thin men who watched them with flat eyes. "It'll never do you any good," he said before pulling Dawit outside.

44

Tᴀʜᴇ ɪɴsᴛᴀɴᴛ ᴛʜᴇ ᴏғғɪᴄᴇʀ sᴛᴇᴘᴘᴇᴅ ɪɴᴛᴏ his cell, the lights snapped on. Hailu sat up, blinking away blindness, and watched this large man come toward him. The officer approached his bed so quietly he thought for a moment that all sound had gone the way of the dark and fled with the closing door.

The officer was thick-boned and meaty. He wore a clean, formfitting military uniform with a red medal.

"Get up," he said, then came a startling clap like thunder breaking free of the sky. His hands were bulging knots of muscle and scarred flesh.

Hailu had no more time to think or begin counting before he was pulled from the bed. Rough palms kept him steady while he stumbled. His eyes watered from the light that flickered. It seemed brighter than before, brighter than any light he'd ever seen.

"It hurts," Hailu said. "Turn it off." Then he realized no sound had come from him.

"Stay alert," the officer said.

Hailu fell into the chair shoved behind his knees and did nothing when calloused palms slapped his cheeks hard once, twice, three times. Instead, he clung to the officer's broad shoulders without protest. He wondered where the scent of lemongrass was coming from. He wanted to pause all motion and try to remember where he'd stopped counting, pick up where he left off, feel the breeze from his cane field, touch Tizita's soft hand again, but everything was swaying and tumbling and only the strong shoulders of this angry man saved him from falling into oblivion. Somewhere in between the buzzing somersaults of his brain, Hailu saw a dash of sky-bright blue behind the officer and he knew if he could reach out and touch that color, he could bring Selam to him.

But then the questions started.

"Why did you kill the girl? Didn't you think we'd find out? Did you think you could lie?"

The sky went away and only words whirred above his head.

"Did you become a doctor so you could kill people?" The officer flashed a gold tooth and it glinted in the bright light. "Maybe you picked the wrong profession, Doctor," he said.

The officer didn't wait for a response. He pressed his elbow into the center of Hailu's chest, kept pressing, didn't stop, the same relentless pressure bearing down slowly, methodically. The pain bent him onto his knees.

"Dr. Hailu," the officer whispered into his ear, "who told you to poison the prisoner?" The officer knelt, sat him upright, and gave Hailu full view of a broken nose. "We know you. Patriot, father of two, widower. You trained in England, married your wife before you left, your first child was born while you were abroad. Your granddaughter Tizita will be entering her second year of school soon. You might not see that. What a pity." The nostrils flared, and Hailu couldn't hear the rest of the officer's words through the ringing in his ears. A sharp burn coursed through his back, set his spine on fire, shot embers into his head. His ribs grazed his legs, slender as twigs.

"Dawit told someone about what you did. Your own son betrayed you, and we can bring him in unless you tell us everything." The officer chuckled. "Father and son."

Hailu traced an image of Dawit's mouth whispering his name into an eager ear and pushed the picture aside. He didn't know his son sometimes, but he knew the man Dawit was growing into, and this man wouldn't betray anyone, not even him.

His head was clearing. The ringing was drifting into a sorrowful moan. He was starting to hear his own breaths. Hailu knew if he tried, he could summon the strength to speak, but he didn't trust his voice to float out of his throat so cleanly. Certain words would surely catch and clip inside his mouth; his son's name deserved more than that.

"The Colonel takes over after me. He's not going to be so gentle." The officer's eyes searched his furiously. "You only get this chance, right now."

"She was already dead," Hailu managed to say.

The officer's arms swung and he grunted from the force of each effort. Hailu tried his best to move away from the momentum of that solid fist, but the rough hand that gripped the back of his neck held him suspended in an agony that sent spasms down his back. He marveled, in the sliver of light that cut into his swollen eyes, about the wonder of an arm that could swing with such abandon and still maintain such perfect precision.

SOLOMON AND DAWIT were deep in the forests of Sululta, nearly thirty minutes out of Addis Ababa. Tall trees with tangled roots rose from rich, red soil and stretched to the sun. In the distance, the bray of cattle and a herder's shrill whistle bounced through densely clustered leaves.

Dawit shouldered an unloaded rifle, an old Beretta, its weight getting heavier by the minute. He aimed at a tree stump. The empty gun pushed a clipped, dull thud into the quiet valley. He inhaled the scent of eucalyptus and waited for more of Solomon's criticism.

"Guide the barrel with your eyes, rely on the sights," Solomon instructed. He jerked the barrel higher. "Don't you know where the trigger is without looking?" He chewed on a stick, working his jaws. "Forget it."

Dawit raised the rifle and aimed. "Let me try again," he said.

Solomon pushed the barrel down. "We've stayed too long and you've got other things to do. Let's go." He tapped on the gun. "This model has two safeties, don't forget. Lock them."

They didn't speak inside the car. Solomon turned on the radio and listened to news of the Derg's maneuvers against Somalia. As they got closer to the city, Solomon fished in his pocket for a crumpled slip of paper. He flattened it carefully on his leg, then tossed it to Dawit.

"Here," he said. "Anbessa wants you to start working. Read the paper, then tear it up. It's your location for the next few weeks." He held up a hand. "No questions yet. Just listen."

Dawit took the paper and opened it. It named a region and neighborhood of Addis Ababa: *Wereda* 12, *Kebele* 11. His own. His heart sank. He'd imagined moving in the shadows of night in clandestine operations far from anyplace he knew, hiding in secret homes and spending days and nights in underground locations surrounded by rugged, loyal compatriots. He'd never thought he'd be assigned to his own neighborhood.

"While we get ready for the big assignment, Anbessa thinks we need to work on new tactics of fighting. He likes what you did, picking up that body." Solomon sighed. "But we need a more efficient system than yours." He slowed for another car.

They were approaching Mercato, an area so congested and busy no one would notice Dawit getting out and going home. They pulled into an alley and sat in silence as a muezzin's chants rose from Anwar Mosque.

Solomon stared at a row of shoppers filing past stores. "The Derg started what it's calling the War of Annihilation a while ago. You know this. We've been fighting back. But now it thinks it can intimidate us and scare people by leaving those bodies all over the city. That can't happen. If we lose hope, we lose this war." Solomon's cigarette pulsed a bright red.

"I can do it," Dawit said. He wasn't afraid of carrying one of those bodies, he was horrified by the thought of finding his father amongst the decaying. He shivered.

"It's simple, but those are the hardest plans sometimes. Look for bodies, start before curfew. Take them to a location you'll need to find. Have someone who knows people help with identifying and contacting the families. This means you need help, one or two others. No job should ever have more than three." Solomon exhaled long and hard. He shook fiery bits of ash out the window. "Start before curfew, get done before curfew. Break as few rules as possible." Smoke floated up and hung in Dawit's face before Solomon flicked the cigarette out. "You'll start when I give word." He motioned for Dawit to get out. "Don't do anything foolish."

The Derg used the forest near his house as its execution ground; he'd avoided it as much as he could. It was close to the new jail, and in that new jail was his father. He stepped out of the car and nearly stumbled, his legs weak.

Dawit leaned into the car for support and saw Solomon watching him closely. "What about target practice . . . ?" he asked, simply looking for something to say.

"Soon. You need something not so old, anyway. We still have to continue," Solomon said. He paused and looked at him. "Can you handle this?"

Dawit nodded. He imagined driving past that dark forest at night and coming across his father waiting on the roadside for him, barely standing, somehow managing.

NOW I KNOW it is not dark at all. There is moonlight that refracts from the sun and brings order to the sea. Here sunlight blooms. I have no need for bones and cartilage, blood and breath. I can forget. Hailu swung on a pendulum. I know now that time sinks to the bottom of the sea and rises again in curves. My reflection is only an illusion, only flesh and water manifest in a drop of moonlight that shudders at what it sees on this dead land I once called my home. Hailu didn't know how long he'd been unconscious. His face was bruised, his eyes swollen, the room dark and quiet once again. It took several moments for the ringing in his ears to subside, and it was only then that he heard the moan. The girl had returned and she was bleeding in the center of his cell. She raised a hand towards him. Would he do it all over again? Then once more there was nothing but the ringing in his ears, then the slide into the belly of unconsciousness.

45

MELAKU WAS RESOLUTE AND FIRM. "You know I'll help," he said to Dawit. He ran a cloth across a dusty shelf. "I know all the families in this neighborhood. At least the women," he said, winking.

The transformation in Melaku had been gradual as he'd explained the mission, but Dawit saw it now in its entirety: his thin frame stood taller, the wrinkles around his eyes had flattened and smoothed, his movements were as crisp as a dancer's.

"Anything for my country," Melaku said softly.

Dawit felt such a rush of affection for the old man that he had to stop himself from hugging him. "It'll be dangerous," he said.

"You've said that already," Melaku said. "Living is dangerous these days."

Dawit saw Melaku drift into a long silence. "I need to get one more person," he said.

"Sara," Melaku said immediately. "Is there even a question?"

Dawit shook his head. "There's Yonas," he said.

"She's the best option," Melaku said. "She's a housewife, and in their eyes, a simple woman." He smiled. "Though we know otherwise."

"If she tells him, he'll stop us," Dawit said. "I want Lily."

"Do you think Sara would have married the man you think your brother is?" Melaku stared at him. "Your family is your most loyal ally."

"We can't have a country full of people like Yonas," Dawit said.

"Or full of people like you," Melaku said. "A government of fighters won't know how to lead, only create more war. You think bravery is measured in resistance."

"My father's in jail because he took him there," Dawit said, feeling hot tears rush to his eyes. He bit his lip and turned away.

"You're upset because you weren't the one to take him, and you know it. Enough of this. You're wearing out my patience." He straightened a few matchboxes on the dwindling shelf. "Talk to Sara."

—

LILY MET HIM at Melaku's kiosk. Her hair had grown, her curls now grazed her chin. "What's wrong?" she asked. "Why are we meeting here?"

"Come inside," Melaku said, opening the side door. "Soldiers walk by here all the time." He closed the door behind them.

"Is the *kebele* store in this area getting as big as the one in mine?" Lily asked. She leaned out the window as she glanced down the road. "They're organizing them well."

"Get back." Melaku patted a stool next to Dawit. "They get their eggs and milk from the same farmers I used to, what's there to organize?" He dusted off his counter with careful hands. "They've taken over everything."

Lily glowed, earnest and excited. "This new system of distribution is the best solution, everyone has what they need, no more and no less. Capitalist methods only exploit the weak."

"Solution? This is nothing but control." Melaku laughed. He looked at Dawit. "Even the Russians are asking me to get them things. The day Communists stop wanting their American jeans, then we can talk about exploitation."

Lily continued as if she hadn't heard him. "I talked to villagers last week to write a report on medical clinics. They need to learn about hygiene and vaccinations," she said, lost in the heat of her enthusiasm. "They need more than food, but we build these changes in small steps. I finally learned that after being a *zemecha*." She smiled at Dawit, then grew serious again. "All of us need to contribute what we can. They give produce, we provide other resources." She sat back, pleased.

Dawit had seen Lily caught up in her convictions before. She focused on nothing else but the goal. "The Derg is the one exploiting," he said, speaking slowly. "They use the emperor as an excuse to take away our freedoms and rights—"

Lily interrupted him with a hand on his leg. "Can't you see that we have to work with the government, use our leverage to educate them on true socialist policies? It doesn't happen fighting them." She avoided Dawit's glare and turned to Melaku. "Already a few forums have gotten concessions and we're establishing a joint committee."

"We?" Dawit asked. He moved so her hand slid off his leg. "What do you mean?"

"Committees can go to hell," Melaku said. "This government sets up committees for everything. Soon there'll be a Derg committee to teach us how to wipe our backsides the socialist way."

There had been a time in the early days of the revolution when Dawit had known what to expect from Lily. The person that was emerging after her work as a *zemecha* and her meetings with her *kebele* officer was someone more prone to government rhetoric. He suddenly realized the foolishness of his plans to ask for her help. They'd seen less and less of each other in the last few months, she'd become more withdrawn.

"Does this have something to do with your scholarship to Cuba?" he asked. He saw her grimace, then grip her hands together.

"I don't know if I'll get it," she said.

"So you have to prove your dedication to them." Melaku polished the counter with a corner of his shirt, his back to them.

"It means I have to study hard," Lily said.

Melaku shifted some boxes from the floor to the counter. "I have to do some work." The silence stretched into tension.

"We'll leave," Dawit said.

Lily sat rigidly in the center of the room. "I'll know about Cuba next week," she said, turning to Dawit. "I'm a finalist."

"Good luck," Dawit said.

"You know I deserve it," she said, refusing to stand up even though he was already at the door.

"Do you think those bodies you see on your way to your precious school deserved it? This government doesn't give anyone what they deserve." Dawit felt the first jolt of a heart being stunned into a new kind of submission. "Let's go so Melaku can do his work." He held out his hand. Tenderness for her was fighting its way past his anger.

She stood, clasping her hands together. "I have to go anyway," she said. "I have a meeting." She didn't let her gaze stray from his face, and Dawit saw there, too, her love for him. "Come with me."

A loud clatter made them jump. Rows of tin cans had fallen to the ground. Melaku grumbled as he picked them up. "Get out of here, both of you," he said. He stood, cans in his arms, and nodded to Dawit. "Go home."

Outside, near his father's car, they stared at each other with the awkwardness of young lovers.

"Every day I drive, I think one of those bodies could be my father," he told her, aching for their familiar intimacy, trying to force it into this strange moment between them.

"And every day, has it been?" she asked. "They're systematic. There haven't been that many bodies. If we work with them, we're safe." She touched his arm, let a finger trail under his sleeve and caress bare skin. "They're not hurting your father. They need his expertise."

"How do you know?" She seemed so sure, her gaze into his eyes held none of the uncertainty that sent quakes through his world.

"I work with the people making policies. They're human, just like you and me. They have families. They believe in a better Ethiopia."

"How can you say that? Who do you think is killing so many of us, then? Don't you hear about the same executions that I do? Do you know how many students are in jail?"

She dropped her head, chewed on her full bottom lip. "They're not innocent, Dawit." She tried to touch him again, but he moved away. She let her hand drop. "Sacrifices need to be made sometimes, change always causes pain." She looked deep and steady into his eyes, into him. "It's not easy."

Dawit found himself caught in the reflective gaze of a complete stranger. He looked away and got in the car and drove home.

NEITHER BROTHER SPOKE at the dining table, they had not talked to each other in days, their conversations dwindling to stares as one week without their father turned into another, and days continued to pile upon days.

"Emama Seble brought some eggs for us," Sara said. She sat between them. "She says Shiferaw's trying to nationalize her hen."

Tizita kept her face close to her plate as she picked at her food. The little girl had grown noticeably thinner since Hailu's arrest.

"Eat," Sara said. "You didn't eat your lunch today." She spoke to

Dawit. "Melaku's been struggling, he doesn't want to say it. The rations are getting smaller. No one's selling him food."

Dawit pushed away from the table. "I'm full." He carried his plate to the kitchen and left them at the table.

Sara looked at Yonas. "Go talk to him."

"He doesn't want to talk to me. You should go." Yonas patted Tizita's head. "Did you do your schoolwork?"

Tizita nodded.

Dawit was in the kitchen leaning against the wall when Sara walked in. His eyes were closed.

"He's coming home," Sara said. "I promise you. He's alive and he's coming home." She put her arms around him and held him tight. She rubbed his back in wide circles, the same way she comforted Tizita. "He's a strong man."

Dawit stepped out of her embrace. "I can't look at him anymore without wanting to hit him. The longer Abbaye stays in jail . . ." He stopped and put his hands on her shoulders. "He shouldn't have taken him to the jail, he should have asked me for help. We could have done something to help him. How can you forgive someone who does that?" His eyes, dark and confused, sank into Sara's and held on. "How did you forgive him for letting Tizita fall?"

"You're not being fair. Those are two different things. One was an accident."

"And the other he could control, right?" Dawit said. "If he could control some part of it, why couldn't he do the right thing?" He reached to hold her close, the awkwardness of his gesture sending her backwards into the dimly lit kitchen.

"You're twisting things." She held his arms to his side. "What's wrong with you today? How do you know you could have made Abbaye stay?"

"Am I?" he asked. "How can you love someone who does the complete opposite of what you would do?"

"What's going on?"

"Lily's gone." Sara's supple and lean figure was silhouetted against the soft light from the dining room. He dropped his gaze.

"What do you mean? Did she get the scholarship?" Sara asked.

He sunk to the ground. "She's left me." Tears ran into the corner of his mouth and he licked them away, sniffing loudly, a small boy again.

Sara sat facing him, a comforting hand on his knee. "I'm so sorry." She handed him a handkerchief.

"Emaye was right. Lily was never going to marry me," he said, blowing his nose.

"Lily believed she was going to marry you. I think she changed. It's these times, everyone's changing." She lowered her eyes to her hands. "You can't help it."

"But you haven't changed. Even Yonas"—he let out a bitter laugh—"even my older brother is still the same. I thought I knew her."

"You did know her, you still know her. This revolution." Sara shook her head. "It's turning everything upside down."

"She's going to Cuba. As soon as she gets her scholarship she's leaving." He wrapped his arms around his knees. "Even if I didn't see her, it was enough to know I would soon. Now . . ."

Sara hugged him and held him tight. "I'm sorry."

He clung to her, leaning into her so heavily that it nearly tipped her over. His hand found the back of her head and he turned her face towards him. He looked into her eyes and without a word touched his lips to her cheek, then pressed, and Sara let him. She didn't resist when he took her chin and raised her mouth to his.

She pushed him away. "You're not thinking right." She smoothed her hair and wiped her mouth with the back of her hand before walking out and leaving him alone.

46

Y ONAS STEERED THE CAR TOWARDS THE edge of the road and raked over the faces of pedestrians staring back at him in confused fear. This slowing down and looking had become a habit, starting the moment he woke up, when he waited for the familiar sound of his father's footsteps and resigned himself once again to the silence of another cold morning. He felt Hailu's absence in the radio that was no longer turned on, in the straight-backed blue chair no one ever used anymore, in the blanketed emptiness of his parents' bed, in the unbearable tension sitting between himself and his brother.

He'd gone to church today to ask forgiveness again for being the son he was and the man he'd grown into. He'd shut his eyes in prayer and tried to push away the image of his mother throwing her pills away. He felt renewed shame remembering her confidence in his obedience. She had been right. Despite the suffering he knew his mother's illness was causing his father, Yonas had never said a word about the skipped medication. If he'd only resisted his father's instructions, if he'd just done what he really wanted to do and gone to Dawit's room to wake him up, his father might be safe.

He eased the car next to Melaku's kiosk and barely had a chance to knock before Melaku opened the door.

The old man was abrupt. "No. Not again. Go home to your wife and daughter, they need you more than I do." He began closing the door. "Stop coming here so much."

"Sara's cooking. Tizita's pretending to sleep," Yonas replied. "That girl never sleeps anymore." He stopped the door with his foot. "I wanted to see how business was."

"Couldn't be better. The Russians discovered my *arake* is better than vodka," Melaku said. He held out two eggs. "This is all I have. Take them home. You've been spending too much time here," he repeated. "Both you and your brother should leave me alone and talk to each other."

"Please," Yonas said.

Melaku stepped aside and sighed.

Yonas sat down and folded his hands on his knees. "Tizzie keeps asking about Abbaye."

Melaku nodded. "You're losing weight, and you look tired."

"I'm fine," Yonas said. He waited.

"We're not going to talk about the same things over and over again," Melaku said. "I have a conversation with your brother, then the same one with you. I'm fed up," he said, smiling. "We're not doing anything for your father by worrying like this right now. You pray and take care of your family. If I hear something, I'll tell you." He sighed. "Same things I told your brother. Now, help me talk about something new."

Yonas returned his smile and looked around. "Can I open them?" he asked, pointing to the shutters.

"Not yet," Melaku said, checking that they were latched. "Seble comes here early and complains that I have no food." He shook his head. "She should go buy from the *kebele* store instead of harassing me."

Yonas laughed softly. "She's hiding her hen," he said. "Shiferaw is trying to nationalize it, I think just out of spite."

"God help him if he does," Melaku said.

"She asks how you are sometimes." Yonas watched the old man's face flush underneath his weathered skin.

"That woman needs to stop her meddling."

"She's just concerned." He stole a sideways glance at the old man and nudged him. "Has Emama Seble always worn all black?"

"She still doesn't wear all black." Melaku grinned.

BERHANE RAN INTO SOFIA'S arms and clung to her. "I saw it. I saw it," he said, pointing past the dusk-lit shanties to the long thin road. "It was like this"—he arched his back in a painful bend, nearly tipping over. In his eyes, a manic wildness that made Sofia nervous.

"What are you talking about?" she asked.

"I saw a body. It was like this," he repeated. Sofia stopped him from another back bend. "It was dead," he said.

"Where? Where were you?" she asked.

"Near the lion, it was a girl and she was tied." He licked his lips. "But

I wasn't scared. I looked at her." He smiled the excited smile of a new discovery. "Her eyes were open."

Sofia shook him. "What are you talking about?" Her mind struggled to connect one frightened thought to the other. Her little boy had seen one of those bodies, one of those she'd only started hearing about recently.

Robel came up behind her, worried. "I didn't know he saw, I was trying to find him."

"You have to watch him," she said. "You're the elder brother." She turned to Berhane. "You have to work somewhere else. You can't go back there." She shook Robel though she didn't need to. "Move to Peacock Café, they have a big parking lot and it's busy." She lifted Berhane's chin. "You have to run the other way if you see something like that again. It's bad for you to see it."

"Okay," he said.

"Peacock Café is far." Robel held his hand. "I'll keep him near me. We make good money near the school."

"I'll give you bus money. You're moving starting tomorrow," she said, her decision final.

BERHANE'S STOMACH WAS full from too much tea and bread, round as a moon and satisfied. And because Robel wasn't there to tell him to stop, he puffed his stomach out even more and walked with his legs angled outwards, the way he'd seen the fattest, richest men do. Peacock Café was bustling, and he liked walking by the parked cars in the lot and looking at his reflection. He made a face at his misshapen self on one door and giggled.

"Today's news!" he called out. "Get today's news!"

A hand shot out of a black car with mud splattered above the tires. "Here!"

The shiny black car honked and he sped up and exchanged a newspaper for coins. Peacock Café was full of patrons taking their afternoon tea and Berhane prepared himself for another pocketful of heavy, clinking coins.

"You! Over here!" another customer called out.

Berhane approached the small car slowly; the man's hands shook. His mother said only people with shame in their hearts had shaking hands.

"Ten cents," Berhane said. He squinted so the smoke from the man's cigarette wouldn't get in his eyes.

The man took the paper, slipped a note inside the front page, then handed it back to Berhane. "Give this note and the paper to my friend over there." He pointed to a car three spaces over. "Don't tell him it's from me," the man said. "He'll know already."

He dropped one *birr* in Berhane's hand. The bill nearly flew away in the wind before Berhane clenched his hand.

"It's too much"—Berhane began to hand him change—"I just need two coins."

"Keep it, for candy." He smiled and Berhane noticed his teeth were perfectly straight and small.

"I like your teeth," he said to the man.

"Then buy milk." He put another coin in Berhane's hand and smiled.

Berhane made his way to the man's friend. "Here," Berhane said to the small man bent over his cup of tea. "From your friend."

"Eh?" The man waved him away with a bony hand. "I didn't call for you." He sipped his tea delicately and pretended Berhane wasn't standing there.

"Your friend said for you to take this note and this." Berhane handed him the newspaper, the note on top.

"What man?" The man began to roll up his window. "Where?" The tray attached to his window tipped, his teacup slid to one side of the tray.

"He's gone," Berhane said, confused. "Don't you want the paper?"

"Go away!" the man exclaimed. "Get away from me!" Berhane saw his forehead was peppered with sweat.

"But he paid me already," Berhane said. He tried again to give the paper to the man.

The man started backing his car up, ignoring the tray tilting on his open window and the teacup that crashed to the ground. The car jerked as he spun his steering wheel. "Go away! Get away!" he cried.

Berhane heard a loud crack above him, then saw a bullet drill its shape into the windshield. There was the burning smell of smoke. The man slumped over and the car horn blared and died. Berhane stood on tiptoes to see the man and saw blood dripping on the car seat from his head.

"Are you hurt?" he asked, but his voice sounded too far away for anyone to hear. It wasn't until his ears stopped ringing and his eyes started watering that Berhane saw soldiers running towards the car, their guns drawn and aimed at him. He dropped his papers and slowly raised his hands the way he'd once seen a man do in the streets when soldiers surrounded him.

"Move! He's been shot!" the soldiers yelled. They brushed him aside. One pointed to a building nearby. "It came from that way. The balcony."

Berhane stepped away from the cluster of military uniforms and heavy boots and ran down the street to find his brother. It wasn't until he nearly collided with Robel that he saw he was still holding the note the other man had given him. The jingle of coins against his leg slowed as he stopped to hug his brother.

"I was coming for you. What happened?" Robel asked.

"A man was shot, the other man's friend, and I couldn't give him this note." Berhane pushed the piece of paper into his brother's hand. "He didn't want it."

Robel shoved the note in his pocket and pulled Berhane down the street. They made their way through the throngs of people who'd begun to crowd the parking lot and whisper through cupped palms.

They made their way to another café and sat behind the building on the steps. Robel hugged Berhane. "Don't be scared. Are you okay?"

"The other man gave me paper money for milk," Berhane said, talking fast. "He had nice teeth."

"Did anyone see you with the note?" Robel asked.

Berhane shook his head. "The man didn't give me his name, and the other man was really scared and the bullet went like this into the window and he fell like this." Berhane pantomimed and then tipped over, his eyes rolled into the back of his head.

Robel unfolded the paper. "I'll get you a sandwich," he said. "Don't tell Emaye anything about this." Robel scrunched his face as he read.

"What's it say?" Berhane asked. He took the note from Robel and held it close to his face.

Robel stared at the paper in Berhane's hands for a long time, then finally read it aloud to his brother. "The essence of our existence is the destruction of the Derg."

47

DAWIT DRANK TEA IN THE DINING ROOM and read the morning's headlines in *Addis Zemen*. A mid-level government official had been gunned down. No witness had come forward to identify the gunman. Major Guddu, the newspaper reported, was taking a personal interest in this latest assassination of one of his most beloved comrades and would not stop until the killer was found. Sincere condolences were sent to the wife and children of the deceased on behalf of all revolutionary Ethiopia. Investigations would begin immediately and any who witnessed the crime were urged to come forward. High schools and the university were closed until further notice.

"Did you read what happened?"

Dawit looked up to find Yonas carrying a book bag overflowing with papers under his arm. His normally close-cropped hair now curled sloppily and uncut around his ears, his eyes were ringed in dark circles. More and more, Dawit caught his brother staring off into the distance, his jaw slack in a look of stunned defeat.

"Schools are closed," Dawit said. "Why the bag?"

"I'm going to try to get into my office and do some work. They'll be looking everywhere for the shooter, you know that, don't you? They think whoever did it is part of an underground group, something student-led." Yonas searched Dawit's face.

"You think I know something?" Dawit looked past his brother to the living room. The curtains were closed tight, like they'd been since his father's arrest.

"Maybe," Yonas said, glancing at the front-page headlines. "Why else would you be reading *Addis Zemen*? Why would you care what the Derg is saying about this?"

"And if I did know?" Dawit flipped over the newspaper. "What do you want me to do, turn myself in? Maybe I'll ask you to drive me," he said.

His older brother took a deep breath and spoke slowly, as if to a child. "He knew which one of us would do what was necessary, no matter how hard it was." He cleared his throat. "You're too selfish and irresponsible."

"You're as obedient as a trained dog." Dawit knocked the bag out of his arm and strode out, leaving Yonas to pick up the papers.

HAILU TRIED TO focus on the arm dangling a long chain and hand-cuffs in front of him, but his vision blurred. The borders of his bed bled into the hazy outline of the officer's shoes. Straight lines undulated like coiling snakes. All sharpness was gone in the world, his body noth-ing but bruised bones and swollen flesh. His mouth tasted of iron, his tongue was coated with a thick, sour film. No matter which direction he pivoted his head, pain lodged even deeper into his neck.

The officer's voice spilled over him laced with static. Hailu cupped a hand to his ear and leaned forward.

"I don't think you're any match for the Colonel, even if you do bring people back to life," the officer said. "Hold out your hands." He snapped the handcuffs on.

Hailu's ankles were shoved together and cuffed. His hands and legs were attached to a heavy silver chain. His bones felt as if they'd slide out of socket trying to drag the chain around. He wanted to sit down on the bed but the officer kicked him in the back and sent him tumbling to the floor. His teeth smashed together as loudly as the handcuffs that hit the concrete.

The officer laughed. "Get up."

Hailu staggered to his feet and kept his head bent, waiting for orders. He had no energy to prepare for what lay ahead.

"Walk to the door. Keep your eyes on your feet." The officer shook the chain like a leash. "Come on," he said, opening the door.

The soft, swaying lines in Hailu's world spun in the gust of clean air just beyond his cell. He leaned into the space untainted by dried piss and shit.

"To the left," the officer said, prodding him from behind. "Eyes low."

There was no sign of life on either side of the corridor, only the same never-ending expanse of concrete that was in his cell. There were three other cells down that hallway, and no sound or hint of light seeped through the thick doors. There was a finality about those locked rooms that nearly buckled Hailu's knees.

The last room to the left was larger than the rest, its door as thick and impenetrable as marble. A dim thread of light laced out from a crack at the bottom of the door and came to rest at Hailu's feet. The officer cleared his throat and waited.

The door opened quietly. The officer pulled him by the chain, then laid it so gently on the ground it didn't make a noise. It took several seconds for Hailu's eyes to adjust to the lighting. It was a soft, golden glow.

The Colonel sat at a spotless desk. Polished medals hung in neat rows from his military uniform. His face was expressionless. A thick scar ran along his hairline. Hailu felt the man's grim interest, his simmering anger, those small eyes drilling a hole into him. He kept his attention on his chain, worked his tongue and throat to loosen his voice.

The Colonel nodded to the officer, and a guard so unobtrusive Hailu hadn't noticed him escorted the officer out. "Sit down," he said to Hailu, pointing to a metal chair.

It was suddenly harder to breathe. Hailu sat down and felt the chair give way under his full weight.

"This jail is the pride of the state, clean and efficiently run. We don't waste any unnecessary energy." The eyes again—calculating and memorizing Hailu's features in quick strokes. The Colonel continued. "I fought in the war with your youngest uncle, he was a good friend of mine, a true fighter." He stared at Hailu. "I see the resemblance."

Hailu's uncle was known for his ruthlessness in the war against Italy. It was said that he shot any of his men who flinched when ordered to charge Mussolini's front lines. Those who fought in his regiment had been no different in their distaste for weakness.

"You don't have to talk." The Colonel unfolded a crisp handkerchief on the desk, following the creases with the long nail on his little finger. "But you will want to soon." His tight smile belied his words. Hailu sensed his impatience. The Colonel slid his chair closer to the desk and leaned forward. "You killed a young girl. The girl came in alive," he said, wiping his mouth with his handkerchief. "She left dead."

Hailu thought of Selam and his sons and wondered how much Tizita had grown in the last few weeks.

"Pay attention," the Colonel said, his voice louder. His hands were interlaced, gripped tightly. "You remember her, Dr. Hailu?"

Hailu sensed this man knew all the answers to anything he could ever ask.

"Do you remember her, Doctor?"

Hailu nodded. He smelled her again, that nauseating stench of flesh burned by electricity. Hailu wanted to go back to his cell, to the familiarity of his waste and his smell and get out of this warm, soft light.

The Colonel waited, hands clutched together. Then he stood up.

"Let's start from the beginning," the Colonel said. He paced in front of him, in steps cut to fit the room's dimensions. "She came in alive, she was improving, and then she was dead. You killed her." He bent over Hailu, his eyes cold, his voice tight. "She was sixteen." His face twisted. "Why did you do it?"

His control frightened Hailu more than the officer's unhinged anger. "She was already dead," Hailu said. He wondered if the Colonel caught the whimper that escaped from his lips. "She was already finished." Then he braced himself for the assault this truth generally brought.

"How could you think that?" The Colonel walked behind him. Hailu tried to turn, but he held him still with a sharp twist of his ear. "She was a special prisoner," the Colonel said. "You were told that. There shouldn't have been any doubt. No doubts at all. I leave clear instructions so there is never any doubt about what I want done." The Colonel's breath fanned his cheek. "I do this because most people are ignorant and lazy. What part didn't you understand?"

"I tried to save her," Hailu said.

The Colonel's moist hand wrapped around his neck, a thumb pressed on his jugular vein. Tiny bones bent from the increasing pressure. He squeezed harder. I will feel light-headed, there will be pain, but I won't die, Hailu reminded himself.

"Your nurse has already confessed. She told us everything." The mention of Almaz forced him upright. The Colonel moved in front of him and sat again on his desk. His hands were elegantly draped over one slim knee. "It wasn't difficult. We already had her daughter. What do you know about these stupid children who pass out pamphlets and play their little rebellious games?" he asked, looking up at the ceiling.

Hailu couldn't breathe.

The punch came so fast Hailu had no time to brace himself. It knocked him backwards and nearly tipped him over. The pain was dull, his body by now accustomed to the blows, but the leaden weight of the hit wouldn't leave him. He struggled to get up off the ground with his chains.

The Colonel took it all in, as calm as ever. "Your loyal nurse," he said, smiling, "told us you ordered her to help you, that you'd fire her if she didn't. It was your idea to steal the poison from the hospital." He took his handkerchief and wiped each fingernail. "Is this true?"

"Where is she?" Hailu asked, sliding back onto the chair and trying to avoid falling sideways. What pain did they subject her to for her to lie like that? Hailu's head ached, thoughts stalled, he looked up. The light in the room suddenly flared so bright his eyes watered. Selam laughed, her laughter like the chime of a thousand bells.

"Tell me what she was like when they brought her in." The Colonel was standing again, walking back and forth in a military stride, his eyes straight ahead. "The soldiers watching her have died in the line of duty. She was buried before we knew what happened. So we're depending on you. Tell me what she looked like. Tell me everything she said."

The Colonel put both hands on his shoulders. Sharp fingers dug into tender nerves. Hailu tried to move to prevent the nerve damage he knew was slowly crawling into him. The Colonel pressed harder.

"Let me go home," Hailu said. "My family."

"You want to go home," the Colonel said, laughing a laugh that held no warmth. "What are we without our family, Dr. Hailu?" he asked. "What are we but shells?"

"She was so sick," Hailu said, and wondered if the Colonel could hear him. "She was so small," he added, and heard nothing but his own breaths.

"Start talking and I'll stop," the Colonel said, squeezing all the air out of Hailu's lungs. "Let me show you how it's done." The Colonel told him Yonas's class schedule, his office room number, and the café where he bought tea.

Hailu spoke. He told the Colonel of the girl and her flowered shirt, her perfect eyebrows and stylish trousers. He talked until he realized there was nothing coming from him but moans, and Hailu learned that Dawit had quit coming to the jail to ask about him, that no one came anymore. As Hailu sank gratefully into a pillow of black, the Colonel told him things Dawit said, things about a father and an older brother too cowardly to resist the regime.

Hailu gave up and looked for Selam, but Selam was gone. He curled up in the dark, wondering how Selam could have left him, and why she'd taken the sky with her.

48

A LOUD KNOCK POUNDED ITS WAY through their quiet living room. An angry voice demanded to be let in. Sara had no time to think about anything but getting Tizita upstairs.

"Go! Go!" she screamed at the startled girl.

Yonas jumped up from the sofa and ran to the door. Ethiopian Television reported the nightly news:

> *After three more assassinations of our comrades this week, house-to-house searches are under way to rid Ethiopia of reactionary enemies. The Derg condemns the so-called Revolutionary Lion Resistance as an agent of subversion and counterrevolution. The War of Annihilation will destroy all enemies and free Ethiopia of bourgeois oppressors.*

The television cut to the inside of a classroom, where several bodies dangled from ropes.

"What is it?" he called out.

"Don't open it!" Sara shouted. "Not yet." She yanked Tizita towards the stairwell. "Go!"

The door was kicked open. A group of three soldiers with rifles aimed at Yonas and Sara strode into the living room.

"We have nothing! There's nothing here!" Yonas said. He moved to hold Sara and froze when the rifles all pointed in his direction. "There's nothing here," he said calmly, raising both hands in the air. "Sara, come here." He dropped his arms as Sara stood next to him. "We've nothing to hide. Please, go look. Everything's upstairs, we've nothing to hide." He spoke in a near whisper and put himself between the rifle and his terrified wife.

Two of the soldiers raced through the living room while one soldier remained, his gun still trained on Yonas and Sara.

"Tizita," Sara said. She rushed towards the two soldiers making their way up the steps. "Tizzie!"

"She's our little girl, she's upstairs," Yonas said to the nervous soldier, his voice even and soft. "My wife is going to get her and bring her here. That's all."

Upstairs, Tizita's wails broke above the gallop of heavy boots. "Emaye!"

"Tizzie, stay there. I'm coming," Sara called, trying to push past a soldier. "I have to get her," she said. "Let me through. I don't care what you take. She's only a child! Move!"

"Emaye!"

"Tizita, don't move, stay there. Close your eyes, don't look at anything." Sara squeezed into her bedroom and clung to her daughter.

IN HIS ROOM, Dawit sat in his closet, waiting for the door to burst open. He'd pushed his notebook and a stack of papers under the bed though they contained nothing but homework. He knew he should get up, open the door, and walk out into the living room to stand by his brother and Sara. He understood that the man he wanted to be would have done that without hesitation. He could hear shouts, Tizita's cries, Sara's angry tone with soldiers. But nothing came from his brother, and he knew that on this night, he would have to share the blame for that shameful silence.

ADDIS ABABA WAS buried in dark clouds of gun smoke. Waves of arrests swept swiftly through the city. Bullets fell like rain. Blood flowed in currents. Winds blew the rotten stench of the dead through deserted streets. Dotting the surrounding highlands and marching steadily into frightened neighborhoods, the Derg's urban militia gathered more members, hefted Soviet rifles on their shoulders, and swarmed the city.

Snipers and firing squads worked relentlessly. A pulsing, steady rhythm bore down on the stunned city while on a narrow patch of barren land, moonlight closed around a pregnant woman pleading at the foot of a man with stones for eyes and a plunging bayoneted rifle in his hand.

49

ERHANE HELD AN EMPTY FANTA BOTTLE to his lips and blew into the top. He grinned and bowed to an imaginary audience. "Thank you, thank you," he said. His newspapers were stacked against the tire of an empty car at Peacock Café. It was a slow day. No one wanted to buy newspapers. Berhane, bored, played in the vast parking lot while Robel shined shoes two blocks away. The sun poured over his head.

"You." The soldier was short and chewed on a stick. He pointed at Berhane with a crooked finger. "Come here."

Berhane straightened. The grin turned into a nervous smile. "Me?"

The soldier grabbed him by the shoulders. He slapped him hard across the back of his head. Berhane winced and let out a sharp cry.

"Shut up," the soldier ordered. "I told you to come here." The soldier led him to a corner where there were no cars. "Do you work here every day?"

Berhane nodded.

"What did you see when you were working here and that man got shot?" the soldier asked.

"Nothing," he mumbled.

The soldier slapped him. "What did you see the day the man got shot?"

"I don't know. Nothing," Berhane said, cringing from the next slap he knew was coming.

The soldier hit him across each cheek, harder this time. "You want me to keep hitting you?" he asked.

"No," Berhane said, starting to cry, tears mixing with snot. He looked for Robel; he was all alone.

"Then tell me what you saw and I'll leave you alone." The soldier looked around. "If you don't tell me, more of my friends will come and they're very mean."

Berhane nodded, wiping his nose with the back of his hand. He saw traces of blood. He could feel his knees shaking.

"The bullet went like this," Berhane said, moving his hand in an arc. "It went into the car and hit the man and the man died. The soldiers came." He braced for another hit.

"Who shot him?"

Berhane protected his cheeks with his hands and ducked his head. "I don't know."

The man crouched so he was eye level with him. Berhane saw dust in his thick eyebrows. "See, you lied to me, you said you didn't see any-thing. How can I believe you now?"

"I'm not lying. I swear. The bullet went into the car, I don't know where it came from."

"What else did you see?" The soldier gripped his shoulder. "What else did you see?"

"Emaye, I want Emaye!" Berhane couldn't escape the next hit. It was so powerful it sent him sprawling into the dirt.

"One man bought a newspaper and he told me to give it to the man who was shot," Berhane said, lying on the ground.

The soldier leaned down over him. "What man?"

"I don't know him." Berhane crawled away from the man. "Robel!" he said. "Emaye!"

The soldier grabbed him by both shoulders and pulled him so close Berhane could see the twitch in his eye.

"He just gave me money for the newspaper and candy," he wailed.

"What else?" the soldier asked. "Tell me everything and you can go home."

"He gave me a note," Berhane said.

"Where is it?"

Berhane fished in his pockets and pulled out the note. "You can have it," he said. "I want my mommy."

The soldier snatched the note and read it. He stood up, shoved the note in his pocket, and dragged Berhane by the arm. "Come on," he growled.

Berhane resisted. "I want to go home." But the soldier yanked him towards his truck. "Robel! Robel!" Berhane screamed. His cries were cut short by the fist that slammed into his mouth and knocked him back to the ground.

"Get up! You're coming with me to jail."

Berhane stumbled ahead, dizzy and disoriented, clinging to the soldier's hand as he was shoved into the back of a military truck. He had a thought, fleeting and brief before a foot came out of nowhere and sailed into his stomach, that perhaps he would finally find his father.

SOFIA'S STOMACH CONVULSED. "Sara..." She turned to the other woman. They were in the kitchen peeling potatoes for that night's dinner, each lost in her own thoughts.

"What is it?" Sara asked. She brushed peelings off her skirt. "Should we do more? Bizu said she'd help after she rested."

"I have to go," Sofia said. She looked confused and stunned. "I don't know why, but I have to go home. I'm sorry." She scrambled to stand, knocking potatoes to the ground. "I have to go. My sons. My children." She ran out, her apron still on.

THEY SAT, MOTHER and son, in the empty belly of a bare room sweating and crying. Sofia began to pace, repeating the same questions to Robel that she'd been asking for hours. They'd searched the areas near Peacock Café and Sidist Kilo all afternoon. Sofia had even offered her savings, a small bag of bills and coins, to confused taxi drivers and shopkeepers who eventually shook their heads.

"Where did you see him last?" She wrung her hands. "How could he just disappear? He'd never leave his newspapers like that, never."

Robel wrapped his head in his trembling hands. "I didn't hear anything. I dropped him off as usual, then I went to check on him." He paused. "He wasn't there." He pulled at Sofia. "Let's go to the police."

Sofia nodded, as she'd done hours earlier, but she didn't move towards the door. Her eyes stared off into a distant space. "They won't help. They never help." She suddenly dropped to her knees, her forehead touching the ground. "I beg you," she prayed, one hand in the air, "give him back, I'll give you my life."

Robel cradled her. "Emama, let's go to the police."

She sat up, her fingers finding the edge of her shirt, ripping the fabric. "I promise, whatever I've done to be punished like this, I promise to pay. Keep my husband, keep Daniel, give me my son. My light." She tore her shirt, the thin cotton coming apart at the shoulders, exposing a straight, elegant collarbone. She began to pound on her breasts, her moans reverberating, her chest a deep-barreled drum.

"Emaye," Robel cried, holding her arms down and planting his head on her chest. "Stop, please."

"Daniel!" she wailed. "Where is my son? Help me!" She tipped to the floor, dragging Robel with her. "Why is God angry?"

Robel gently eased his mother to the ground and folded a pillow under her head. "I'll be back soon," he said.

She stared at the ceiling and a hand traced the crucifix that hung around her neck as she repeated her youngest son's name.

THE POLICE STATION smelled like vomit. Just inside the gate, a group of women and a cluster of girls sat huddled in a tired bunch. They were dressed in black, their tear-stained faces hidden behind their *shammas*. A soldier paced back and forth in front of them.

Robel shoved himself into the middle of a long line, then pushed through the queue to squeeze into a cramped office. He ignored the mumbling and muttering behind him. He slapped a hand on the counter and got the attention of an agitated police officer.

"Stop that," the policeman said. "If you want to report someone, just drop the name in the box over there." He pointed to a square white metal box near the entrance.

"I'm looking for a small boy, my brother." Robel put a hand to his chest. "This tall."

The policeman shook his head. "No boys today. We just brought in those women from a funeral for an anarchist." He rolled his eyes. "Don't they know the laws about mourning for enemies?" He smiled tiredly at Robel. "You seem like a smart boy."

"My brother sells newspapers at Peacock Café. He was gone when I went to pick him up. I need to find him."

The policeman sighed. "Maybe he just went to play with friends.

I have two sons," he added. "They leave the compound all the time, even when I tell them not to." He patted Robel's hand reassuringly. "Go home and wait, he'll come back." He turned and walked back to his desk and soon became lost in a stack of papers.

Robel stood at the counter until another officer walked by. "Get out of here. We're busy," he said. He shoved Robel away from behind the counter. "Go on."

Robel walked out, defeated. He saw one of the soldiers kick a thin woman and raise his rifle butt above her head. She curled up at his feet, a pile of bones and black cloth.

BERHANE SAT STRAPPED in a metal chair that was bolted to the ground. In front of him, two large men in uniform hunched over a box of long needles and ropes. One of them, the tallest, tugged on two ends of a long rope and brought it close to Berhane's face.

"This one should work," he said.

Berhane whimpered as he felt his legs lifted and tied to the chair. The man stood up, satisfied, when he was finished. Berhane's feet dangled, the end of the rope dragged on the floor.

"Don't make me do this," the man said. He patted Berhane's head. "Just tell us the name of the man who gave you this note."

"I don't know. I don't know. I don't know!" Berhane cried, terrified. His tears caught in his throat and he coughed them up. "I don't know, I'm not lying. I promise."

The man pulled one of the long needles out of the box and waved it in front of him. "Do you know what I'm going to do with this?" he asked.

Berhane shook his head, too afraid to speak. He tried to jerk his arms free, but that made the rubber strap cut into him. The man put the sharp tip of the needle on his thigh. It felt cool and sharp against his skin.

"I'll push it all the way through. Do you know how much that'll hurt?" the man said.

Berhane saw the shorter man wipe his upper lip. "Enough," the short man mumbled. He couldn't bring himself to meet Berhane's gaze. "Enough. He doesn't know anything." He slid the box closer to himself. "He's telling the truth. Stop."

The tall man turned around, angry. "He knows. They always know." He swept the needle through the air and Berhane's eyes followed every motion, ready to scream when it touched him. "They think they can use kids now and we won't dare question them? He's not a child"—the man pointed at him. "This is our newest enemy."

Berhane was so intent on watching the short man run to a corner and kneel that he lost track of the needle. It stabbed his thigh before he had a chance to scream. It went through his leg, its coolness warmed by his blood, and he thought he heard the tip hit against the metal chair before the man ripped it back out, flesh sliding from the end. Berhane gaped at the gushing wound in his thigh and realized the voice wailing into his ears, slamming through his hot, pounding head, was his own. The needle came down again. Berhane saw it arc slowly through the air, a brilliant ribbon of red floating through silence and nothingness.

SOFIA STARTED AWAKE. "Robel," she said, shaking him, "wake up." They were huddled under one blanket. She sat up and held Robel, tears rolling down her face. "I sent him there, I made him start working at that place."

"It's okay, Emaye," Robel said, rubbing her back. "We'll find him. Don't cry." He swallowed the tears that rushed to his throat. "I promise. I'll find him for you." What he didn't say was that now there were two people lost to them, and that if there was a God, maybe they'd finally found each other.

50

SOFIA SANK TO THE GROUND AS SOON as Sara opened the gate to let her in. She fell to her knees, her arms outstretched, crawling towards the other woman.

"They took my son," she moaned. "They took him. Someone saw them take him. They beat him. They beat my son." Sofia was gasping for air, her eyes vacant. "Who is this God I pray to?" she asked. "Who is he to do this to a small boy?" Sweat poured down her face. She swayed, almost tipping over.

Sara dragged her through the gate and closed it quickly. "Stand," she told her. "Get up, let's go inside before Shiferaw sees."

Sofia struggled to her feet and pressed against Sara as they walked into the house. Once inside, she collapsed onto the sofa.

Sara rubbed her hands. "Tell me what you heard." Her eyes were gentle, sad.

"Another newspaper boy saw him taken in a military truck. He watched a soldier hitting Berhane." She rose up angrily. "Why couldn't he do anything?"

Sara sat next to her and held her. "He's just a boy, they'll let him go."

"I had a dream," Sofia said. "Daniel and Berhane, walking together." She began to sob. "I made him work at that café, I moved him from the square."

"They'll both be okay," Sara said, trying to smile. "That means they'll be okay."

Sofia shook her head. "Daniel's dead. I've known. I've known for so long." She dropped her head. "He was killed the same night the emperor's officials were executed. I couldn't bring myself to tell my sons. I wanted them to still believe in something, to hope, until they were old enough to understand." She turned anguished eyes to Sara. "Do you think I killed my son? Do you think he did something foolish trying to find his father?

You remember how he always talked about finding him. I tried to stop that, to just get him to pray. But this is my punishment for lying." She was still, rigid as stone. "This is God's way. In the end, we always pay."

THE BURNING CANDLE in the dark room grew brighter as the sun set through Emama Seble's window. The old woman sat hunched over a bowl of *dabo kolo,* tossing the kernels of baked dough in her mouth.

"You should be glad they didn't go into Dawit's room and find him. They only took Hailu's medical bag. But you keep wanting to test God," Emama Seble said, shaking her head. "Just leave things alone."

"There was a woman who was eight months pregnant. All she did was work at a printing press that these murderers thought was counter-revolutionary. And another *kebele* dog killed her. A pregnant woman!" She put her head in her hands. "Now they have little Berhane, that sweet boy." She wiped her eyes. "What if they'd taken Tizita?"

Emama Seble grew quiet. "They executed the man who killed that woman. He died with his own demons, he did worse to himself. There was justice."

"It's not enough." Sara wrung her hands. "And what about Berhane? How can we do nothing?"

Emama Seble brought Sara's hands to her chest. "So you think stepping into the battle will help your family with Hailu gone? What can you do to bring this boy back to his mother? Nothing."

"My mother fought in battles, my father almost died in one. It's the way I was raised."

Emama Seble scooped another handful of *dabo kolo.* "You can't grab a gun and march into the streets." She flicked an eye towards an open window and stood to close it. She lowered her voice. "Listen to me. Stay alive, do what you can to keep living. Be a sister to Sofia, comfort her son. What matters is life."

"It's how you live."

"And your daughter? After all you did to keep her with you, now you're going to risk your own life?"

"I don't want her growing up thinking we didn't fight back," Sara said.

Emama Seble shook her head.

"I'm a daughter of patriots," Sara said. "They charged at Italian rifles with spears. My aunt was burned from those chemicals they dropped from the planes, but she tried to fight as soon as she could."

Emama Seble seemed to sift through words, choosing carefully. "So much anger. You can't see what you have," she finally said. She put her hand on Sara's knee. "How much more will you ask from God? Hasn't he given you enough?"

"I'm not going to wait patiently while people are dying," Sara said. "Maybe you don't understand."

"You forget I was one of the women who lived through the Italian occupation." Emama Seble put a hand on her stomach. "What they did to us was another side of the war."

"I know," Sara said quietly.

"We all talked about your mother, how she fought in the bed with one of them and strangled him. All the women in Addis celebrated." She stared into Sara's eyes. "She was brave. Brave enough to give birth, unlike some of us." She touched her face.

"Those rumors aren't true," Sara replied, her voice trembling. "I know who my father is."

"Then you should know there's no need to fight. It won't make you any more Ethiopian," Emama Seble said. "It won't bring back anything you think you've lost."

"It's not enough just to pray," Sara said.

Emama Seble sighed. "We all have our own ways and times to die, including our enemies. Don't rush God's work."

"Nobody gets punished enough. If we don't do something, we have to suffer for their wrongs for generations," Sara said. "My mother knew this."

Emama Seble shook her head and lit another candle. "Go talk to Melaku," she said. "That man is foolish enough to agree with you."

MELAKU'S DOOR SUDDENLY flew open and the unhinged lock clattered noisily to the floor.

"Emaye!" he cried out, startled into the child's habit of calling out for his mother. He groaned in frustration when he realized it was Emama Seble, and that she'd kicked his unlatched door open with her foot.

"Can't you knock?" he asked. He tried to slow her entrance into his home, but she shoved him aside and examined the room with critical eyes.

"Who comes for tea this early?" Emama Seble pointed at the empty teacup sitting next to his. "You're too old for night guests." She sank onto the bed, frowning at the squeaky coils. She leaned back slowly.

Color rose to Melaku's cheeks. "Seble?"

She rolled her eyes. "Don't be so vain." She propped a pillow behind her. "We need to talk about Sara."

Melaku collected himself. "Did the soldiers find anything besides Hailu's bag?"

Emama Seble's eyes didn't leave his face. "Sara's coming to talk to you."

"About what?"

"What do you think?" Her hands were folded in front of her. "Why else would I be here?"

Melaku let out a short laugh. "Not everyone is part of the resistance."

Emama Seble leaned forward. "Take care of her. I'll hold you responsible."

"I'm not in any underground movement." He pointed to the empty teacups. "In fact, these bastards searched everything last night and took my best teakettle. What do you need a teakettle for? I asked them. But they took it just in case it was counterrevolutionary. I don't have anything."

"Your lies work on other women, not me," Emama Seble said.

"What makes you think you know everything about me?" he asked sharply.

"Just be ready when she comes to you." She stood up and looked around. "Clean this place."

Melaku walked to the door and opened it. "Haven't you misjudged me before? Isn't this why we're both alone now?" He saw that she wasn't making any move to leave. "Go," he said. He felt her eyes sliding from his ankles to his shoulders.

She stepped close. "I wasn't the one who made bad choices," she said.

"You're not always right," he said.

Emama Seble walked out and slammed the door. It hit the frame, then bounced open again, leaving the rusting metal latch to clank loudly.

SARA SMELLED OF CLOVES and cinnamon, a musky sweetness that Dawit breathed in. She hunched into the flickering candle, daylight dying above her head, shadows cascading through her hair.

"I want to do it," she said. "I have to."

They were crouched inside Melaku's kiosk, the old man standing guard at the counter.

"They have Berhane," Sara said, choking. "They killed a pregnant woman and now they have this little boy. What if it were happening to me?" She covered her face.

Dawit wanted to comfort her, but then he thought of how he'd crouched in his room while she shouted at soldiers fearlessly, and he found himself shamed into silence. He nodded instead.

"I won't tell Yonas," she continued. The candle flame spread under her breath. Again, the scent of cloves and cinnamon, and Dawit imagined honeyed tea boiling under an umbrella of mint leaves and spices. He remembered her silhouette in the kitchen, the flush of her caramel skin, the quiver he wanted to believe he detected in her lips.

"It's just us," he said. He fought with the guilt his thoughts left behind. "We have to start immediately. If you don't think you're ready—"

"You shouldn't even question it." She dusted dirt off her skirt. "We're family, we help each other," she said. "You're my brother."

Melaku looked down at them. "I know of a small hut that's impossible to see from the roads. It's not far from here, in the hills of Entoto." He grinned. "I haven't used it in years."

Dawit sat back. "How will you leave the house without Yonas finding out?"

"He reads at night, then sleeps in Abbaye's bed," she said.

Dawit was startled. "Since when?"

Sara hid her expression behind a veil of hair. "Recently."

"What about Tizita?" Dawit asked.

"She sleeps with Yonas, to be near Abbaye, she says," Sara said.

Her face, Dawit noticed, had grown more fragile in the last few weeks. Her high cheekbones pressed through tight skin, her eyes sunk into dark hollow circles.

"You'll need to help me carry them—the bodies—to the hut," Dawit said to her, watching her expression closely. She only looked more determined.

Melaku nodded above them, waving to a pedestrian on the road. "I'll identify them."

Sara grimaced. "I'll tell the families, the mothers . . ."

Dawit fought to keep his voice steady, overcome for a moment by their loyalty. He reached for Sara's hand. "I should have come out of my room when the soldiers were there," he said.

She pulled away. "No you shouldn't. They wanted to arrest any student they could."

Melaku hummed to himself, then stopped. "Hurry," he whispered. "Soldiers."

Dawit went outside. Sara stood behind the counter, ready to serve the next customer. There was a group of soldiers lazily walking by, laughing easily amongst themselves. One looked up, settled his gaze on Sara for so long his companions moved on ahead of him.

51

ONE DAY, HE WOULD TELL HIS FATHER THIS: that the eyes die first, that we make our way to dust and ash blindly. Dawit would tell him of the night he learned of this, the night they found the still-breathing woman by the road, her broken bones and open wounds covered in grass and dirt. Sara had taken a blanket from the car to cover her, her face grim and pained, but the woman's eyelids had fluttered, then widened, and Dawit had watched her breath leave her body through her eyes. He'd stared, stunned, as a cloudy film covered them and seemed to travel through the length of her, stiffening everything in its course. He'd sat for longer than he should have, peering into her flat gaze and dilated pupils, fascinated by how terror fell away from her face and left only a gaping mouth. One day, he would ask his father if he knew that death shows no mercy on a fighting body, that those who struggle suffer rigor mortis more quickly than those who lie submissive and let death creep slowly. He would tell Hailu that this vengeful rigidity lasts no more than two days, that the body's eternal desire for motion eventually takes control again, and limbs become pliant. He would tell him everything. He would even confess, never letting go of his father's hand, that a stiff body could be broken, unsnapped from its rigidity by the simple will and exertion of his youngest son, then reshaped to fit in the back of a Volkswagen already full of the smell of decay.

THE BODIES WERE easy to find, sloppily discarded by the road just beyond the new jail, dumped from roaring trucks in the first hours of dark. Dawit, Sara, and Melaku worked tirelessly, in the lull of soldiers' shift changes and mealtimes. Dawit lifted the corpses, Sara helped drag them into the car, then both of them drove past homes into the hills, then to a dense patch of trees and shrub to a hut where Melaku waited to let memory guide him towards recognition. They discovered that soldiers who patrolled the area were inexperienced and lazy, that the Colonel kept the best in his jail monitoring his private collection of prisoners. They learned that bodies left alone for one day raised less suspicion than those they picked up immediately. And as family after family from neighborhoods beyond their began to gather at Melaku's kiosk at dawn, desperate for news of their missing, they realized that they were not enough and would never be enough to rid the roads of this latest blasphemy.

DAWIT AND SARA stopped at a barefoot boy lying faceup on the road, no more than fifteen years old. His shoulder was dislocated, face swollen, neck broken. A note was pinned to his torn cotton t-shirt:

> I AM AN ENEMY OF THE PEOPLE.
> MOTHER, DON'T WEEP FOR ME, I DESERVED TO DIE.

Dawit got out of the car and worked quickly, flinching each time the wind scattered small rocks and blew the sound of hurried footsteps past his ear.

"Hurry," Sara said, glancing at her watch. "It's late." She focused past Dawit, towards the edge of a row of trees. "I'll see if anything fell," she added. Some nights, they'd found torn slips of paper with the victim's name, hidden in pockets or clutched in tight fists. Simple gestures of rebellion by those who refused to have their lives extinguished in anonymity.

He lifted the boy into the back of the Volkswagen and gently laid him on an old, frayed blanket, careful not to smudge the car seat with blood. He forced himself to keep his gaze away from the body, away from more tangible evidence that there was no God, that all his life he and this boy had prayed to nothing.

Dawit and Sara drove uphill, towards Melaku.

"I'm so afraid of finding Berhane, or—" Sara stopped and pushed her hair back under her scarf. "What's the point in saying anything?" she whispered. She slept less than he did during the day, and the exhaustion was showing. "There must have been a celebration that kept them busy, there's only one tonight." She rubbed her eyes, then sniffed her hands and grimaced. "The smell never comes out."

Dawit squeezed her arm. "You're so tired," he said. "Maybe we'll take a break tomorrow."

She shook her head and looked out the window. "Stop," she said.

There was another crumpled body in the grass. A naked man. He had a wide forehead and long lashes. His white hair was stained with bloody patches and his dried lips caved in where his front teeth should have been. His ears had been cut off, burnt flesh curled around his eardrums, and he had a bullet hole through his chest. He could have been an older uncle, his father's colleague, an elder statesman. But in this city, on this road, he was nothing but another warning, a rotting message to the living.

Dawit bent to lift the dead man when bright headlights sprang behind him and threw tall shadows in his path. He stepped away from the body, hoping tall grass would hide it. Sara, further back from the road, dropped to her knees, then lay flat on the ground, hidden.

"Don't come out," Dawit hissed. "No matter what." He ran his fingers along the seam of his shirt collar and felt the tiny vial of cyanide. Sara had hers on her necklace, behind a cross pendant on a gold chain long enough to reach her mouth.

A military truck crawled to a stop behind his car. Squinting against the harsh lights, Dawit walked to the Volkswagen as casually as he could, dusting off his hands and yawning with exaggerated stretches.

A slender man wearing a military-issued jacket approached with an AK-47 tucked under his arm. Dawit glanced at the truck to see if another soldier was inside. There was no one else. This was a soldier on his way home.

"What are you doing?" the soldier demanded. He was a few feet from Dawit but still hidden in the glare of headlights.

Dawit didn't know how to respond.

The soldier lifted his rifle and aimed it at his chest as he walked closer. "Answer me! What are you doing?" he asked again.

Dawit tried to see the soldier's face. He saw only a silhouetted figure blocking more of the glare as it got closer. The crooked outline of the soldier's finger hung in the light, poised gently on the trigger.

"I'm collecting these bodies," Dawit replied. He was surprised by how easy it was to admit the truth.

The soldier stopped. In the distance, Dawit heard the deep-throated breathing of a pack of hyenas. The soldier kept his AK-47 leveled on the center of his chest.

"It's almost curfew," the soldier said, as if he could think of nothing else to say. His voice cracked as he spoke and Dawit realized that he was young.

"I'll go home after this." Dawit made a mental note of the quietness that had crept back to them again. The hyenas were gone.

The soldier lowered his rifle and glanced into the backseat.

"It's just a body," Dawit said. He could smell the soldier's sweat. "You must be on your way home."

"He's a traitor to the revolution. What are you going to do?" His finger still rested on the trigger.

"He needs to be buried. He'll stink soon."

The soldier shook his head. "No funerals for the enemy. Let the hyenas eat."

"It'll be just a burial. No funeral." But soldier wasn't going to leave him alone.

"Dump it out," the soldier said. "Do it now or I'll shoot."

"Comrade," Dawit said, holding his hands in front of him, "can a dead boy still be an enemy?"

"Get it out!"

They stared at each other until Dawit nodded. "Okay. I'll need help. It's heavy."

The soldier nudged him with his rifle.

"Open the door and take the body out," he said. "And then you're going to jail."

Dawit turned away quickly, hoping his face revealed nothing of the fear he felt. "All I wanted was to get it out of the way. The hyenas come here, then they disturb the area." He opened the door to the backseat with shaking hands.

The soldier cleared his throat. "Hurry up."

Dawit lifted the small body. "I can't do it alone. Help me hold the other side. Don't drop him."

"What difference does it make?" the soldier grunted as he moved closer and grabbed the other half of the body.

The soldier strained with the weight of the boy. Dawit didn't think, didn't allow himself the luxury of doubt. He wrapped his arm around the soldier's neck until the young man's chin lifted and stiffened. The soldier arched and flailed, trying to keep his balance.

"Please," the soldier said.

"Quiet," Dawit whispered, his own knees weak.

He cupped the soldier's chin in the center of his palm and pushed it hard into the curve of his elbow. The soldier's neck was turned as far as it could go without snapping.

"Please," Dawit said, his throat starting to hurt. He swallowed back the tears. "Please don't fight." Two owls cooed from high above a tree.

The soldier stilled for that split second, his Adam's apple moving up and down against the inside of Dawit's arm. Dawit closed his eyes and asked forgiveness from the mother he knew was waiting for her son to come home. With a deep breath, he twisted the soldier's neck, surprised by its pliancy, its snap muffled by his own startled gasp. The soldier slumped to the ground with the boy in his arms. Dawit slid the AK-47 to the floor, pushed the boy back into the car, then stripped the soldier of his uniform. He shoved the clothes underneath the front seat and dragged the body into the grass.

"Help me get this body!" Dawit said to Sara. "Hurry." Then he stopped when he saw her standing with her hands covering her mouth, her eyes filled with terror.

He went to her and held her, both of them shaking. "Mekonnen did this," he said. "I did this. Not you." He kissed her forehead, his heart pounding, his senses attuned to every noise in the night. "Don't think. Push it away until this is all over." He pulled her hands from her mouth. "Let's go."

They hurried to the old man and struggled to put him in the car, on top of the boy. Dawit grunted to mute the sound of bone on bone. Then they got into the Volkswagen and drove away.

SOLOMON SAT IN the dark storage room of a small shop in Mercato, paper and pen in hand. He nudged Dawit. "Don't fall asleep. How many?" he asked. "We can't stay here long."

"Four since we talked. I know we missed some a few nights ago." Dawit rested his head against the wall. Its hard coolness soothed his headache. "I'm hungry."

He'd been with Sara and Melaku just hours earlier, the three of them afraid but resolute. Now, all he could think about was how hungry he was. He hadn't slept yet.

"We have to finish this." Solomon had the composure of a secretary taking dictation. He surveyed the boxes of newsletters and ammunition tucked under blankets, then glanced back down. "Injuries."

Dawit didn't want to imagine the body of the girl he picked up tonight. The wounds on her stomach had made even Melaku cry out. He tried to close his mind to the face of the man who was close to his father's age. "The usual," he replied.

"I need specifics, there's nothing different tonight." Solomon dropped the pen and pulled out a cigarette. "Don't get lazy."

"She was maybe sixteen, broken bones. Burns from an iron on her stomach, deep cuts. The man, teeth pulled." He grimaced and looked at Solomon. "Cigarette burns."

Solomon nodded and wrote. "How many?" He waited, then snapped his fingers. "Mekonnen! How many?"

"What's the point?"

"We're building a case." Solomon tightened his mouth around his cigarette. "One day there'll be a trial, these people will be brought to justice, and everyone will know what really happened." He paused and stared ahead. "Any news about the little newspaper boy you know?"

Dawit shook his head, his face clouding. "There was one more. A boy, maybe nineteen, in a soldier's uniform. Not far from Kidane Mehret Church, the one on Entoto."

Solomon stopped writing. "A soldier?"

"A boy on his way home." Dawit drew circles on the dusty floor. "He was alone."

Solomon stared straight ahead, his face expressionless. "Did you get his gun?"

"You should be writing this down." Dawit pointed to the paper, to the spot where Solomon's unfinished word vanished into an expanse of white.

Solomon tapped his cigarette case and shook out another. "Where's his gun?"

"In the suitcase." He pointed behind him to a corner in the room. Dawit stared at the stacks of boxes ahead of him which blocked any light from entering through the windows. "He looked scared. He begged me not to do it."

"Do you think he would have let you go if you begged?" Solomon asked. "The only advantage you had was quickness, not compassion."

"I don't know anything about my father." Dawit turned so Solomon wouldn't see his quivering chin.

Solomon exhaled a large puff of smoke. "You're doing something for him, what you did tonight helps them all." He stood and picked up the suitcase. "After this soldier, I think we need to move you. Things might get too hot for a while."

Dawit sighed.

"I'll walk out first." Solomon rubbed his head, his eyes red from fatigue. "Nothing happens overnight, but every act counts." He gave Dawit a small salute before taking the suitcase and leaving.

FROM A FADING TEAHOUSE with plastered walls, a hushed name traveled like a current and grew into a tide of admiration: Mekonnen. Mekonnen collects the bodies. Mekonnen guides them to angels. Mekonnen, avenger of the weak, has heard our cries. And from mouths that whispered stories under candlelight and incense, Mekonnen, killer of soldiers, grew large and strong, more powerful than a thousand raging armies.

52

AT FIRST, SARA THOUGHT SHE COULD get used to the sight of those lifeless bodies. She was sure that the deaths of so many she'd called hers had prepared her for the evidence that dying leaves behind. She was confident that she was ready to face the steady succession of corpses. She had enough anger, she'd told herself, to carry her through the risks of stepping into each long night. She was shielded from the ordinariness of nausea and shock. But Sara was beginning to feel the weight of tragedy and injustice. Her steps were slower, she held her daughter longer. She craved her husband's strong arms but pushed him away, aware that his presence would only raise questions she couldn't answer. She walked alone in the space created by her breached loyalty, caught between what couldn't be said and what needed to be told. She knew that her husband was asking without words and she turned from him more often, hoping her love could one day bridge the distance that shouldered them now and ripped them further apart.

"I CAME TO TALK to you," Mickey said, "I can't talk to Dawit."

Mickey and Sara were in the courtyard of the Ghion Hotel, its thatched-roof design a modernized version of the countryside huts that dotted Ethiopia. They were surrounded by blooming rosebushes and jacarandas, brilliant red hibiscus, and large, leafy trees. The staff, dressed in black and white, unobtrusively cleared plates and refilled teacups as hotel guests chatted discreetly. At one table, Russian and Cuban men pored over documents with Ethiopian officers. At another table, two young Ethiopian men and their female companions leaned in close to each other, their hands over their mouths, while stealing looks at the table of military officers.

"It'd be better if you tell him for me," Mickey said.

Sara pushed her chair a little further from Mickey, her arms folded across her chest. "He's been to your house looking for you," she said. "You never even tried to contact him."

"I didn't know, my mother didn't mention it."

"Why didn't you come see us once you found out Abbaye was in jail? You wait until now?" she asked. "You've known him since you were a boy, he's been like a father to you."

Mickey held up his hand. He stood up. "Let's walk in the garden." He'd lost weight around his face, though his stomach was bigger. His shoulders and arms seemed more muscular, but his walk, plodding and graceless, hadn't changed.

They made their way to the back, where a lush, vibrant display of roses and bougainvillea drenched the courtyard in color. Mickey linked arms with her. "It's for show," he explained. He continued. "The minute they took Gash Hailu, they started watching me to see if I was connected."

"Connected?" Sara took some pleasure in seeing her spit land on Mickey's face. She knew he'd be too polite to wipe it away in front of her.

Mickey pushed his glasses up and blinked. He cleared his throat and pulled on the front of his shirt, then stopped. "It's complicated . . ." he began.

"There's nothing so complicated you can't explain."

"He's alive," Mickey said. "He's kept away from the other prisoners, even most of the guards. I can't get to him. I've tried."

"Try harder," Sara said. "If this were your own father, what would you do?"

Mickey shook his head. "He did something. He's being accused of something big or else he wouldn't be isolated like this."

"What do you mean?"

Mickey wiped her spit off. "If he didn't have information they needed, they'd have killed him already. I don't know what it is."

"Who'd know?" Sara asked. "You aren't telling me anything."

"The Colonel." Mickey folded his arms over his round stomach. "He's been the only one near him since his first week."

"The Colonel?" An image of a thin-nosed, sharp-eyed man flashed in front of Sara. She'd heard about this Colonel, seen pictures of a man who stood so straight some said his spine had been replaced with a metal rod when he'd been injured fighting against Somalia. She'd heard rumors of his ruthlessness with prisoners of war, of his terrifying, methodical means of torture and murder. "Are they hurting him?"

"Most likely." He lowered his eyes.

She shook his arm. "Can't you do something?"

"I swear on my mother, I've tried. I love Gash Hailu." Mickey swallowed hard. "You people who call yourselves revolutionaries, what do you know about politics?" he whispered. He squeezed Sara's hand so hard she winced.

"I don't know what you're talking about," Sara said, pulling her hand out of his grip.

"You do what you need to do to feel good about yourselves, then you go home and turn your back on all the ugly details." He was full of contempt. "You turn your backs on the rest of us."

He smirked. "We're the ones in the middle of the blood trying to turn the gun away from a brother so it points to a stranger. That's the war we're in, it's not this child's game you're playing."

He took her hand again and caressed it, his touch gentle now. "You don't know what you're doing," he said, the edges of his thick mouth curling. "I'm the one keeping you safe."

Sara pulled away. She pushed up his sliding glasses and held the bridge of the frame tight against his forehead. "Earn the kindness he's shown you," she said, and left him.

53

O N A GRASSY HILLSIDE ROAD ABOVE the sounds of traffic, Yonas rolled his father's Volkswagen to a stop and turned off the ignition. The soft churn of the dying engine settled into the nighttime calls of a distant bird. The air was chill and a sharp wind drilled through an open window in the backseat and Yonas wrapped his thick brown sweater tighter around him for warmth. This was the sixty-first day of his father's imprisonment and he still hadn't been able to get any word about charges. He knew about Dawit's continued early treks to the jail. He understood his brother's need to feel like he was doing something to get their father out. What he didn't understand was Dawit's secrecy, the self-imposed solitude of his grief. Sara, too, had become more withdrawn, more sullen and distant. Tizita shied away from him, clinging instead to her mother, constantly asking about her friend Berhane. There were hours when he felt nothing but waves of helplessness and fury. And as the days edged into a new month, he found himself longing for the comfort of Sara's presence, for Dawit's innate confidence and strength. He spent more and more time in the prayer room trying to drive out the questions of where his wife went with his brother at night.

"TELL ME FROM the beginning," the Colonel said. He stared out of the tiny window in the small room. Threads of rain spiraled against the pane as thunder shook the sky outside. The light flickered, then shivered back on. "Tell me what she looked like."

Hailu sat in a chair that was bolted to the ground, his hands tied behind his back, his bare feet roped together in front of him. Electric wires were clamped to his ears, the ringing in his head as loud as a thousand unleashed bells. He nudged his front teeth gently with his tongue; they were loose. What felt like an insect crawling down the side of his face was a drop of blood rolling from his mouth to his jaw. The punches the Colonel had pounded into him had been carefully aimed and precise. He was hit again and again on the jaw, just to the side of his mouth, and the impact forced the lower half of his face to buckle and snap against the swinging fist. It was after only the third punch that Hailu heard a splintering tree and knew his jaw was fractured. The crackle and brush of falling leaves deep inside his head told him his eardrum was damaged.

"Tell me," the Colonel said, still facing the window. His hands were neatly folded behind his back. There was no trace of Hailu's blood on him. He'd remained as immaculately clean as ever, as composed and controlled as a priest at prayer.

Hailu replied the same way he'd been replying, his memory for new words failing him. "She was weak." He saw the Colonel's hands tighten and his fingers pale from squeezing.

"Yes," the Colonel said, nodding. "Weak. What else?"

"She had cuts on her legs."

"And?" The Colonel nodded, brushing aside the detail.

"The bottoms of her feet had been burned, then whipped."

"This is a lie," he said, softer. "I know this is a lie, Doctor. But please go on. I have plenty of time to get the truth from you." He tipped towards Hailu, his face watching his mouth intently.

"She'd been raped," Hailu said through clenched teeth.

"It's a privilege to be alive." The Colonel backed away from him, he was talking fast, sweating. He began to pace. "To have the chance to see your children again, isn't it?" He wiped his hands on a stark white handkerchief. "Do you love your children, Doctor?" he asked, staring at Hailu.

Hailu's jaw was too rigid to talk. He tried to nod and found that his head felt welded to his vertebrae. He followed the Colonel's pacing with frantic eyes he was sure would bleed again if moved too fast. He felt his head being pulled back by a fistful of hair until he was staring, wide-eyed, into the bright beam of the lightbulb. The Colonel's face hovered above him.

"Tell me you love your children."

"I love them," Hailu said.

"Tell me what you would do if Dawit was brought in front of you right now and strapped into another chair. I could do that, you know. We have him."

"No," Hailu said. "No." But he didn't know what he was protesting, he didn't know anything anymore. For a fleeting moment, he thought he saw Dawit huddled in the corner, tired and bruised, but when he blinked, there was nothing.

Hailu flinched as the Colonel's hand came to rest on the electrical switch. He tried to stop the whimper that fled from his lips as his body jerked and burned and froze all at once. The bells clanged behind his eyes, he smelled his hair singeing. A hundred red ants scurried inside his stomach. He was cooking, his blood reaching the boiling point in milliseconds that stretched into eternal minutes. The ants were trying to chew their way out. If he hadn't already emptied his bowels in the last rounds of shocks, he knew he would have loosed shit and piss onto the floor again.

The Colonel watched it all with disinterest.

"What are we without our children, Doctor? If we could stop their suffering, what is our own?" The Colonel wiped his face, his eyes, dried the sweat that had collected on his upper lip. "What is our own?" He lifted his hand off the electric switch to take Hailu's. He used his hand-kerchief to avoid the wounds. "Are you a good father?" he asked, curious. He caressed Hailu's hand, paternal and affectionate. "Would your son call you a good father?"

Hailu's head sank into his chest. "No," he said. "No."

"Wouldn't you give anything to get another chance to right your wrongs?"

Hailu didn't know when the Colonel had moved across the room to watch him with intense concentration.

"Wouldn't you give anything to fix your mistakes?" the Colonel asked, his back as straight as the wall behind him.

"Dawit," Hailu said. "Dawit," he said again, aching for a memory of a good moment between them.

The Colonel sagged against the wall. "Wouldn't you want to kill the man who stood in your way?" Then, slowly and clearly, the Colonel said: "I'm asking you to tell me the truth. What did she say to you? Whose name did she give you?"

"She asked for her father. That's all she said, 'Abbaye.'"

The Colonel strode in front of him and landed another blow on his face with a fury that exploded from every pore. "You're playing games! Don't lie to me! I can kill you this instant!"

Hailu caught a thread of panic in the Colonel's voice.

"Don't say that to me again!" The Colonel began to choke Hailu. "Don't say that," he said. "I know what you're doing."

A fist slammed into Hailu's face. Another tooth swam in his mouth, then down his throat. The room spun.

"She was brought in a plastic bag," Hailu groaned.

"A plastic bag?" The Colonel fell back, his hold loosening from Hailu's neck. "A plastic bag? No. She wasn't. She wasn't taken to Girma. She wasn't taken to that monster." He held his head. "She wasn't to go there." He paced again, his attention on his steps, on his feet, his teeth gnawing on his cheek. "You only wanted to fix your mistakes."

The Colonel rested his hand on the electrical switch again. Then he continued talking, his whole body shaking. "Are you telling me they disobeyed my orders and took her to that butcher? Are you expecting me to believe you were merciful in killing her? Is that it?" The Colonel stood over him, his eyes wet, his head moving from side to side. "What have I done?" he whispered again and again.

DAWIT AND SOLOMON sat in a hut in Sululta. Dawit shivered, his thin shirt no defense from the nighttime chill. He'd assumed this would be a short meeting, and now Solomon was telling him something different.

"I need to get in touch with my family," Dawit said. "They'll worry," he added when the man didn't respond.

"We can't take that chance. The military's crawling all over Addis looking for Mekonnen the killer of soldiers." Solomon had a rifle on his shoulder, a cigarette smoldering at the corner of his mouth, both objects seemed permanently attached to him. "Right now, they don't know you're Mekonnen. You'll stay in hiding until it's safe. If they catch you, they'll find ways to make you talk, believe me. This is the only way to keep us all out of danger." Solomon lit a partial cigarette and took three deep draws before throwing it on the ground. "Practice loading faster," he said, extending his weapon to Dawit.

—

"HE DIDN'T COME home last night," Yonas said to Sara. They were in the prayer room, trying to hide from Tizita, who'd clutched at Sara's skirt all day asking for Dawit. "I called his friends, no one's seen him since yesterday." He drew the curtain on the window. "It's not like him."

"Lily doesn't know anything." The echo of gunfire rustled past the window. "She was here. She'd told him she was leaving this week and he was supposed to see her today."

Yonas paced. The floorboard creaked under his steps.

"She'll hear you," Sara warned, pointing to the door. He stopped.

Yonas looked long into Sara's face. He smoothed the red velvet cloth draped over the table. "Do you know something?"

"Like what?" Sara tried to smile but her lips only trembled, then slipped back into a grim line.

He kept quiet, intent on her expressions, on the secrets they both knew she kept.

"Don't do that," she said. She waited for him to respond. "Say something," she said.

He gave a jolt. "His suitcase. Where's his suitcase?" He pushed Sara aside and ran down the stairs. "Did they take him away when we were gone somewhere?"

Sara found Yonas in Dawit's closet rummaging through the piles of clothes and shoes. He yanked a suitcase from the bottom of a heap. "It's here." He clung to it, turning away from her. "It's here."

54

THE MORTICIAN OPENED A THICK METAL DOOR. "We keep them in here until their families come," he said to Yonas, wiggling a toothpick in the large gap between his teeth. "It takes a while for some, they don't want to admit the truth." He let the door shut behind him. "Tell me what he looks like, I'll go in and check."

"He looks like me."

The mortician shook his head. "You all say the same thing. Do you have a picture?"

Yonas fumbled inside his shirt pocket. "I didn't think—"

"Any birthmarks, scars, age?"

"He's twenty-seven, tall like me, he wears a green shirt a lot, it's his favorite." His younger brother's image came to him in fragments: the wide openness of his grin, the laugh lines around his eyes, the strong lines of his jaw, the frailty of the ankle he'd broken as a small boy.

The mortician tapped on the door. "We're full in here, I need more details. Some of the families don't have a hundred and twenty-five *birr* so we're waiting for them. Not enough cold storage in this entire city."

"A hundred and twenty-five *birr*?"

The mortician sighed wearily. "The bullet fee. If a bullet was used to kill your brother, I have to charge you for it before you can get the body. Policy. I thought everybody knew."

Yonas was too stunned to say anything.

The mortician seemed to take pity on him. "Listen," he said. "I'll try to see if I can find him, but I don't have much time." He went into the room.

It had been nearly a week and Dawit hadn't come home. Sara, finally panicked after what seemed too long to him, had walked from house to house in their neighborhood asking for his whereabouts. Yonas had gone to his father's jail and worked his way down the long line of people asking about his brother. Many knew him, but none had seen him in a week.

"They might have got him, he was one of the loud ones here," said a tired-looking man with deep wrinkles around his mouth. "He was a good boy." Then the old man had sank onto the top step of the jail. "They know which ones to get."

The mortician came out of the room. "Nothing. Did you check the roads around your house?"

"I've checked everywhere."

"You have to do it every day. If you can't, I know someone. He's very good, cheap," the mortician said.

"Cheap?"

At this, the thin man laughed. "He's smart. He should charge extra for going into the hills and checking in the river, but who can afford that?" The mortician took him by the elbow. "Come back with a picture, I'll have my friend look."

"Let me go in." Yonas fished in his pockets and pulled out money.

"Go home."

Yonas pressed the money into his moist palm and squeezed it closed.

"Have it your way," the mortician said, slipping the money into his pocket. He swung the door open and turned his head away from the smell. "Excuse the mess."

The mortician handed Yonas a small box of toothpicks from his jacket. "They help keep the smell out, at least I like to think so." He smiled, then let the grin slip off his face. "If he's in there, I can't let you have the body until you pay. They shoot them after they're dead if they killed them some other way, just to collect the fee."

THEY WERE LINED UP in rows in various stages of decay and undress. They lay on dulled metal gurneys shoved into each other. From somewhere, the jagged breathing of a hungry hyena drifted by. He fumbled in his pocket for his father's prayer beads.

Jaws slack from agony and shock, hands tangled in a web of broken fingers, and the same heartbreaking gaze of a trapped animal on every face. There wasn't enough air in the room. Yonas realized his breathing came in quick, short takes; he began to get dizzy, began to feel the weight of breathlessness, and a pocket of something warm and black and overpowering rose from the center of his chest and worked its way up. He knew when it reached his head he'd faint. Dawit wasn't in this room, couldn't be.

55

SELAM BLUE AND BRILLIANT SITS in the cold gray of his concrete cell, her crosses bright as new leaves after a rain. She opens her arms and Hailu feels his heart slipping out of his body. She is as young as when they married, when it was just the two of them discovering each other. He sits up, feels trapped by this aged body, by this strange lack of sound, listens for the tiniest echo of his breathing, brings a hand to his mouth, feels his breath against his palm, can't hear himself. Ice climbs up his spine, twists its way into his stomach, rests in his bones, sinks to the marrow. Selam is fading. A weight tugs at his head, closes his throat, paralyzes him. His jaw aches, he breathes through his nose, inhales mucus, feels like he is drowning even as he tells himself that it is impossible.

BOOK FOUR

56

"**R**EVOLUTIONARY MOTHERLAND OR DEATH!**"

Clouds of dust swarmed around a group of prisoners marching past numb-faced onlookers. They moved with military precision, stiff legs rising and falling in rhythm. Bored soldiers stood at each street corner with rifles tilted casually towards the prisoners.

"Long Live Marxism!" the marchers cried.

"Louder, anarchists! Stand straight!" a long-necked soldier shouted to an old man leaning on a young girl. He ignored the flies that crept near his eye.

The young girl raised her hand to her mouth to shout louder. She pushed the old man off her shoulder and adjusted the tattered collar of her red shirt. A deep gash exposed the pink of open flesh on her collarbone.

"Viva Proletariat Ethiopia! Viva Guddu!" she cried with the rest.

"Raise the signs higher! Don't slow down!" the soldier yelled at a row of boys holding handmade signs against their bony hips.

Berhane limped off to the side. "Viva Guddu!" he cried. He dropped his sign and pulled his sagging shorts over his waist, revealing angry, infected wounds on each leg. "I don't have a belt," he whimpered to the boys marching on without him. "Wait for me."

"I said don't slow down!" The soldier raised his rifle. He edged his finger towards the trigger and leaned his face closer to the rifle's steel frame. "Didn't you hear me?"

Berhane scrambled to pick up his sign. "I'm hurrying!"

He looked up just in time to see the hollow-eyed stare of the gun and hear his own sharp breath. The soldier pulled the trigger. The loud pop of exploding gunfire silenced the marchers. A puff of smoke bloomed over the fallen body.

"Keep marching!" the soldier yelled, veins drawn on his neck. "Or you're next!"

The marchers fell into a silent pantomime, their stricken glances at Berhane hastened by the menacing aim of the soldier's rifle. They shoved crooked-lettered placards higher, then put one foot in front of the other. Left right left right. They walked in perfect unison.

"I can't hear you!" the soldier shouted.

"Victory for the Masses!"

"Revolution Is Joy!"

"Death to Imperialism!"

In the sun, the crooked letters, red and sloppy, shone against the dirty brown paper.

YONAS HEARD THE gunshot and turned. There was a small boy lying facedown on the road. He shook his head and tried to get through the crowd without another glance. People around him squeezed together, an immovable mass of prayers, and stared at the fallen body. Yonas tried to push through but he was blocked by chests and arms, legs and hips, trapped by the pressure of too many living bodies. He gave up and looked at his watch. It was just past noon. He'd waited two hours to get fresh meat and onions.

Out of the corner of his eye, he caught the unflinching momentum of bare feet trampling the small figure in a steady march forward.

"Revolutionary Ethiopia!" the marchers cried.

The crowd began to thin as the last row of marchers filed past. A group of women hurried by with tears running down their faces, their hands stifling screams.

"You!" the soldier shouted.

A stooped woman dressed in black looked at Yonas, shook her head in pity, then grabbed her friend and walked faster.

"Stop! I'm talking to you, with the bag," the soldier said.

A few people slowed. Their glance followed the soldier's gaze to land on Yonas. Others quickened their steps. Some stopped completely, a weary sadness etched on their faces.

Yonas stood still, his eyes on his bag. He pulled his shoulders down, hunched into himself, and prayed. He avoided the soldier's glare.

"Help me get this rubbish out of the way." The soldier was a skinny man. The whites of his eyes were the color of rust. The barrel of his rifle pointed at the small boy on the road. "He shit himself."

Yonas looked at the dark stain that flowered from the back of the boy's shorts and crept down his thin leg.

He was small. He looked the same age as Tizita.

"Did you hear me?" the soldier asked, standing in front of Yonas. He turned to wink at his comrades who were gathering around the two men. People dropped their heads and shuffled uncomfortably in place as the soldiers brushed past them.

"I thought we killed all the deaf last week," one of the other soldiers joked.

"This one didn't hear the announcement," another quipped.

"What are you going to do, Lukas?" another said. "Call Mekonnen to get this body?" The soldiers laughed.

The sun bore heavily on Yonas, patches of sweat fanned the back of his light blue shirt. He didn't move. He only stared at the boy in the road and tightened his grip on his plastic bag. His fingernails cut into his palms.

"I said get over there and move it out of the way!" Lukas shouted. "You should be down the road helping with the marchers, not here," he said to the other soldiers.

The soldiers smirked. Lukas pushed close to Yonas. His sharp nose grazed his chin. He stretched his neck. "Move this body out of the road if you don't want to die."

"Professor Yonas?" A soldier with soft eyes and a high forehead sprang from the line of men. "Is it you?"

Yonas calculated how late he already was in getting home. Sara was waiting for the meat. He'd promised Tizita that he'd help her with her homework. She was learning the Amharic alphabet. He was going to show her how to write her name. He was going to sit and talk to her as he hadn't done in a very long time. She was seven. The dead boy, could he have been any older?

The soldier shook his arm lightly. "Professor, drag the body out of the road. It's already dead, there's nothing else you can do."

There was the twirl of a safety latch, released.

"Lukas! Just wait, he's going to move it. Professor, please," the soldier said.

Yonas's limbs felt thick, slowed by a pressure he could feel in his chest. He put down his plastic bag and walked towards the boy. He grasped the skinny ankles and pulled. Sticky flesh gave way under his palms and he saw garish rope burns on the boy's legs. He leaned down to turn the body onto its back, to lift it by its armpits and avoid exposed wounds. He flipped the body over.

"Hurry up!" Lukas said.

Yonas drew back, startled. Berhane. "I know him," he said softly. "I know this boy."

"You've got one minute!" Lukas barked.

"Take it to the side," the other soldier pleaded.

Berhane's face was swollen and cruelly bruised, nearly unrecognizable if not for his large front teeth and equally large eyes. Yonas could see, even in this vacant stare, the last traces of the little boy's wide-eyed curiosity. He turned his head and dragged the child out of the road. Then he knelt next to Berhane and shut his vacant eyes, once again seeing his resemblance to Sofia. He folded the boy's arms across his chest.

"Gabriel, take care of his soul, give him no memory of this," he prayed to the archangel. "Send him to his father."

The soldiers ambled on, kicking stones in a mock game of soccer. Tagging behind them, Lukas carried Yonas's white plastic bag, swinging the bag casually. It rose and fell in the air, the pool of blood from the meat dulled to pink through the plastic.

"Death to All Enemies!" the marchers cried in the distance.

Yonas waited until the soldiers curved into the bend of the road and disappeared, and the anthems of the frightened marchers faded into the sky, then he walked back to Berhane and lifted him in his arms and hugged him. He cradled his head, cupping it so it wouldn't loll back, then he carried the boy back to the car and laid him in the backseat, tucked under a frayed blanket he hadn't known was there.

57

THE NIGHT WAS THICK WITH FEAR. Echoes of gunfire pounded relentlessly on the horizon. The prisoners had been taken to the soccer stadium, marched past Revolution Square into the heart of the city, and ordered to sing of their loyalty to Guddu and the Derg. Their fervent cries of revolution and Communism were soon eclipsed by sudden and continual rounds of shooting. All over the city families listened in their homes in helpless anger and sorrow. Anbessa, it was rumored, had climbed up a tree that overlooked the soccer field and begun to pick off one merciless soldier after another. Whispers carried from one eager ear to the next told of a row of angels, enraged by the bloodshed, who surrounded him with swords, deflecting bullets and blinding soldiers who dared look in his direction. And underneath those whispers, other stories bloomed, of three men who moved with the fierceness and speed of fire: Mekonnen killer of soldiers, Anbessa destroyer of roadblocks, Solomon the wise.

BEHIND A FADED DOOR, Emama Seble knelt, solemn and spent, over Berhane, the small body wrapped in a crisp white sheet. Sofia and Robel clung to each other, watching her every move. Melaku stood just behind them, rocking back and forth, his mouth moving in rapid prayer. From a row of candles, bright yellow flames curled into long strips of smoke. In the distance, bullets drilled through the last remaining marcher.

Emama Seble turned to Sara and Yonas. "I don't know what you expect," she said. "I'm just a simple woman." Sweat fell down her face and collected at her neck.

Sofia held Robel tighter. "Help him," she pleaded.

Emama Seble smoothed the sheet lovingly. "I can't." She sat back. "He's dead."

"Emama . . ." Sara began.

Emama Seble held up her hand. "Your daughter was only sick. If there's life, there's a chance." She wiped her eyes and turned to Sofia and Robel. "I'm sorry."

Melaku sank into a chair. "We'd hoped . . ."

Emama Seble was drained, she seemed to have shrunk inside her clothes, her sweater hung loose and wrinkled across her chest. She gestured towards Sofia. "What's the point in false hope? Why give her something you'll have to take away?"

"Where's my little boy?" Sofia whispered. "He should be home now." Her glazed eyes searched Emama Seble's. "You know where he is."

Robel held her hand and rubbed it, his mouth trembling. "Let's go home, Emaye," he said.

Sara and Yonas led Sofia to the door.

Emama Seble stopped them outside. "We have to bury him. Find out how." She pointed to Sofia and Robel going into Yonas's house with Melaku. "Don't leave her alone once she understands he's gone."

A WAIL SHATTERED the sky, startled sparrows out of trees. A low mournful cry dipped into guttural sobs. Sofia pounded her chest, face upturned to wilting stars, her remaining son curled at her side, wrapped around her legs. Her grief knew no refuge, found no shelter.

"Daniel," she said, her voice a whisper. "Where is mercy?" She grew louder. "Where is justice?"

"Emama." She was deaf to Robel's cries, his anguish eclipsed by hers.

Sara knelt over them, her eyes swollen from tears.

"It can't be," Sofia said. "It can't be. I don't believe it. You're lying!"

Sara put a hand over Sofia's mouth. "They'll hear you, be quiet. Shiferaw keeps walking past the window."

They were in the living room of Sara's house, the doors locked. Bizu drew the curtains, protecting them from intrusive eyes. She sat next to Sofia, murmuring, "*Aizosh, Aizosh,*" in comforting tones.

"What else can they take?" Sofia said.

"You have a son," Sara said, pulling Robel upright. "You have him." She nudged him forward.

Robel tried to wrap his arms around his mother. "Go away," she said. "I'm cursed."

"It's okay," Sara said to Robel. "Go upstairs. Get rest."

"Come with me," said Bizu, holding out her hand.

Robel, drawn and shaken, refused. "I can't leave her." His lips trembled. "She's alone."

Sara hugged him, aching at the way he clung to her desperately. "She's got you. You're everything to her now. She's lucky to have you still." She wiped his tears. "Go take a nap in our room. She'll be okay." She could see the boy's struggle. "Go. Then we'll eat. You haven't eaten all day. We have to bury him tomorrow." She smoothed his hair.

Robel stared at her, stunned. He looked at his hands as if expecting Berhane to materialize between them.

"Go upstairs," Sara said, putting his hand into Bizu's.

Once he was gone, Sara laid Sofia down on the sofa. "Rest," she said. She covered her in a blanket once reserved only for Hailu. She held Sofia when she struggled to sit up. "He's safe. You're both staying here for a while, don't worry about anything."

BEYOND THE COMPOUND, underneath a tree, Yonas counted coins and bills into Shiferaw's open palm. The *kebele* officer stared at the mounting pile greedily, his permanent smile spreading like a thread across his face. "It's going to be extra because now you want to keep it overnight," he told Yonas. "I'm taking a bigger risk." He worked a finger into a hole in his sweater. "Just take it back to the street. The mother's seen him now."

Yonas pulled the man's hand away from his sweater and held his wrist. "I brought what you told me. I've cleaned out my savings. We have to bury him."

"Are you crazy?" Shiferaw protested, pulling out of his hold. "Where?" He waved his arms to encompass the neighborhood. "Anyplace they see freshly dug dirt, you know they'll come and dig the body out. Especially after tonight and all that shooting." He shook his head. "Take it somewhere in the hills and put it under rocks. Burn it. I don't care, but you can't put it anywhere near here. They'll take me to jail." His grin widened, his finger finding the hole again. "Next time they'll slice my nose off."

Yonas slapped the man's hand from his sweater and raised his chin. He searched Shiferaw's face. "And my brother?" he asked.

"It's not enough." Shiferaw held out his other palm, then flinched when Yonas reached for his throat. "Okay, okay. I have a family too," he said, backing away. He cleared his throat. "These fanatics don't pay me enough for what they did to me. They cut my face and leave me with one sweater. They give the best nationalized homes to these foreign advisors." He spit in disgust. "No one's said anything about your brother. I'd hear it if they found him."

Yonas turned away, unwilling to let the man see the relief in his face.

"Take it into the hills. Tomorrow is Major Guddu's birthday, they won't be watching," Shiferaw said as Yonas walked back into the gate and into the compound.

THE VOLKSWAGEN WOUND its way up the hill. Sara sat in front. Robel, Sofia, and Emama Seble rode quietly, dazed, in the back, the wrapped body across their laps. Sofia concentrated on the landscape of rolling hills and the bright yellow of *meskel* flowers. She tapped on the window as they came to an alcove tucked away from the road. There was a leafy tree sheltering the mouth of a small cave.

"Stop, "she said, beating on the window. "This is it." She stumbled out as the car came to a halt. She leaned against the large tree and sat down. "Right here. We'll dig here." She inspected the sky. "He'll face the sun every morning."

Sara sat next to her. "The men will dig," she said. "Let's go wait over there." She pointed to a spot several paces in front of them.

"Give me the shovel," Sofia said, standing. She stared ahead of her without seeing anything. "Bring it here."

Robel and Yonas led her away. "Emama Seble said it's my job," Robel reminded her. He wrapped his arm around her, supporting her.

"No," Sofia said, staring at a spot on the ground. "I'll do it."

The old woman, still sitting in the Volkswagen, frowned. "Sofia, go sit with Sara, let the boy do this."

Sofia followed Sara woodenly.

"He needs to do this for himself," Sara said. "Be gentle with him."

"Why can't I look at him?" Sofia asked.

The sun burned the belly of the sky, cut deep orange streaks into the horizon.

They sank onto the hard, rocky earth, their black dresses tucked beneath their legs. Sofia stared at Sara as if seeing her for the first time. "I'll wear black for the rest of my life," she said. "For both of them." She pulled a small plastic bag out of her handbag and took out a faded shirt. "It's Daniel's," she said, holding it up to her face. "There's still the scent of him in the bag. I'm giving it to Berhane so he'll have his father. How selfish of me to keep it to myself. I couldn't even share with my children." She folded it carefully and put it in the bag again.

Sara took the bag. "Keep it. You can give it to Robel. You gave them so much of their father. Memories." She patted the other woman's cheek but Sofia didn't respond, a silhouetted statue against the fading sun.

"Do you think he was afraid?" Sofia asked. "At the end, do you think he cried for me?" She covered her hands with her ears. "I hear him." She wrapped her arms around her legs. "How can I put him in the ground after all he's been through . . ." She hugged herself. She couldn't stop moving.

"That body's not your son anymore," Sara said, holding her still. "It's just a shell."

The women watched the sun arc and slide through the sky, a cooler breeze descending on them as the horizon darkened.

"We're ready," Emama Seble called out.

They walked back to the tree, and at the sight of the short, shallow grave, Sofia fell to her knees and held out her arms. "Give him to me," she said. "Give me my son."

Emama Seble and Yonas laid the body in front of her. Sofia began to unwrap the sheet. "I will look at him," she said, talking to no one. "I will look at what they did and never forget."

Emama Seble held her back. "Don't do this. Don't punish yourself."

Sofia shrugged her off and rolled the sheet away from Berhane's face. "I don't even have a photograph of him. Nothing's left but this." She fell back at the sight of his wounds. "Daniel, what have they done to your son?" She turned away, her hand in her mouth, fighting not to scream. Then she started unwrapping the sheet again, talking to Berhane as she worked. "I met your father on Timket, in a big field called Jan Meda, did I ever tell you . . . ?"

Robel buried his head in Sara's chest. "I can't look," he said.

Sara led him over to Yonas and the boy clung to the man. She sat next to Sofia and took hold of the other end of the sheet, stripping it from the body. At the sight of his ankles and the punctures on his thighs, she stopped and glanced at Sofia, who refused to take her eyes off her son's face as she continued talking to him.

The two women worked under the dead sun and didn't stop until a wan moon hung above them like a curious eye.

Sofia kissed each cheek and each hand, and smoothed the creases in his wrinkled shorts. She shifted the rigid body onto her lap, then she cradled it as best she could. Rocking softly, she began to hum, her voice like a blowing feather, the sounds evidence of a grief that could not be contained within the confines of language.

"Daniel," she finally said. "He's mine no more. Take him and wait for me." She paused, then looked to the car where Robel stood, shaking. "Wait for both of us."

A LION KNEELS. Berhane climbs on its back and they race through a field of *meskel* flowers to the top of a bright green hill where his father waits on his white horse, his hair like a dark sun around his head. Berhane rushes through the wind, becomes the wind, sails to the tip of the sun, and falls into the Nile. He swims, free and cool, in the golden light of dusk. His father holds out his hand.

"You've come," Berhane says.

"I've been looking for you."

Berhane climbs onto the back of the horse and holds on tight as they ride through the hills, leap over creeks, and rush headlong into the orange sky.

58

HAILU'S CELL DOOR SLAMMED OPEN and two soldiers dragged him towards the immaculate reception area he hadn't seen since walking in. Soldiers worked quietly at their desks, ignoring his noisy shuffling towards a row of sleek metal chairs. He didn't have enough strength to sit up in the cold chair he was pushed into. A balding soldier handed him papers that slipped through his hand like dust. The pen they waved in his face fell to the ground as soon as they gave it to him.

The soldier, picking up and testing the pen, said, "Bring a new Biro, the Colonel doesn't like old ink." His shout produced another pen and a few smirks. "Sign," he said, pointing to the paper on the desk in front of him.

The letters shifted dizzyingly in front of Hailu. Two soldiers steadied him by the arms. His head tipped, dragging the rest of his body down, before someone finally held his forehead and anchored him.

"Don't you want to know what you're signing?" the balding soldier asked, his raised eyebrows causing deep ripples in his forehead.

The rest of the soldiers looked up from their documents. Hailu saw the soldier's mouth moving, his pointed eyebrows, but couldn't decipher the words. His head felt thick, heavy.

"It's your death warrant," the soldier quipped, pointing at the paper. "Sign it or we'll kill you."

They laughed.

Hailu scraped his signature across the page; ink blots and smudges spotted his palm as he dragged it along.

The soldier put the signed paper into a folder and handed it to a comrade. He lifted Hailu by the elbow. "What did you say to him?" he asked, patting the bald spot on the top of his head. "How could he let you go after you killed his daughter?"

Hailu couldn't hear above the buzzing in his ears. He stood with his hands folded in front of him, his head down, waiting to be led to the

Colonel. He was pulled towards the front door instead, then prodded from behind. At the door, he was handed his suitcase, now empty, and pushed out, blinking wildly in the chilly fresh air. The door shut and locked.

He stood still, dry-mouthed, waiting for soldiers to fling the door open and drag him back. He waited for the mocking laughs and taunts at his gullibility. He waited until he stopped shaking, until his legs steadied, until a thought sank in and became solid: he was free. Free. There was no warning, there would be no ceremony, but he was free. He could walk down this road and, with each step, become just another man wading through his day, time constricted to twenty-four hours once again. Minutes neatly divided into segments guided by the sun.

Hailu squinted against the dropping light. He took a step down the dusty ribbon of road that would lead him home and shifted the empty suitcase in his hand. He looked over his shoulder at the square gray jail and searched the landscape for soldiers. He waited unbearable minutes for the Colonel's commanding stride to grow increasingly louder. There was nothing.

He glanced around him. Eyes were on him, peering from distant hills, and shuttered windows, from calibrated military binoculars. Ethiopia had become a country of watchers. He imagined the figure he made: a lone man with a battered suitcase, staggering over rocks and potholes. There was the momentary thought that he was a vulgar and frightening sight. He was close to naked, his trousers cut and torn, holes revealing parts of him indecently. But the thought evaporated in the cloudiness of a dulled and bruised mind. He didn't care. All modesty had disappeared during the interrogations. The Colonel had turned him into nothing but a mass of damaged nerves and soft bones. He'd been repeatedly stripped of all inhibition, one indignity after another. He didn't care that his clothes exposed every part of his emaciated figure. He didn't care that this warm palm of sunshine was part of his world again. He didn't care about any of it.

If he'd had the same heart he was born with, he'd have wondered about Yonas and the guilt he knew his son carried. He'd have considered what he'd say to Tizita, how he'd explain where he'd been and why. And he'd have weighed his words with Dawit, chosen only the kindest. But no thought entered his head; no emotion nudged his heart into existence again. He moved mechanically, dragging one leg in front of the other and letting that momentum pull him towards the next step. He searched the space his body lurched through for Selam, some hint that she was with him, but there was only the sound of small rocks snapping and crackling under his bruised and beaten feet.

PEOPLE STOPPED TO STARE, groups separated wordlessly to let him through. The air stilled around his head and above him, a bird's song snapped in half and crumbled into silence. Hailu had the appearance of a man dragging death with him through life—a Lazarus damned. His back curved deeply, his stomach caved inward. His skin hung loose, tucking and folding where once there had been flesh and fat.

A woman approached him, a cup in her hand, her eyes moving over the length of him, then modestly turning away. "Abbaye," she offered. "Drink some water."

Her voice sounded rich and pure, as clean and gentle as a spring. It made tears well in his eyes and he swallowed them to quench the dryness in his throat. He continued walking, afraid to reach for the cup in case the momentum hurled him to the ground. The woman brought the water to his mouth and tenderly cupped the back of his head, steadying him for a sip.

"I'll walk with you, just open your mouth," she said.

Hailu obeyed, long since unable to resist any command. The water flowed down his throat in a rush, it flooded his stomach and the coolness of it, the complete pureness of its taste, startled him. There was nothing in this water but its brilliant, shining, sweet wetness.

He felt the woman take his arm. She slid her *shamma* off her shoulders and wrapped it around his. "Where are you going?" she asked.

"Home," he said. His voice sounded dry and brittle, thin. "Home," he said again.

She held his arm closer to her side. They walked until she could go no further. "I'll get reported if I don't go to *kebele*," she said. "Walk with God."

She released him and Hailu felt like a startled bird flung into the sky. His head spun from the renewed imbalance in his steps and he stumbled forward, staggering into the next lonely step. He groped the empty space in front of him for something, anything, to guide him onward, straight-backed and dignified, to his front door, but he was met with the sound of leaves, empty of their birdsongs, shivering in the wind.

THERE WAS A KNOCK at the door.

"Go get it, Tizzie," Sara said. "It's probably Emama Seble."

Tizita charged out of the kitchen and bounded through the living room. She stopped at Abbaye's red radio, quiet and dusty, and kissed the front of it as she secretly did every time she passed by. Then she listened at the door to make sure soldiers weren't at the other side.

"How do you know if they're there?" she'd asked her best friend at school, Rahel. Rahel's brother had been taken from their house at night by soldiers who knocked first.

Rahel had tilted her head knowingly. "They smell like goats."

Tizita stood by the door now and pressed her nose against it. She smelled something bad. Rahel told her if you didn't open the door the soldiers would take everyone. She opened the door, holding her nose.

His eyes were far back in his face and his slack mouth revealed yellow teeth. Two were missing in front and his tongue licked between the spaces like a thirsty dog. His face was hammered in on the sides, his nose was crooked and big and swollen. There was wild hair in patches across his jaws and pimply, bumpy skin in the pale naked pockets.

Her nose burned, her eyes stung, her throat hurt. She stepped back and began to shut the door.

"Tizzie," the man said. "Tizzie?"

She looked at the man's skinny arms and saw scabs and scratches and black burned holes, and knew she was staring at one of the ghosts people said Emama Seble talked to. She slammed the door, scared, and ran back to her mother.

SARA'S SCREAM WAS formed in the friction between horror and elation. She stood at the threshold of the doorway transfixed by the image of the man she saw shivering in the sun, his mouth opening and closing around air. She screamed again, clutched her heart, and stepped back from the door.

"Sara," he said, standing still, afraid, it seemed, to move without instruction. A rotting tree stripped of roots, drained of water and sun.

"Abbaye," she cried, holding her arms out even as he stayed grounded in place. "It's you," she said, reassuring both of them. Ululations flew from her mouth, their shrill shivering tempered by raw grief. She swallowed, tried to stop the tears, but her throat shook the cries loose, released the loneliness and fear that had begun long before Abbaye's arrest, that had been planted at the death of her own father. "You're home."

"Who is it?" Tizita asked. She'd stiffened rigid as a board.

"It's me, Tizzie." He began to sway, his body finally buckling, toppled by the little girl's fears.

"My father. My father." Yonas dropped next to them. "Abbaye."

Hailu leaned solidly against Sara, a heavy stone. Sara sank to the ground and held him across her lap. He moaned and his decaying breath floated to her face.

—THERE. THERE. OVER THERE. A speck of dust floats on an angry wind and settles in the wet eyes of a man with a mouth open to the moon. He crouches in his military uniform, wild-eyed and haggard on barren earth, his eyes dirty pools of light. There the Colonel stands on the edge of a hillside road, above a dimmed city, and marvels at the thickness of the black night. On a hilltop high above Addis Ababa, he sheds his uniform, Colonel no more, naked to the wind. He stands, tender-skinned and bent-backed, a grieving father with clouds in his eyes. There on a lonely hillside, stars bend to a sudden wail. Trees sway to the shivering in his heaving chest. A startled owl blinks at the dull thump of bullet spinning through skull bone.

THE RIFLE WAS HIS ARM, ATTACHED TO the rhythm in his chest, hot and heavy and solid against his shoulder. Dawit aimed and shot and hit the target, heard the boom and bang of cracking wood, felt the ringing in his ears, smelled the sharp tang of lead, understood the power and charge of a thing both deadly and seductive, loaded again. Birds scattered overhead, a distant herder's whistle rose and dropped in the startling quiet of gun smoke and sweat.

"Much better," Solomon said, standing next to him, cotton shoved in his ears, a grudging smile on his lips. "I'm surprised." He slapped him on the shoulder. "Enough for one day. Let's go back."

Dawit sighed gratefully. A deep tiredness had set in. "I have to go home," he said. "Lily's already left for Cuba and I don't know anything about my family."

"We have to wait until they find a new anarchist to chase. It won't be long, they've been arresting everyone."

"Because of me?" Dawit asked. He grew agitated. "What if they punish my father? I have to go."

"Slow down," Solomon said. "Your father's home."

Dawit dropped the rifle. "I have to go." He grabbed his jacket from the ground. "I have to see him."

Solomon blocked his way. "Stop," he said. He pushed him back. "That's your problem, you don't listen."

Dawit tried to walk around him. "I need to make sure he's all right. What if they come back for him?" he said.

"Do you think he'll be safer with you in the house?" Solomon asked, pushing him back again, then resting a hand on his chest. "The Colonel had him released, then killed himself. An old farmer found his body."

"The Colonel?" Dawit staggered backwards. "The famous one?" He'd read about this man in his history class.

Solomon nodded. "The same Colonel, one of our greatest war

heroes, had his own daughter arrested, a high school student. She was helping us pass out pamphlets at school. I heard he wanted to scare her, teach her a lesson, but she got into the wrong hands. Bureaucratic error."

"What does that have to do with Abbaye?" Dawit asked.

"They took her to Black Lion Hospital, the interrogators and soldiers involved. They didn't want the Colonel to find out. Girma was the one who questioned her."

Dawit took a sharp breath. Everyone knew of Girma the Butcher, the handsome, elegant man who worked with a human-sized plastic bag over his victims. Few made it out alive. Those who did, it was said, were the unlucky ones.

"My father treated her?" Dawit asked. "He was taking care of her?"

Solomon nodded. "They say he killed her himself, gave her poison so she wouldn't go back to jail." He watched Dawit's expression closely. "You didn't know?"

"We don't talk," he said. "He doesn't talk to me."

Solomon looked sad. "Girma was planning to threaten her into keeping her mouth shut, then send her back home to the Colonel, healed and obedient, and earn himself a promotion." He chewed on the inside of his cheek. "She was friends with my little sister."

"How do you know all this?" Dawit asked.

"Girma told us. He was trying to flee the country and not so cooperative, but after a few nights of"—Solomon paused—"talks with us, he told us everything."

"Where is he now?" Dawit asked.

"He was hit by a car right after we released him. Unfortunate."

Dawit shook his head, dizzy with information. He still felt his father's disapproval, even from this chasm they found between them. "He never told me."

DUST FLOATED IN the strip of sunlight angling across the bed, the trajectory of their movement testimony to the day's passing hours. Hailu lay in Dawit's room, and tried to break minutes and seconds into their smallest increments, into that perfect moment just before the brain recognized pain.

"You disappeared again," Sara said as she brought a spoonful of porridge to his mouth. "Eat. It's not too hot." She smiled with the tenderness of a new mother.

Cigarette smoke slid up his nose. Hailu turned away, afraid to stare at the Colonel. Dawit had yet to visit him, no one had spoken his name. He looked up and found the Colonel leaning into the shooting pains that clawed at his throat.

"Just a little." Sara nudged the spoon against his closed lips.

Tizita ran into the room, making him jerk.

"Tizita!" Sara said. "I told you not to run in here." She patted his shoulder.

Tizita patted his legs, unaware that she was hitting on places where wires had been attached. He moaned.

"Stop touching him." Sara slapped her hand away. "He's still healing."

"Where did he come from?" she asked.

"I told you," Sara said. "From prison. He was there for a long time. That's why he's like this."

Tizita crept closer to Hailu. With a shy finger, she traced the outline of a closed cut above his eyebrow. "Does that hurt?"

Hailu stayed still, reminded himself that the Colonel wasn't coming.

"I think he likes that," Sara said. "He usually pulls away."

Hailu closed his eyes and let her voice drift above his head.

"I'm sure your teeth will grow back," Tizita said. "Mine did." She paused. "I think he's dreaming again, Emaye. His legs are running."

61

THE KIOSK WAS SHELTERED FROM intruding eyes by the black blanket Melaku draped over the shutters. Dawit let his eyes roam through the dim light. Robel stood in front of him, his feet shuffling on the dirt floor. The boy was small for his age. Dust and chunks of dried mud filled the creases between his toes. He wore no shoes and his ankles stuck out jaggedly at the ends of bony legs that dangled out of shorts too large for him. His faded shirt was stained and exposed a flat belly. His thick eyebrows nearly met in the middle.

"I'm sorry about your brother." Dawit knew his tall frame dominated the cramped space and dwarfed Robel. He hunched into the wooden stool. "He was a wonderful boy. I promise you we'll do everything we can to get back at them." He'd managed to beg Solomon for one night in his neighborhood to speak to his family. "How is your mother?"

"He was smart. He should have been in school." Robel's arms were clamped stiffly to his side, his hands balled into fists.

Sara watched from the corner, waiting for her turn to talk.

"If your mother loses anyone else, do you know how sad she'll be?" Dawit asked. "I know you want to do something. I came here just to tell you, so you understand, the best thing for you to do is take care of your mother. Let the rest of us fight."

Robel's clear brown eyes met Dawit's, brimming with anger. "They took my father, too." His mouth trembled. "I was supposed to look after my brother."

Dawit saw that this small boy could grow into a full-blooded adult menace, a destructive force borne of grief that had been treated as inconsequential. He pretended to think for a moment.

"My mother used to show me stones like this one." He picked up a tiny pebble and rolled it between his fingers. "This can't do anything, it's too small. But inside a shoe, it can make a grown man stumble. Do you understand?"

Robel frowned, shook his head, but was listening intently.

"You're my pebble. I want you to tell Melaku anytime you hear something when you're working. You hear men talking, right?"

Robel nodded enthusiastically. "They don't think I can hear them."

"Good, that's perfect. We need you. And you have to promise me you won't tell anyone you saw me."

"I won't," Robel said, looking back at Sara.

"I won't tell anyone you were here," she said to the boy. "Not even your mother."

"Stand straight. Put your feet together." Dawit's heart ached at the sight of the eager, obedient boy. He gripped his shoulders and looked him in the eye. "Seyoum. That's your new name. Any message you send me through Melaku, make sure it's from Seyoum." He paused. "I'm Mekonnen."

"Mekonnen," Robel said, looking up at Dawit in awe.

SARA AND YONAS SPOKE in soft voices across a divide that was larger than the dining room table separating them. The weight of betrayed trust rolled in the undercurrents of tension.

"You knew? All this time you knew and you didn't tell me?" Yonas asked. "I went to that, that morgue, and you knew?" His words strained against his own disbelief.

"I didn't know then. I just found out he's been hiding, he wouldn't tell me where. He said to tell you he's all right."

"No." Yonas shook head. "You knew, I could tell something was different, you weren't as worried, you didn't even start looking until a week after he'd been gone. Don't tell me you didn't know."

Sara spoke in even tones. "You'll have to trust me." She stood up. "I need to check on your father."

"What else is going on?"

She stopped and turned around. "What do you mean?"

"There's more."

"There's nothing else," she said. Fatigue and love softened her tone.

"You don't think I know about the late nights? You go somewhere and don't come back until curfew. I used to pace until you came home. I knew you were with Dawit, and what could I say?" He swallowed hard.

"After all the things I didn't do that I should have done . . . How could I blame you?"

Sara shook her head, surprised. "It's not what you are thinking."

"How do you know what I'm thinking?"

She stiffened. "You're my husband and there's never been a moment when I didn't know that."

"You've always been a bad liar, Sara. Like me," he said, smiling ruefully. "Can't you tell me one of your many secrets after all these years?" He reached for her and drew her near. "What is it?" He kissed her cheek, then each eye, and settled his mouth on the top of her head. "On my life, I swear never to tell anyone."

She leaned on his strong chest, tired, and began to tell him about the bodies, the identifications, the nausea and the stench, the broken bones and destroyed families, the wailing mothers and stunned fathers. She told him of the late night drives in the womb of a shuttered city, the crawls under starlight and trees. "We worked as fast as we could, but the next day, there'd be more. And the mothers, the mothers," she said. "I had to tell the mothers."

He tightened his grip on her, squeezed gently, and kissed her. "This was dangerous." He shut his eyes. "You were so close to so much danger. Melaku was helping?"

She nodded.

"That's why he looked so tired all the time. Did Emama Seble know?"

"Do you have to ask?"

They both grinned. He grew pensive again. "What's next?"

She pressed deeper into his embrace. "Curfew has been moved from midnight to dusk. Dawit is hiding. There's nothing to do now but wait for him to come home, for Abbaye to get better, for us to be together again."

"He's not any better."

"He needs sleep," she said. Hailu called for Selam in his sleep each night, sat up in mid-conversation with her, then dropped back to the bed dazed and mumbling.

"We can't bring a doctor to check on him," Yonas said. "Who'd get near him?" Almaz had been dragged out of bed soon after Hailu's arrest and executed in front of her daughter. "Nothing is getting better."

62

THE COLD WINDS OF THE DAY BEFORE had settled into a gentle breeze. Stray blooms of bright *meskel* flowers lined the road. It was the beginning of Ramadan and everything was closed, including Melaku's kiosk. Sara went there now to visit with the old man.

"Look at the sky, look!" he exclaimed, pointing to the spot where others were already staring, their mouths hanging open. Melaku tipped out of the window of his kiosk, body draped on the counter.

In the center of the sky, surrounding the burning sun, were halos of vivid colors—red, yellow, orange, blue—with dark, nearly burnt edges.

An old woman, her wrinkled face set in a stern frown, shook her head. "It's a curse. See that dark lining at the ends? Satan's setting heaven on fire." She sighed sadly but remained transfixed by the colors. "He's winning."

"It's a blessing!" one neighbor shouted. "Things will change."

Sara felt herself sway under the red-circled heat. Her mother had described such a sun on the day she'd decided to take the Italian's life. She'd told her that even as she closed her eyes, froze her body, and began to squeeze the general's neck, the colors from the sun had stayed under her eyelids, brightening her darkness.

"Don't stare so long," the old woman warned her.

Sara saw several patrons run home, but more emerged from their compounds and gathered in groups on the road. There were so many people it was beginning to look like the start of a procession. Several were on their knees praying with upturned palms. Sara noticed soldiers looking up as well, confusion and curiosity on their faces. Their forgotten guns leaned clumsily against their thighs or drooped behind their shoulders. Shiferaw stood apart from everyone, gawking into the sky with his deformed smile.

"What do you think it is?" she asked Melaku.

"It's a sign of forgiveness," he replied. "It's a sign of redemption for the people we've become." He rubbed his eyes. "Come inside."

He gave her a stool and offered her a Coca-Cola. "It's my last one. Our socialist friends don't realize this is an imperialist drink." He sat next to Sara and patted her leg, all energy drained from him, suddenly older and tired.

"Save it," Sara told him, setting the bottle back on the counter. "Are you all right?"

He was already lost in thought. "I used to be a good man," he said.

Melaku's words traced the days when he stood atop a shaky wooden lookout and swung a slingshot at the hyenas that prowled near his father's goats. He wove a tale of the young son of a peasant who found himself in an emperor's palace and used his songs to mingle with noblemen and princesses, senators and princes.

"Then I met a girl," he said. "But her father wanted grandchildren worthy of palaces. Elsa. My Elsa. I wasted all my money on this spoiled girl while my father was breaking his back in the sun. He died while I was in the palace," Melaku said. "I was too busy wooing Elsa to go back when they told me he was sick. I thought I had time."

"If you knew you'd have gone back," Sara said.

He continued, leaning forward. "What do we ever know about the time we have? What do we know about anything? When they installed a box at the police station to inform on reactionaries, I put Elsa's husband's name in it. They took both of them, even her father, an old, old man by then. They had to carry him and his wheelchair out of his house. When I realized these new officers were nothing but murderers, I tried to get them out but I couldn't. They're gone."

He draped both hands over his head and pressed into his temples. "I asked for a sign that I could forgive myself. Show me there's still light underneath all this I said. I started helping Dawit, penance for all the people I destroyed." He moved his hand across his chest. "Show me, I said, because my heart couldn't feel. I watched for signs every day, every night we collected a body, I worried I'd find Elsa, I prayed I'd find Elsa, I prayed to get caught. But I see something today in this sun. I've seen it." He pointed outside. "This sun."

—

"DID YOU SEE THAT?" Dawit asked, pointing to the sun. "All those colors. What is it?" Dawit tried to distract himself from Solomon's instructions on his new assignment, details about his new weapon, reminders to aim for the cleanest kill. All happening that day.

"You're good, almost better than me." Solomon reached in the back of his car and took out the suitcase Dawit had once given him, the one that held a dead soldier's rifle. Inside was the same AK-47. "Remember this?" Solomon asked, holding up the weapon. "I saved it for you. It's been tested, works well, you don't need to squeeze as hard as the older model I gave you last week. Everything else is the same." He pointed to the trigger, then clenched his fist to hide a hand that was shaking more than usual. "Practice some rounds now, then we have to go."

Dawit took the weapon and tried to control his shivers. He was holding the gun of a man he'd killed, on his way to kill another. He looked into the sky again. There had been a time when all he'd wanted to do was help the defenseless.

"What's wrong?" Solomon asked.

"Do you think this means something, the sun? I've never seen it like this," Dawit asked, trying to hide his thoughts.

"Are you scared?" Solomon slammed the trunk shut. "We can't depend on signs."

"No." There was a tightness climbing in Dawit's chest. The first waves of nausea descended.

Solomon put an arm on his shoulder. "I'll drop you off at Revolution Square, there's a big rally. You'll see a line of Mercedes and jeeps. When you hear the first shot, aim for the second-to-last car and start shooting. Simple."

"Who am I aiming for?" Dawit asked, beginning to sweat.

"Anyone in that car. With enough of us, we'll have full coverage. As soon as you fire, get lost in the crowd. Meet me back here." Solomon took in the clearing in the forest. "If you're not here by curfew, I'll have to come back the next day."

"People will see me with the gun."

"I've brought a uniform for you." Solomon sized him up. "It'll fit. You'll be second in line to shoot, people will think you're aiming for the first shooter. Don't waste a second. Aim for the backseat. Keep shooting until you can't. Run with the crowd."

Dawit wondered if Solomon could smell the sourness in his breath. Fear this strong had a taste.

"I don't care who else you get, and if you don't get him, there's a good chance somebody else will. We failed the first time, we know what to do now." Solomon flexed his hands. "I don't mind fear, I hate doubts."

"I'm sure," Dawit replied.

Solomon clapped him on the back. He took the time now to look into the sky. "My father told me about a sun like this once." Then he shrugged and handed Dawit the uniform.

SARA LAY ON TOP of Yonas, chest to chest, mouth against mouth, and told him everything. She watched him listen to her stories, attentive and loving. She let his hand trail the top of her head and find the scar. "I'm my mother's daughter," she said. "My father was Mikael Abraham. They ran away to Qulubi and I was born there, the daughter of Abraham's son."

"You are my wife," Yonas said. "I don't care about anything else. Your history began here, with me."

She brushed her lips over his. "It started before you." She smiled into his eyes. "But we mold ourselves out of our fates, don't we? My mother once said this to me." She let her stomach rise and fall into his, felt the softness of flesh on flesh, rested in his muscles and strength. "I'll stop grieving for what I never had, for those two. I promise."

He hugged her tightly. "Both of us will stop grieving for those who are happier with God."

"We'll be a family again," she said. "With Dawit."

Yonas blinked back tears as Sara kissed the corner of his mouth. "You two will have a chance to talk when this is over. He's hiding to be safe, and he's safe. He'll come back," she said.

HAILU DREAMS: a truck on the road to his house roars its way to his gate, soldiers clamber out of creaking doors, scurry with a thousand legs and a hundred shouts to his window. They dangle Selam's picture and tear it to shreds, extend a photograph of a newborn Dawit, and with milli-pede legs and reptile hands rip his baby's picture in half and Hailu hurls himself out the window into a cool breeze and a ringed dark sun and he hears above the cacophony of cockroaches and rats, above the buzz of angry locusts, his own voice come back to him, virile and steady.

THE ROADS WERE DESERTED THAT AFTERNOON, no jeeps patrolled the area, and there were no soldiers pacing in front of homes.

"It's so quiet," Sara said to Emama Seble. They were at Hailu's bed, waiting for Yonas to bring Tizita from school. It was almost five o'clock. Sara looked out the window. "They should be here."

"A big rally today," Emama Seble said. "Guddu's making a new announcement. There's lots of traffic. Yonas called, didn't he? He was going to go shopping before coming home."

Sara nodded. "He's waiting until the roads are less crowded. He told me there are schoolchildren practicing marches." She stopped. "He cries about Berhane. I hear him at night but he stops when he knows I'm awake."

"You've told him?" the old woman asked.

Sara nodded. "He thought there was more between Dawit and me."

"Who wouldn't?" She glanced at Hailu. "No news?"

"Nothing yet." Sara unwrapped a bandage around Hailu's chest and laid new leaves on the wounds. They were healing, slowly.

Emama Seble touched his cheek. "He's getting better. He's fighting back."

DAWIT STARED AT the spectators in Revolution Square. People jostled each other and milled around. He felt the anticipation and tension in the air, the electric charge of too many bodies moving too quickly with little thought, and it made the wide-open space stifling. He turned to face Finfine River and the pale golden walls of what was once called Jubilee Palace, then looked towards the imposing Africa Hall, the shining dome of St. Estifanos Church, and settled his gaze on the trees around the square. He caught the glint of a sniper's sunglasses through thin leaves. Soldiers flanked every corner, their ammunition belts strapped solidly across their chests and waists, eyes methodically roving past pedestrians and schoolchildren. They raked the horizon, paused at scattering groups of young people, furrowed their eyebrows at black-clad mothers, and ignored him. Dawit's eyes were locked on a certain row high in the bleachers where two men dressed as soldiers sat far apart, legs crossed identically.

The *keberos* started, rolling steady drumbeats over the tempered whispers of civilians. The drummers slapped cowhide worn thin from years of use, and drilled cavernous beats into the echoing field. For a moment, people stopped their shuffling, soldiers paused mid-scan, and all eyes shifted to the young boys and girls bearing down wildly on their drums. An expectant gasp rose like a bubble to the sky. Dawit sensed what he knew everyone else sensed: that angels were speaking, reminding them that there were others also who shouted with them into the heavens. They were not alone.

A whistle blew outside, trilling screeches that broke the reverie. Children's voices climbed into the sky, excited and shrill. The distant rumble of engines and thick tires grew louder. Military police marched towards the road in twos and threes and Dawit followed, a solitary figure walking in clipped steps towards the nearest exit.

"Don't walk with them but stay close," Solomon had told him. "You'll stand at the intersection closest to the stadium and watch for the second-to-the-last Mercedes. Aim for the passengers. Keep shooting. Don't stop, don't worry about who else you hit. Run with the crowd." Then he'd shaken his hand and gripped it tightly. "And if you get caught"—he'd slipped a tiny cyanide capsule into his palm. "Let the angels hear us today."

The cavalcade moved at a crippling pace. The crowd was silent, transfixed by the oily sleekness of cars sliding over the road like a single black snake. Dawit slipped behind two women and looked around. All eyes were trained on the procession, mesmerized by the regal progress of the entourage. Schoolchildren broke the silence again with a song that praised Guddu's latest triumphs against cowardly enemies. Drumbeats drove them on, their marching strides grew wider, their arms swung with wild exuberance. And despite the words, despite the

sickle-and-star flags, despite the terror resting behind every spectator's stare, the crowd could not help swaying to the exhilarating rush of
being witness to such power and force.

From a corner across the street, Dawit saw Solomon, and behind
him was Anbessa. Solomon nodded and walked into the crowd. Anbessa
stepped forward, and Dawit thought he saw him wink and grin before
carefully resting his rifle higher in his arm. There were five cars still
remaining, then a row of soldiers, then the last two cars.

They came, one after the other, in certainty and calm. The soldiers
went by, caught up in the fervor of an audience ordered to cheer and
clap on the threat of death. The children shouted. The drums thudded,
unstoppable. And Dawit imagined that even the trees bent and bowed
from the momentum. Anbessa raised his rifle.

Dawit raised his own, scanned the last row of soldiers, made sure
none looked his way. Then he released the safety and began to count.

The car slipped into view.

The driver was a crisply dressed chauffeur with a long nose and grim
mouth. Then came the passengers in the backseat. Dawit slid his finger
on the trigger and set the sights on the man closest to him. What he
saw made him falter. Mickey: dazed, blinking rapidly, smiling benignly,
waving blandly through the window. Dawit looked up quickly and saw
Anbessa was intent on the car, his shoulders taut, all his concentration on the passengers, none on the soldier across the street from him
pointing a rifle at an old friend, confusion rising and crashing against
his stomach.

—a fat hand lifting him after a fight, the constant pushing up of
black-framed glasses, the nervous smiles, the short breathy laughs that
masked a calculating mind, the sweat, the obsessively ironed clothes,
the stained uniform that cursed night that turned this friend inside out
and upside down and then sent him back into Dawit's life unrecognizable with a heart bludgeoned and cut to fit bite-sized into the mouth of
a venomous monster this boy is no more a boy this man has never been
a man, what has never been can it really be taken away?

Dawit angled the rifle against his shoulder. Before he heard the first
bullet whirling through the air, he pulled the trigger and fired one shot
after another, ignoring the women who dropped in front of him, then
ran covering their heads. Children scattered. Soldiers fell. The Mer-

cedes swerved, brakes squealed, Mickey slumped against the shattered window, holes drilled through his glasses. Dawit shot repeatedly, caught up in the magic of bullets roaring out of a cool polished barrel, exploding with sound, ricocheting off metal and bone. At the first empty click, he looked up, trapped in the tidal wave of panicking civilians, and walked quickly with them. He lost himself in their pressing bodies and became just another soldier trying to find a way out of the mayhem.

64

ALL OF ADDIS ABABA ERUPTED IN CHAOS. Doors were torn off hinges, sons pulled from homes and shot, daughters raped, men and women hanged in public squares. Thousands were herded to prisons where morbid cries and agonized pleas spiraled out of small dark rooms.

"The Red Terror!" the still-breathing Guddu declared in Revolution Square. "The Red Terror will break the backs of these enemies of the state! They have killed one more of our brave! They have tried to kill me once again! And again, they have failed!" He pounded on a podium in front of a new crowd of terrorized and shaking spectators and held up a bottle filled with water the color of blood. "We have recently eliminated the traitor Chairman Teferi Bante for his treasonous acts against the state," he declared, ignoring the surprised gasp from the crowd. "From Nakfa to Assab, we will destroy every Eritrean rebel! All those who want to stop Ethiopia's progress will be eliminated. We will not stop until the gutters flow with the blood of all our enemies! We will fight bourgeois White Terror with Red Terror! Until Ethiopian soil is soaked with their bones and flesh and cries, we will not stop! Death to our enemies! Death to our enemies! Death!" He raised the bottle higher and sent it crashing to the ground. Red-tinged shards of glass splintered and glistened in the sun. A thousand mothers and fathers sank to their knees and prayed. Young men and women braced themselves for a new onslaught of violence. And everywhere, everyone searched the heavens for signs that angels reigned, that they would listen and heed their calls for help.

As bodies piled on top of each other in city streets and public squares, as families stumbled over familiar corpses draped with signs that announced "Red Terror" in cooling blood, as mass graves grew, stories of Anbessa's furious gun battles with the Derg's rattled soldiers, always fought with Mekonnen and Solomon at his side, rippled through homes. The government's search for the three men intensified. Week after week, special forces were sent into the highlands, ordered to burrow into caves and huts, destroy fields and farms, raze villages and climb to the bottom of watery wells. And still, they found nothing. It was as if, the people breathed, it was as if angels had made them invisible. Nightly, prayers were sent up for Anbessa destroyer of roadblocks, Mekonnen killer of soldiers, and Solomon the wise. The Holy Trinity, some dared to say, unafraid to blaspheme a deity who had long abandoned them.

65

A TIRED MONK SHUFFLED IN THE DEEP purple dark of the cave, making room for Anbessa, Solomon, and Mekonnen. His long dusty robe brushed the ground as he bowed and made the sign of the cross in front of an altar of candles and a Bible, then sat on an old leather cushion.

"We have lived here for hundreds of years without any problems. You are safe," he said. "They cannot climb this mountain without this." In his hands was a long, thick rope.

Solomon crouched at the entrance of the narrow cave, squinting into the sun and looking down into the valley far below them. Tall trees below the steep, rocky incline blocked them from view, leaves letting in only fragmented threads of daylight.

"They're looking specifically for Mekonnen," Solomon said, pointing to Dawit. He turned to the monk. "Is there somewhere else he can go if we need to separate?"

"We are many here," the monk said, nodding. "They don't know we exist, we're forgotten."

Dawit stood behind Solomon and stared into the gaping mouth of the bright valley as a raw, sharp wind howled past them. A small, freshly dug grave rose under the wide shadows of a tree far below, surrounded by wilted *meskel* flowers.

"A child is buried there. The mother comes every day and sleeps next to the grave before curfew," the monk said. He looked at Dawit. "He promised us no more floods, but I pray every day for a deluge to wash this all away."

Dawit looked at the man, bent and dignified, and recognized a soft-spoken rage and unshakable loyalty. He dropped to his knees and wrapped his arms around the old monk's legs. "I have done so much," he said. Longing for his home and his family, for his old life and his old friends surged through him.

"Mekonnen." The monk laid a hand on his head. "Don't we serve the God of the warrior King Dawit, that killer of beasts and giants, that appointed slayer of husbands and fathers and the virile sons of weeping mothers? Did our Father not make this Dawit his most beloved, the seed for his own Son? Did he not add strength to his swinging sword? Didn't he put a murderer's rage into his beloved's heart himself?" He made the sign of the cross on Dawit's crown. His voice was tinged with the resolve of the faithful. "My child, Ethiopia, stand up and fight against this new beast that has descended on our country. I will pray for you nothing but blessings, for eyes that see in the night and legs that carry you far and fast, for a life long and peaceful, for children who will not rest until our country is free again."

HAILU WOKE, PULLED out of sleep by the startling light of the sun. It was in the quick jerk of his legs that he understood his body had begun to heal itself, that all this time, while he swayed in dulled intellect and sharpened fear, it had been knitting and patching nerves and muscles. His body was adjusting to an existence without pain. I have swallowed my own teeth, have had nowhere to spew my own refuse, and nearly starved with a stomach full of only guilt and fear. Hailu stared at his legs, at the slight tremor he could not control in his hands, and in the mirror he traced the side of his mouth that would never be fully un-numbed. But the body heals in due course, he thought, and one day soon, I will sleep free of these dreams and uncontrollable spasms I have witnessed in the dying who long to give up. I will live free of all this, far from those days of stench and electricity and probing hands. I will live. The girl. What have I done? Hailu stared once more at his healing legs, his strengthening hands, the mending body of an old man, and he began to weep.

YONAS WATCHED FROM the window of the prayer room, forced his eyes to distinguish the figure that crouched, then sprang inside Melaku's kiosk in one lithe leap. He tried to mold his gaze to the contours of the dim light that flickered, then shut off inside the kiosk, but there was no moonlight. He turned and began to pray.

He heard a familiar sound. It was a soft knock followed by rocks thrown against glass. Yonas was taken back to boyhood days when he and his brother hid from each other, from Mickey, from their parents, from a disgruntled Bizu. It had been his little brother's game more than his, but one he joined in with grudging enjoyment. The rocks came again, a splatter of taps against the window.

Yonas moved swiftly and quietly down the stairs to the small side door. He unlatched the lock and flung his arms wide and let his brother fall into him and he held him firmly, Dawit's soft weeping the only sound separating the tall men who clung so desperately to each other they were nearly indistinguishable in the dark.

"You're home," Yonas said. "You're home."

"I'm in danger," Dawit said. "There's nowhere else to go."

Yonas nodded. "You'll be safe here. I won't let them find you," he said under the shelter of their father's house.

DAWIT GASPED AT the sight of his father. "Abbaye," he said, trying to break through the fog in his father's mind and find the man. "Hailu." He held his father's hand. "I'm here."

Hailu brought Dawit's hand to his mouth to kiss it, then turned away.

"He's usually more alert and much stronger," Sara said. She touched the pillow next to Hailu's head. "He's been crying." She raised his head and felt underneath. "It's soaked. Let me change this. Abbaye, what's wrong?"

"Let's change the pillow and let him rest," Yonas said, his arm around his brother again, drawing himself closer. "You have to go back upstairs and hide before Tizzie wakes from her nap," he said to Dawit. "She shouldn't know you're here, she might say something."

Dawit stood. "She's grown so much," he said. "How long have I been gone?"

Sara touched his arm, drew her hand back and took Yonas's arm. "Too long."

"Does Shiferaw give you trouble?" he asked as they walked out of his old room and up the stairs.

Yonas shook his head. "He's away at meetings. These *kebeles* are going to get more strict."

Dawit paused over Tizzie's sleeping figure. "She looks like you," he said, smiling at Yonas.

Sara stood by the prayer room. "We'll bring food soon." She walked in, smoothed the velvet draping the table. "Once Melaku finds some place, we'll take you there."

Dawit went to the prayer room. "I remember when I never felt bad for anything I did . . ." He trailed off.

"We all have regrets," Yonas said.

A LARGE CLEAR MOON SAT IN THE BEND of the sky. A breeze graced the tops of trees and fluttered curtains that grazed Sara's face. She held Tizita on her lap in Hailu's room, rocking her gently. They stared out the window and watched a stray dog wander aimlessly on the road.

"Sometimes when people leave us, they don't die, they just fly away," Sara said. The whisper was so soft it fell from her lips like a breath, then died in the breeze.

Tizita gazed out the window, leaned into her mother, and listened.

"Sofia and Robel are packing because they're moving, not because they have to go to jail," Sara said. She put her finger on Tizita's right cheek, watched a dimple form as the little girl started to smile, and smiled herself.

"When are they going on the plane?" Tizita asked. "Can I go?"

"You're staying with me." Sara smoothed her daughter's braids. "They'll be here for a while longer. Then they go to America and a church will take care of them."

"Rahel's mommy said if we leave they'll put Abbaye in jail again." Tizita stopped, serious. "He can come, too, can't he? He just sleeps." She looked up.

"We're not leaving." Sara smiled. "He's been getting better. Didn't he pray with you up here yesterday?"

A distant purr outside the window grew louder, then the crunch of thick tires. A door slammed. Shouts ricocheted. Gunshots punctured the night. Another search.

"It's late," Sara said. She sat next to Tizita on the bed. "Go to your room and I'll come back and pray with you."

"Is it the soldiers?" Tizita asked. She clung to Sara and ran her fingers over her mother's short curls. Sara had cut her hair in mourning for Berhane. Her scar rose like a tree root from the top of her head.

"It's just a government car," Sara said. She let out a deep breath as the rumble went by.

"Sometimes bullets sound like the rain," Tizita said, pointing to the ceiling and talking nervously. "It comes down on the roof." She gripped her mother's hand and looked out the window in fear. "Are they coming?"

The car crawled back in front of their house and stopped.

"I will be back," Sara said. She raced down the stairs where Hailu sat in his armchair next to his red radio, now permanently off.

Tizita stood on her grandfather's bed on tiptoes to get a better view of the car. She could hear solid steps entering the compound. Two soldiers marched to the door, their rifles in front of them. The shorter one rammed the butt of his rifle into the door three times. He turned around to say something, then the door flew open.

"What is it?" she heard her mother say. Tizita imagined her planted firmly in their path.

"Get Yonas," one soldier replied. "We need to talk to him."

"About what?"

"Where is he? It's after curfew," the other soldier said. Both of them took a step into the house but Sara stepped outside and shut the door.

"You can talk to me. He's sleeping," her mother said.

Tizita didn't hear her father behind her until she felt the sharp slap he gave her bottom. Her grandfather was with him, his tired eyes now wide.

"I have to go downstairs," her father said. "You should be asleep." Yonas gripped Tizita's shoulders so hard that she shrank from the pain. "Abbaye, lay down," he added. He turned back to her. "Go to your room," he said. "Hurry."

They heard the heavy-soled footsteps at the same time.

"They're inside!" Tizita cried. She threw herself into his arms. The thin gold crucifix around his neck cut into her cheek.

"Don't get scared," Yonas said. "If you're not brave, you'll get everyone in trouble." He settled on the prayer room. "Go to your room and close the door."

Loud voices came from the living room and Yonas ran. Tizita found herself alone with her grandfather, cornered in a room grown eerie with nighttime shadows and hyenas' snorting. She wanted to hug him but he was kneeling, lost in something on the ground.

She went inside the prayer room to ask for help. The tiny square room was painted a light blue. The statue of Saint Mary and her baby was at the center of a long table draped in red. Tizita made the sign of the crucifix, and as she'd done every night for a long time, she asked the angels to watch over Berhane, then started praying for her family.

Tizita prayed with open eyes in case her mother needed her. "Please don't let them take my daddy or Abbaye. Help my mommy not be scared."

The loud thud of falling furniture came from downstairs. Sara's splintered voice rose above the din. "You're wasting your time!"

Tizita knew her mother was looking into the soldier's eyes when she said this, the same way she looked into her father's when they were fighting. She continued praying, hoping her words would let angels know that they needed help right now, even if it was late at night. She struggled against the urge to go downstairs.

Feet pounded up the steps. They were coming towards the prayer room.

"Tell me where he is! Mekonnen is here!"

Her father: "You've been here before. There's nobody here but us."

Tizita closed the door to the room. From the other side, she heard a sickening thud and her father's groan. She pulled back the velvet cloth to crawl under the table and hide, but twisted in that cramped space was her uncle.

Her world started to unravel in that brief second between horror and recognition.

"Dawit?" Their eyes met. She'd never seen her uncle shaking like this. He put a finger on her mouth to be quiet and Tizita saw he'd bitten one side of his lip bloody.

"Bastard. Only a coward needs his gun to hit an unarmed man," her mother said.

"You're in the wrong house." That was her father. "There's no Mekonnen here."

She looked down at her uncle, waited for him to tell her what to do. His shaking was traveling into her body; her knees were quivering. He motioned and she leaned in.

"They're going to look in here," Dawit whispered. "When they open the door, pretend I'm not here." He looked for her agreement and she nodded.

On the other side of the door, she heard her mother. "Has this dirty Russian uniform made you forget you are *habesha*?" Sara spat. "You foolish boy."

Tizita jerked, alarmed, when she heard the piercing slap that forced her mother to cry out and her father to roar in fury. Bodies thudded to the ground. Tizita cried out in fear, then scrambled to push Dawit back under the table and yank the velvet cover in place. She turned just in time to see the flinty determination in the tall soldier's eyes as he strode into the room. Her mother was at his shoulder, pushing to get past him. Her father was outside the door, holding the soldier back.

The soldier raised his rifle and all of them froze, eyes riveted on the barrel.

"I heard you speaking." The soldier reached for Tizita, catlike, until her mother moved past him to pull her close.

Tizita wrapped her arms around Sara's waist. She couldn't take her eyes off the gun. "Don't shoot us," she said. "I was just praying."

The soldier leaned close to her, the smell of rotten teeth on his breath. His eyes raked over the sparsely furnished room as he jabbed each corner with his rifle.

"Enough. You've done enough for your government tonight," her mother said. Her mother kept her eyes glued to the rifle, her nails dug into Tizita's arms.

The soldier lifted the barrel of his rifle to scratch his chin and he spat, aiming for Sara's foot. He paused to stare at the spit that settled on the edge of her slippers. Then his mouth stretched and his stained teeth jutted out in a triumphant smile.

"Move," he said. "Mesfin! Come here!" he shouted for his partner.

The soldier thrust his rifle into Sara, flinging her aside. Sara's head slammed against the wall. He stared down, pleased, as Tizita sank to the ground to help her.

The soldier was already spinning from the punch before anyone knew what was happening. Yonas's next blow sent the soldier careening on top of Tizita and Sara and his weight pushed her further into her mother. Sara wrapped an arm around his neck and Tizita grasped the back of his shirt. They struggled to maintain their hold on the straining body.

"Daddy, I'm holding him for you!" Tizita cried between clenched teeth.

Yonas knew what he needed to do. He grabbed the weapon, grim and determined, and smashed the butt of the gun into the soldier's cheek, then again when the soldier tried to rise, then again. Then the soldier lay still and everything slowed and his daughter and wife slid out from underneath that uniformed mass, and Yonas aimed the rifle at the soldier's heart.

"My son. No." It was his father, standing behind the second soldier, who was looking at his fallen comrade with fear.

Hailu and the soldier walked into the room, and it was only when Yonas looked again that he saw his father had a pistol he'd never known existed, aimed at the soldier's head.

"Abbaye? Where did you get that gun?" Sara asked.

Dawit listened from underneath the table. He squeezed his eyes and bit his tongue. That bulletless gun had come into this house in the fleshy hands of a coward. Had traveled from a killing field to his room and then landed in his father's possession. That gun that had transformed his friend into an enemy and a murderer was now in his father's grip, a cursed weapon that could offer no defense tonight if tested. Dawit started to crawl from under the table to take the weapon from him and offer himself to these soldiers. But then he heard his father speak.

"I'm a doctor. I'm not afraid to watch you die," he said. "I was arrested by the Colonel and kept in his jail for months." He paused, then continued, his voice shaking. "No one can do worse to me. I'll shoot you if you don't leave us alone."

Dawit heard one of the soldiers whisper, "The Colonel," then saw his brother take a step towards the soldier who was groaning on the ground.

"Get out of our house," Yonas said. "Leave my family alone." Dawit saw the edge of the gun barrel press under the soldier's chin and lift his gaze up, away from what sat under the table. The soldier stood.

Tizita was crying. Her legs shook so badly she could barely stand. The soldiers were quiet, still, boys frightened and confused. Then they turned and left, with Sara and Yonas following them. Soon, the house quieted. Only the family remained.

"Dawit," his father said. "My Dawit." The pistol dropped to the ground, his father fell to his knees, and strong arms wrapped around Dawit and helped him stand.

Outside, as house after house was forced open in search for Mekonnen, Emama Seble murmured a prayer that held the power of a hundred. Melaku opened his shutters and sang of resistance and courage, his cries soaring into the night. And Hailu sat on the edge of his bed holding Dawit's hand, refusing to let it go.

Dawit held his father and listened as he began to count. As he counted, his eyes closed, Hailu saw a flash of brilliant blue, as wide and open as the noon sky, and a wild bird on the strong back of a fierce lion racing home.

THIS BOOK IS BASED on the Ethiopian revolution that began in 1974, but I have taken many liberties for the purposes of fiction. My intent has been to convey the essence of the early years of the revolution through my imagination. Though the characters of Emperor Haile Selassie and Prime Minister Aklilu Habtewold are based on actual people, their portrayals are fictitious. The characters of Kifle and Colonel Mehari, who are included among the sixty officials executed by the Derg soon after the emperor's arrest, are fictitious. Major Guddu was inspired by Mengistu Haile Mariam, but he remains a fictional character. The chronology of events has at times been compressed and altered. I have included a condensed list of books that helped my research, and I thank the authors immensely. Specifically, Kiflu Tadesse's *The Generation, Part II* was central in helping to create a sketch of underground resistance groups in Addis Ababa; the late Taffara Deguefé's *A Tripping Stone* was instrumental in conveying the life of prisoners; Nega Mezlekia's *Notes from the Hyena's Belly* and the late Prime Minister Aklilu Habtewold's *Aklilu Remembers: Historical Recollections from a Prison Cell* were significant to my understanding of the political and personal costs of the revolution. I humbly express my gratitude to these writers for sharing their stories so the rest of us may know.

The Derg regime collapsed in 1991 and there are no confirmed numbers of how many men, women, and children lost their lives during its rule. Some reports based on Amnesty International estimates say the death toll could be in the hundreds of thousands. By the end of the most violent period of the Derg's rule, the Red Terror (1976–78), Mengistu Haile Mariam had effectively eliminated all opposition through execution, imprisonment, or exile. This book is dedicated to those who made the greatest sacrifice for their country, and those who have survived to carry on the dream of a better Ethiopia, whether from home or from abroad.

Though the act of writing is solitary, completing any book is the result of the kindness of many. My love goes to my wonderful parents, Mengiste Imru and Yayne Abeba Abebe, for their unfailing support. I am indebted to my brother, Tedros Mengiste, and his wife, Anketse Debebe Kassa, for their leap of faith. I am forever humbled by the wondrous generosity of Mr. and Mrs. Phil and Mary Roden and my dear friend Molly Roden Winter.

A warm thank you to two who guided me through my years at the NYU Creative Writing Program, Melissa Hammerle and Russell Carmony; bravo for creating a wonderful community that allowed so many to feel at home. My gratitude to Breyten Breytenbach, who taught me to trust my vision; to Irini Spanidou, for friendship, honesty, and unwavering encouragement; to Chuck Wachtel, who kindly agreed to be my thesis advisor despite an inhuman workload. My thanks to the director of the NYU Creative Writing Program, Dr. Deborah Landau, for championing my work. A special thank you to the NYU Expository Writing Program and Pat Hoy, for helping me understand what it takes to be a better writer. I am grateful to VONA Voices Workshop for creating a space where so many writers of color can gather and share their stories.

I am so thankful to my wonderful agent, Maria Massie, who believed in this book before it was anything and had faith in my ability to see it through. A loud round of applause to her assistant Rachel Vogel for dedicated attention to all the little details. I am grateful to my skilled editor, Jill Bialosky, who guided this book with sure and steady focus, and to her assistant, Adrienne Davich, for keeping me on schedule and on track with professionalism and warmth. To everyone at W. W. Norton, a heartfelt thanks for the willingness to take this novel on.

I would have stumbled many times if not for the support and insight of my friends. Many, many thanks to the immensely talented members of the best writing group in the world: Katie Berg, Olivia Birdsall, Nicole Hefner Callihan, and Cleyvis Natera. I am profoundly grateful to Breyten Breytenbach's Fall 2004 fiction workshop for that crisp November night when you saw my first rough ideas and offered gentle but honest critiques: Ryan Sloan, Nat Bennett, Eric Ozawa, P.J. Bordeau, Chris Mahar, Ethan Bernard, Luke Fiske, Thomas Hopkins, Martin Marks, Dominique Bell. I owe much to Uwem Akpan, Getachew Abera, Professor Yacob Fisseha and the Michigan State University African Studies Center, Peter Limb at the Michigan State University Library and the staff at the Special Collections Division, Professor Solomon Getahun, Professor Tibebe Eshete, Mahlet Tsegaye and the family of the late Ethiopian Poet Laureate Tsegaye Gebremedhin, Makonnen Ketema, Tarekegn Gebreyesus, Debrework Zewdie, my uncle Ayalew Abebe, Yemane Demissie, Marty McClatchey, Laila Lalami, Mylitta Chaplain, Sarida Scott, Rebekah Anderson, Matt Gilgoff, Debut Lit, the Prague Summer Program, the Virginia Center for the Arts, Yaddo, Bill and Carol Freeman at the Borland House, and Drs. Glenn Hirsch and Tim Muir. My eternal love and gratitude goes to my anchor and light on those toughest of days, Marco Fernando Navarro.

BIBLIOGRAPHY

Gaitachew Bekele. *The Emperor's Clothes: A Personal Viewpoint on Politics and Administration in the Imperial Ethiopian Government*. Trenton, NJ: Red Sea Press, 1989.

Dawit Wolde Giorgis. *Red Tears: War, Famine, and Revolution in Ethiopia*. Trenton, NJ: Red Sea Press, 1989.

Taffara Deguefé. *A Tripping Stone: Ethiopian Prison Diary (1976–1981)*. Addis Ababa, Ethiopia: Addis Ababa University Press, 2003.

Donald L. Donham. *Marxist Modern: An Ethnographic History of the Ethiopian Revolution*. Berkeley: University of California Press, 1999.

Ethiopia: Revolution in the Making. New York: Progressive Publishers, 1978.

Solomon Addis Getahun. *The History of Ethiopian Immigrants and Refugees in America, 1900–2000: Patterns of Migration, Survival, and Adjustment*. New York: LFB Scholarly Publishing, 2007.

Aklilu Habtewold. *Aklilu Remembers: Historical Recollections from a Prison Cell*. Uppsala, Sweden: Nina Printing Press, 1994.

Teferra Haile-Selassie. *The Ethiopian Revolution, 1974–91: From a Monarchical Autocracy to a Military Oligarchy*. London and New York: Kegan Paul International, 1997. Distributed by Columbia University Press.

Fred Halliday. *The Ethiopian Revolution*. Edited by Maxine Molyneux. London: NLB, 1981.

Paul B. Henze. *Layers of Time: A History of Ethiopia*. New York: St. Martin's Press, 2000.

Edmond J. Keller. *Revolutionary Ethiopia: From Empire to People's Republic*. Bloomington: Indiana University Press, 1988.

Harold G. Marcus. *A History of Ethiopia*. Berkeley: University of California Press, 2002.

John Markakis. *Class and Revolution in Ethiopia*. Edited by Nega Ayele. Trenton, NJ: Red Sea Press, 1986.

Nega Mezlekia. *Notes from the Hyena's Belly: An Ethiopian Boyhood.* New York: Picador USA, 2001.

Marina Ottaway. *Ethiopia: Empire in Revolution.* Edited by David Ottaway. New York: Africana Publishing Company, 1978.

Haile Selassie I, Emperor of Ethiopia. *My Life and Ethiopia's Progress, 1892–1937.* Vol. 2, *Addis Abeba, 1966 E.C.* Edited by Harold G. Marcus, Ezekiel Gebissa, and Tibebe Eshete. East Lansing: Michigan State University Press, 1994.

Kiflu Tadesse. *The Generation, Part II.* Lanham, MD: University Press of America, 1998.

Andargachew Tiruneh. *The Ethiopian Revolution, 1974–1987: A Transformation from an Aristocratic to a Totalitarian Autocracy.* Cambridge, UK, and New York: Cambridge University Press, 1993.

Bahru Zewde. *A History of Modern Ethiopia, 1855–1991.* Athens: Ohio University Press; Oxford, UK: James Curry; Addis Ababa, Ethiopia: Addis Ababa University Press, 2001.

www.vintage-books.co.uk